DEAR JUSTICE LEAGUE

Written by
Michael Northrop

Illustrated by
Gustavo Duarte

Colored by
Marcelo Maiolo

Lettered by
Wes Abbott

SUPERMAN created by Jerry Siegel and Joe Shuster.
By special arrangement with the Jerry Siegel family.

SARA MILLER Editor

STEVE COOK Design Director - Books

AMIE BROCKWAY-METCALF Publication Design

BOB HARRAS Senior VP - Editor-in-Chief, DC Comics

MICHELE R. WELLS VP & Executive Editor, Young Reader

DAN DiDIO Publisher

JIM LEE Publisher & Chief Creative Officer

BOBBIE CHASE VP - New Publishing Initiatives & Talent Development

DON FALLETTI VP - Manufacturing Operations & Workflow Management

LAWRENCE GANEM VP - Talent Services

ALISON GILL Senior VP - Manufacturing & Operations

HANK KANALZ Senior VP - Publishing Strategy & Support Services

DAN MIRON VP - Publishing Operations

NICK J. NAPOLITANO VP - Manufacturing Administration & Design

NANCY SPEARS VP - Sales

DEAR JUSTICE LEAGUE

Published by DC Comics. Copyright © 2019 DC Comics. All Rights Reserved. All characters, their distinctive likenesses, and related elements featured in this publication are trademarks of DC Comics. DC ZOOM is a trademark of DC Comics. The stories, characters, and incidents featured in this publication are entirely fictional. DC Comics does not read or accept unsolicited submissions of ideas, stories, or artwork. DC - a WarnerMedia Company.

DC Comics, 2900 West Alameda Ave., Burbank, CA 91505

Printed by LSC Communications, Crawfordsville, IN, USA. 6/28/19. First Printing.

ISBN: 978-1-4012-8413-8

Library of Congress Cataloging-in-Publication Data

Names: Northrop, Michael, writer. | Duarte, Gustavo, 1977- artist. | Maiolo, Marcelo, colourist. | Abbott, Wes, letterer.
Title: Dear Justice League / written by Michael Northrop ; art by Gustavo Duarte ; colors by Marcelo Maiolo ; letters by Wes Abbott.
Description: Burbank, CA : DC Comics, [2019] | "SUPERMAN Created by Jerry Siegel and Joe Shuster." | Summary: "The greatest heroes in the DC Comics universe, the Justice League, answer mail from their biggest fans--kids!"-- Provided by publisher.
Identifiers: LCCN 2019014552 | ISBN 9781401284138 (paperback)
Subjects: LCSH: Graphic novels. | CYAC: Graphic novels. | Justice League of America (Fictitious characters)--Fiction. | Superheroes--Fiction. | BISAC: JUVENILE FICTION / Comics & Graphic Novels / Superheroes. | JUVENILE FICTION / Comics & Graphic Novels / General.
Classification: LCC PZ7.7.N678 De 2019 | DDC 741.5/973--dc23

DEAR JUSTICE LEAGUE

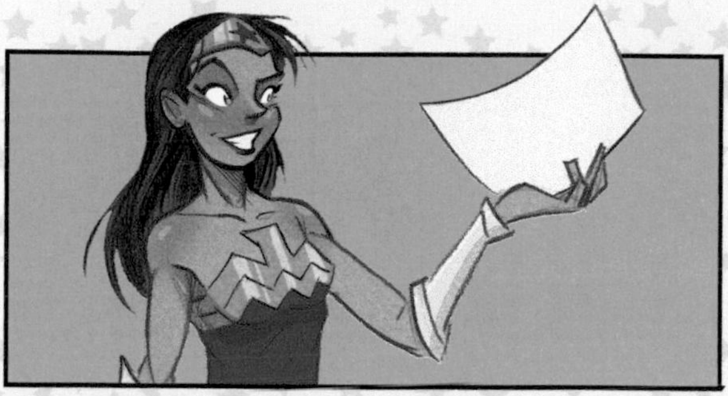

TABLE OF CONTENTS

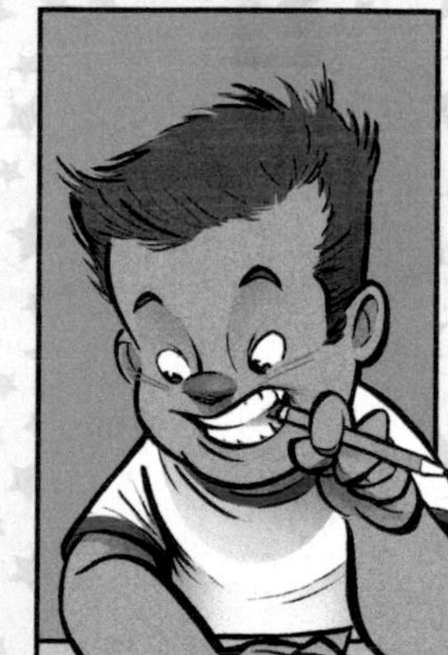
DEAR WONDER WOMAN

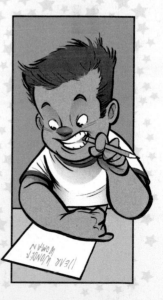

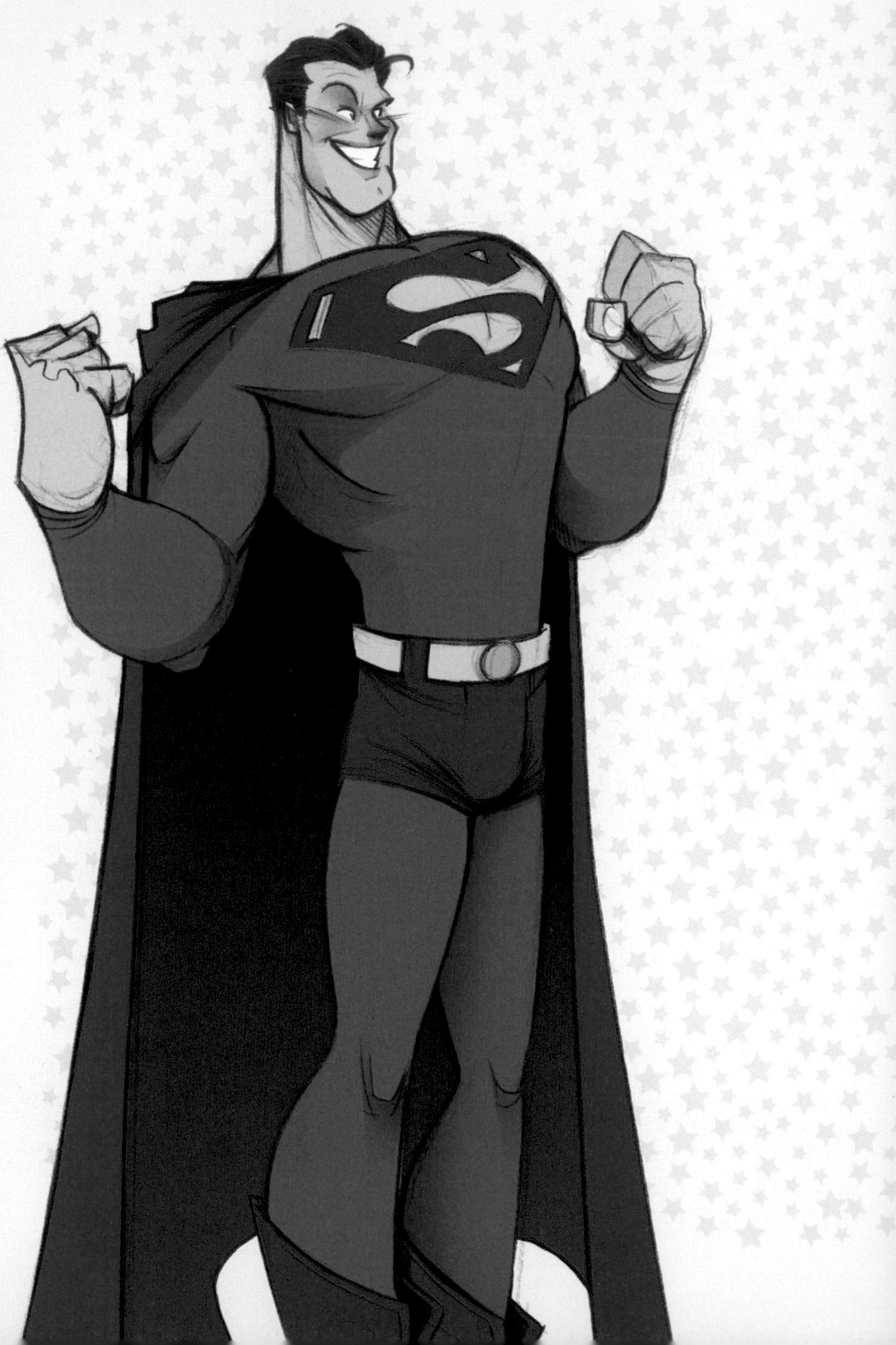

CHAPTER 1

Dear Superman

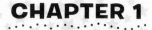

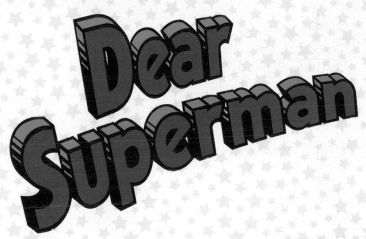

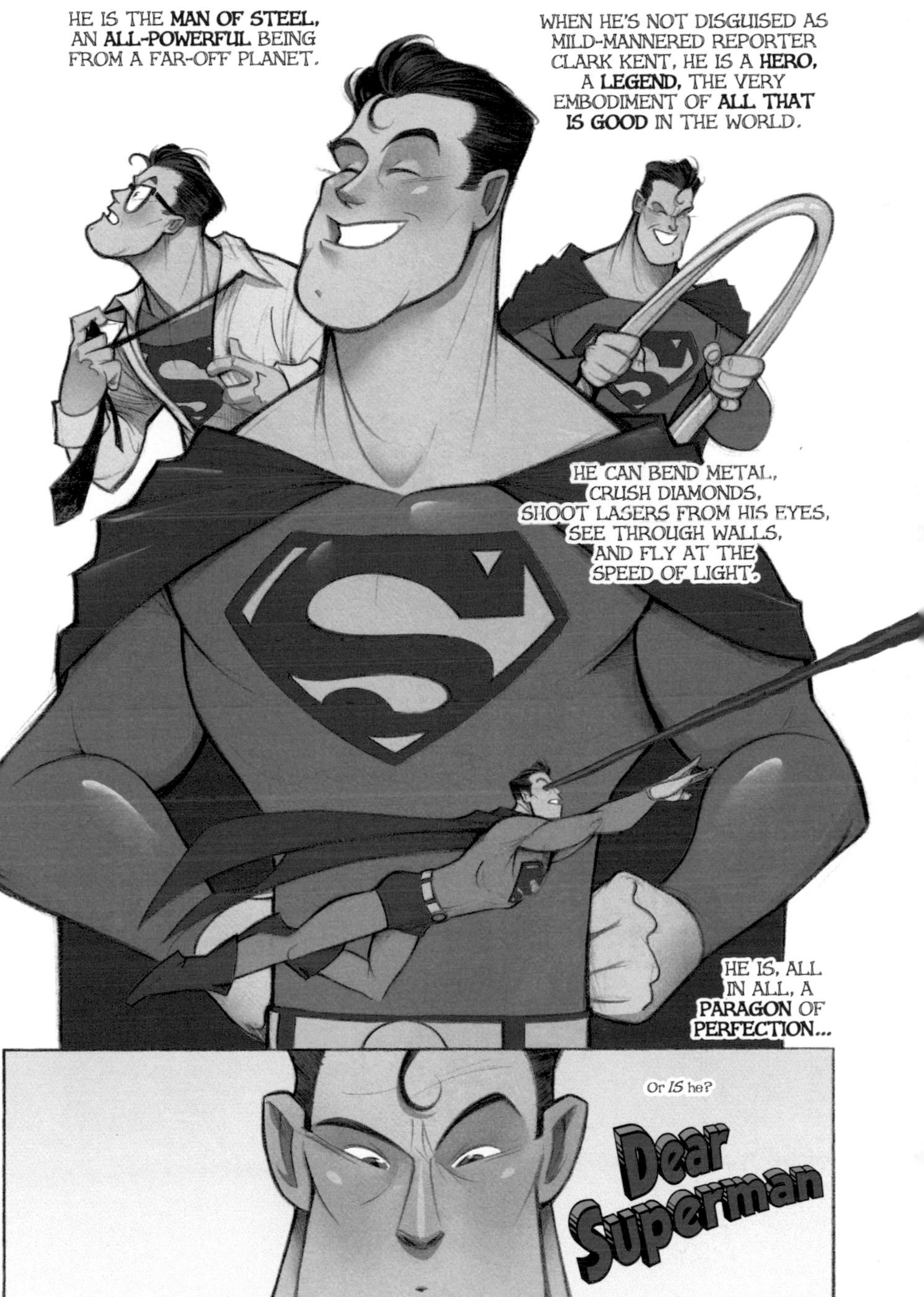
HE IS THE MAN OF STEEL, AN ALL-POWERFUL BEING FROM A FAR-OFF PLANET.
WHEN HE'S NOT DISGUISED AS MILD-MANNERED REPORTER CLARK KENT, HE IS A HERO, A LEGEND, THE VERY EMBODIMENT OF ALL THAT IS GOOD IN THE WORLD.
HE CAN BEND METAL, CRUSH DIAMONDS, SHOOT LASERS FROM HIS EYES, SEE THROUGH WALLS, AND FLY AT THE SPEED OF LIGHT.
HE IS, ALL IN ALL, A PARAGON OF PERFECTION...
Or IS he?
Dear Superman

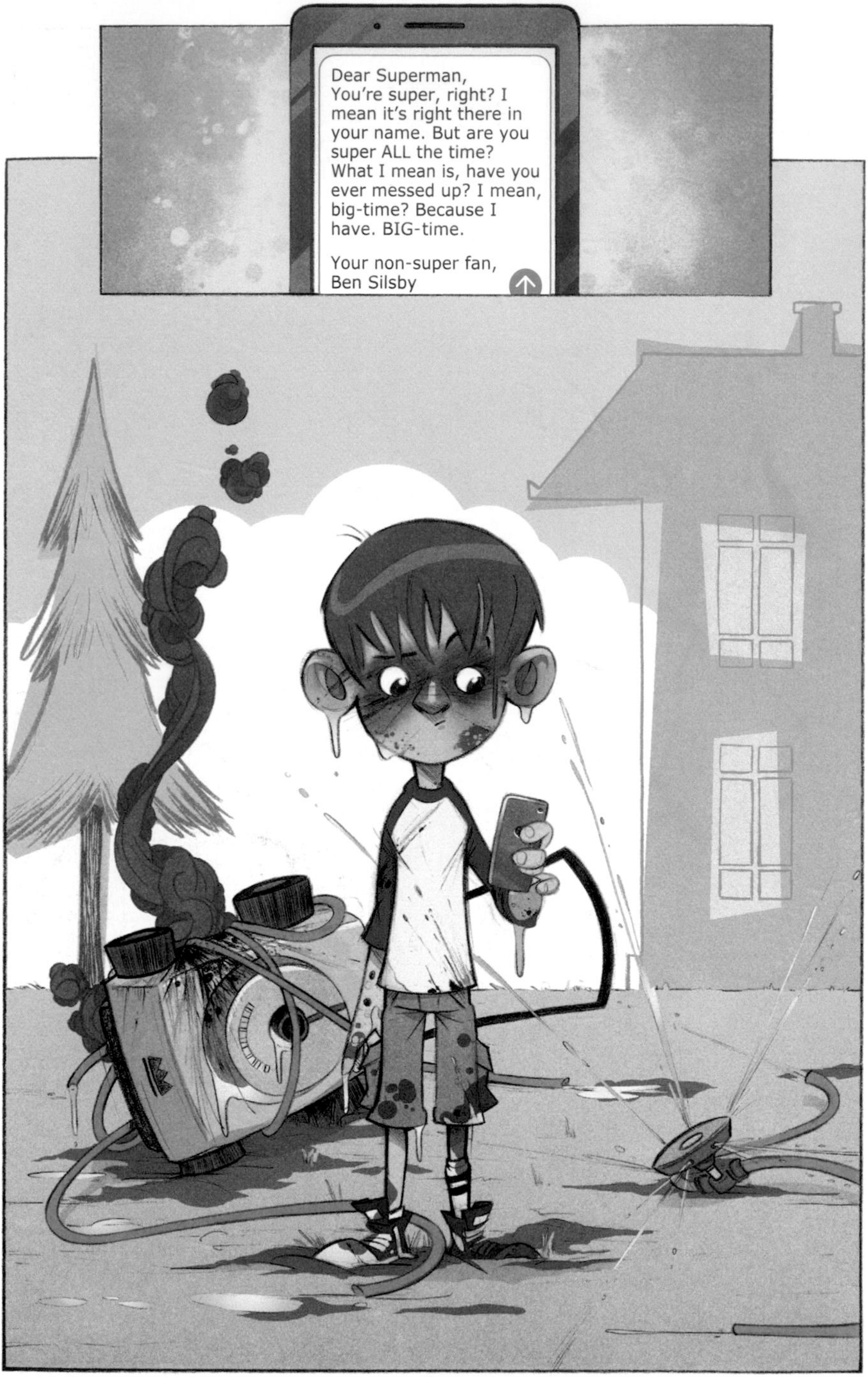
Dear Superman,
You're super, right? I mean it's right there in your name. But are you super ALL the time? What I mean is, have you ever messed up? I mean, big-time? Because I have. BIG-time.
Your non-super fan,
Ben Silsby

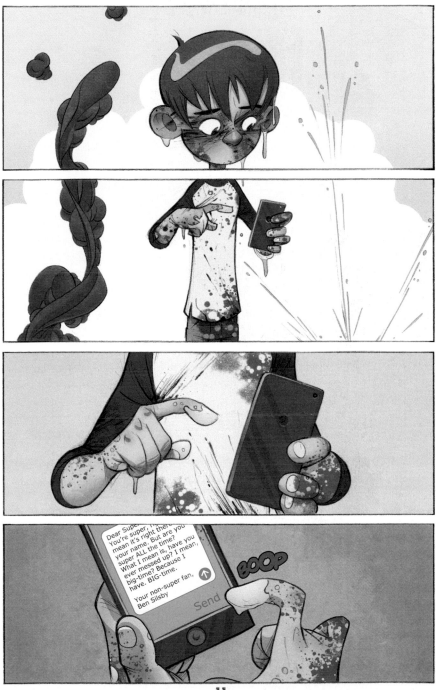

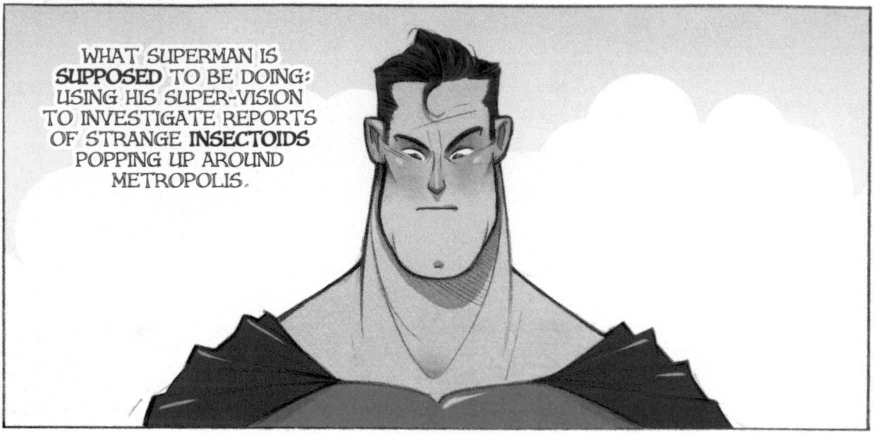
WHAT SUPERMAN IS SUPPOSED TO BE DOING: USING HIS SUPER-VISION TO INVESTIGATE REPORTS OF STRANGE INSECTOIDS POPPING UP AROUND METROPOLIS.

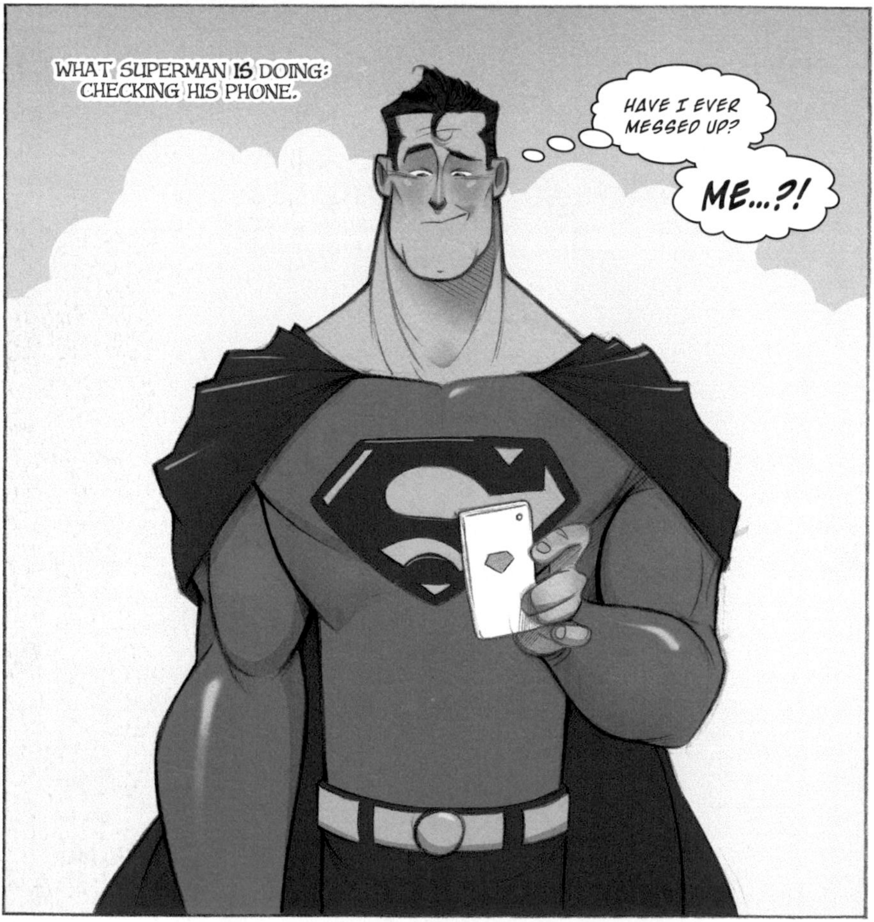
WHAT SUPERMAN IS DOING: CHECKING HIS PHONE.
HAVE I EVER MESSED UP?
ME...?!

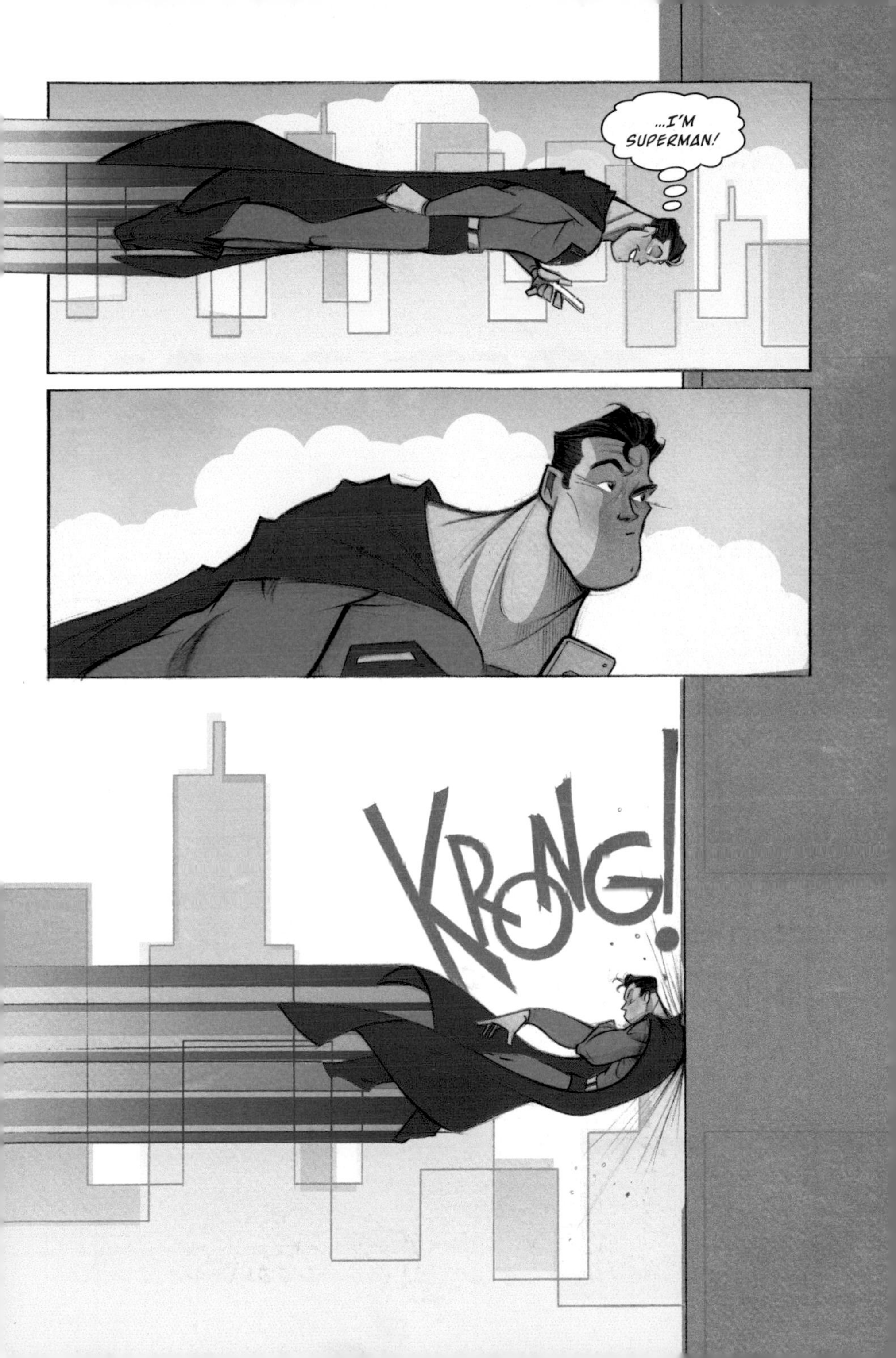
...I'M SUPERMAN!
KRONG!

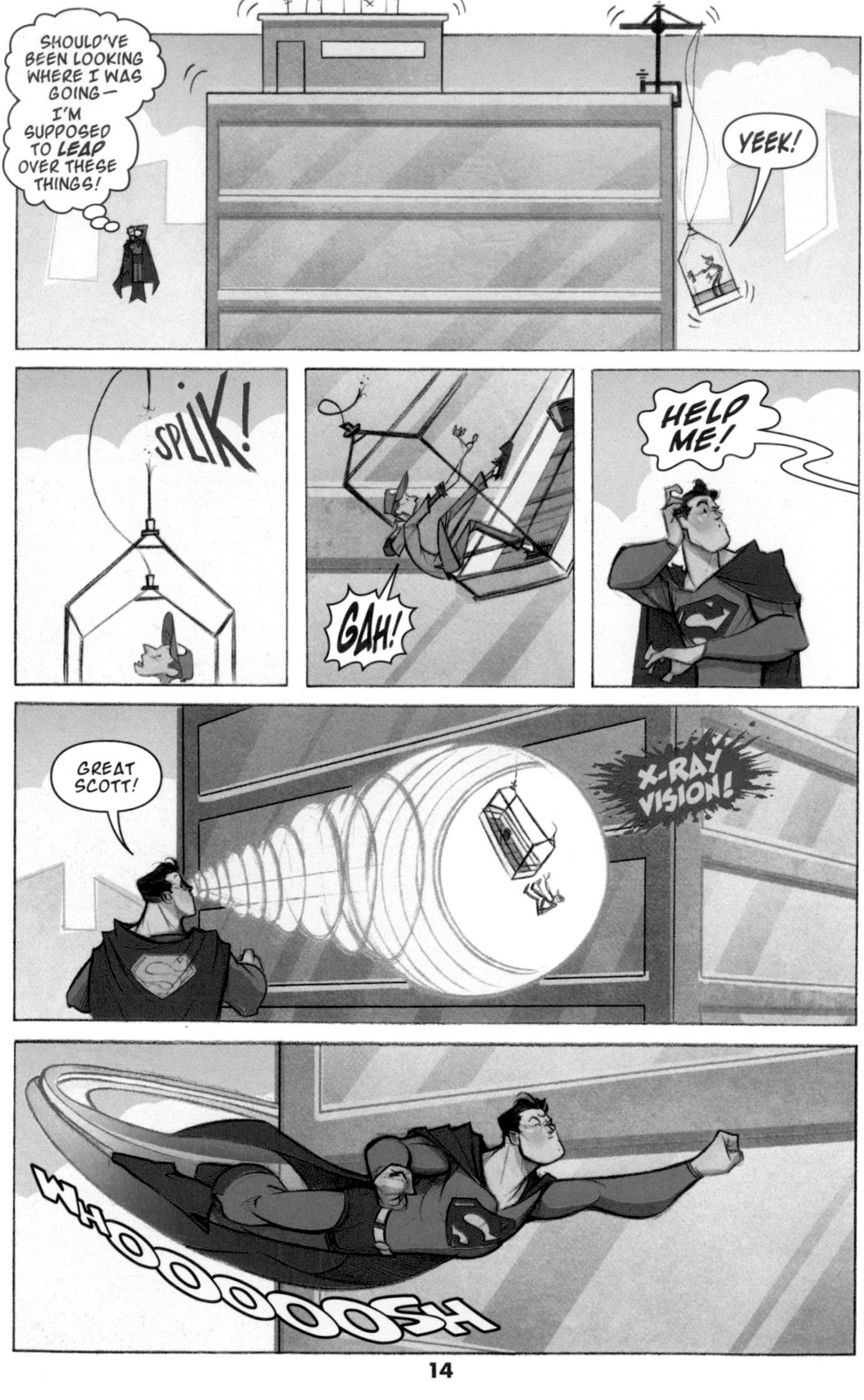
SHOULD'VE BEEN LOOKING WHERE I WAS GOING— I'M SUPPOSED TO LEAP OVER THESE THINGS!
YEEK!
SPLIK!
GAH!
HELP ME!
GREAT SCOTT!
X-RAY VISION!
WHOOOOOOSH

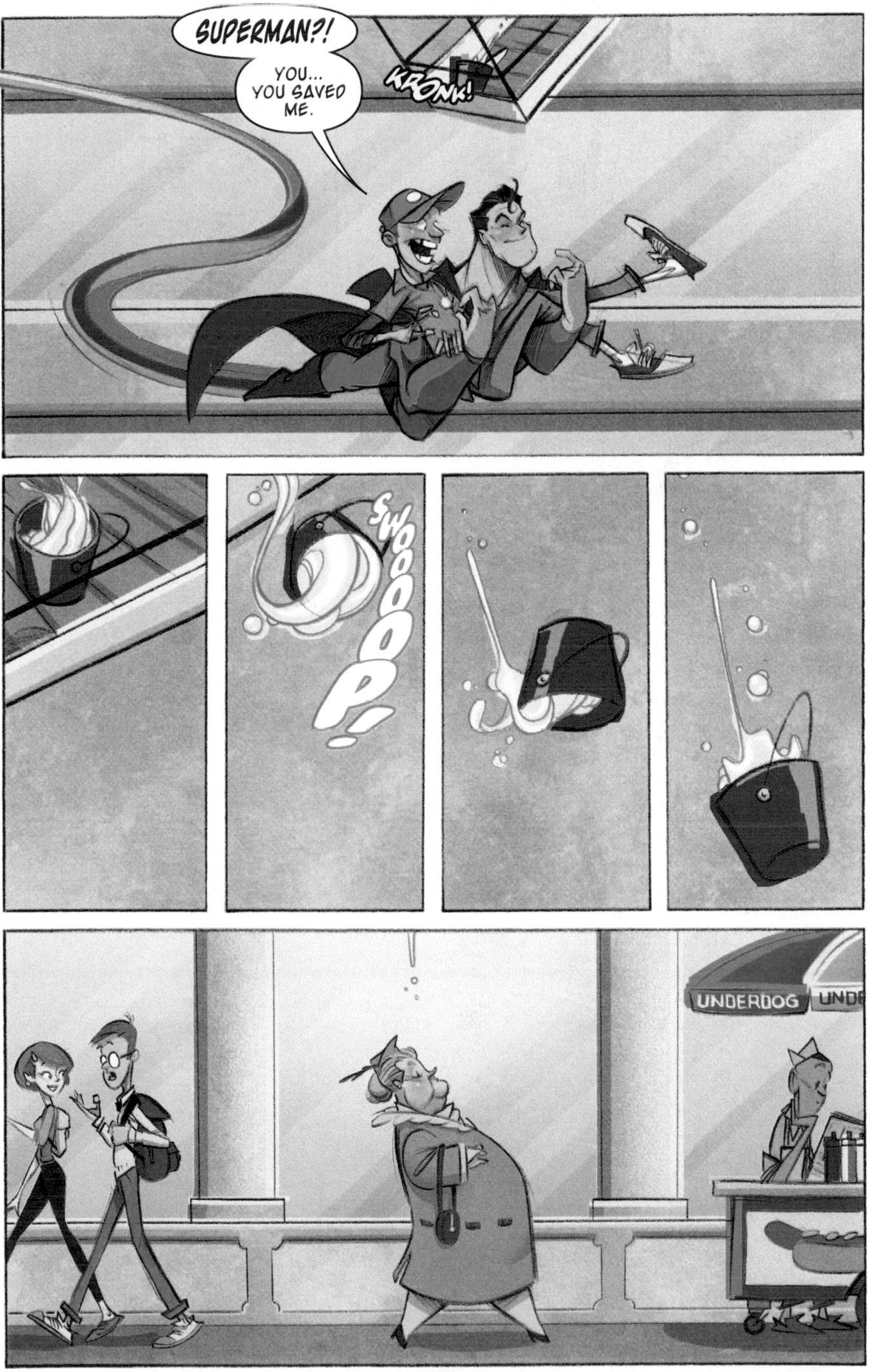
SUPERMAN?!
YOU... YOU SAVED ME.
KRONK!
SWOOOOOP!
UNDERDOG
UNDE

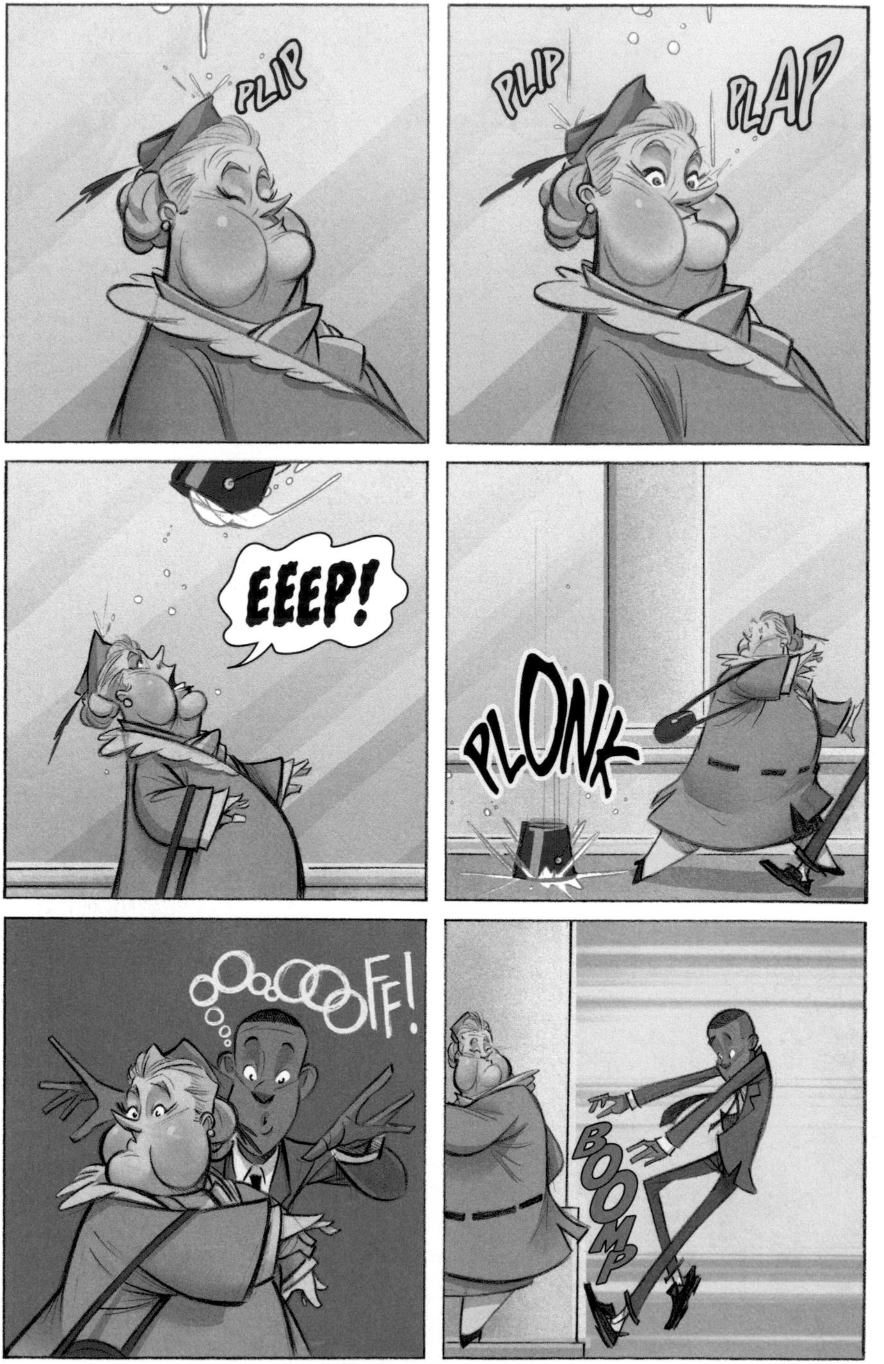
PLIP
PLIP
PLAP
EEEP!
PLONK
OOOOOOFF!
BOOMP

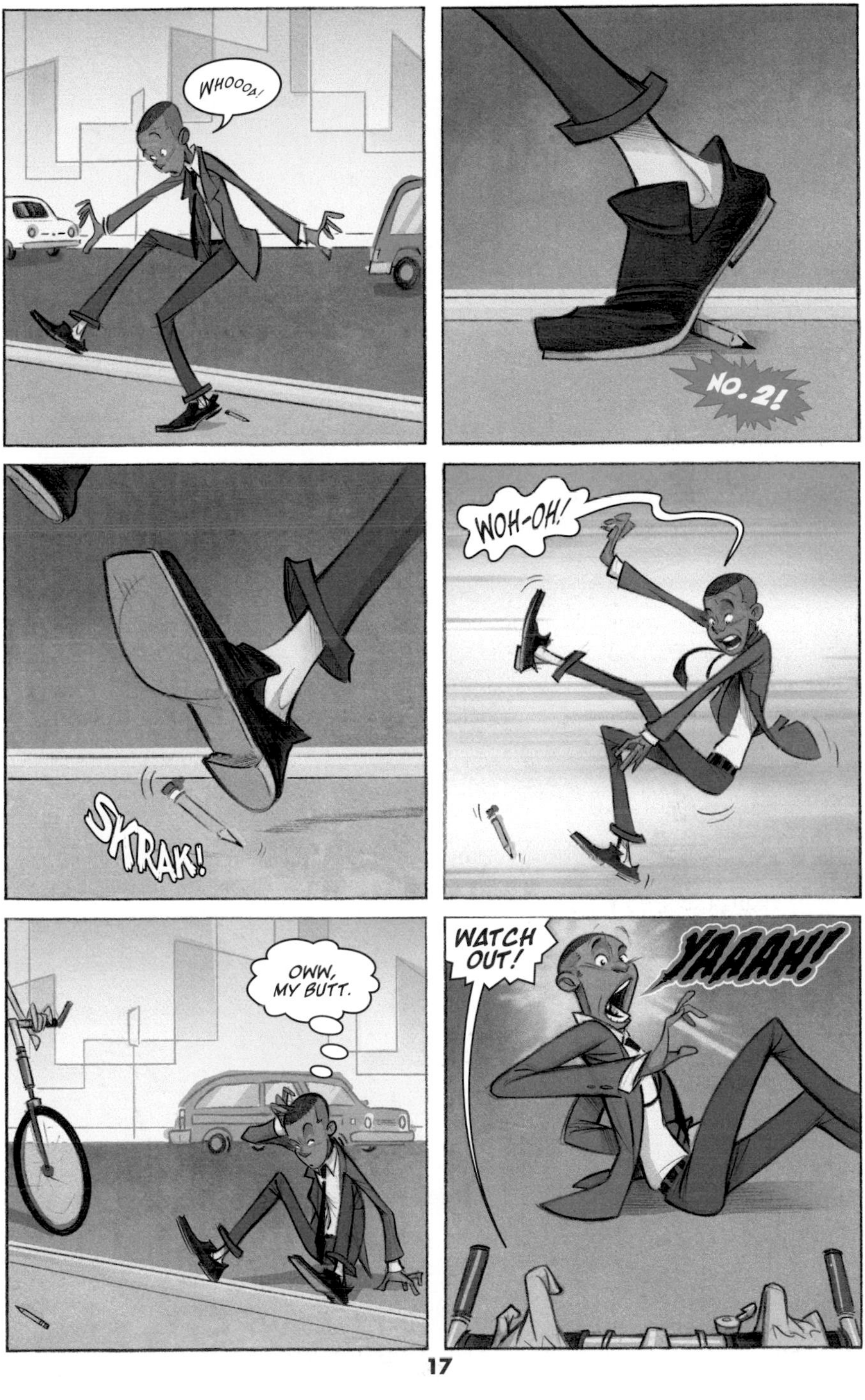
WHOOOA!
NO. 2!
SKRAK!
WOH-OH!
OWW, MY BUTT.
WATCH OUT!
YAAAH!

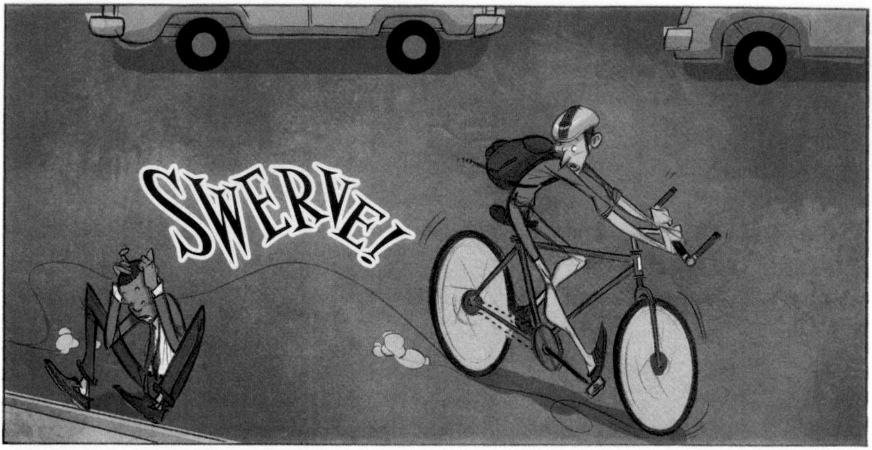
SWERVE!

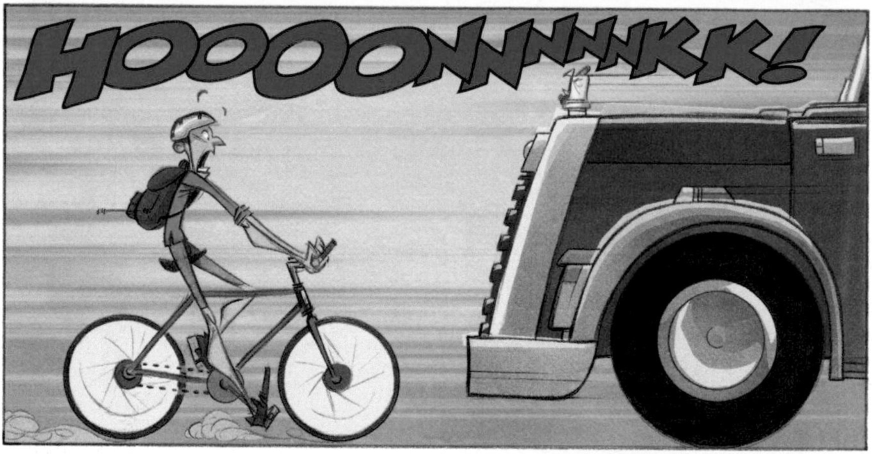
HOOOONNNNKK!

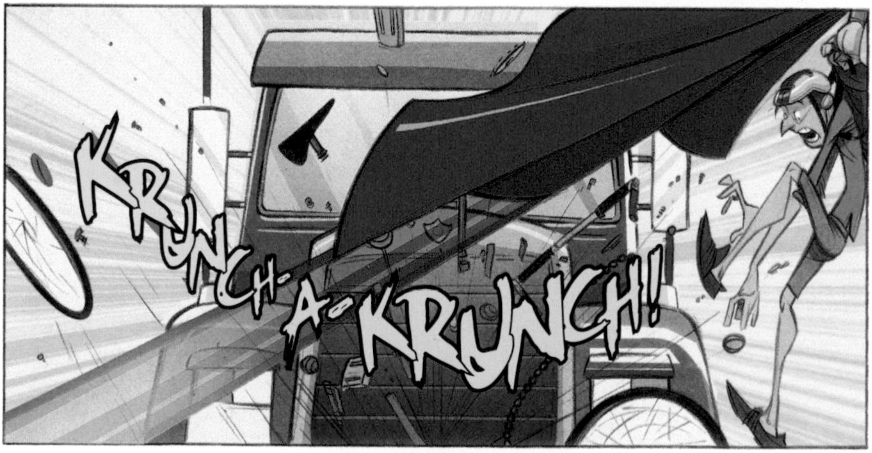
KRUNCH-A-KRUNCH!

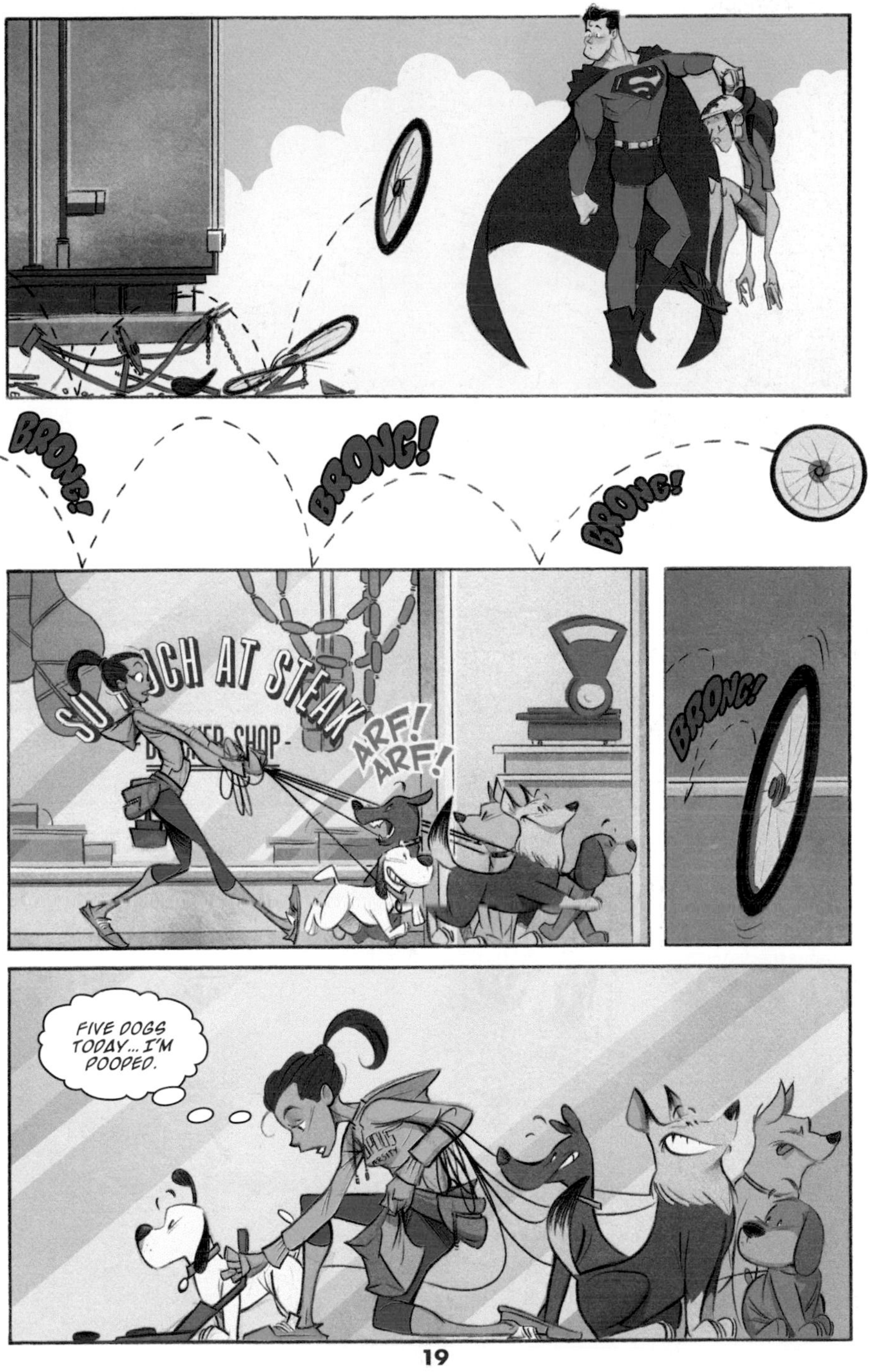
BRONG!
BRONG!
BRONG!
ARF! ARF!
BRONG!
FIVE DOGS TODAY... I'M POOPED.

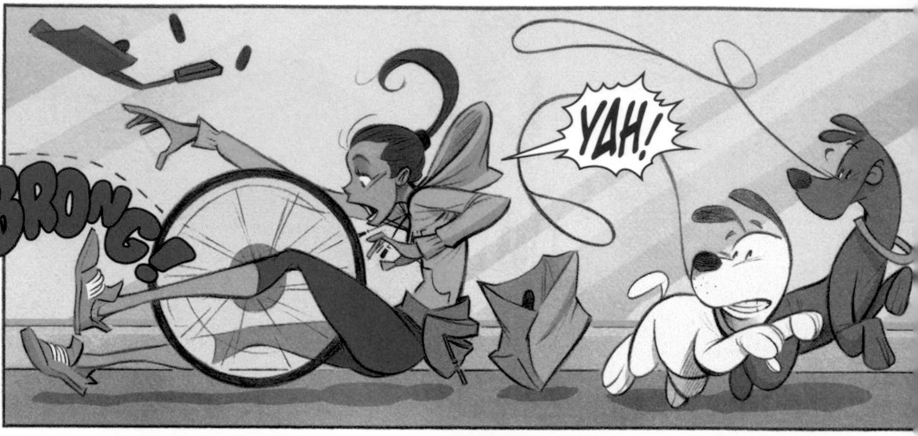
BRONG!!
YAH!

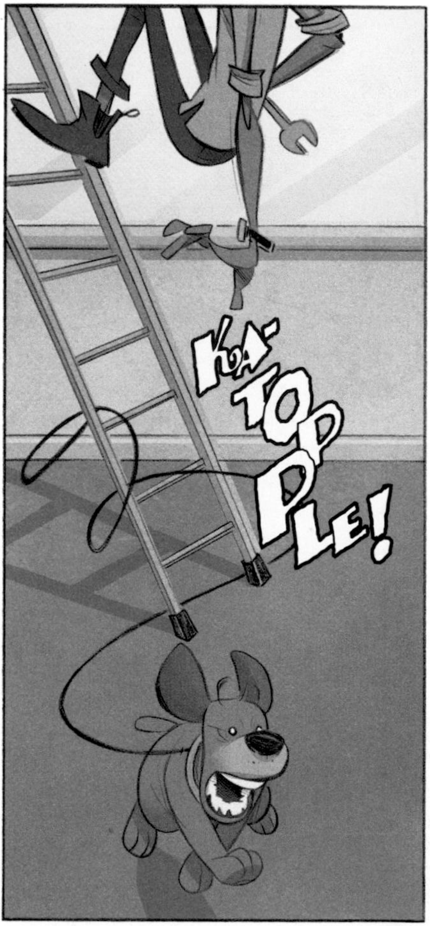
KA-TOPPLE!

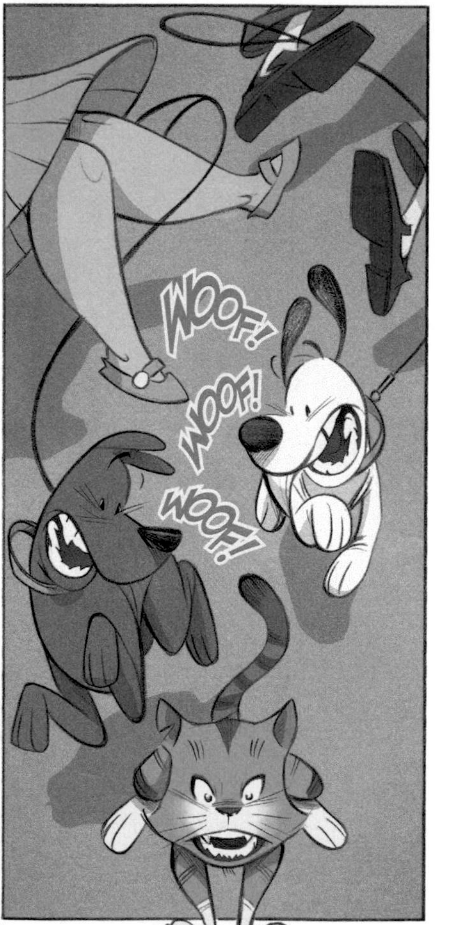
WOOF!
WOOF!
WOOF!

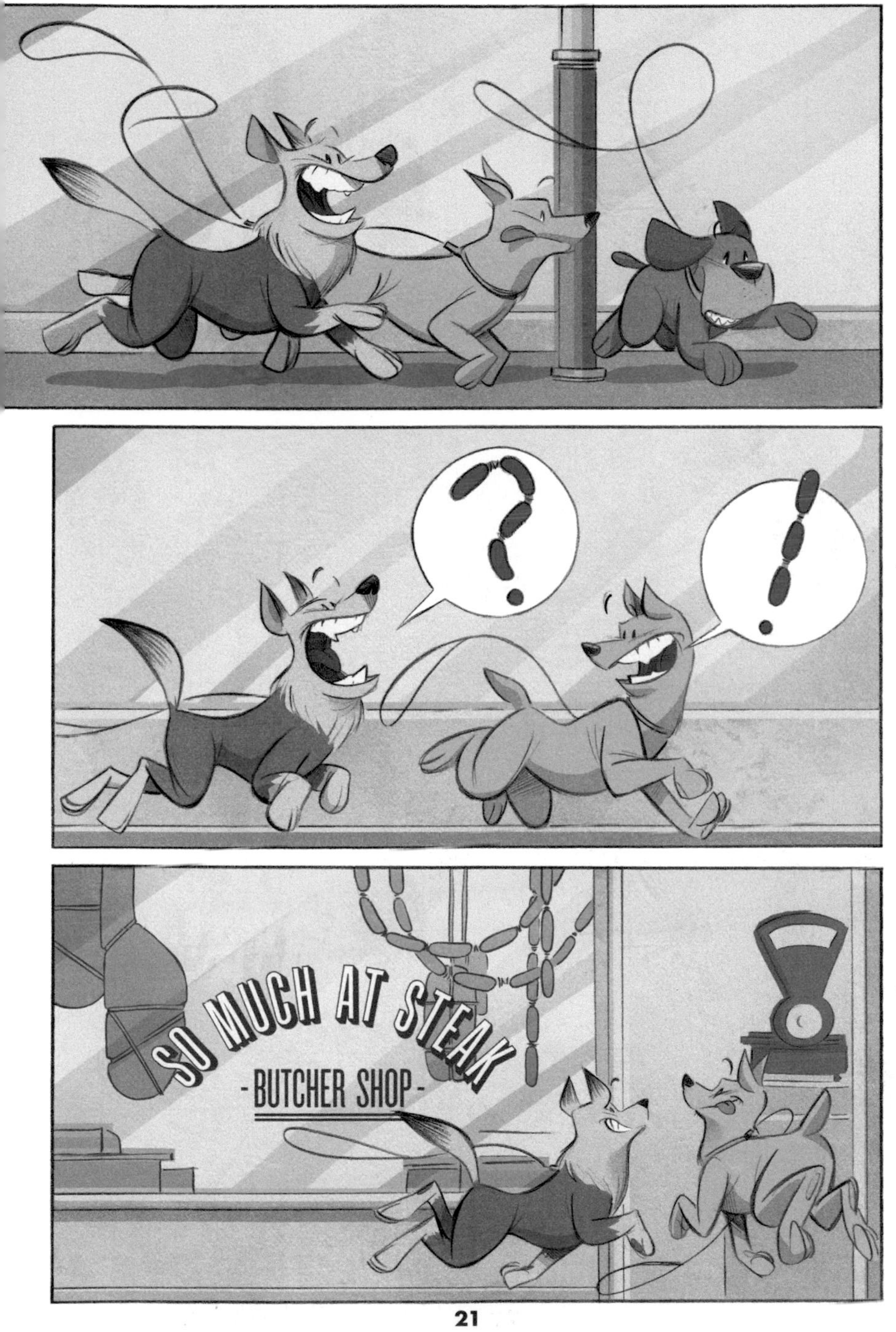
?
!
SO MUCH AT STEAK
-BUTCHER SHOP-

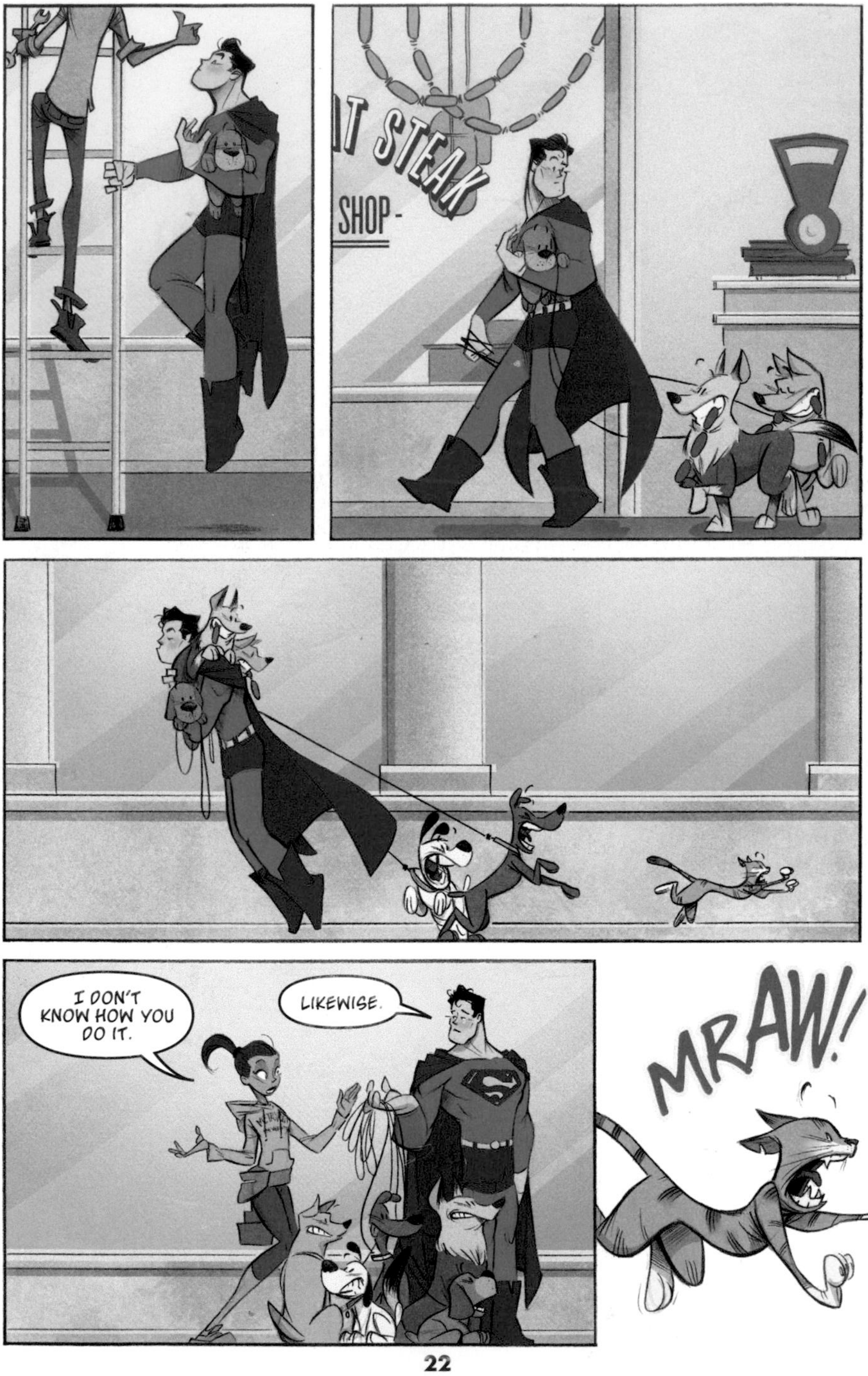
AT STEAK
SHOP -
I DON'T KNOW HOW YOU DO IT.
LIKEWISE.
MRAW!

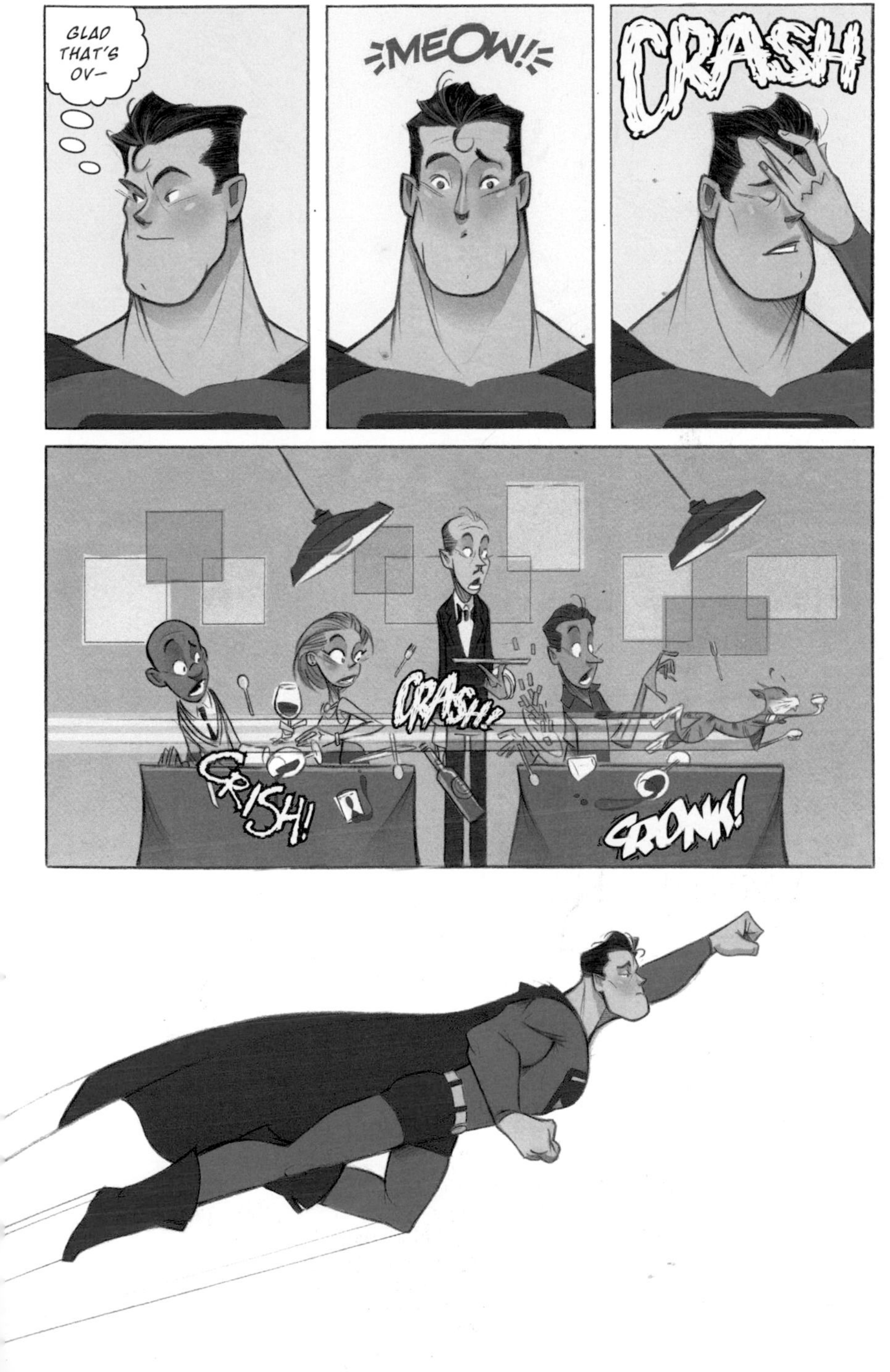
GLAD THAT'S OV—
MEOW!
CRASH
CRASH!
CRISH!
CRONK!

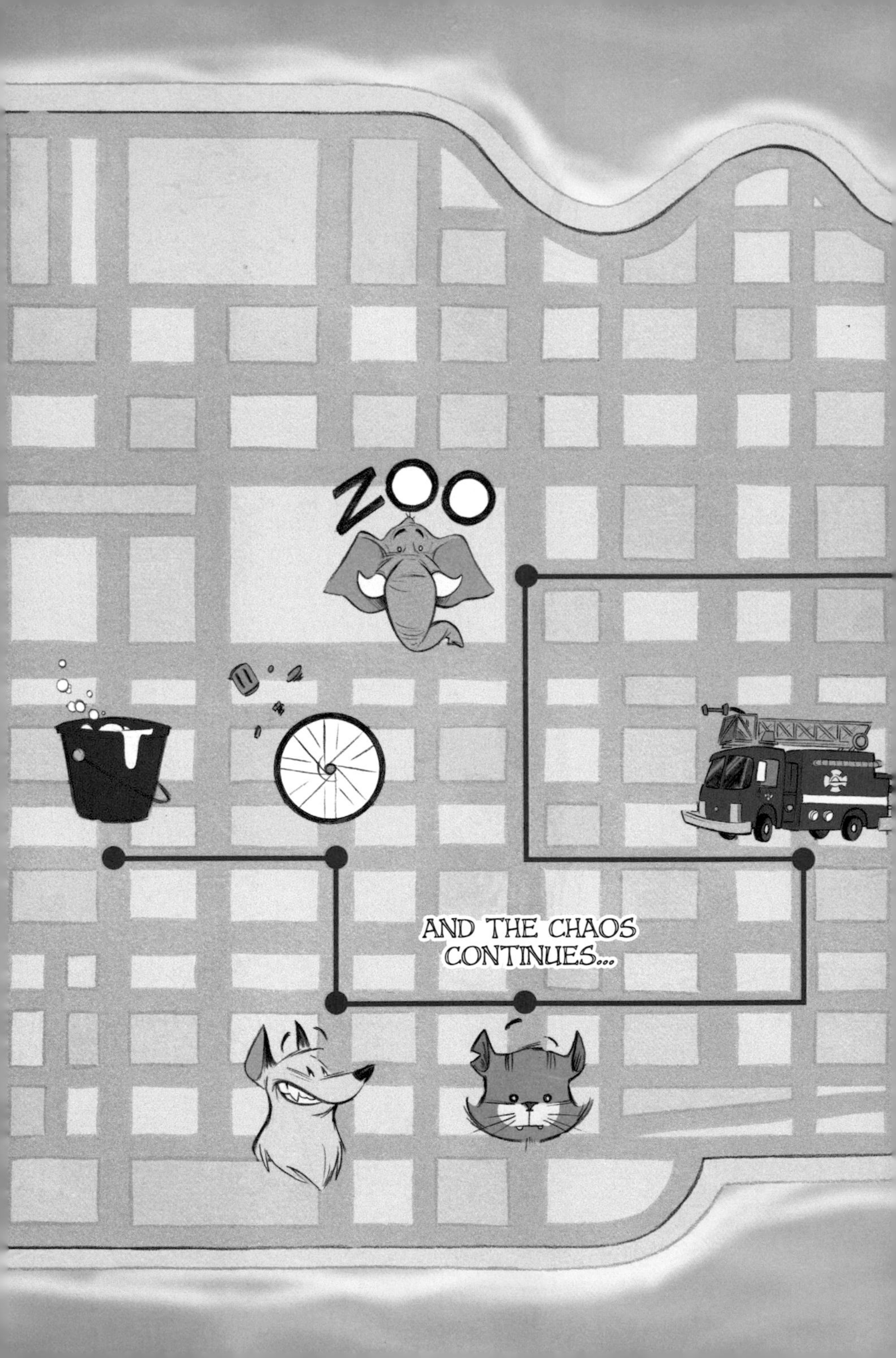
ZOO
AND THE CHAOS CONTINUES...

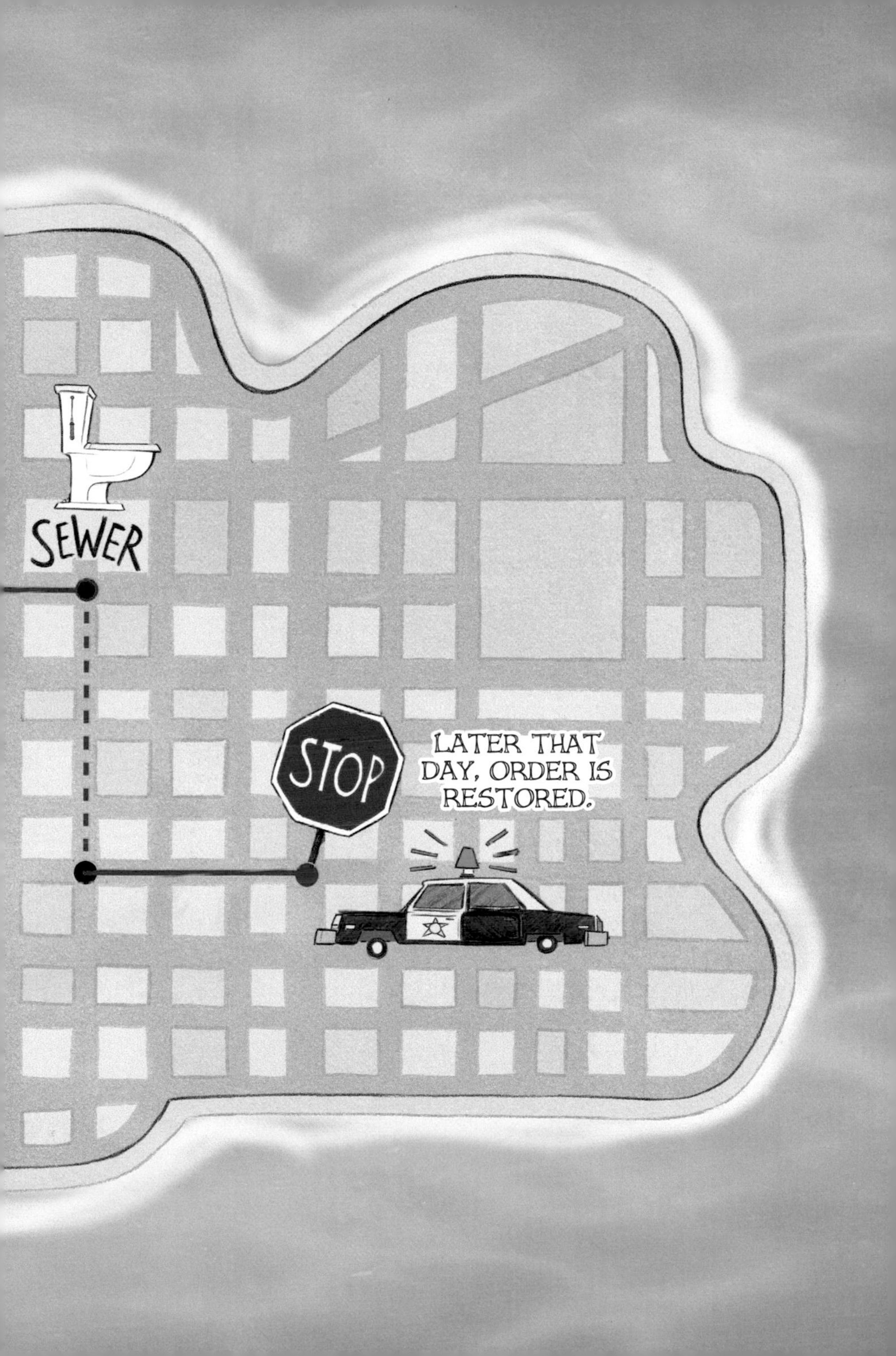
SEWER
STOP
LATER THAT DAY, ORDER IS RESTORED.

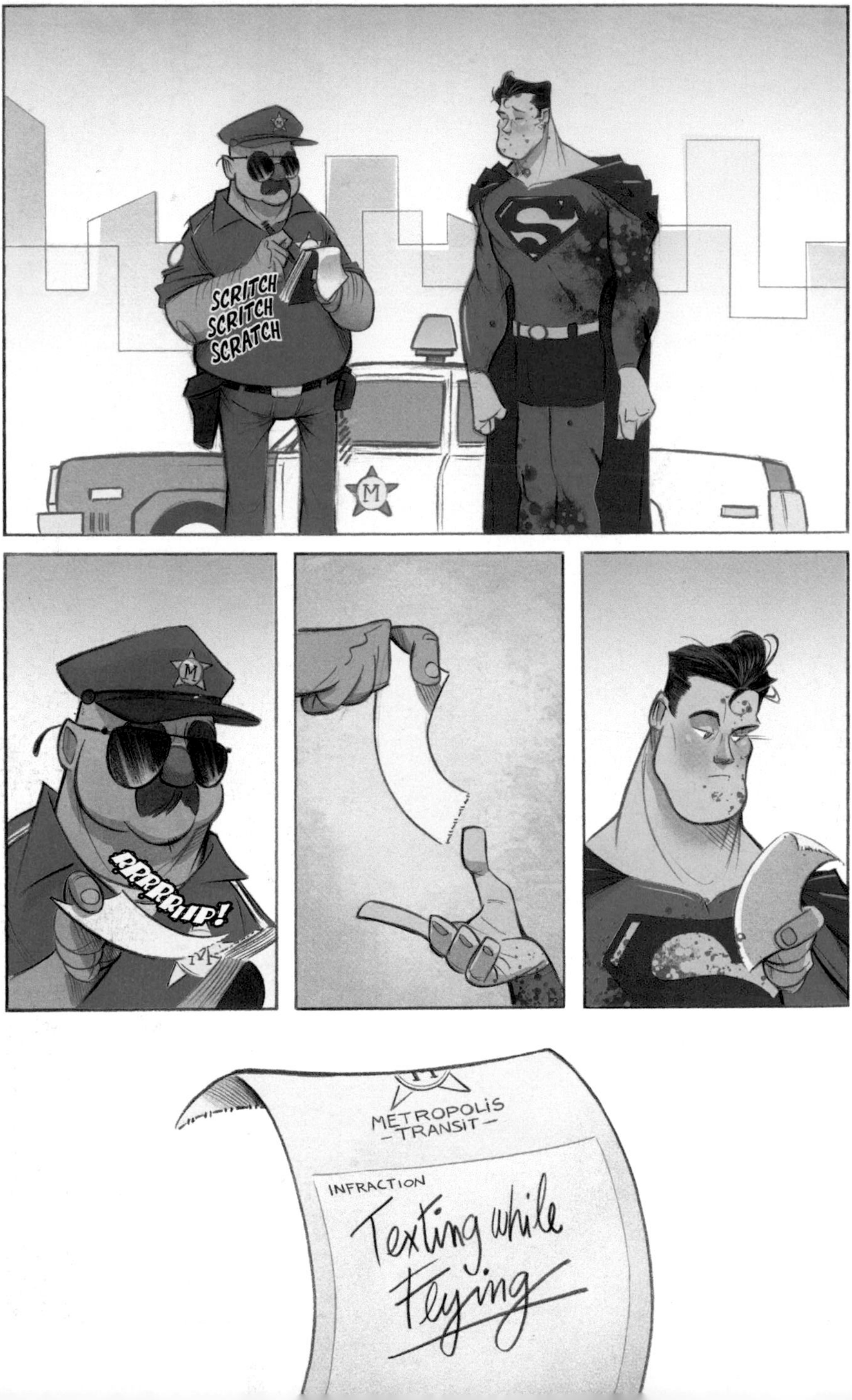
SCRITCH
SCRITCH
SCRATCH
RRRRRIIP!
METROPOLIS
-TRANSIT-
INFRACTION
Texting while
~~Flying~~

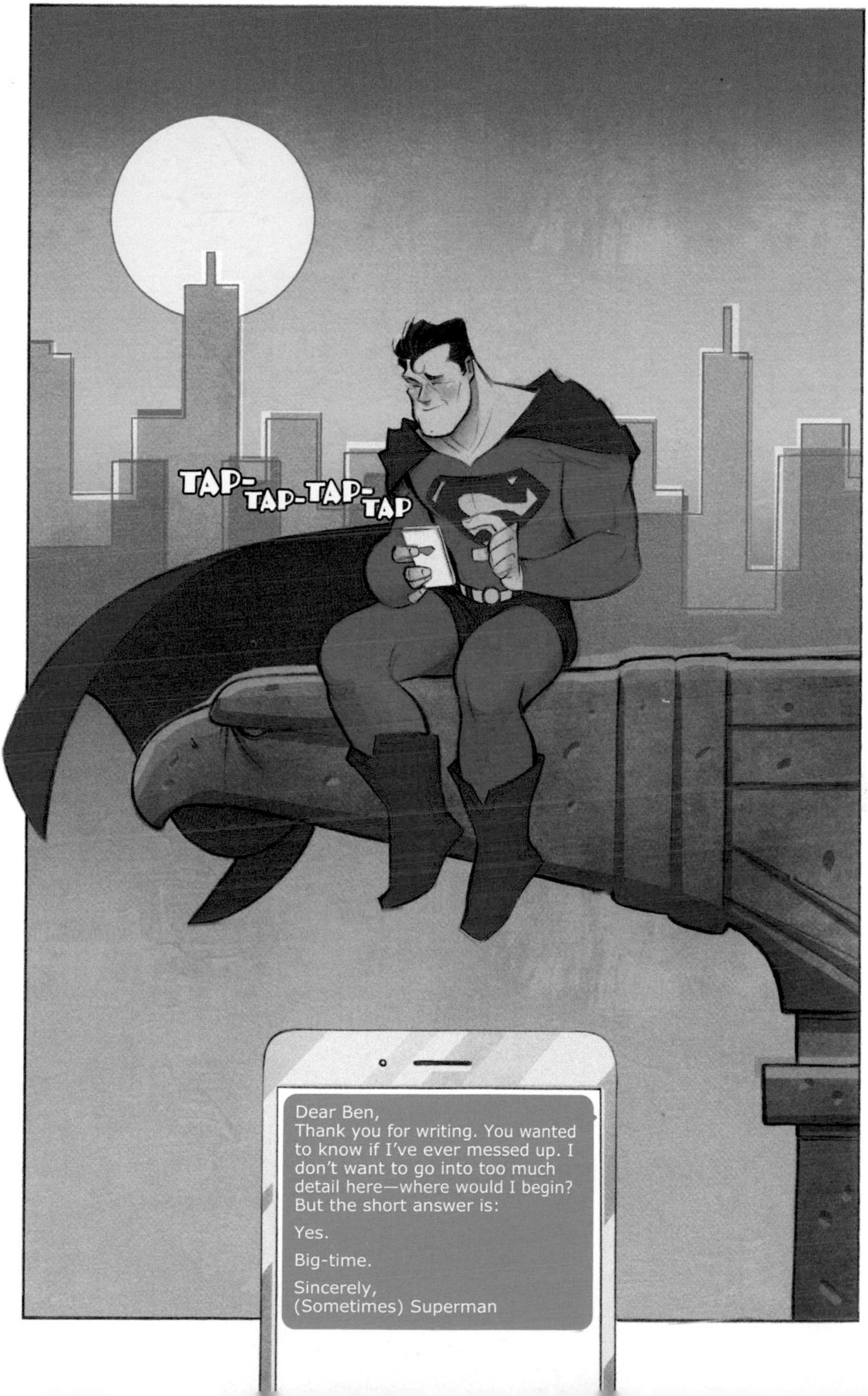
TAP-TAP-TAP-TAP
Dear Ben,
Thank you for writing. You wanted to know if I've ever messed up. I don't want to go into too much detail here—where would I begin? But the short answer is:
Yes.
Big-time.
Sincerely,
(Sometimes) Superman

CHAPTER 2

DEAR HAWKGIRL

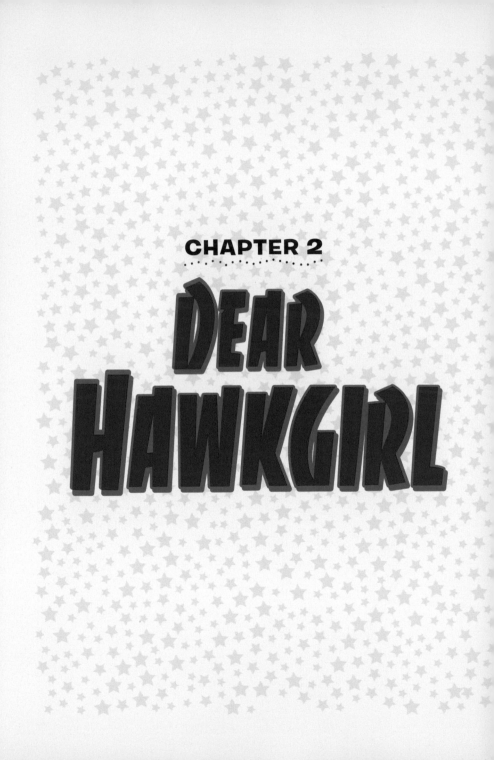

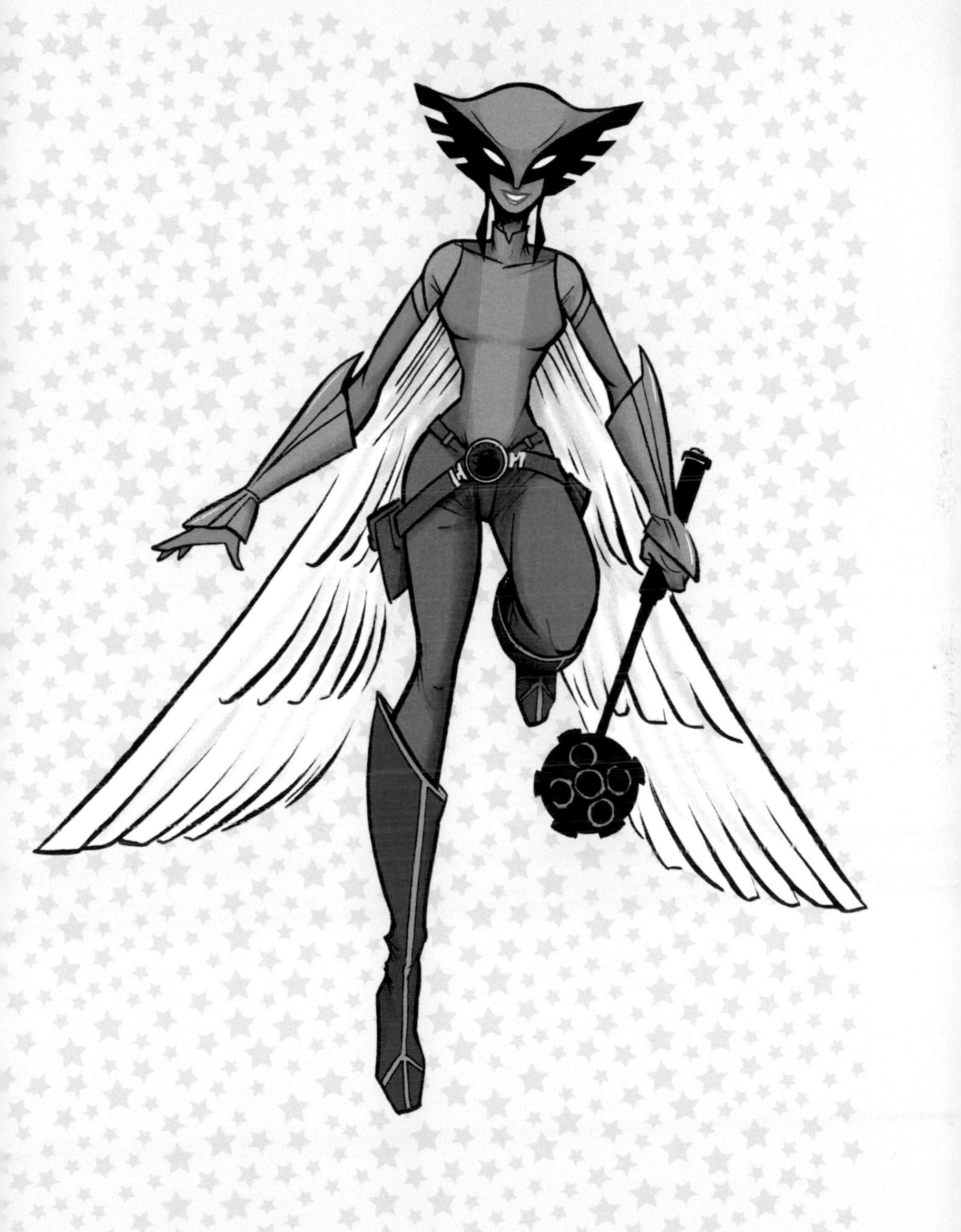

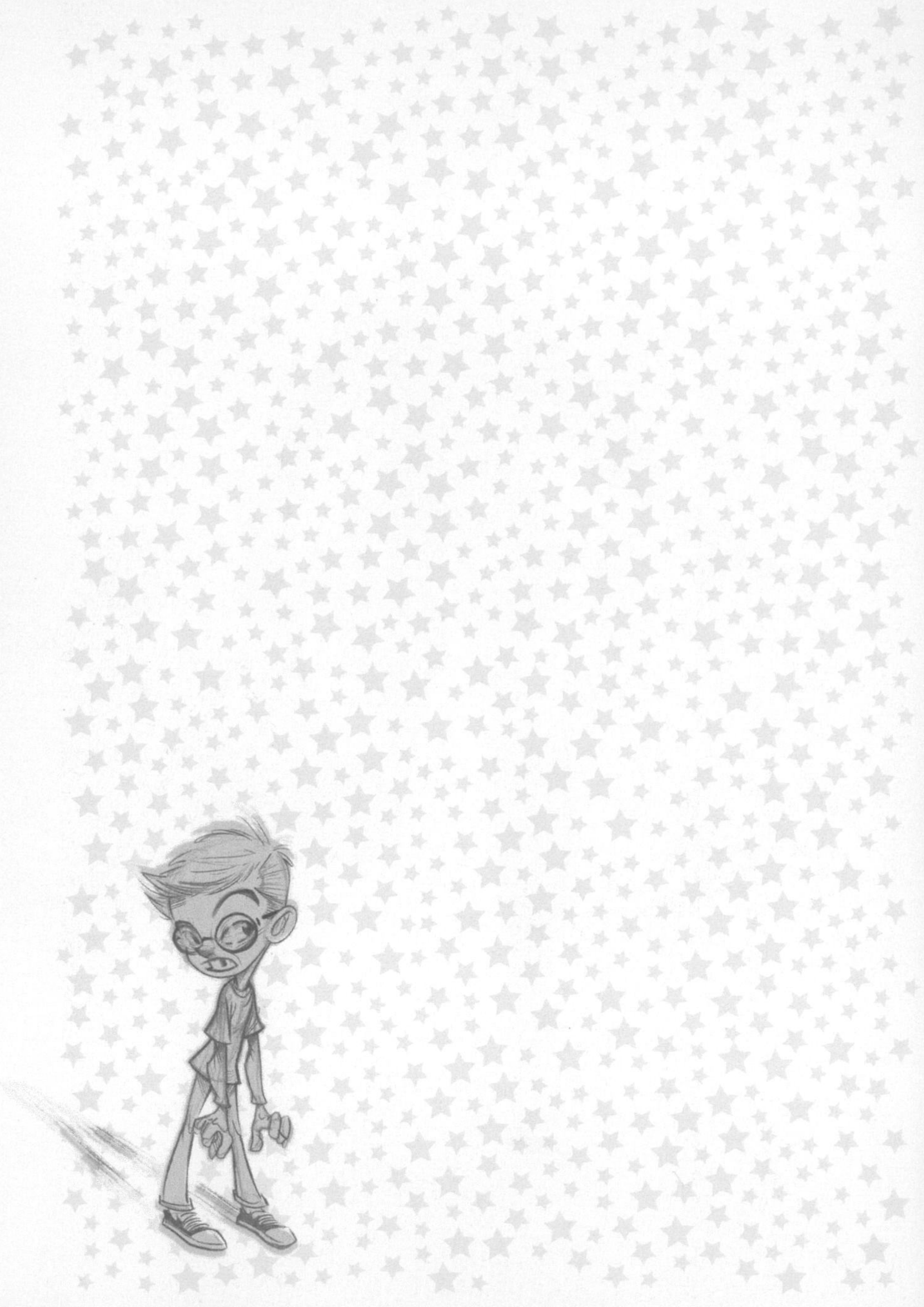

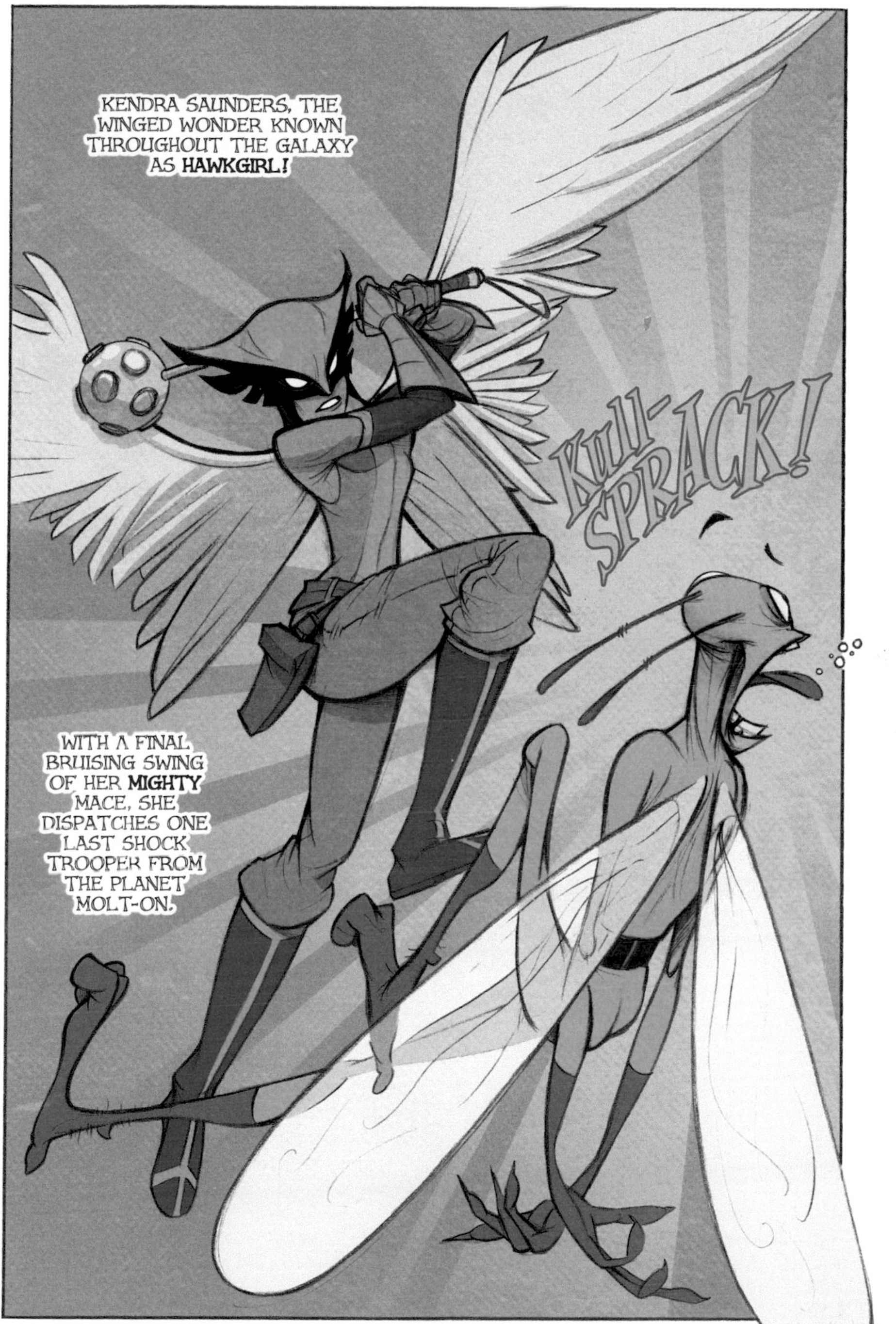
KENDRA SAUNDERS, THE WINGED WONDER KNOWN THROUGHOUT THE GALAXY AS **HAWKGIRL!**
KULL-SPRACK!
WITH A FINAL BRUISING SWING OF HER **MIGHTY** MACE, SHE DISPATCHES ONE LAST SHOCK TROOPER FROM THE PLANET MOLT-ON.

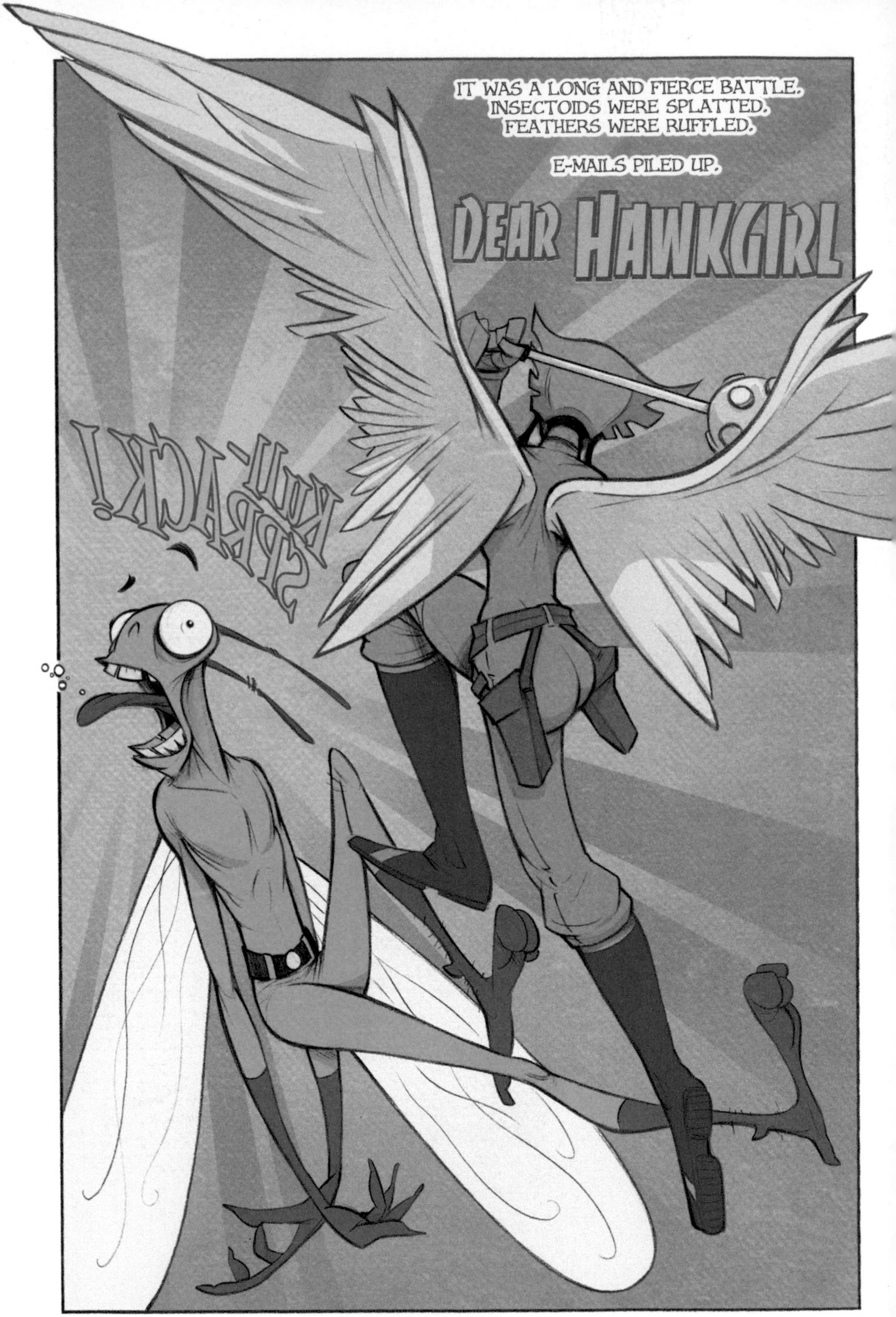
IT WAS A LONG AND FIERCE BATTLE.
INSECTOIDS WERE SPLATTED.
FEATHERS WERE RUFFLED.
E-MAILS PILED UP.
DEAR HAWKGIRL
SPRACK!

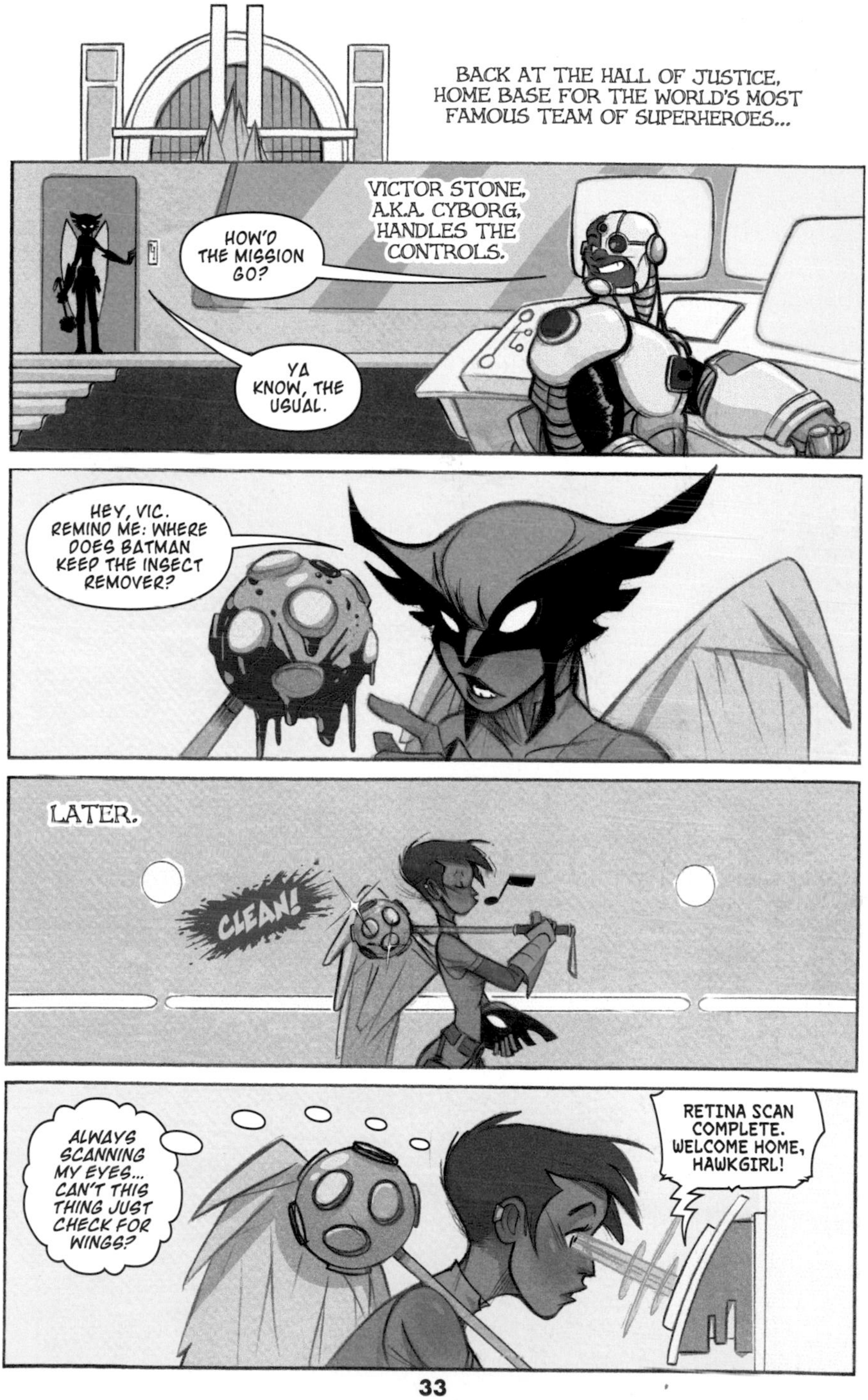
BACK AT THE HALL OF JUSTICE, HOME BASE FOR THE WORLD'S MOST FAMOUS TEAM OF SUPERHEROES...
VICTOR STONE, A.K.A. CYBORG, HANDLES THE CONTROLS.
HOW'D THE MISSION GO?
YA KNOW, THE USUAL.
HEY, VIC. REMIND ME: WHERE DOES BATMAN KEEP THE INSECT REMOVER?
LATER.
CLEAN!
ALWAYS SCANNING MY EYES... CAN'T THIS THING JUST CHECK FOR WINGS?
RETINA SCAN COMPLETE. WELCOME HOME, HAWKGIRL!

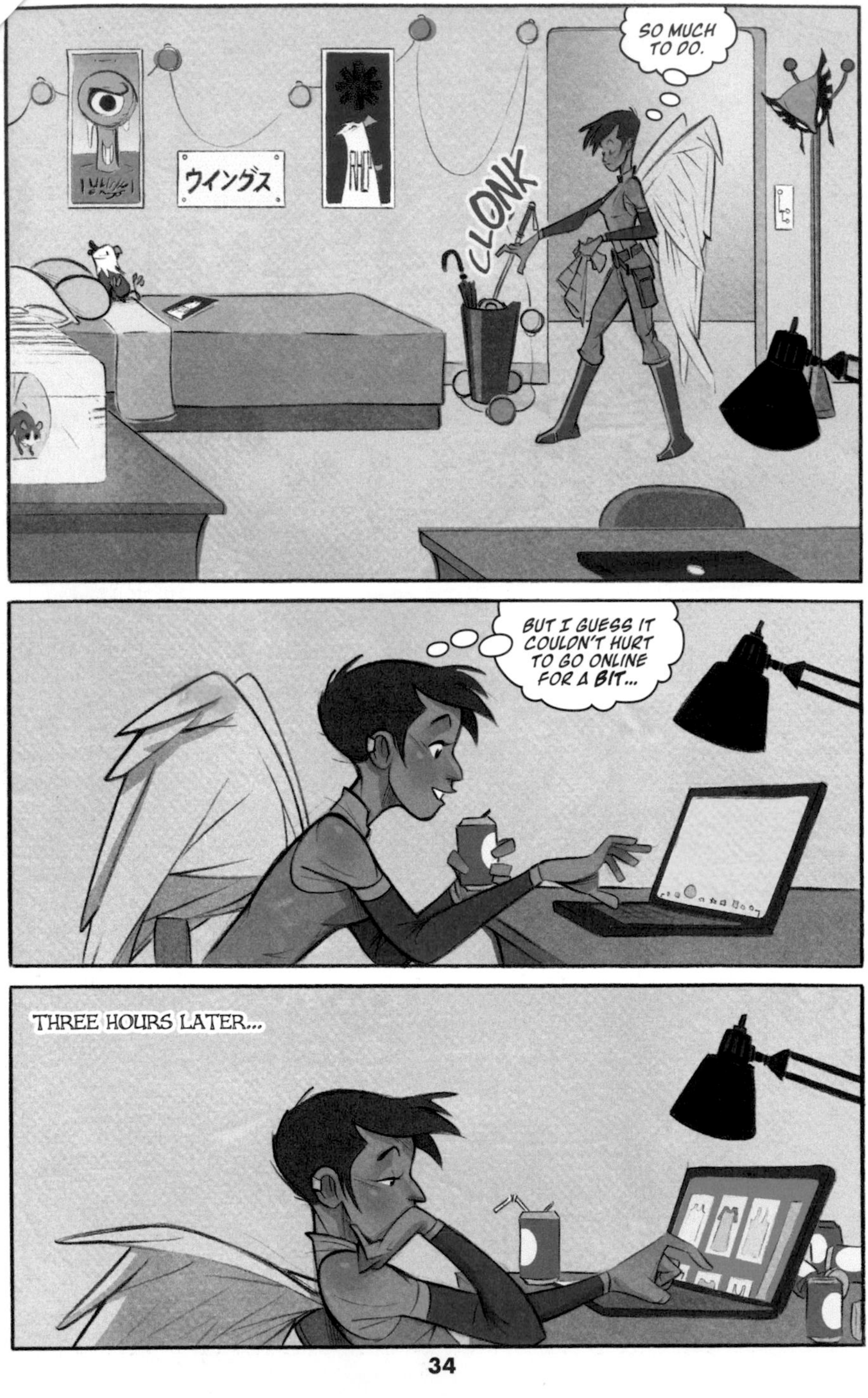
SO MUCH TO DO.
ウイングス
CLONK
BUT I GUESS IT COULDN'T HURT TO GO ONLINE FOR A BIT...
THREE HOURS LATER...

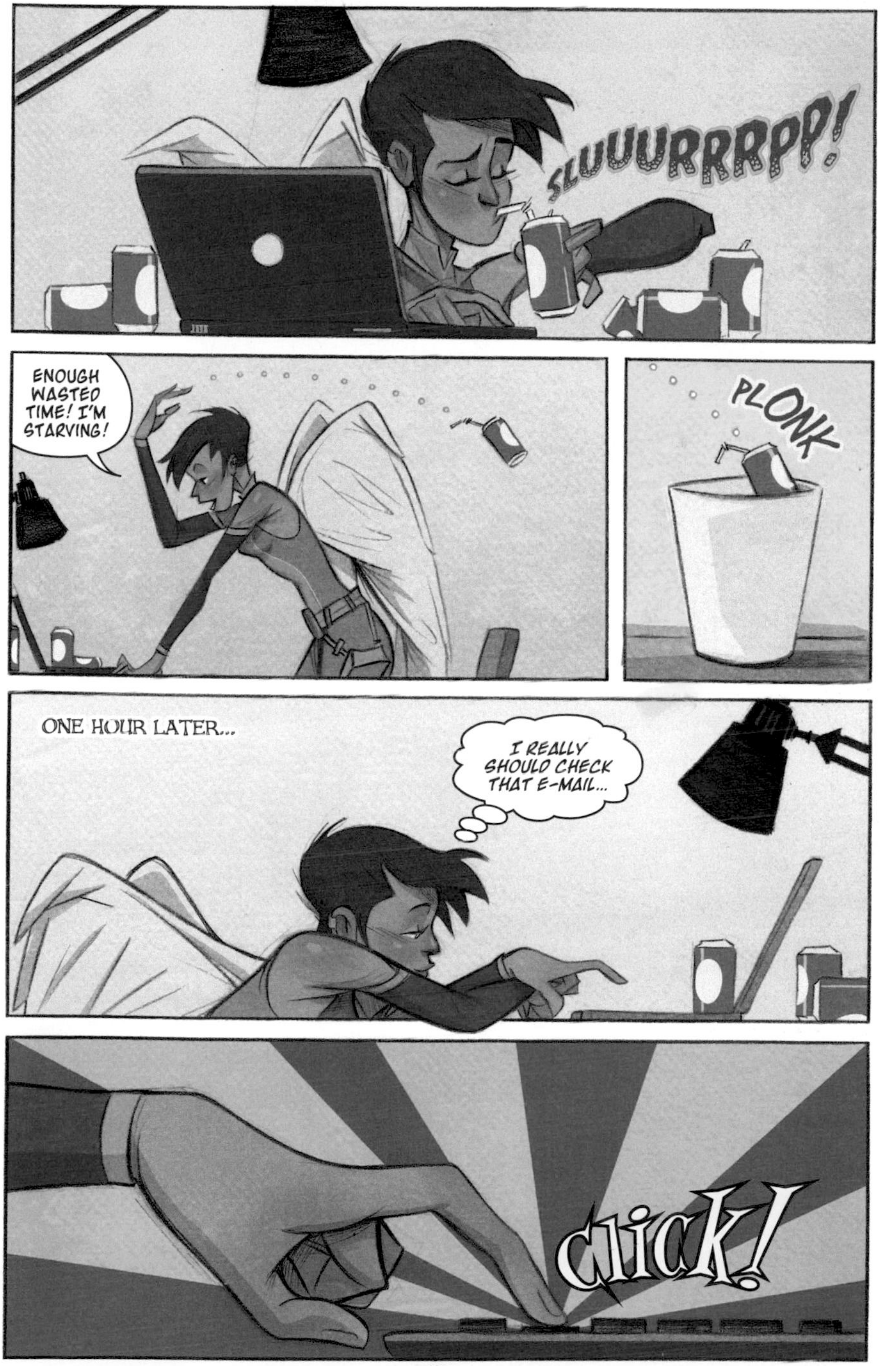
SLUUURRRPP!
ENOUGH WASTED TIME! I'M STARVING!
PLONK
ONE HOUR LATER...
I REALLY SHOULD CHECK THAT E-MAIL...
CLICK!

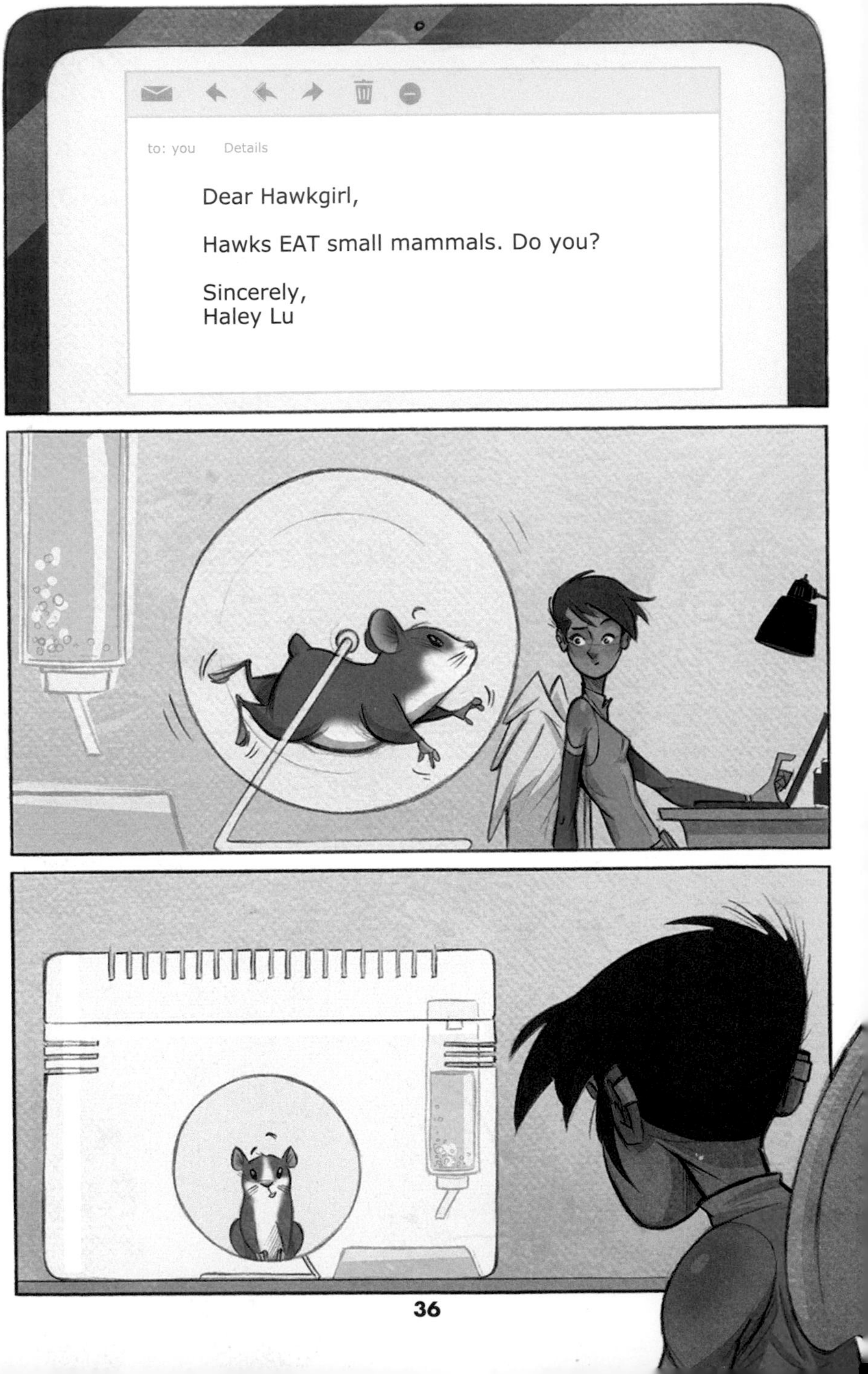
to: you
Details
Dear Hawkgirl,
Hawks EAT small mammals. Do you?
Sincerely,
Haley Lu

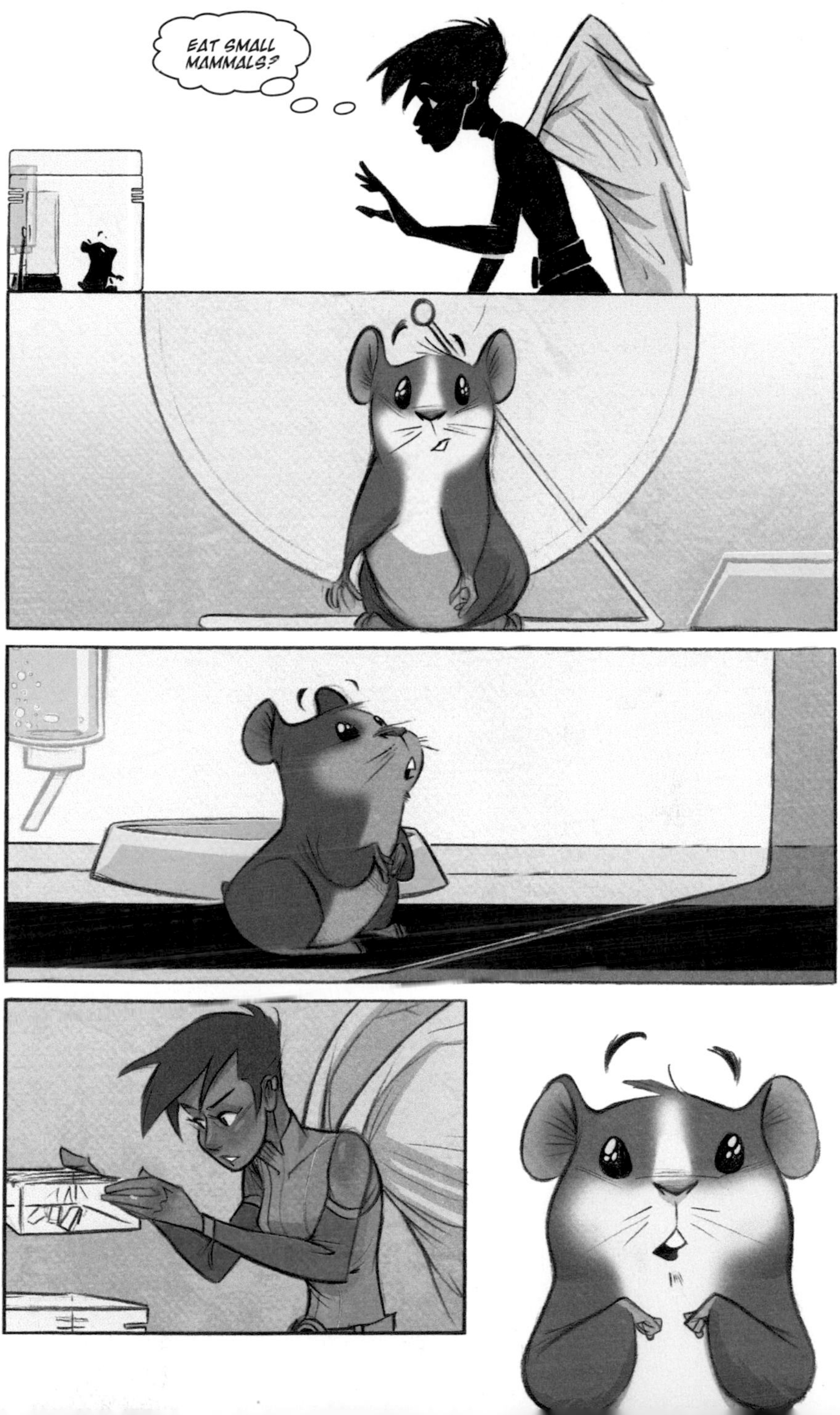
EAT SMALL
MAMMALS?

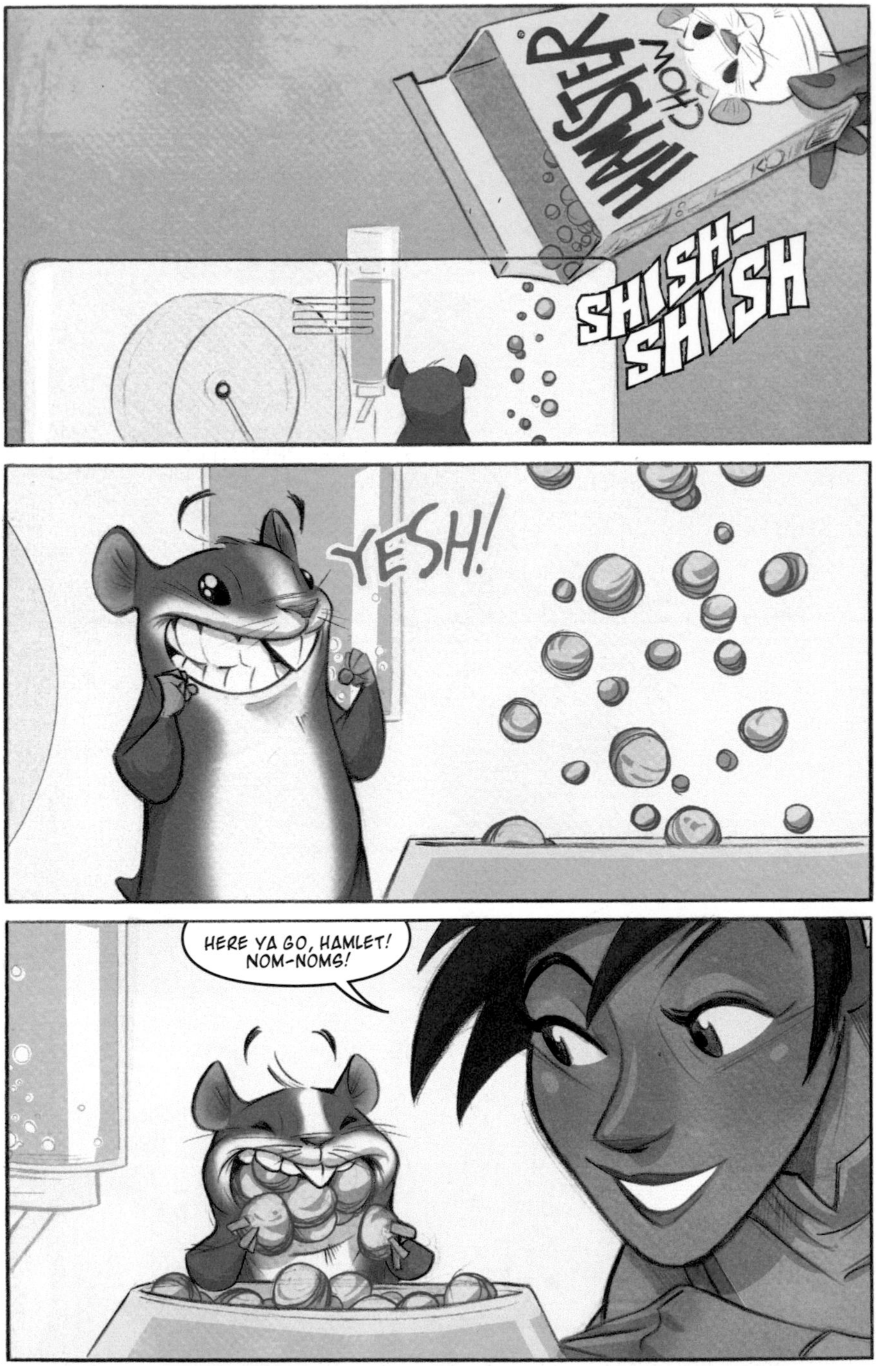
HAMSTER CHOW
SHISH-SHISH
YESH!
HERE YA GO, HAMLET! NOM-NOMS!

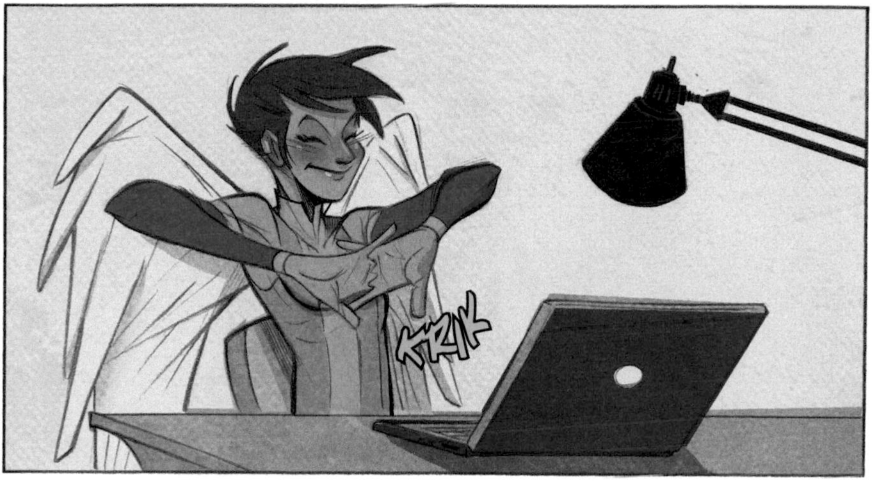
KRIK

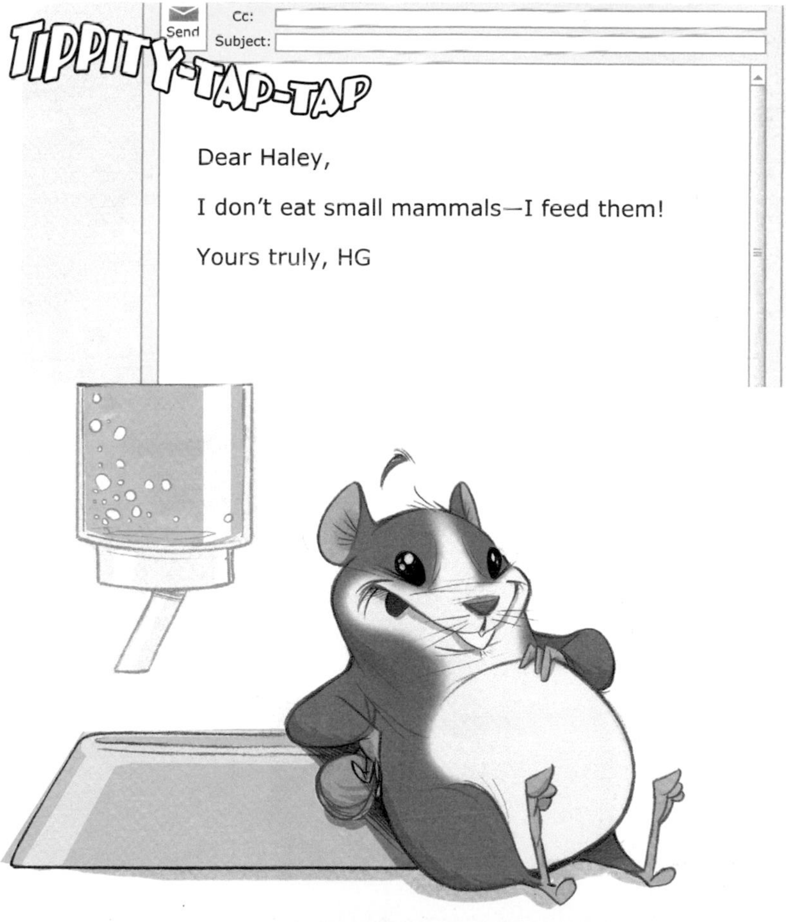
Send
Cc:
Subject:
TIPPITY-TAP-TAP
Dear Haley,
I don't eat small mammals—I feed them!
Yours truly, HG

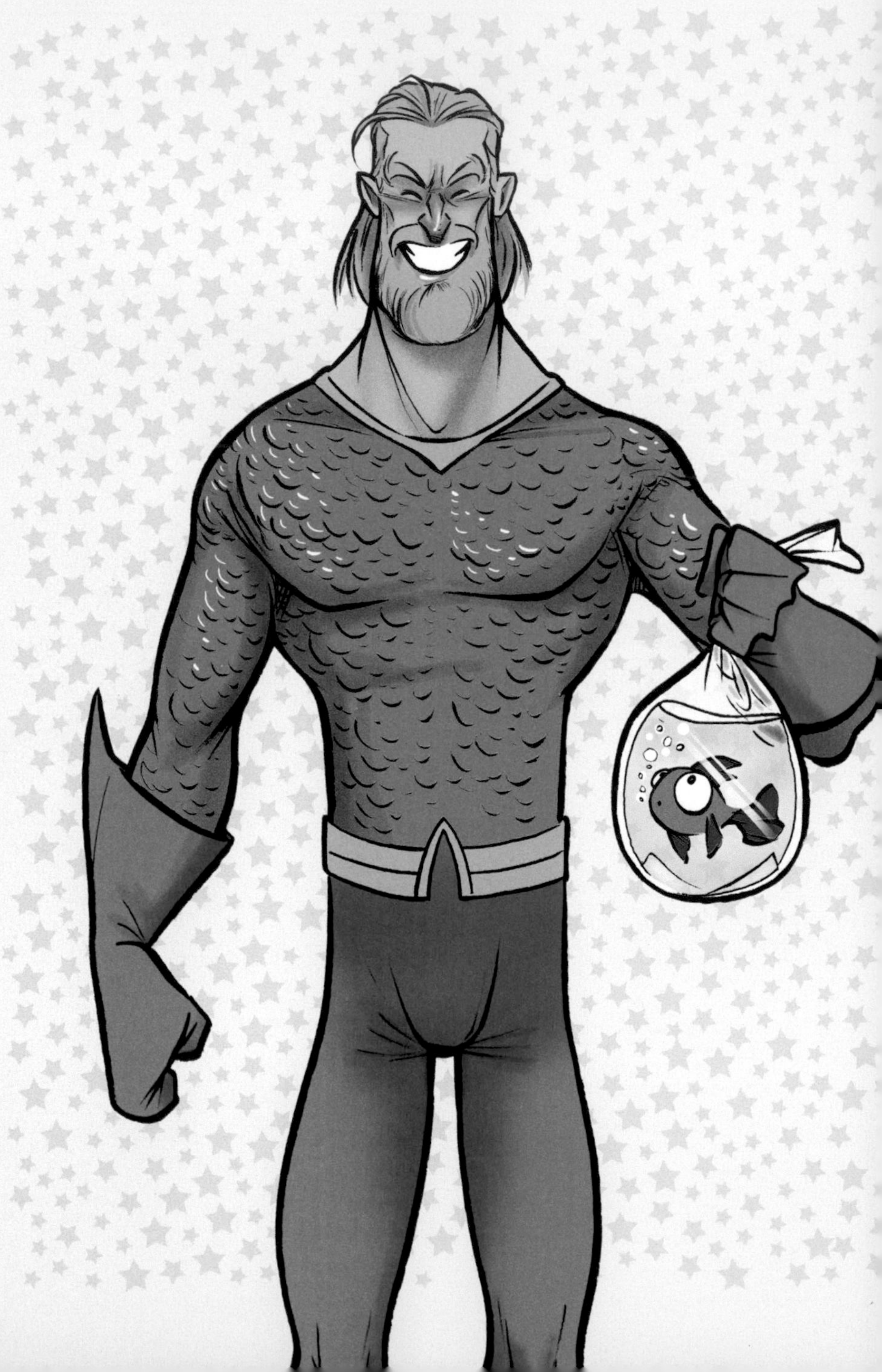

CHAPTER 3

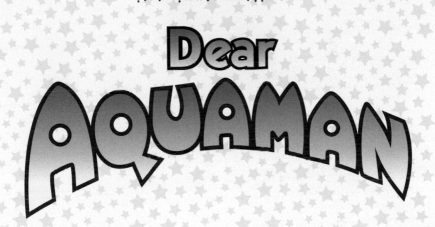

Dear AQUAMAN

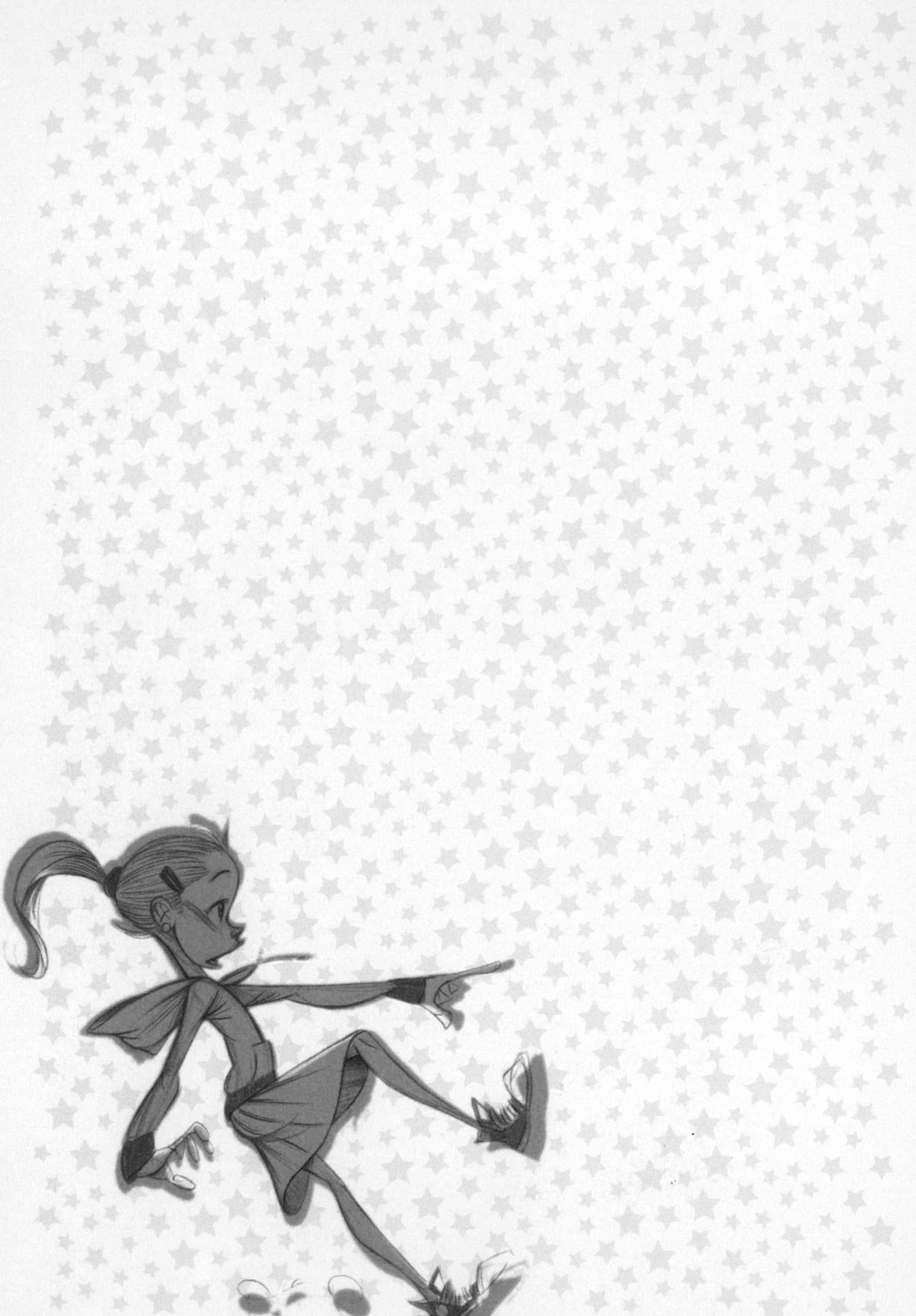

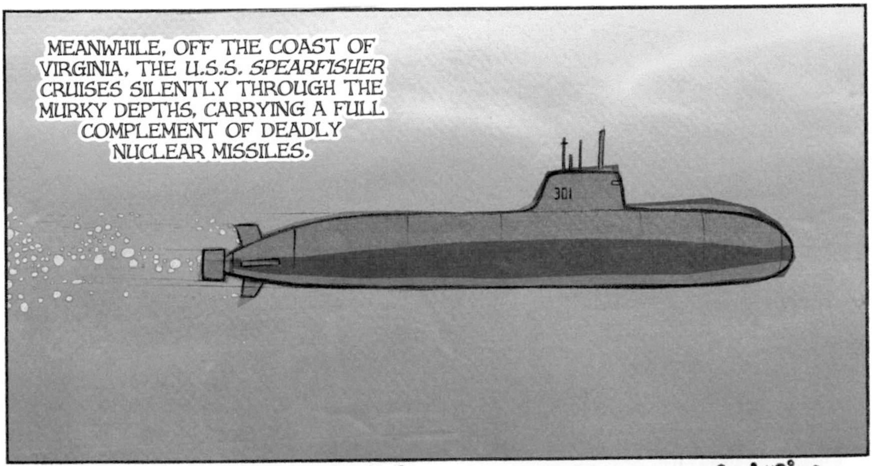
MEANWHILE, OFF THE COAST OF VIRGINIA, THE U.S.S. *SPEARFISHER* CRUISES SILENTLY THROUGH THE MURKY DEPTHS, CARRYING A FULL COMPLEMENT OF DEADLY NUCLEAR MISSILES.
301

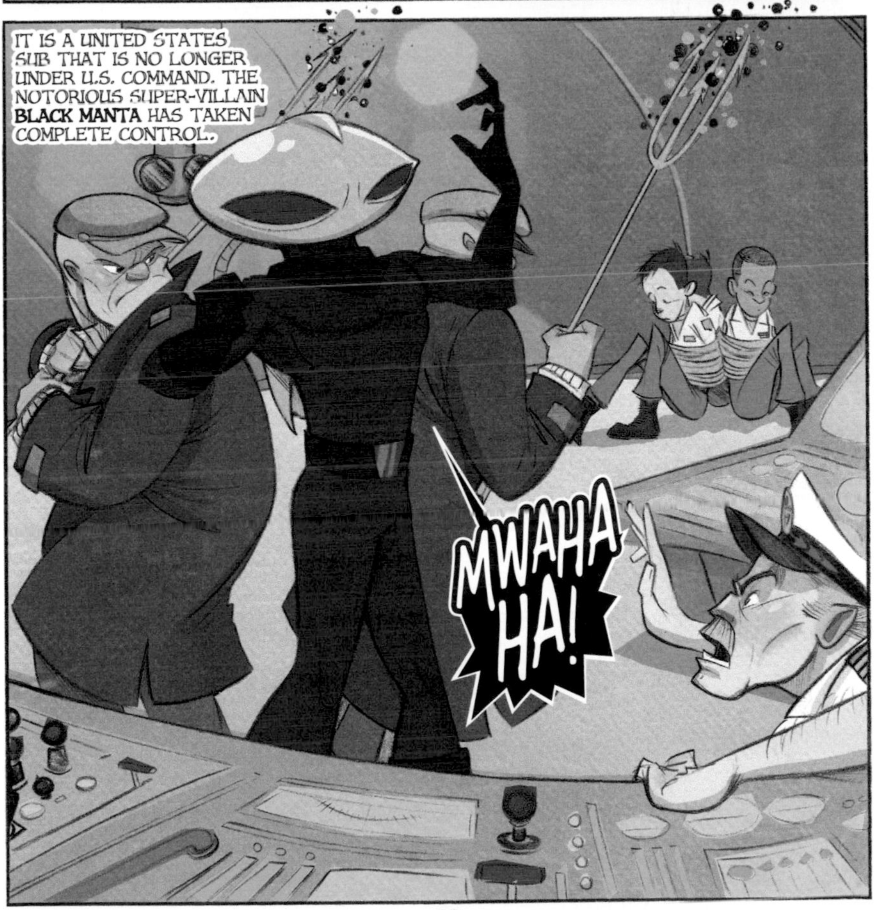
IT IS A UNITED STATES SUB THAT IS NO LONGER UNDER U.S. COMMAND. THE NOTORIOUS SUPER-VILLAIN **BLACK MANTA** HAS TAKEN COMPLETE CONTROL.
MWAHA HA!

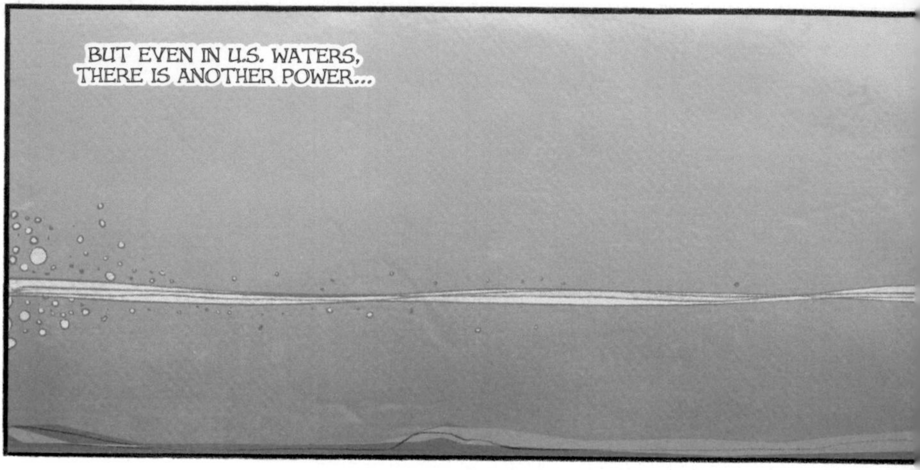
BUT EVEN IN U.S. WATERS, THERE IS ANOTHER POWER...

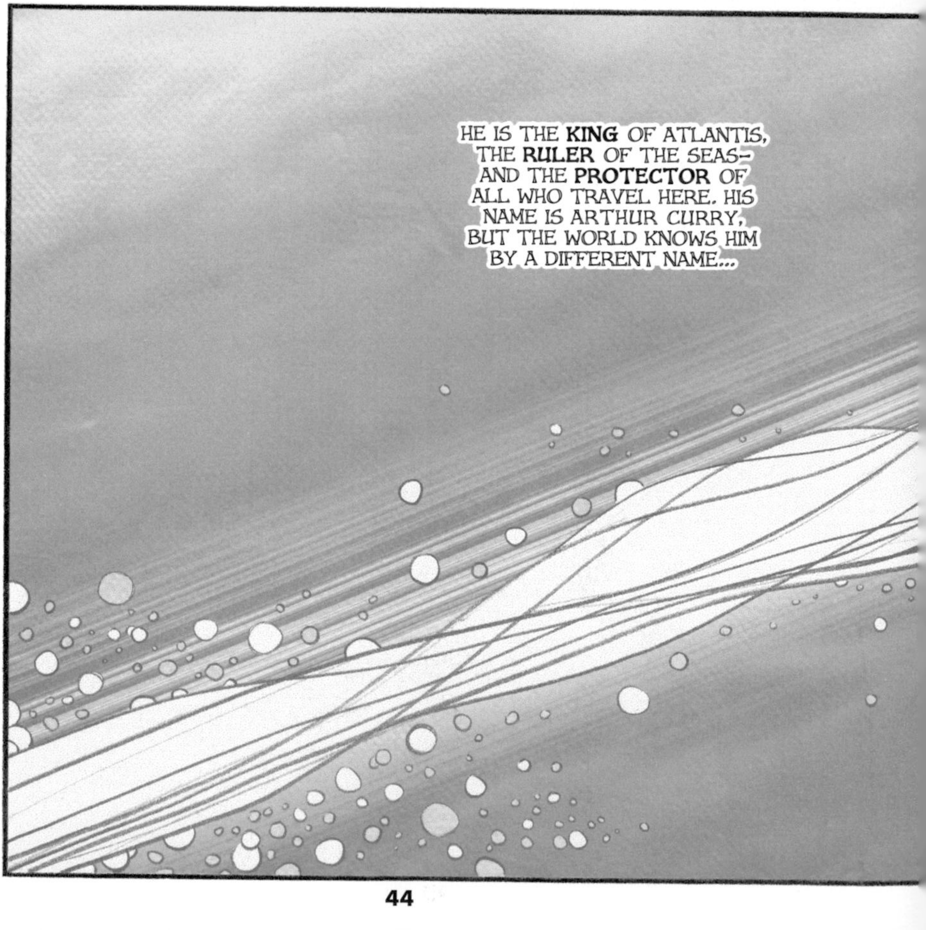
HE IS THE KING OF ATLANTIS, THE RULER OF THE SEAS-- AND THE PROTECTOR OF ALL WHO TRAVEL HERE. HIS NAME IS ARTHUR CURRY, BUT THE WORLD KNOWS HIM BY A DIFFERENT NAME...

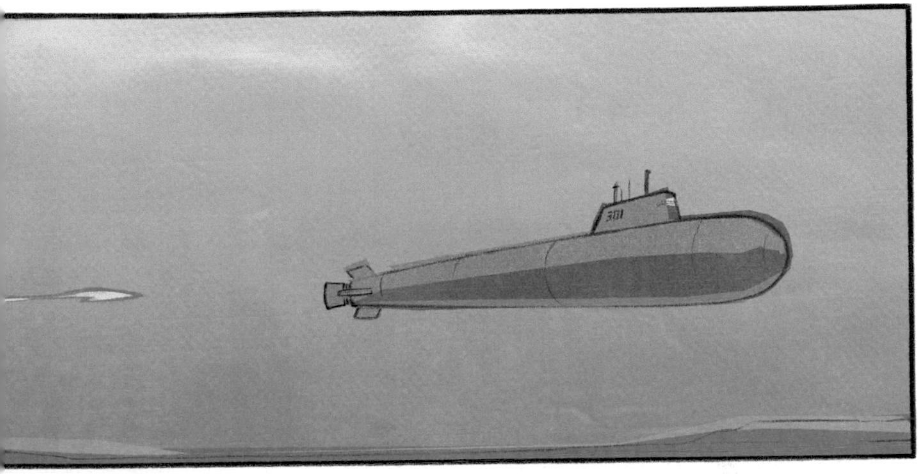

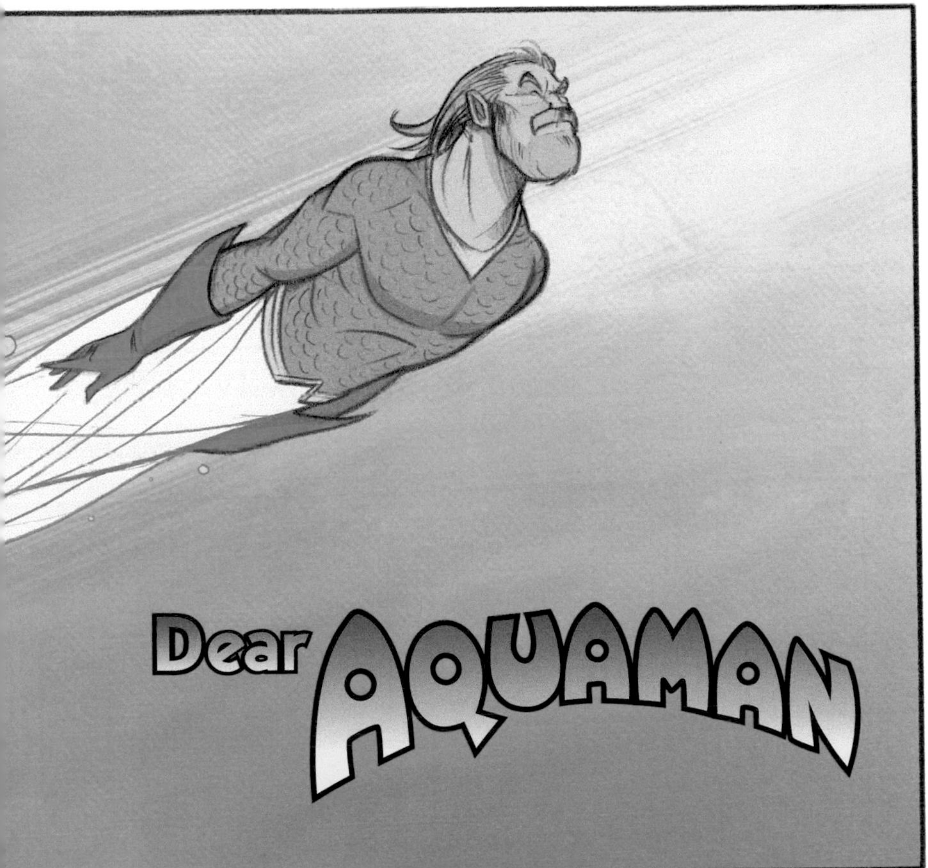
Dear AQUAMAN

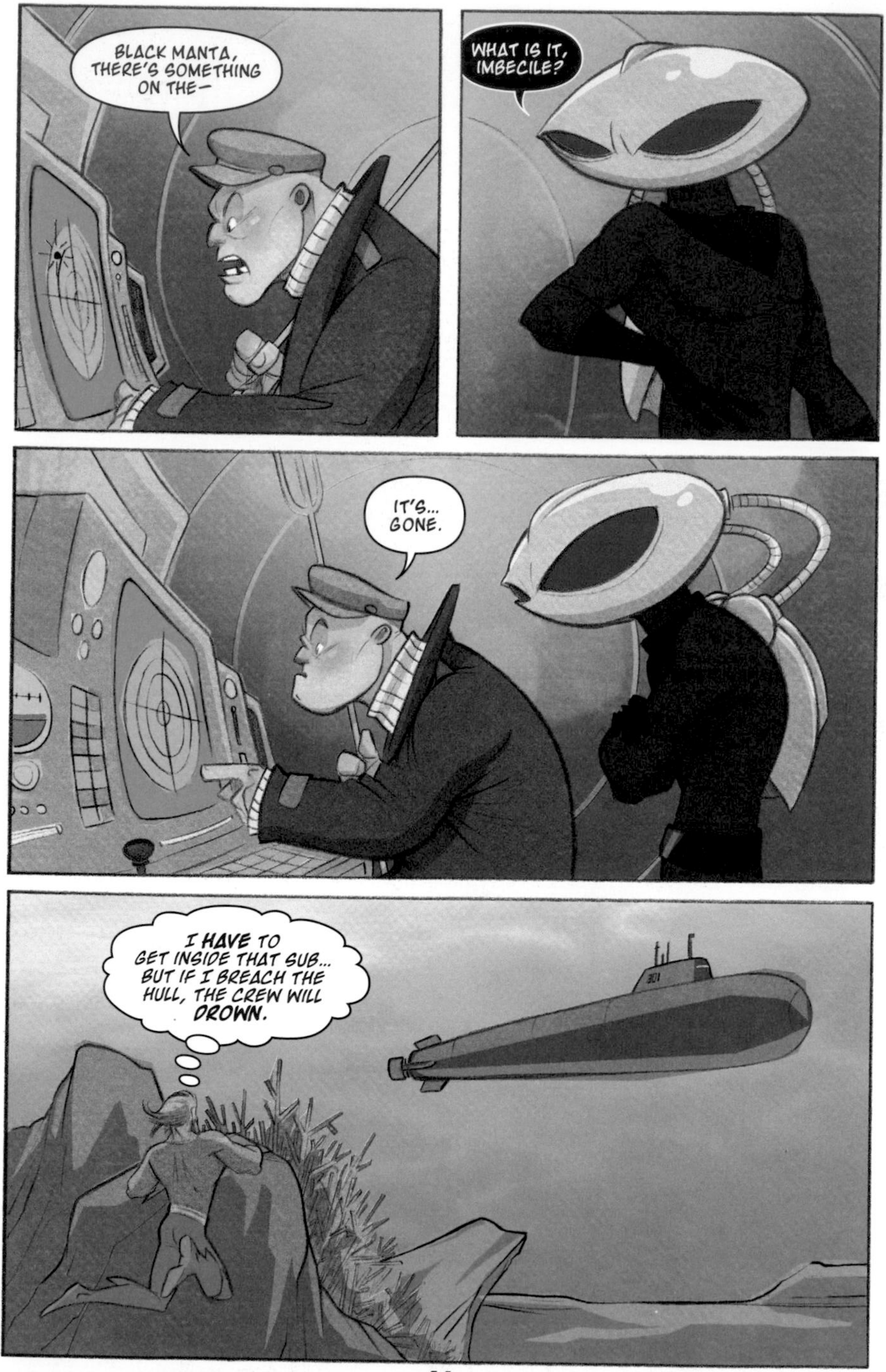
BLACK MANTA, THERE'S SOMETHING ON THE—
WHAT IS IT, IMBECILE?
IT'S... GONE.
I HAVE TO GET INSIDE THAT SUB... BUT IF I BREACH THE HULL, THE CREW WILL DROWN.
301

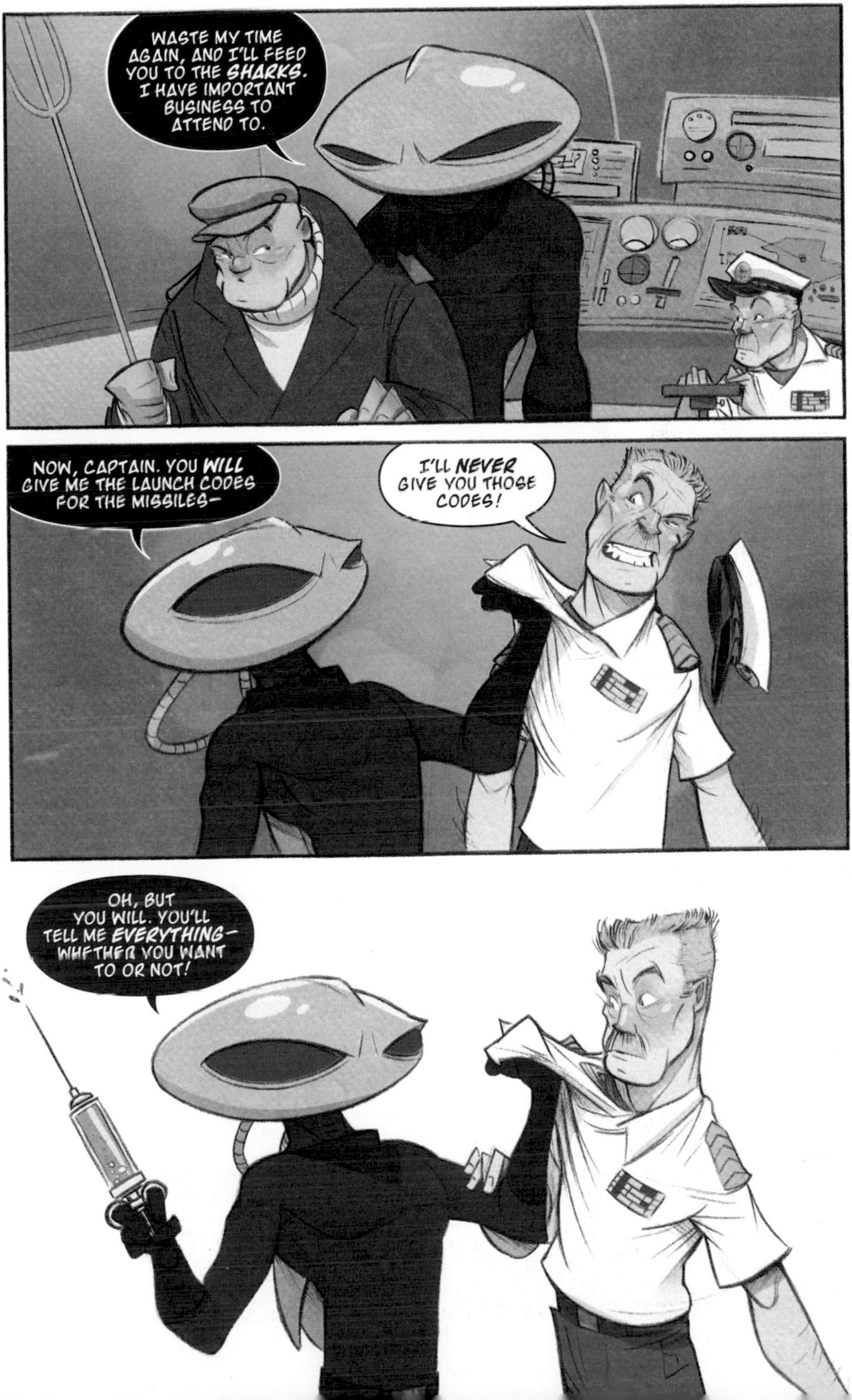
WASTE MY TIME AGAIN, AND I'LL FEED YOU TO THE ***SHARKS.*** I HAVE IMPORTANT BUSINESS TO ATTEND TO.
NOW, CAPTAIN. YOU ***WILL*** GIVE ME THE LAUNCH CODES FOR THE MISSILES—
I'LL ***NEVER*** GIVE YOU THOSE CODES!
OH, BUT YOU WILL. YOU'LL TELL ME ***EVERYTHING***— WHETHER YOU WANT TO OR NOT!

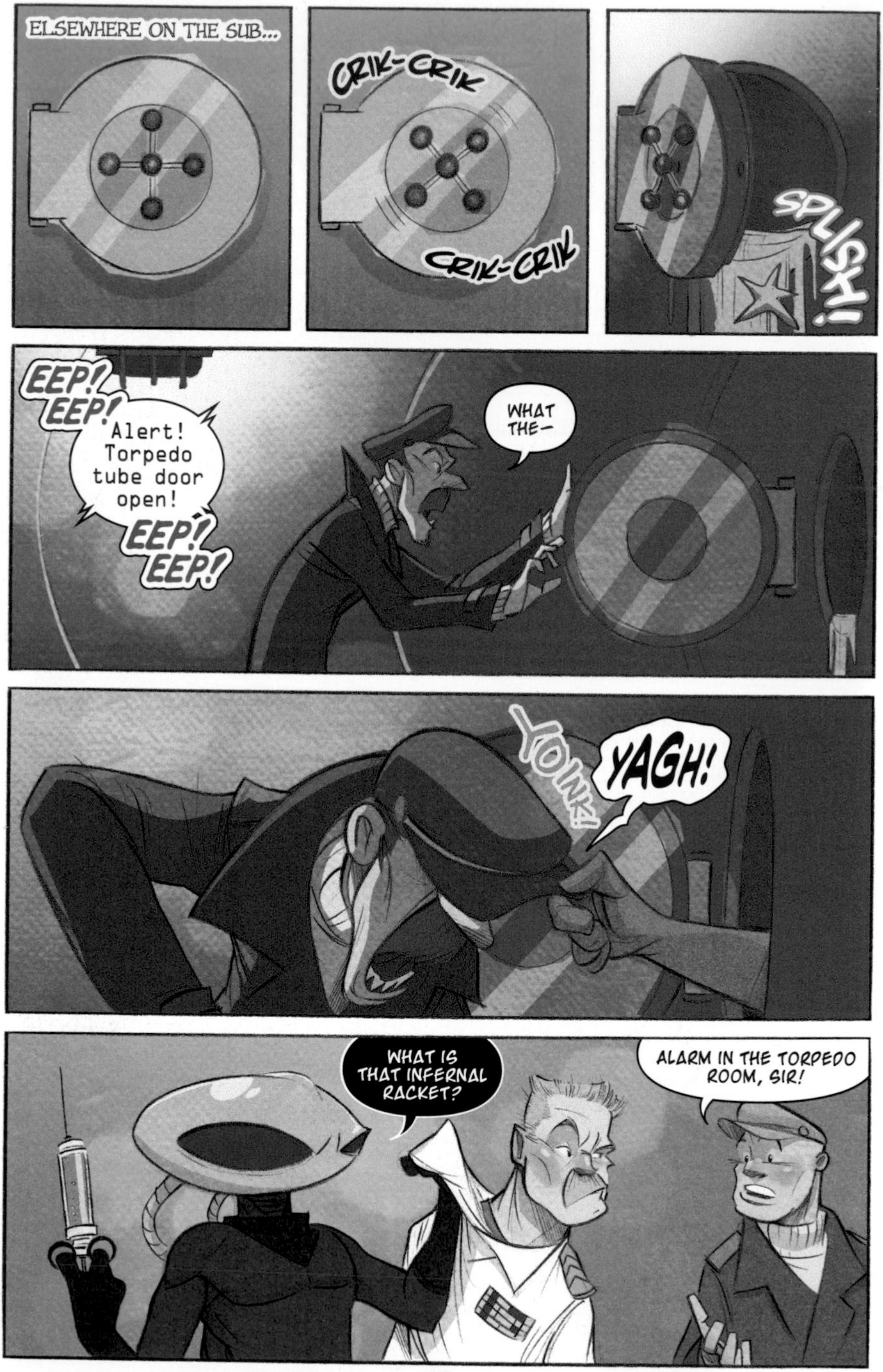
ELSEWHERE ON THE SUB...
CRIK-CRIK
CRIK-CRIK
SPLISH!
EEP! EEP!
Alert! Torpedo tube door open!
EEP! EEP!
WHAT THE—
YOINK!
YAGH!
WHAT IS THAT INFERNAL RACKET?
ALARM IN THE TORPEDO ROOM, SIR!

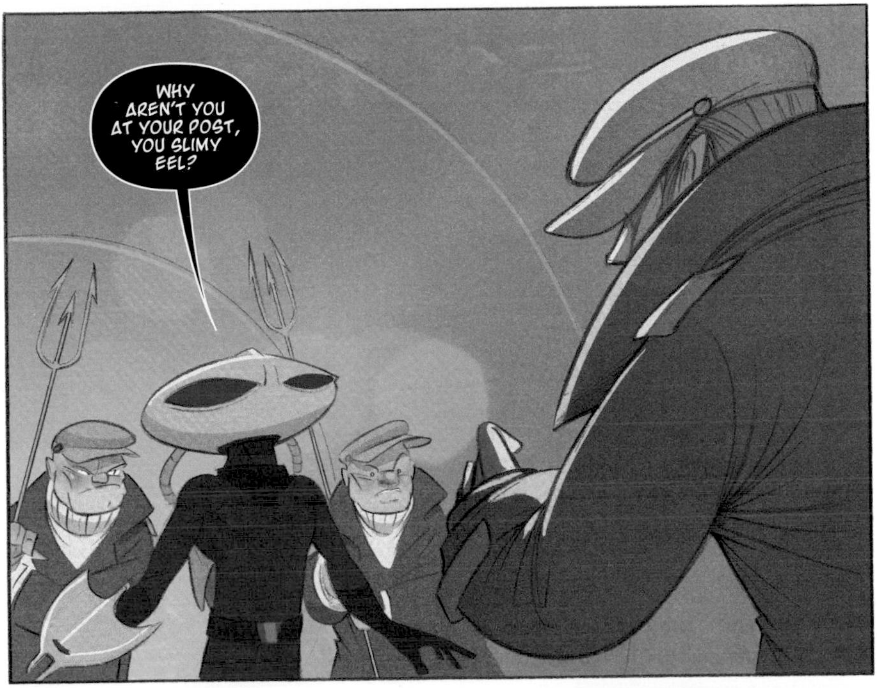
WHY AREN'T YOU AT YOUR POST, YOU SLIMY EEL?

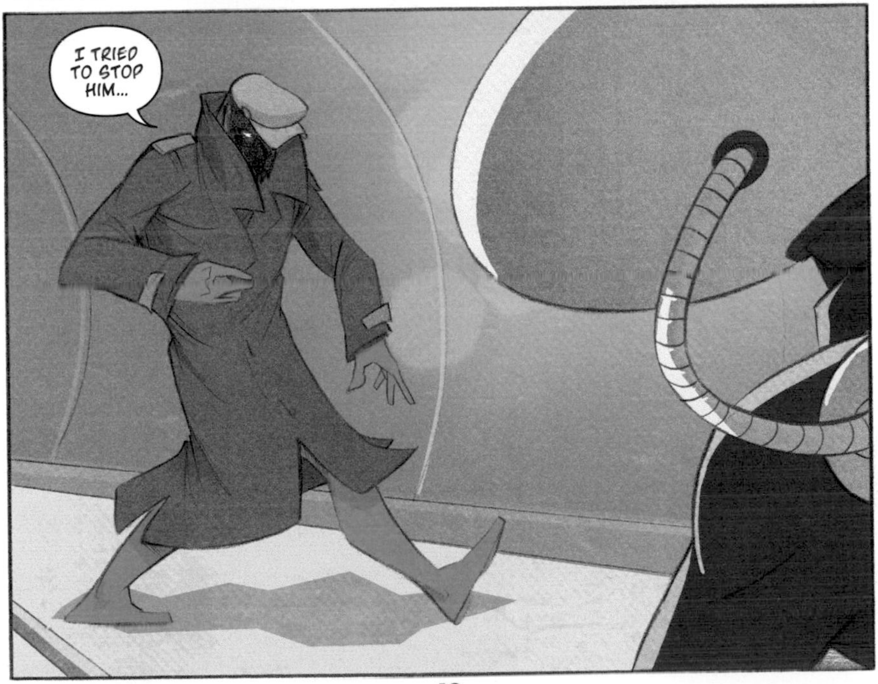
I TRIED TO STOP HIM...

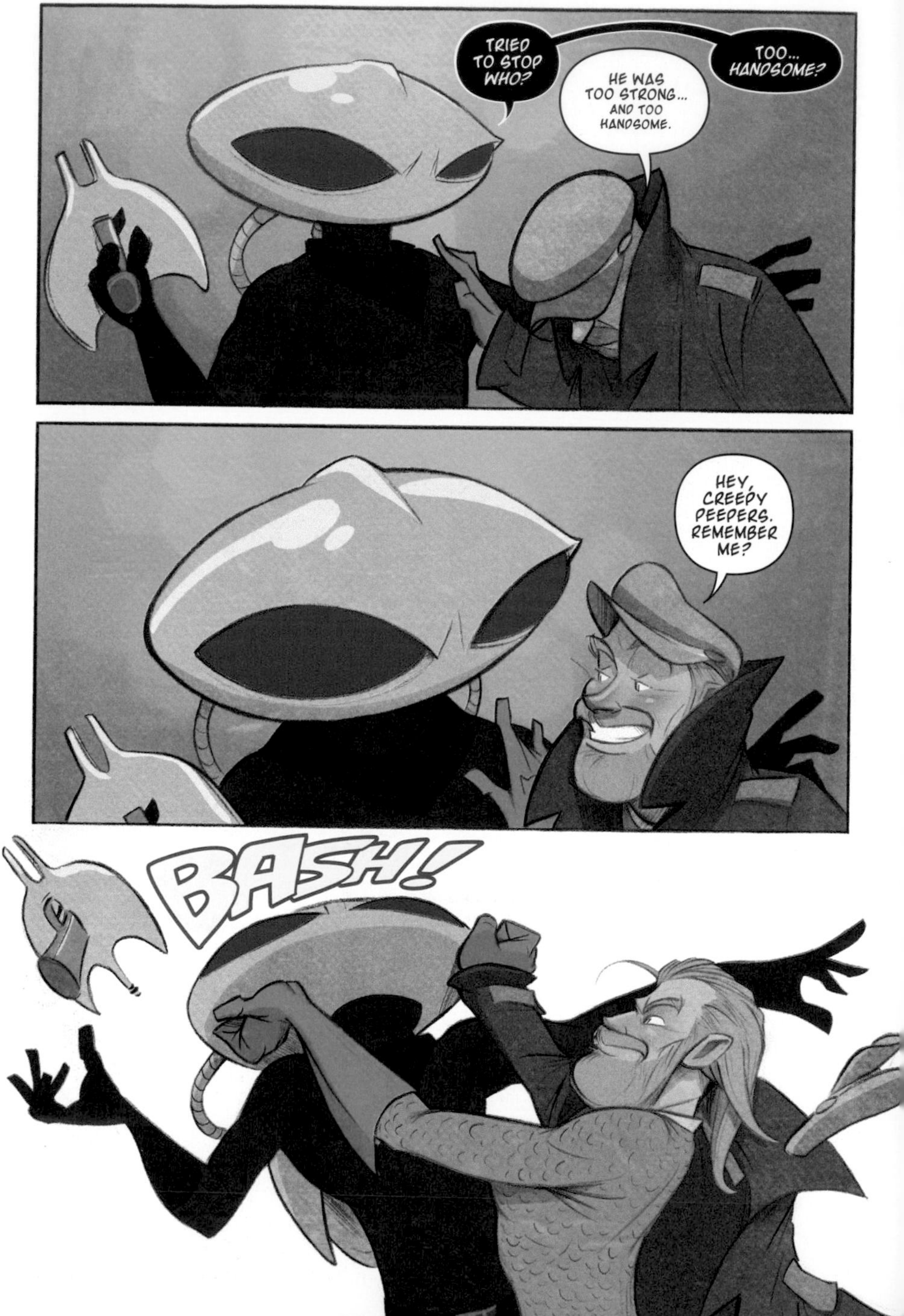
TRIED TO STOP WHO?
HE WAS TOO STRONG... AND TOO HANDSOME.
TOO... HANDSOME?
HEY, CREEPY PEEPERS. REMEMBER ME?
BASH!

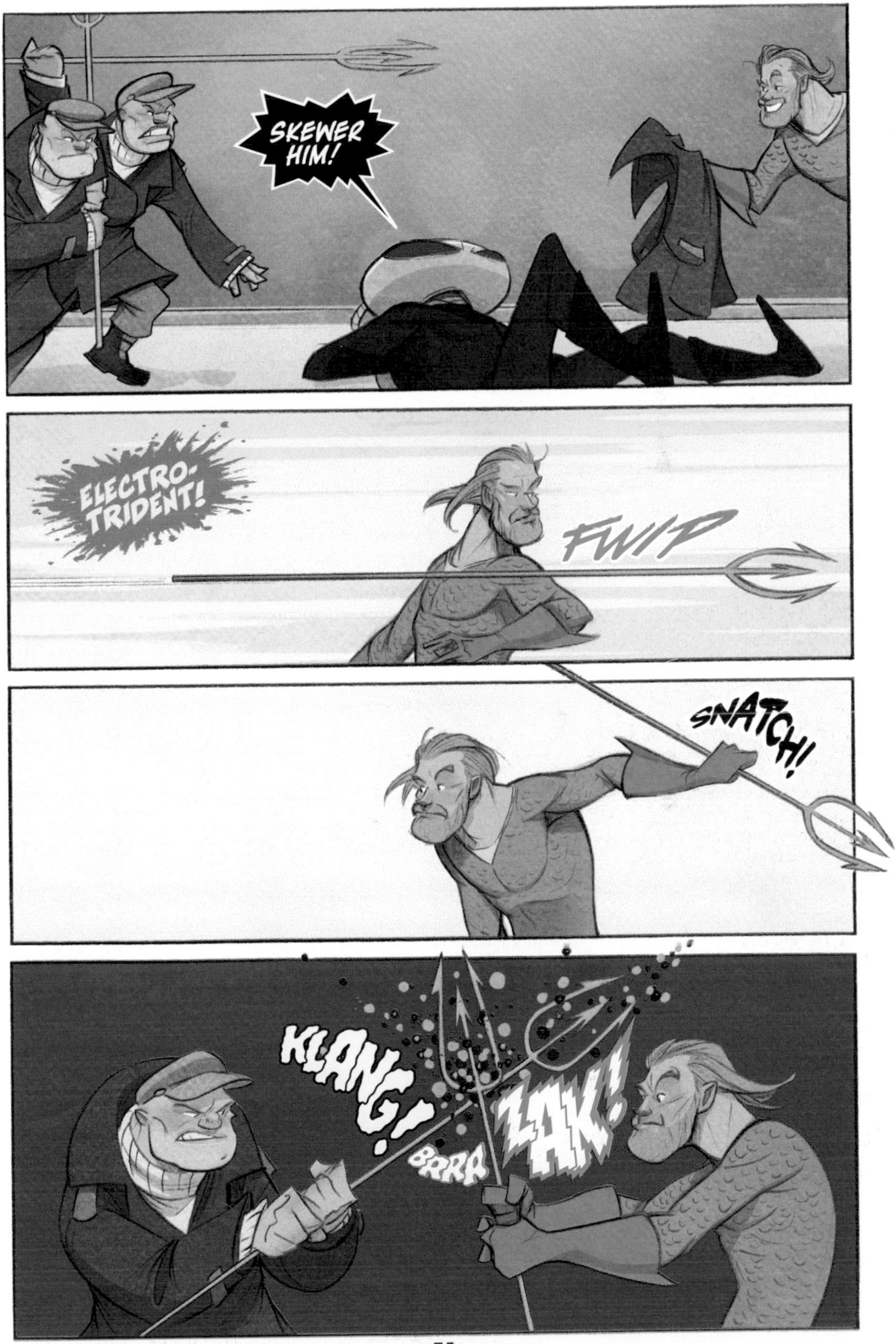
SKEWER HIM!
ELECTRO-TRIDENT!
FWIP
SNATCH!
KLANG!
BRRR
ZAK!

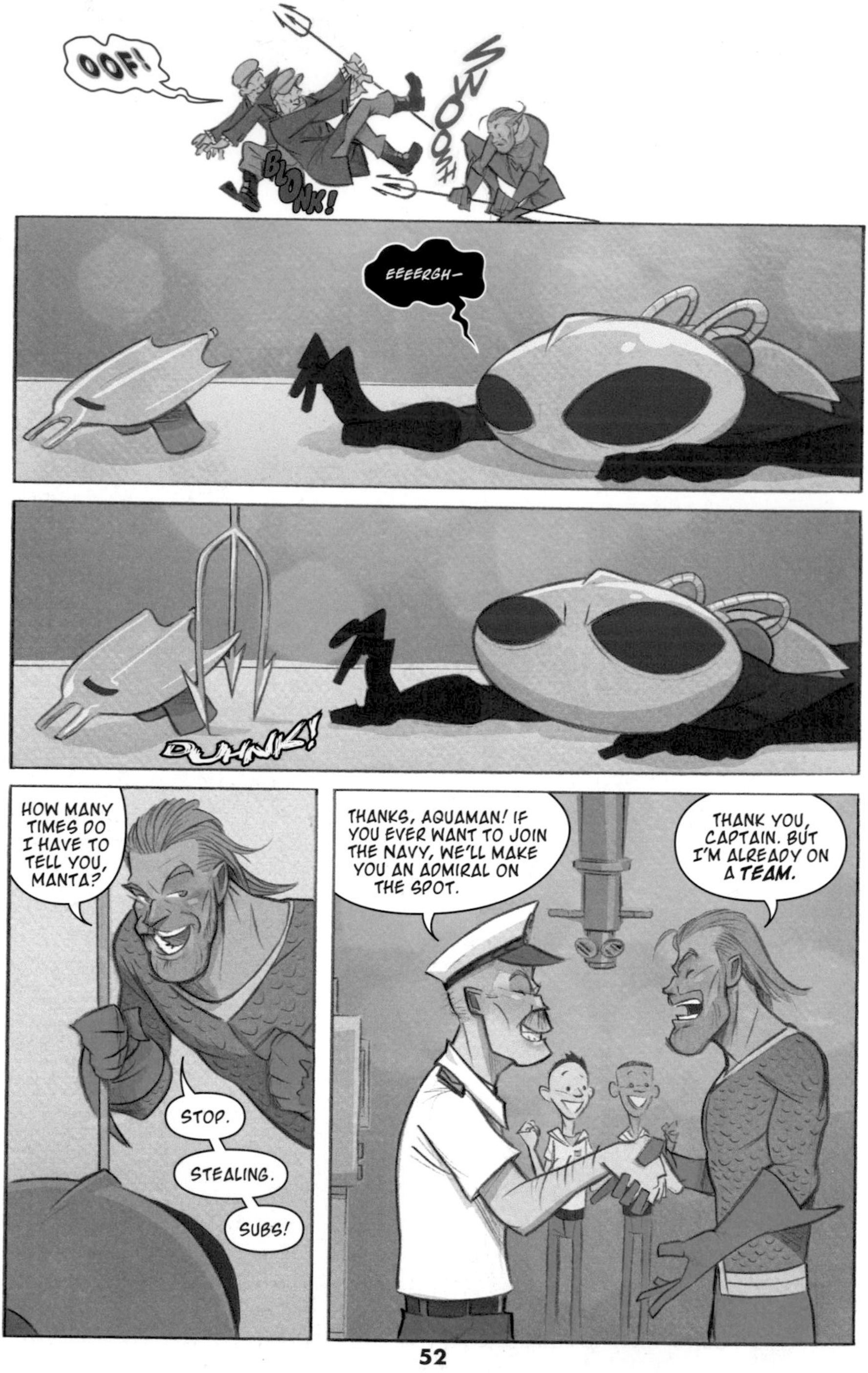
OOF!
SWOOOSH
BLONK!
EEEERGH–
DUHNK!
HOW MANY TIMES DO I HAVE TO TELL YOU, MANTA?
STOP.
STEALING.
SUBS!
THANKS, AQUAMAN! IF YOU EVER WANT TO JOIN THE NAVY, WE'LL MAKE YOU AN ADMIRAL ON THE SPOT.
THANK YOU, CAPTAIN. BUT I'M ALREADY ON A TEAM.

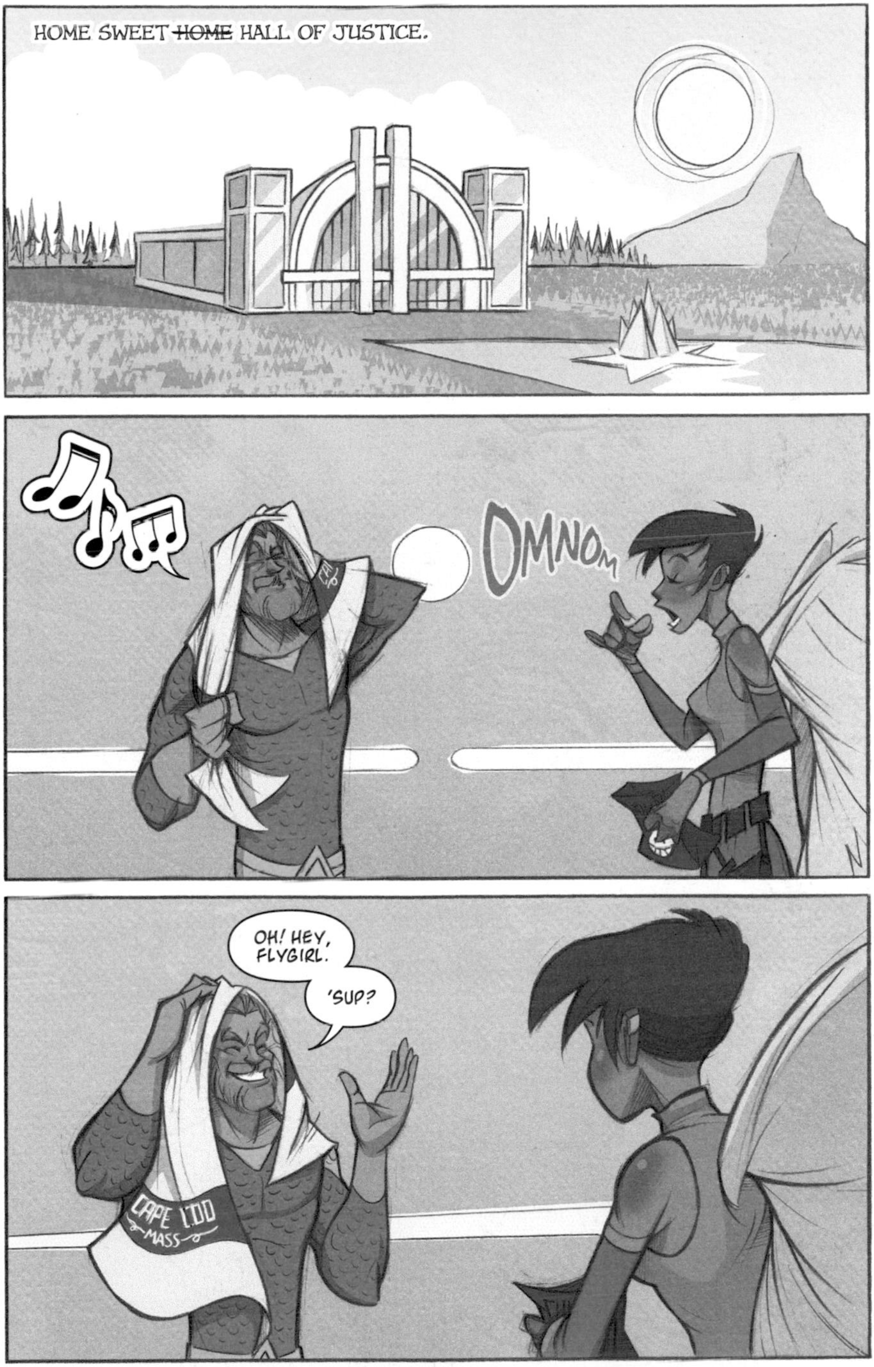
HOME SWEET ~~HOME~~ HALL OF JUSTICE.
OMNOM
OH! HEY, FLYGIRL.
'SUP?

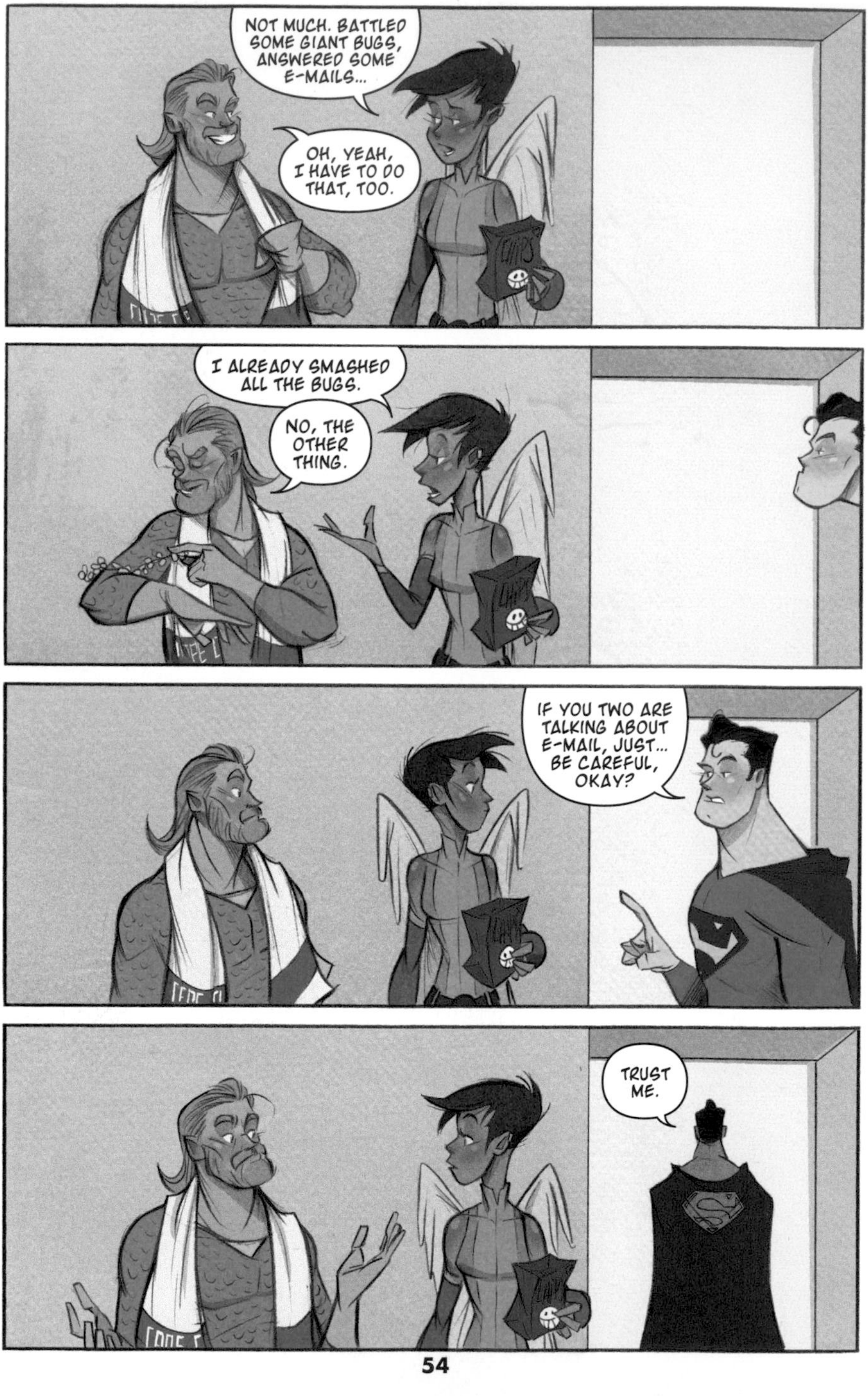
NOT MUCH. BATTLED SOME GIANT BUGS, ANSWERED SOME E-MAILS...
OH, YEAH, I HAVE TO DO THAT, TOO.
I ALREADY SMASHED ALL THE BUGS.
NO, THE OTHER THING.
IF YOU TWO ARE TALKING ABOUT E-MAIL, JUST... BE CAREFUL, OKAY?
TRUST ME.

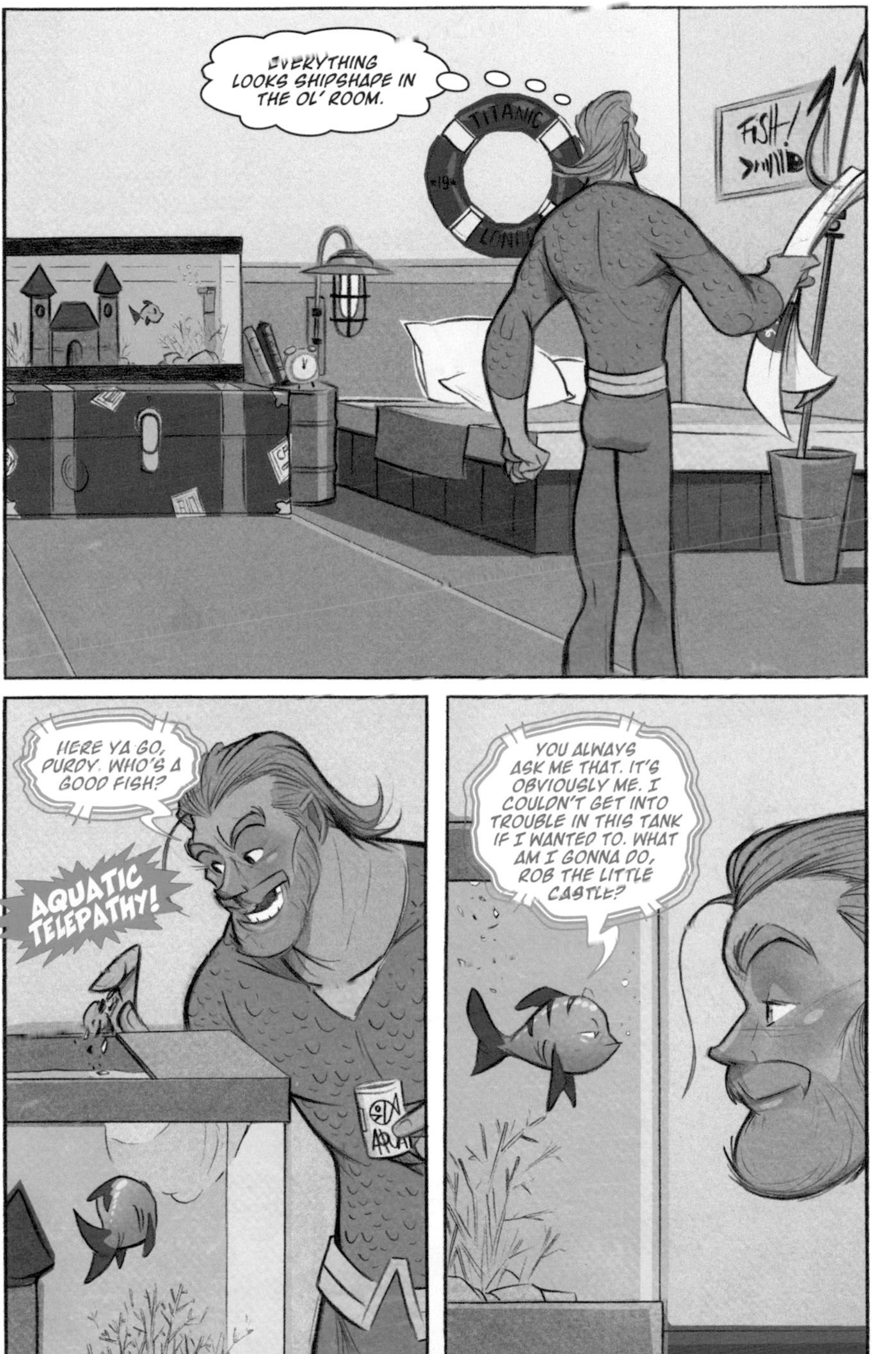
EVERYTHING LOOKS SHIPSHAPE IN THE OL' ROOM.
TITANIC
FISH!
HERE YA GO, PURDY. WHO'S A GOOD FISH?
AQUATIC TELEPATHY!
YOU ALWAYS ASK ME THAT. IT'S OBVIOUSLY ME. I COULDN'T GET INTO TROUBLE IN THIS TANK IF I WANTED TO. WHAT AM I GONNA DO, ROB THE LITTLE CASTLE?

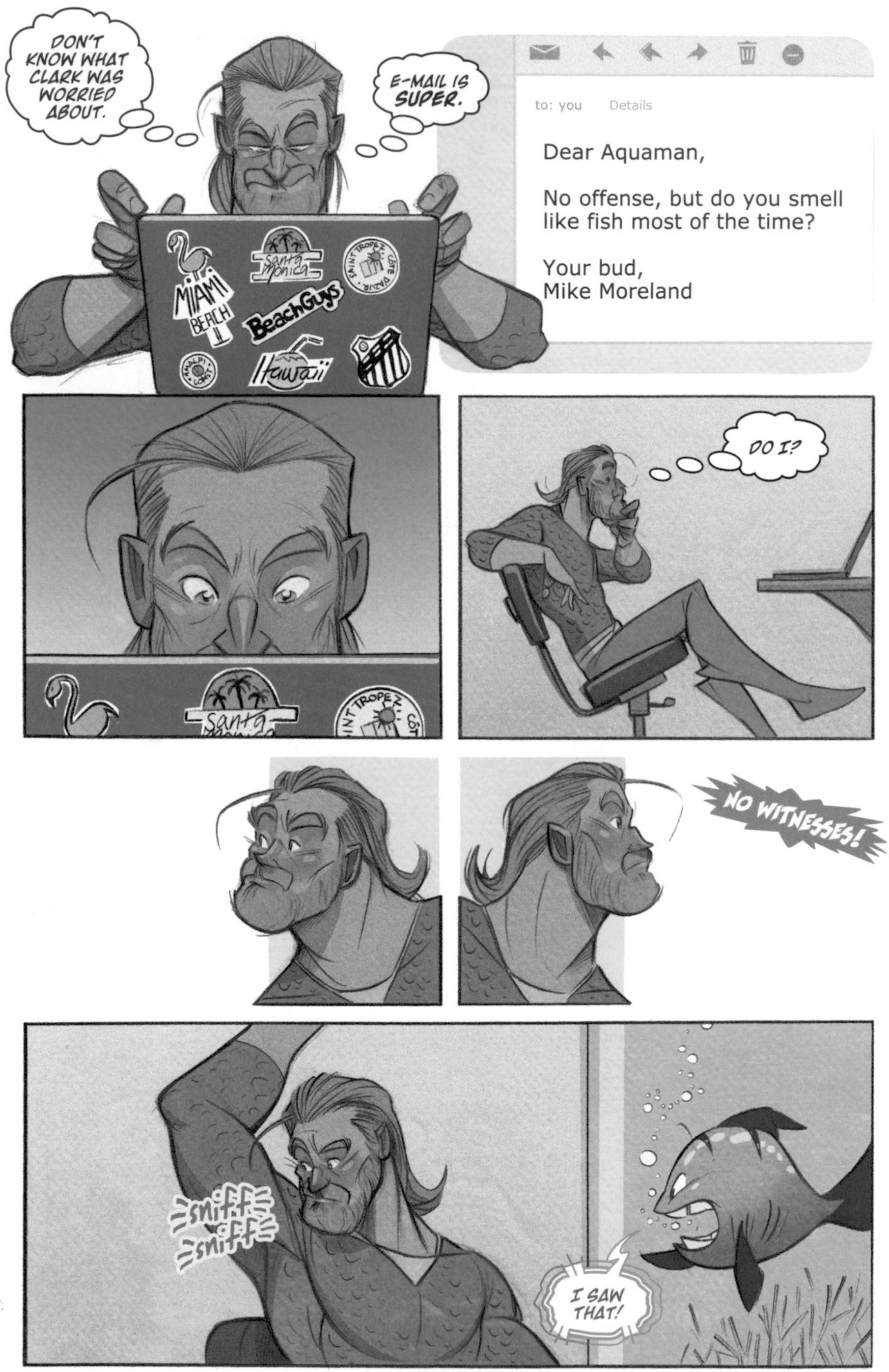
DON'T KNOW WHAT CLARK WAS WORRIED ABOUT.
E-MAIL IS SUPER.
to: you Details
Dear Aquaman,
No offense, but do you smell like fish most of the time?
Your bud,
Mike Moreland
MIAMI BEACH
Santa Monica
BeachGuys
Hawaii
DO I?
NO WITNESSES!
sniff sniff
I SAW THAT!

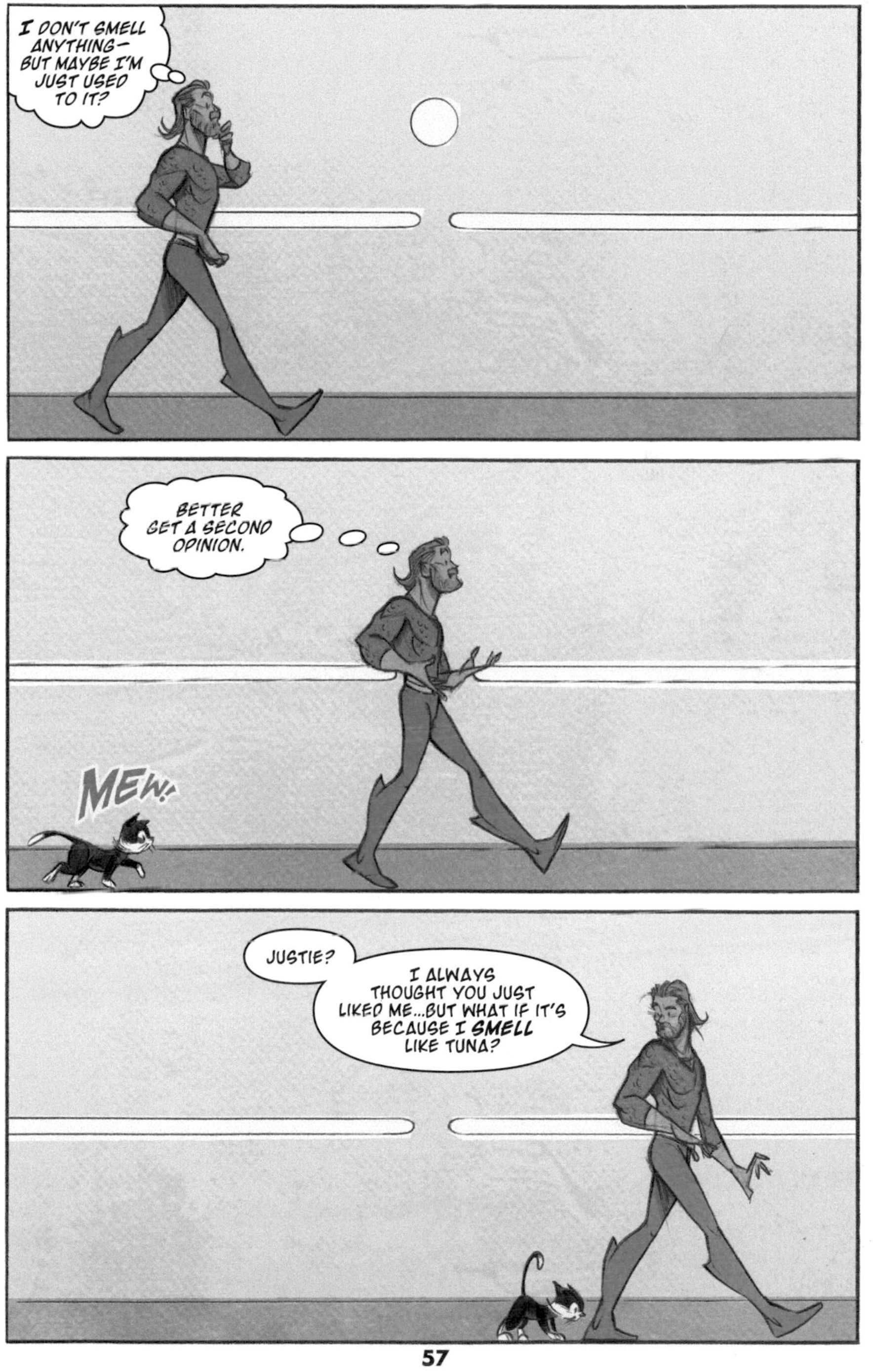
I DON'T SMELL ANYTHING— BUT MAYBE I'M JUST USED TO IT?
BETTER GET A SECOND OPINION.
MEW!
JUSTIE?
I ALWAYS THOUGHT YOU JUST LIKED ME...BUT WHAT IF IT'S BECAUSE I **SMELL** LIKE TUNA?

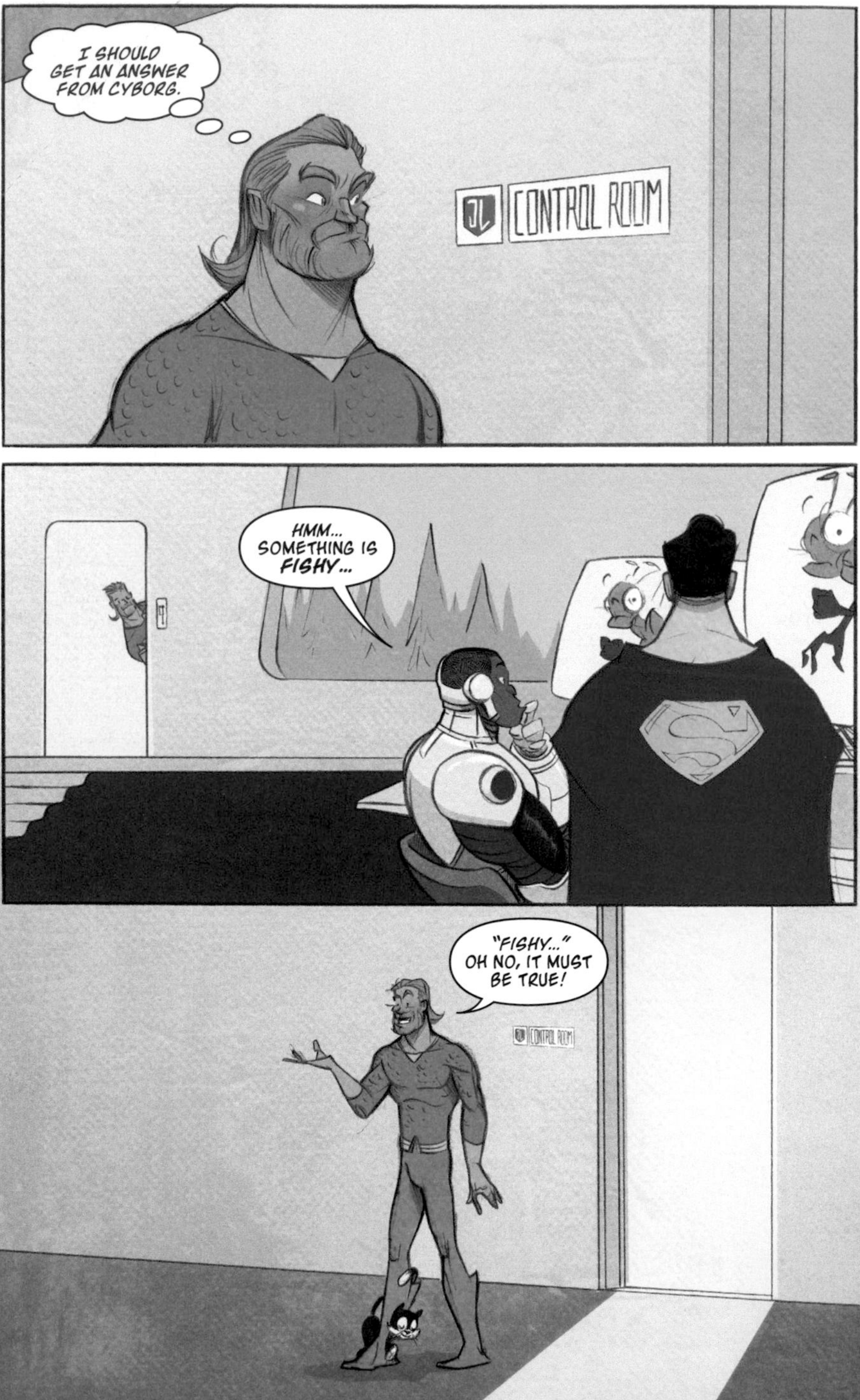
I SHOULD GET AN ANSWER FROM CYBORG.
CONTROL ROOM
HMM... SOMETHING IS FISHY...
"FISHY..." OH NO, IT MUST BE TRUE!
CONTROL ROOM

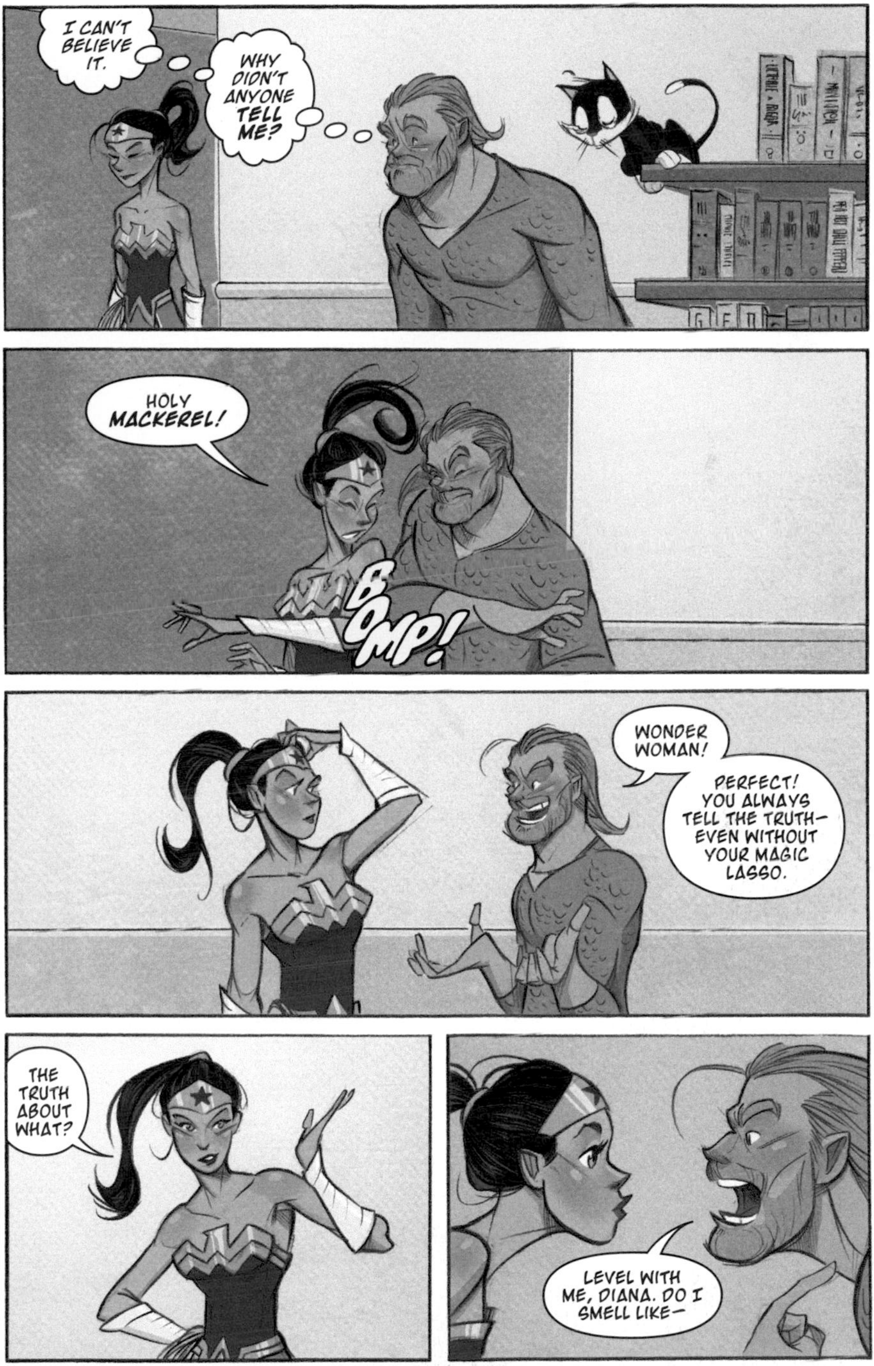
I CAN'T BELIEVE IT.
WHY DIDN'T ANYONE TELL ME?
HOLY MACKEREL!
BOMP!
WONDER WOMAN!
PERFECT! YOU ALWAYS TELL THE TRUTH— EVEN WITHOUT YOUR MAGIC LASSO.
THE TRUTH ABOUT WHAT?
LEVEL WITH ME, DIANA. DO I SMELL LIKE—

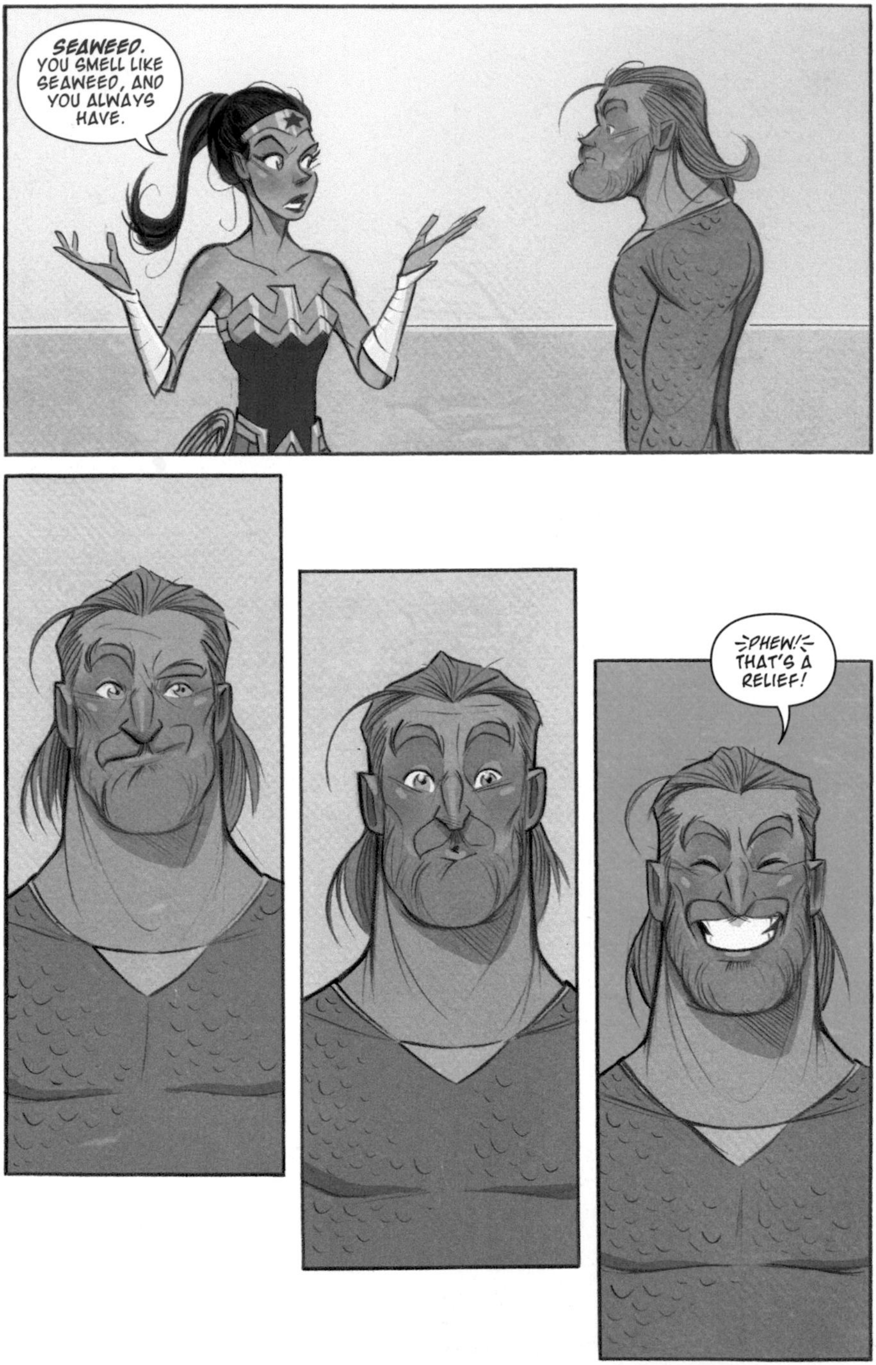
SEAWEED. YOU SMELL LIKE SEAWEED, AND YOU ALWAYS HAVE.
-PHEW!- THAT'S A RELIEF!

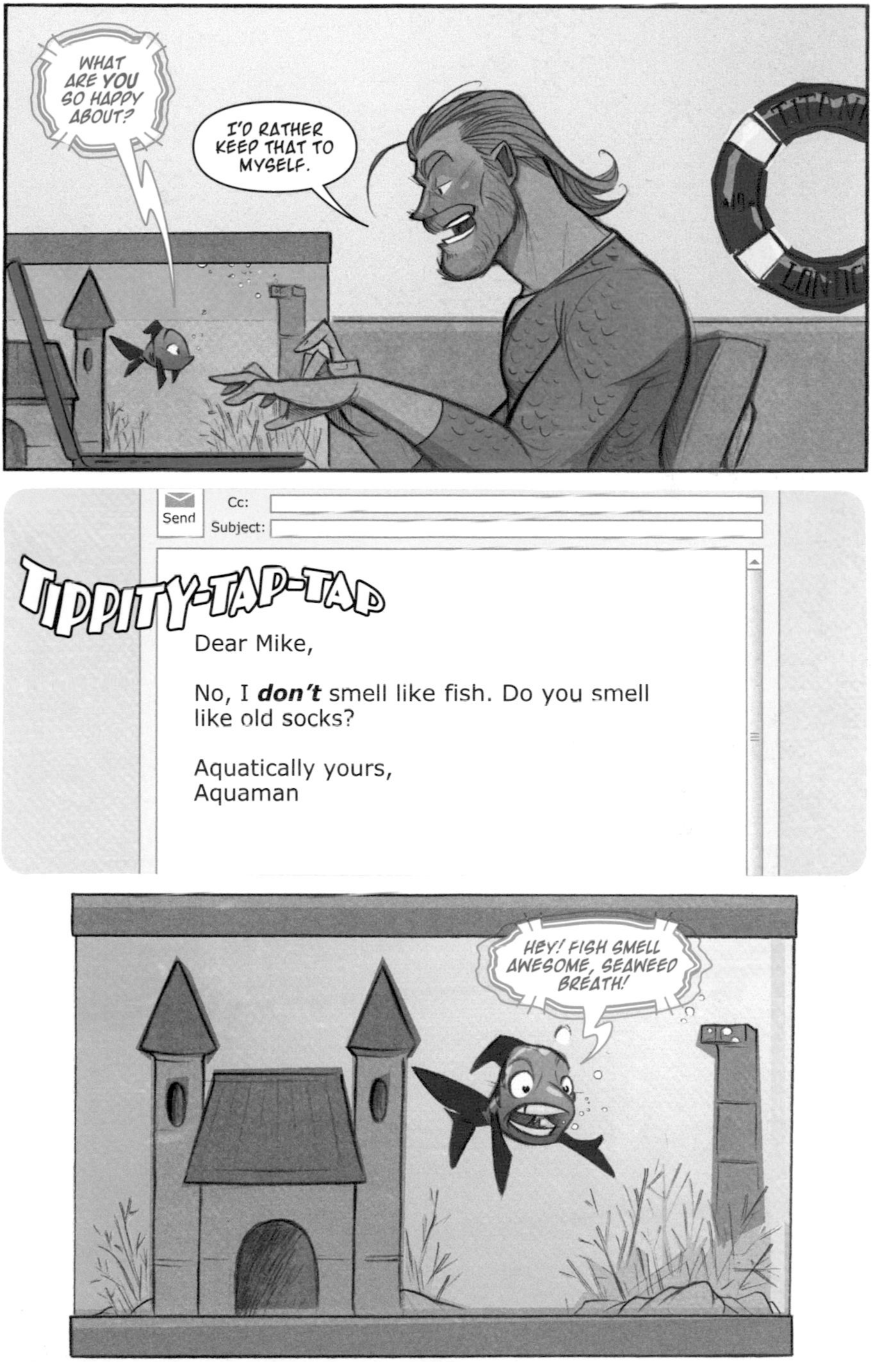
WHAT ARE YOU SO HAPPY ABOUT?
I'D RATHER KEEP THAT TO MYSELF.
Send
Cc:
Subject:
TIPPITY-TAP-TAP
Dear Mike,
No, I ***don't*** smell like fish. Do you smell like old socks?
Aquatically yours,
Aquaman
HEY! FISH SMELL AWESOME, SEAWEED BREATH!

CHAPTER 4

DEAR WONDER WOMAN

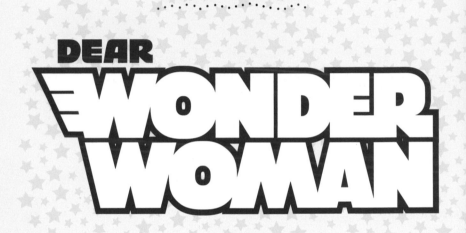

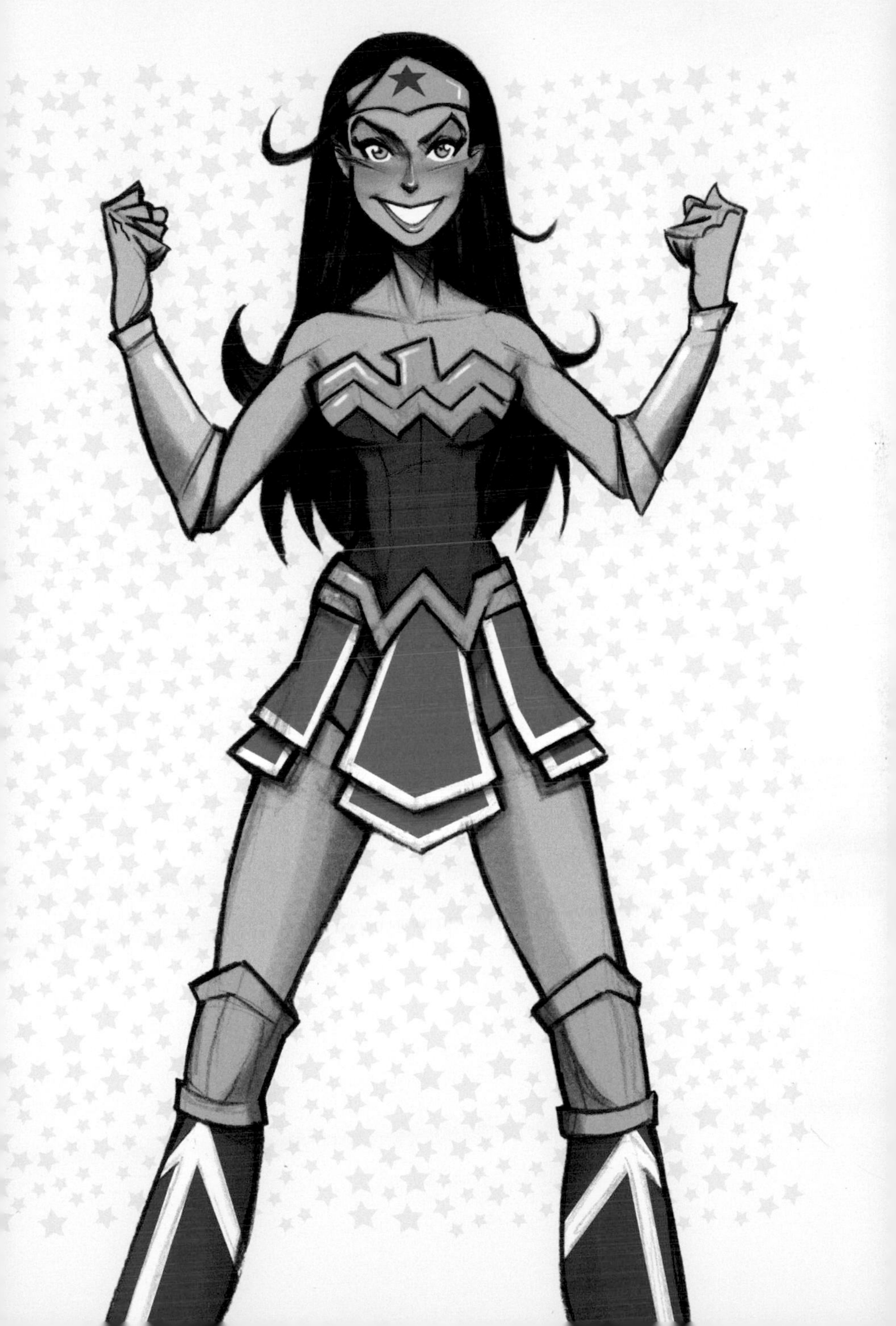

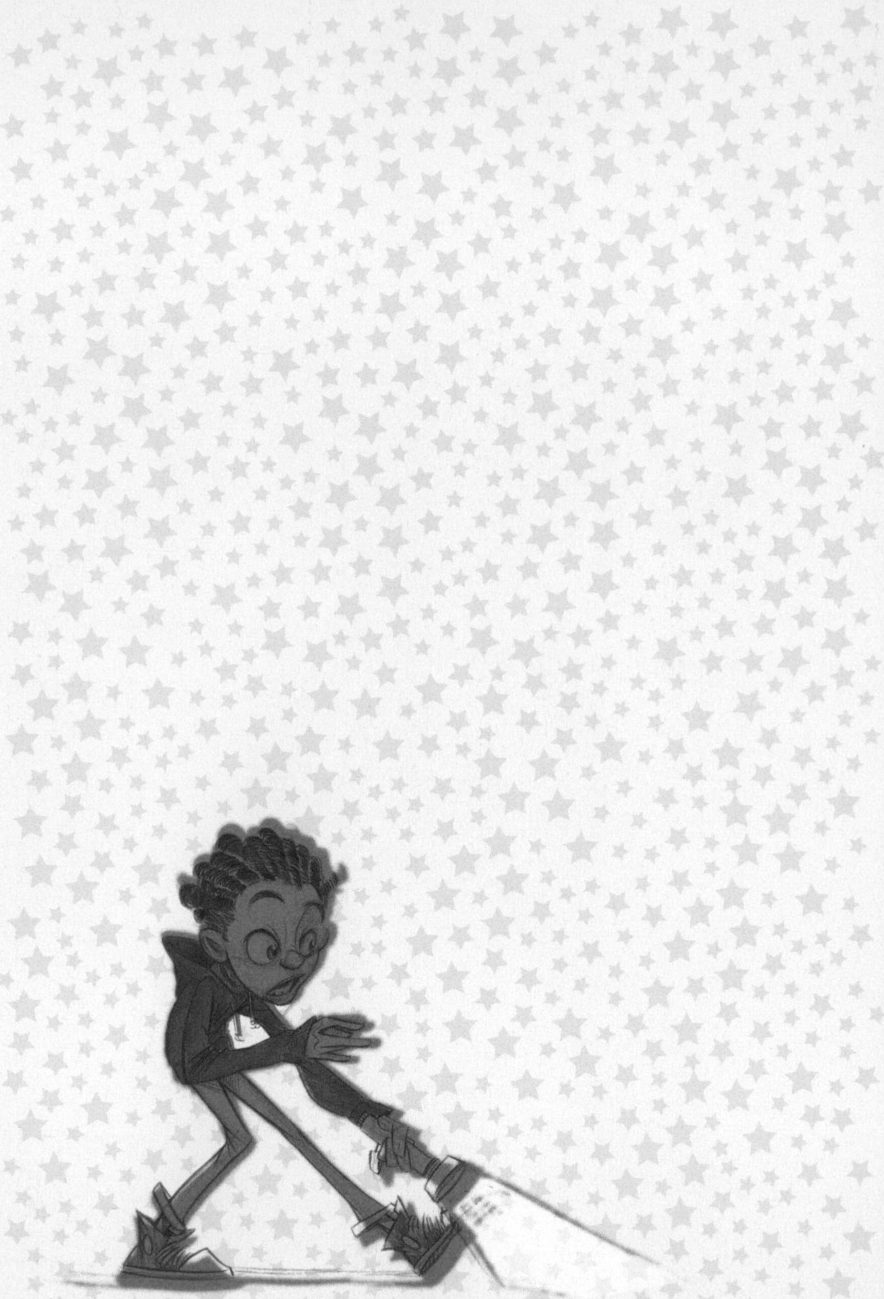

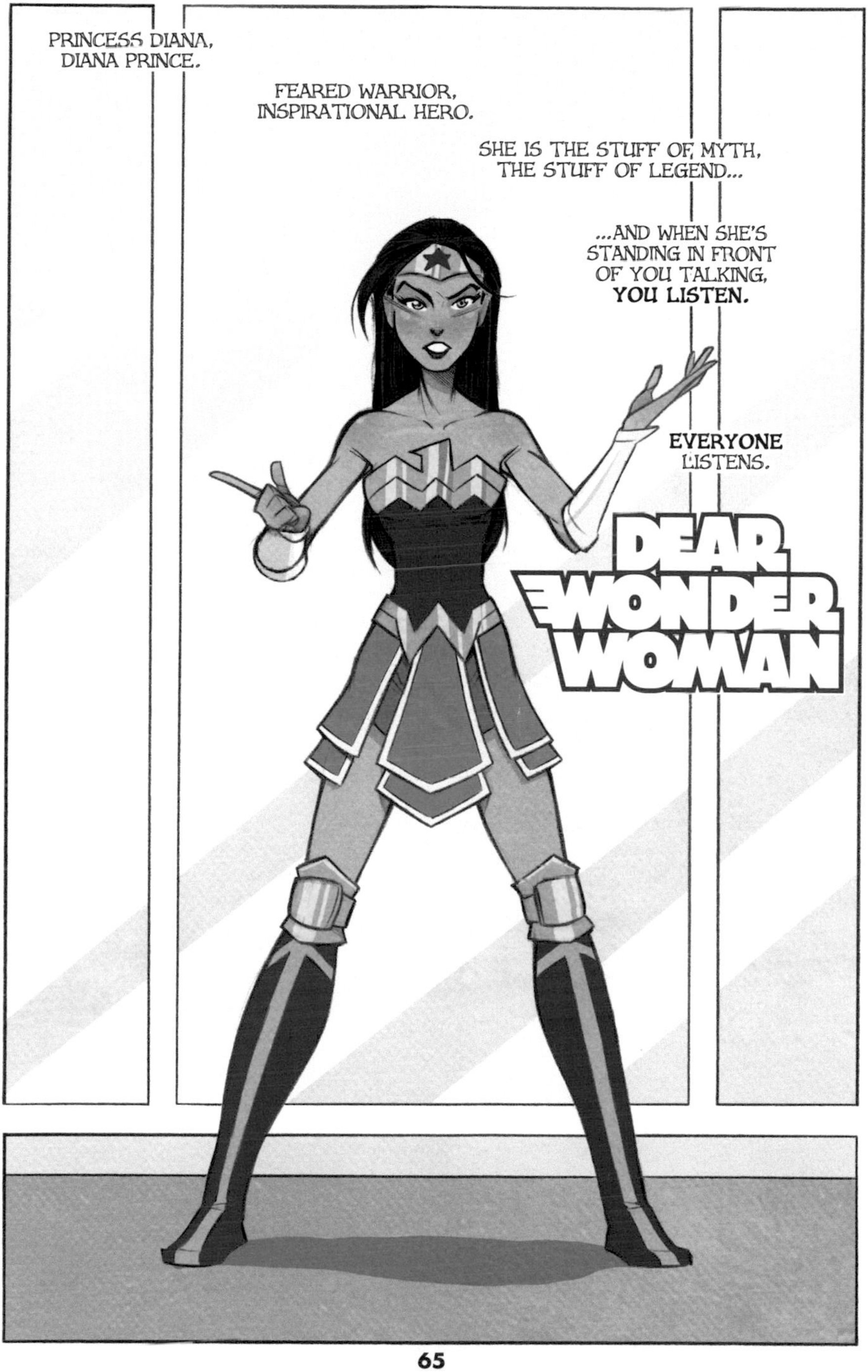
PRINCESS DIANA, DIANA PRINCE.
FEARED WARRIOR, INSPIRATIONAL HERO.
SHE IS THE STUFF OF MYTH, THE STUFF OF LEGEND...
...AND WHEN SHE'S STANDING IN FRONT OF YOU TALKING, YOU LISTEN.
EVERYONE LISTENS.
DEAR WONDER WOMAN

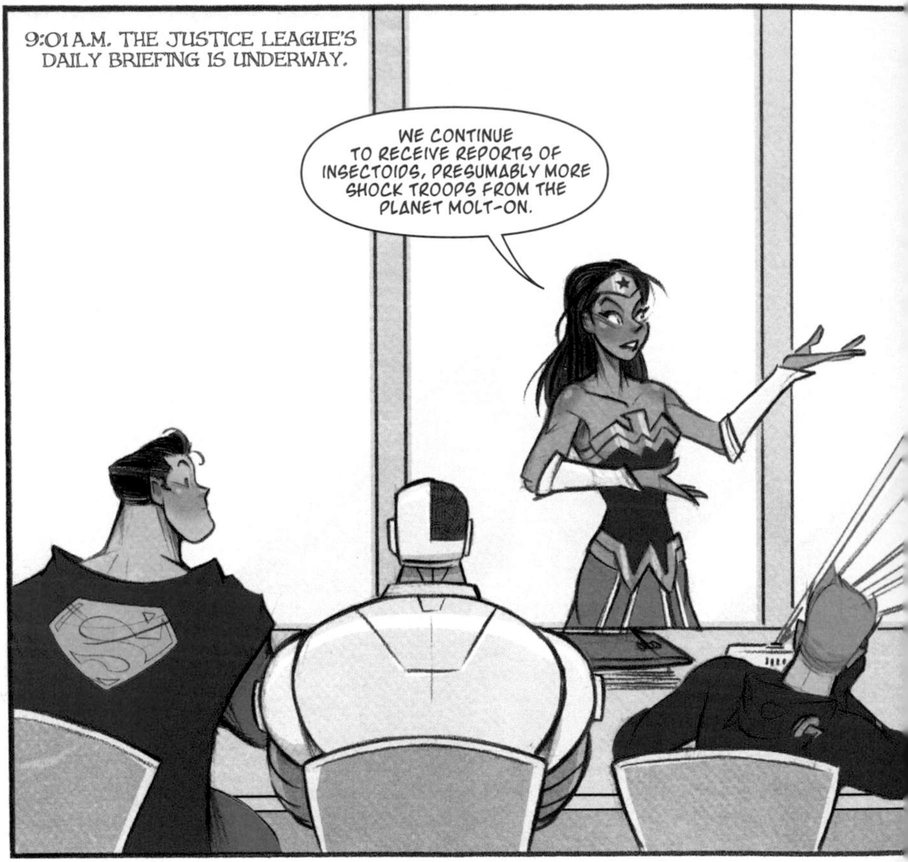
9:01 A.M. THE JUSTICE LEAGUE'S DAILY BRIEFING IS UNDERWAY.
WE CONTINUE TO RECEIVE REPORTS OF INSECTOIDS, PRESUMABLY MORE SHOCK TROOPS FROM THE PLANET MOLT-ON.

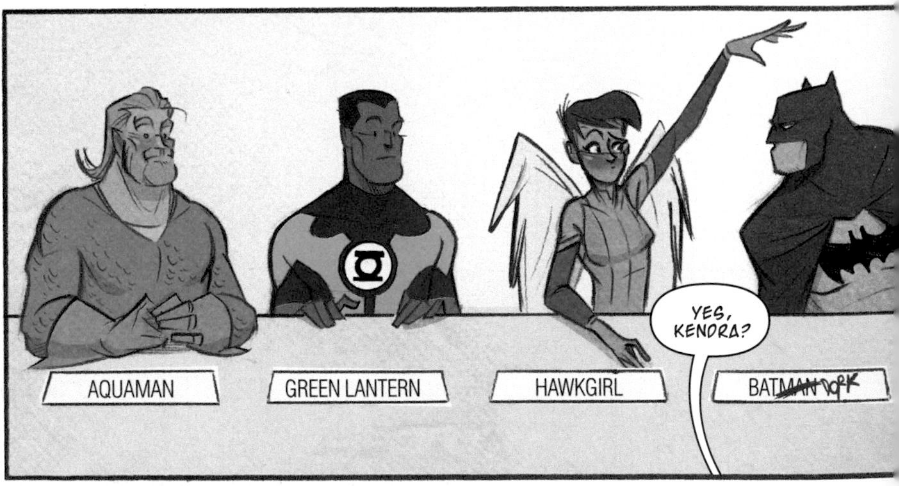
AQUAMAN
GREEN LANTERN
HAWKGIRL
BATMAN DORK
YES, KENDRA?

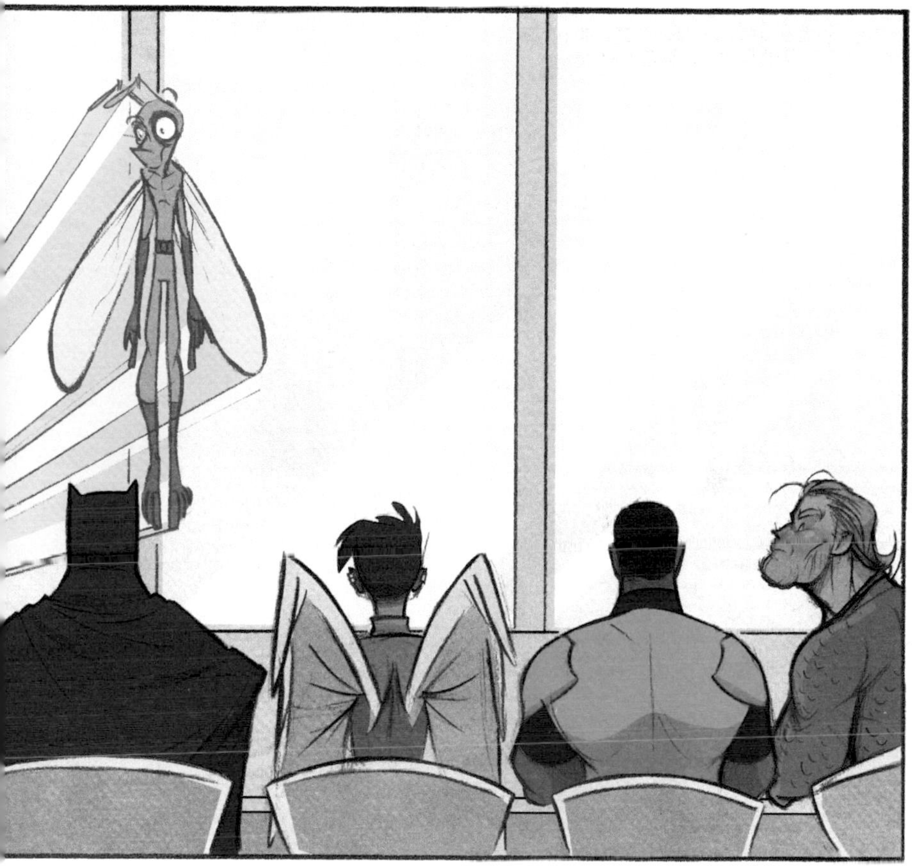

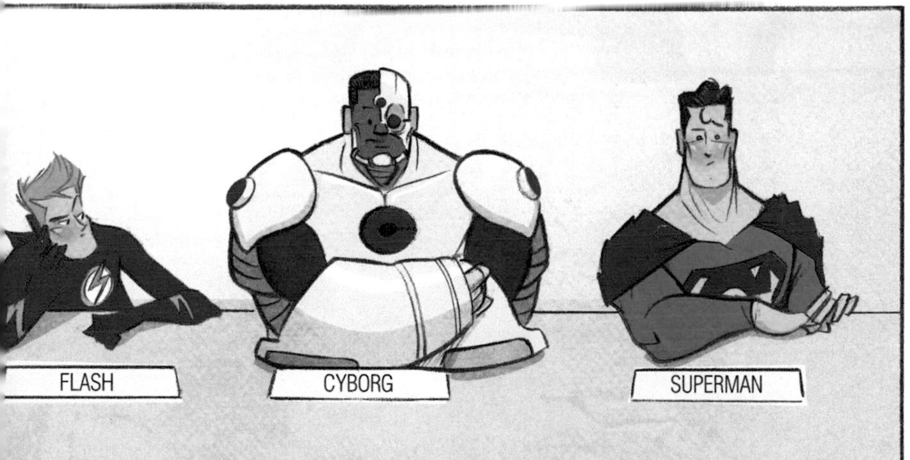
FLASH
CYBORG
SUPERMAN

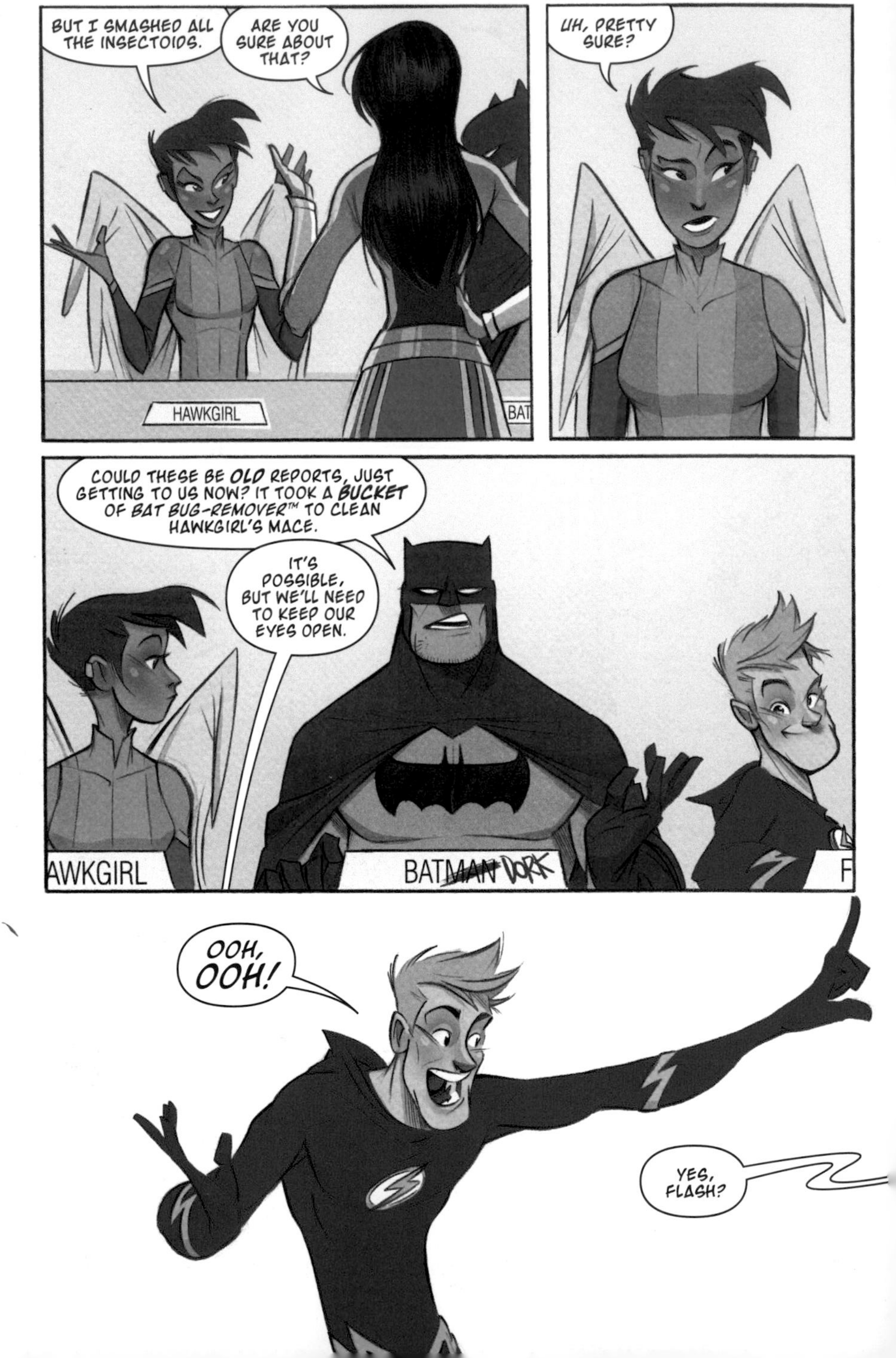

BUT I SMASHED ALL THE INSECTOIDS.
ARE YOU SURE ABOUT THAT?
HAWKGIRL
BAT
UH, PRETTY SURE?
COULD THESE BE OLD REPORTS, JUST GETTING TO US NOW? IT TOOK A BUCKET OF BAT BUG-REMOVER™ TO CLEAN HAWKGIRL'S MACE.
IT'S POSSIBLE, BUT WE'LL NEED TO KEEP OUR EYES OPEN.
AWKGIRL
BATMAN DORK
F
OOH, OOH!
YES, FLASH?

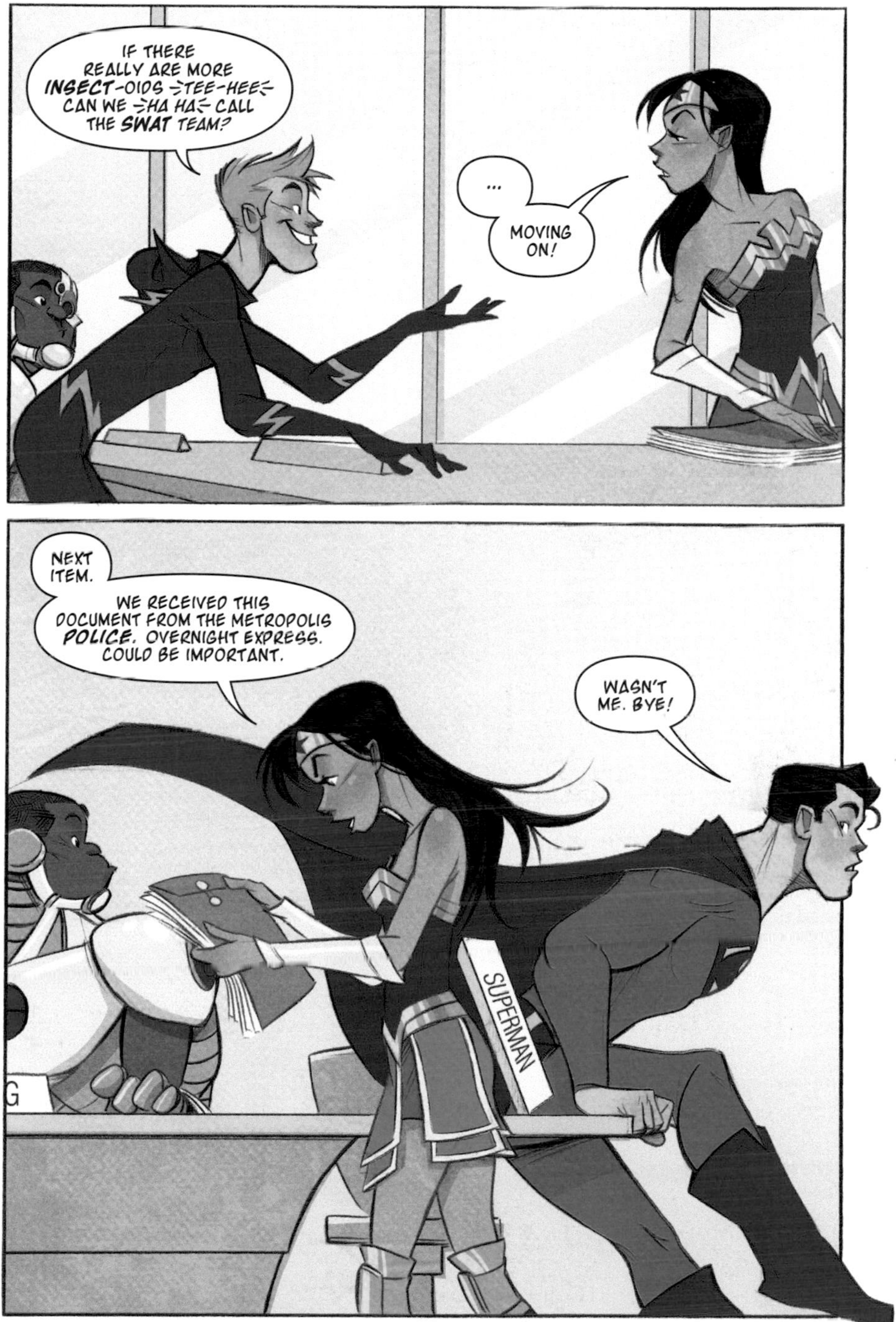
IF THERE REALLY ARE MORE INSECT-OIDS =TEE-HEE= CAN WE =HA HA= CALL THE SWAT TEAM?
...
MOVING ON!
NEXT ITEM.
WE RECEIVED THIS DOCUMENT FROM THE METROPOLIS POLICE. OVERNIGHT EXPRESS. COULD BE IMPORTANT.
WASN'T ME. BYE!
SUPERMAN

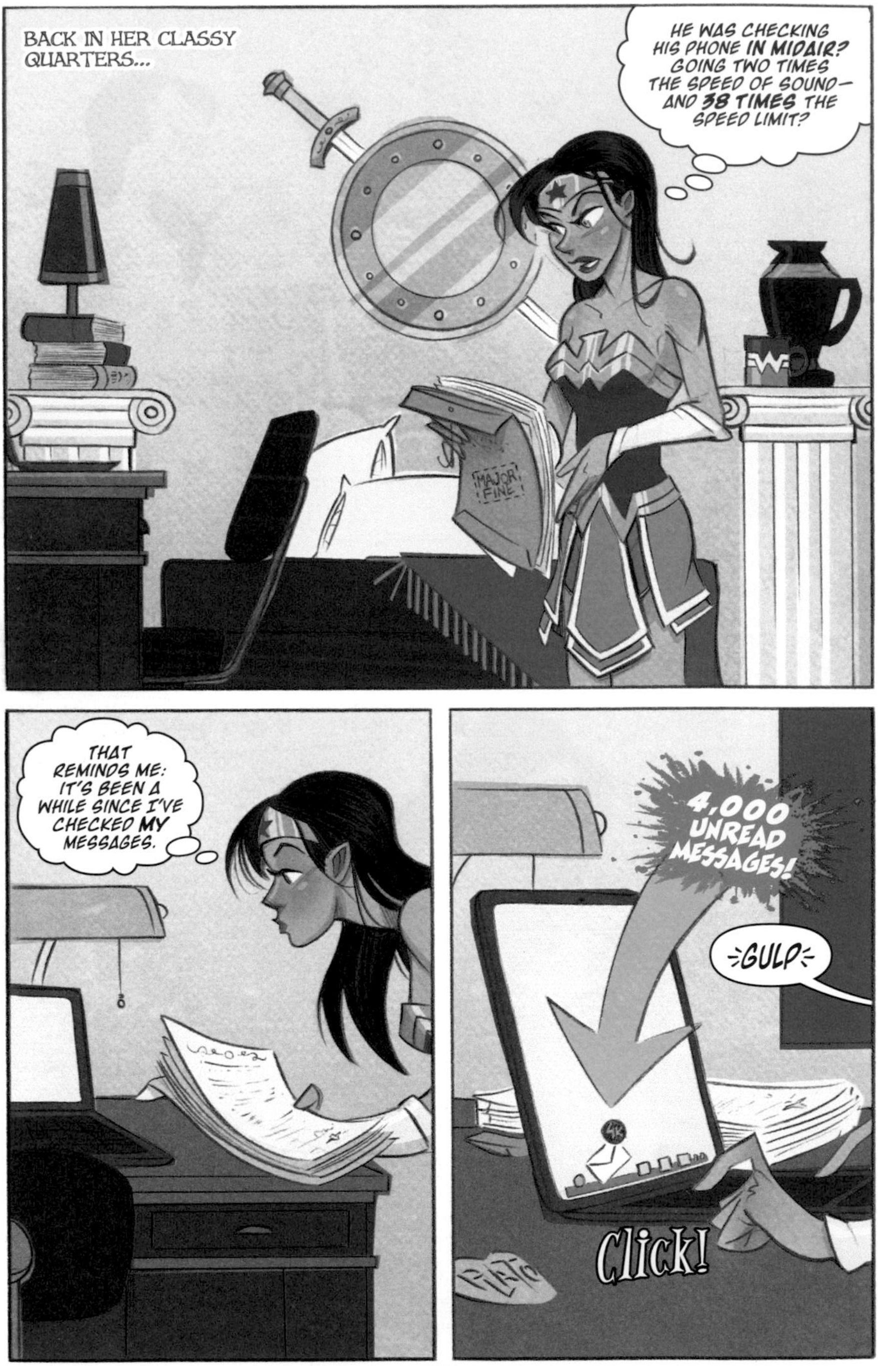
BACK IN HER CLASSY QUARTERS...
HE WAS CHECKING HIS PHONE IN MIDAIR? GOING TWO TIMES THE SPEED OF SOUND— AND 38 TIMES THE SPEED LIMIT?
MAJOR FINE
THAT REMINDS ME: IT'S BEEN A WHILE SINCE I'VE CHECKED MY MESSAGES.
4,000 UNREAD MESSAGES!
GULP
CLICK!

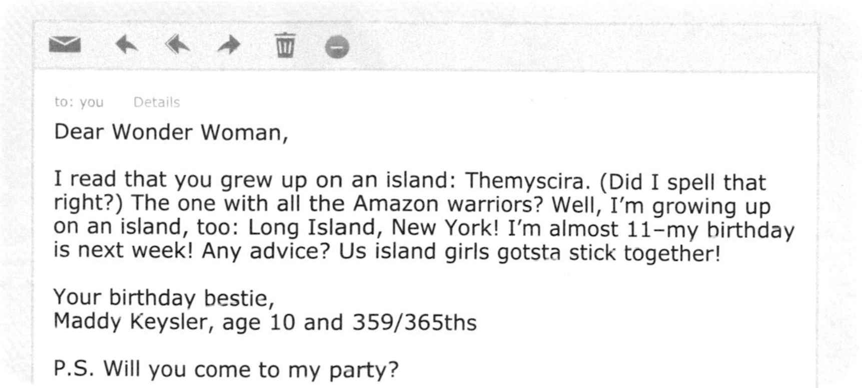
to: you Details

Dear Wonder Woman,

I read that you grew up on an island: Themyscira. (Did I spell that right?) The one with all the Amazon warriors? Well, I'm growing up on an island, too: Long Island, New York! I'm almost 11–my birthday is next week! Any advice? Us island girls gotsta stick together!

Your birthday bestie,
Maddy Keysler, age 10 and 359/365ths

P.S. Will you come to my party?

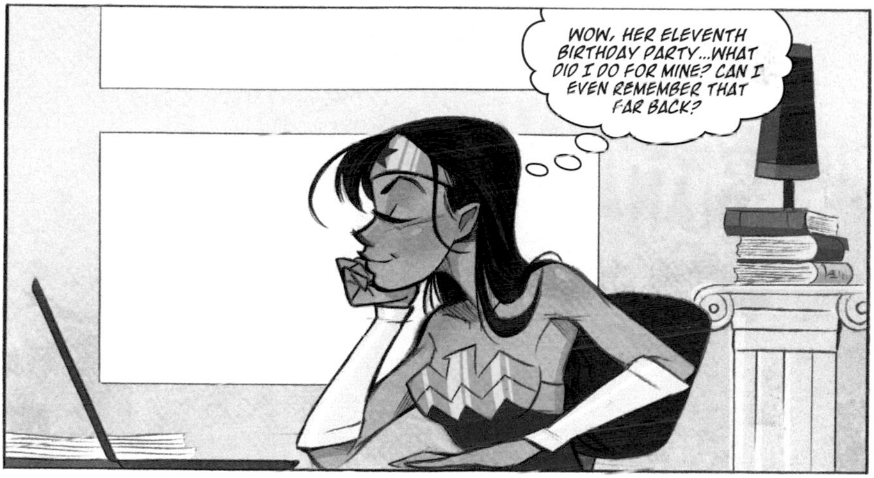
WOW, HER ELEVENTH BIRTHDAY PARTY...WHAT DID I DO FOR MINE? CAN I EVEN REMEMBER THAT FAR BACK?

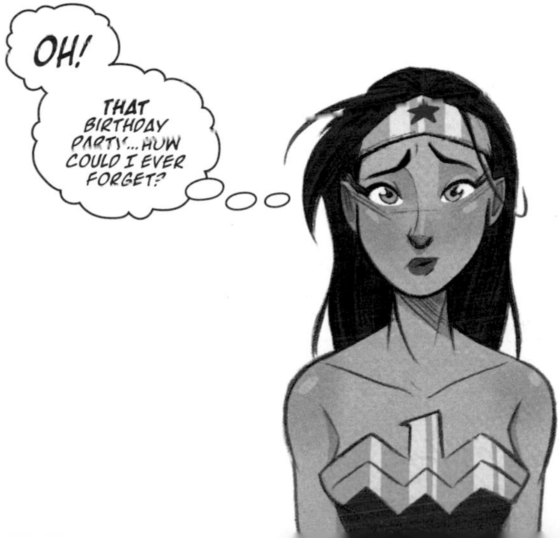
OH!
THAT BIRTHDAY PARTY...HOW COULD I EVER FORGET?

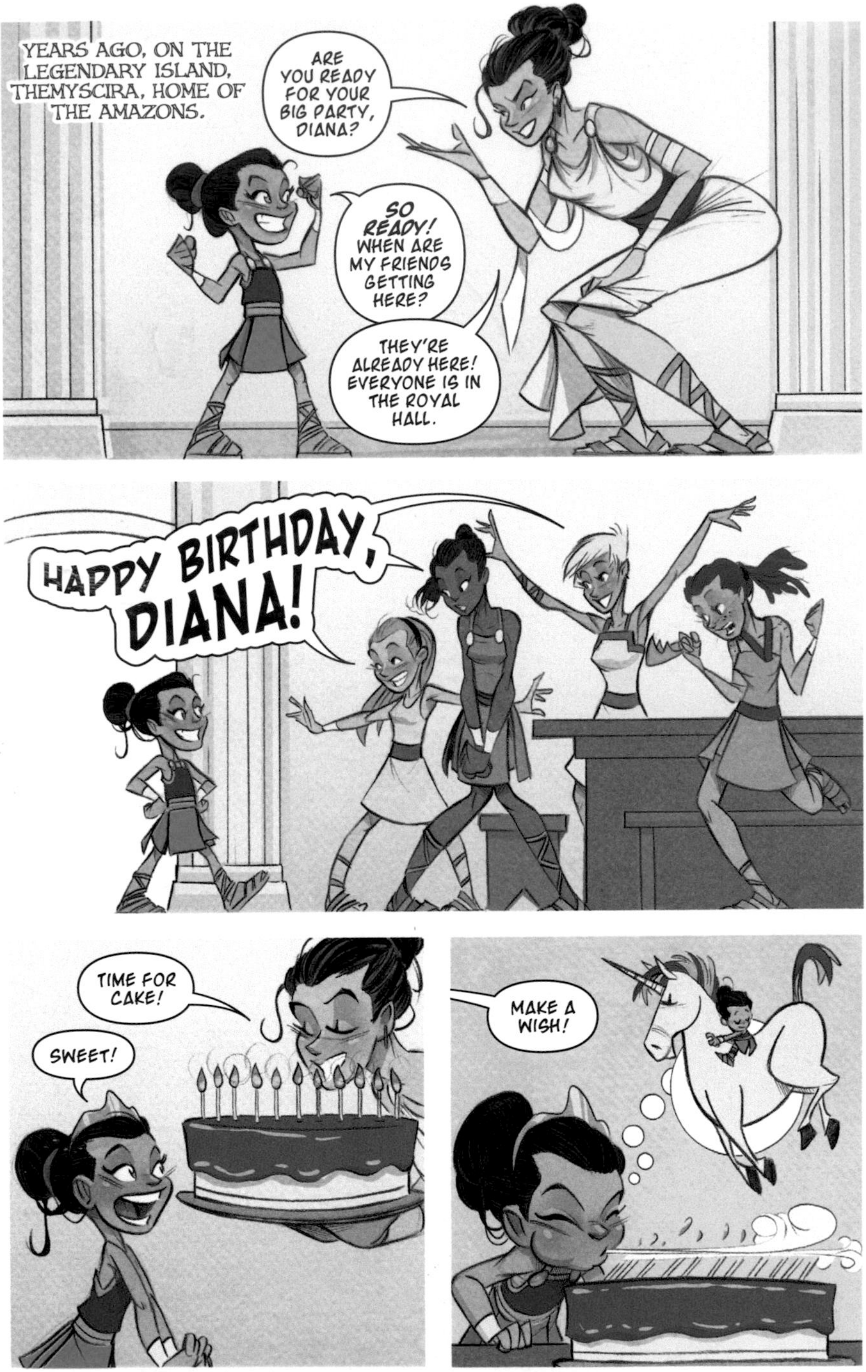
YEARS AGO, ON THE LEGENDARY ISLAND, THEMYSCIRA, HOME OF THE AMAZONS.
ARE YOU READY FOR YOUR BIG PARTY, DIANA?
SO READY! WHEN ARE MY FRIENDS GETTING HERE?
THEY'RE ALREADY HERE! EVERYONE IS IN THE ROYAL HALL.
HAPPY BIRTHDAY, DIANA!
TIME FOR CAKE!
SWEET!
MAKE A WISH!

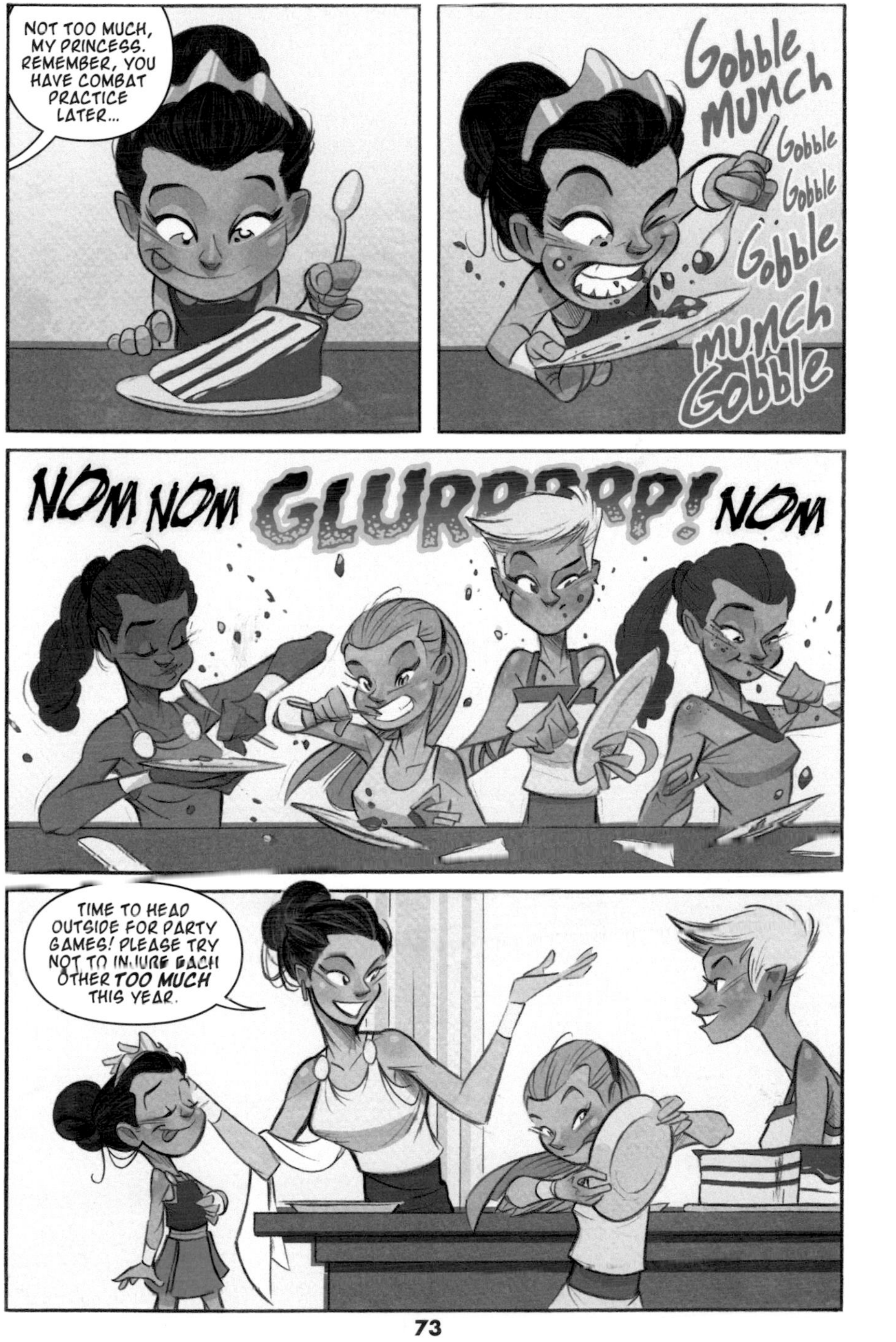
NOT TOO MUCH, MY PRINCESS. REMEMBER, YOU HAVE COMBAT PRACTICE LATER...
Gobble Munch Gobble Gobble Gobble munch Gobble
NOM NOM GLURRRRP! NOM
TIME TO HEAD OUTSIDE FOR PARTY GAMES! PLEASE TRY NOT TO INJURE EACH OTHER TOO MUCH THIS YEAR.

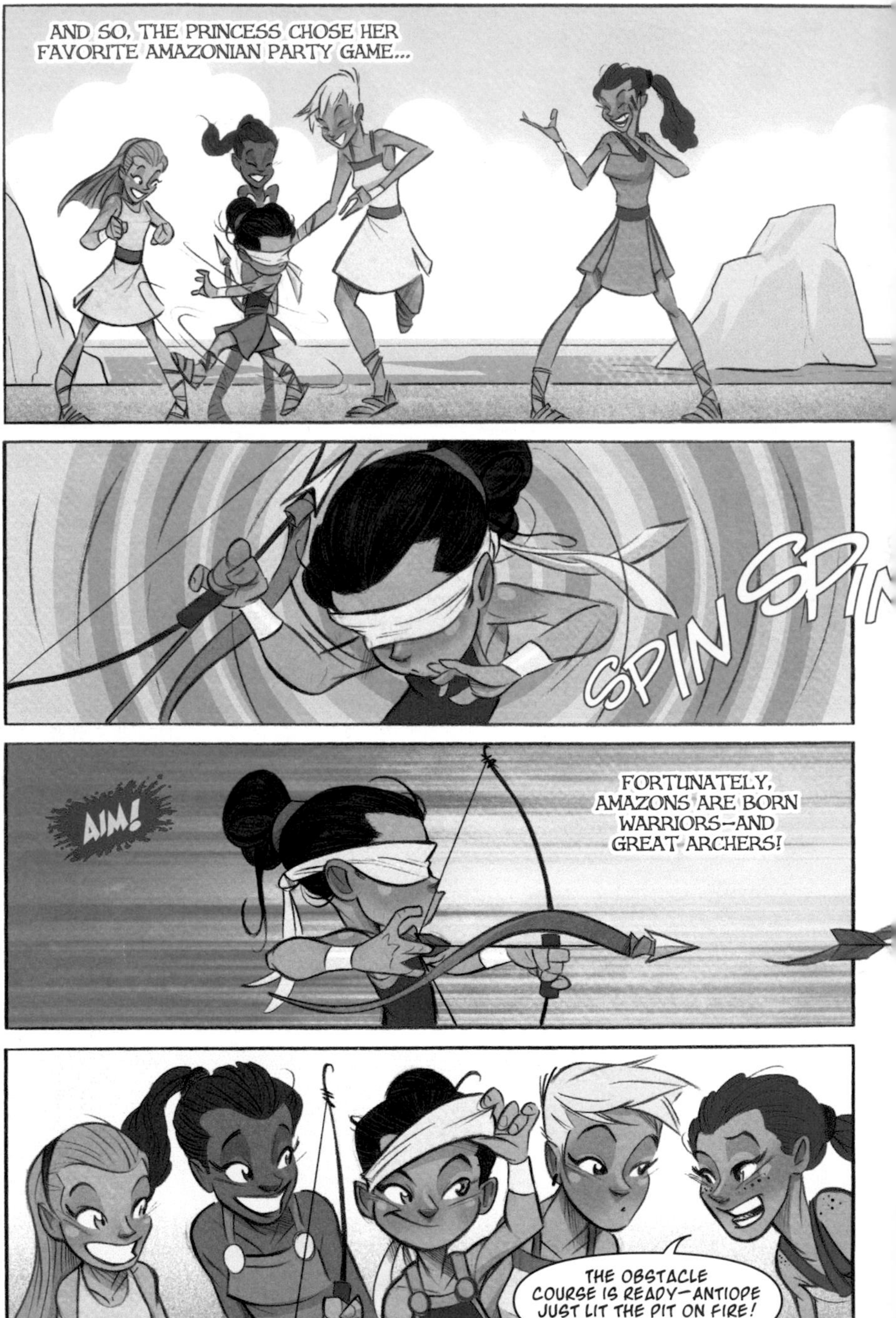
AND SO, THE PRINCESS CHOSE HER FAVORITE AMAZONIAN PARTY GAME...
SPIN SPIN SPIN
AIM!
FORTUNATELY, AMAZONS ARE BORN WARRIORS—AND GREAT ARCHERS!
THE OBSTACLE COURSE IS READY—ANTIOPE JUST LIT THE PIT ON FIRE!

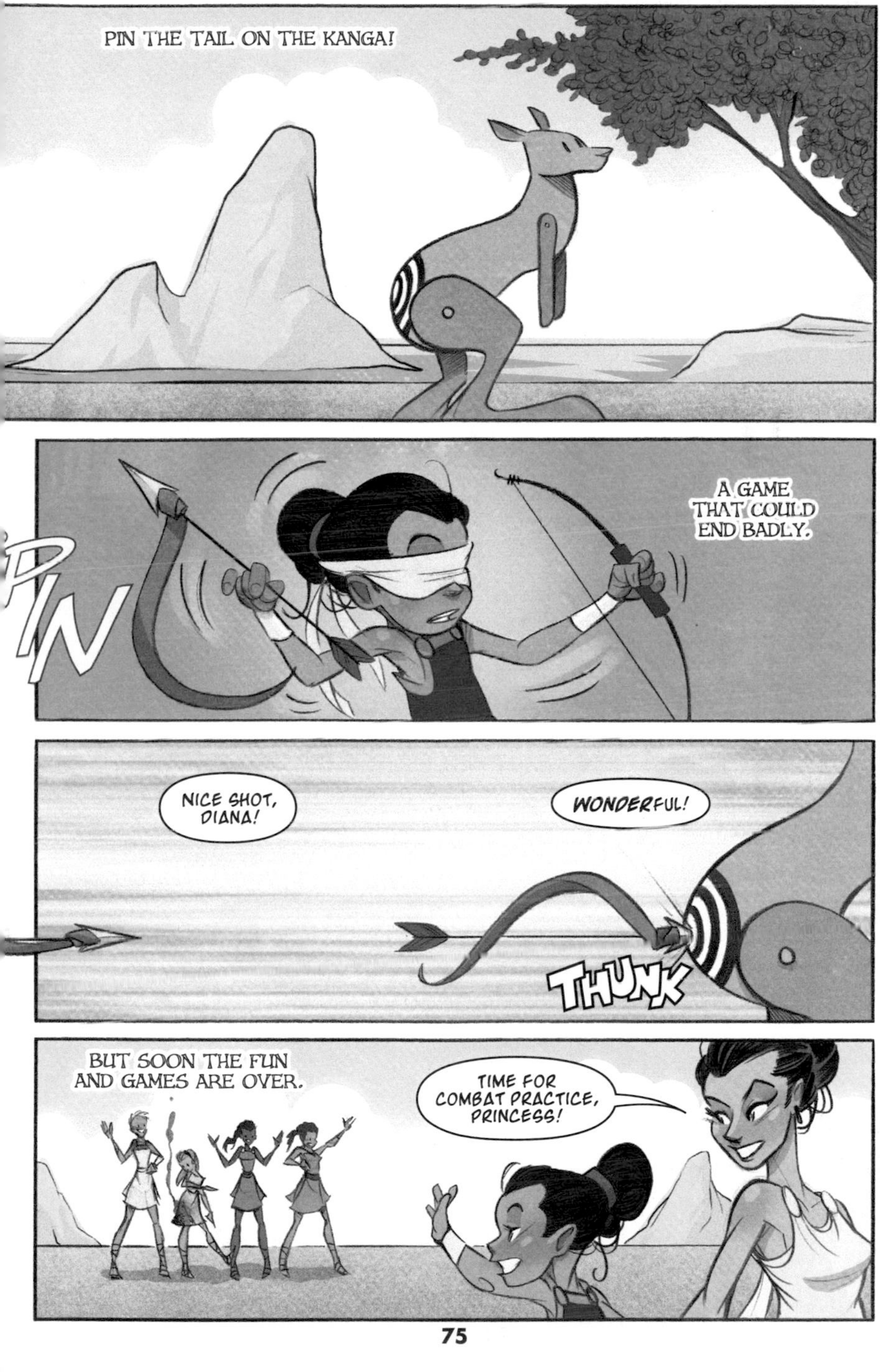

PIN THE TAIL ON THE KANGA!
PIN
A GAME THAT COULD END BADLY.
NICE SHOT, DIANA!
WONDERFUL!
THUNK
BUT SOON THE FUN AND GAMES ARE OVER.
TIME FOR COMBAT PRACTICE, PRINCESS!

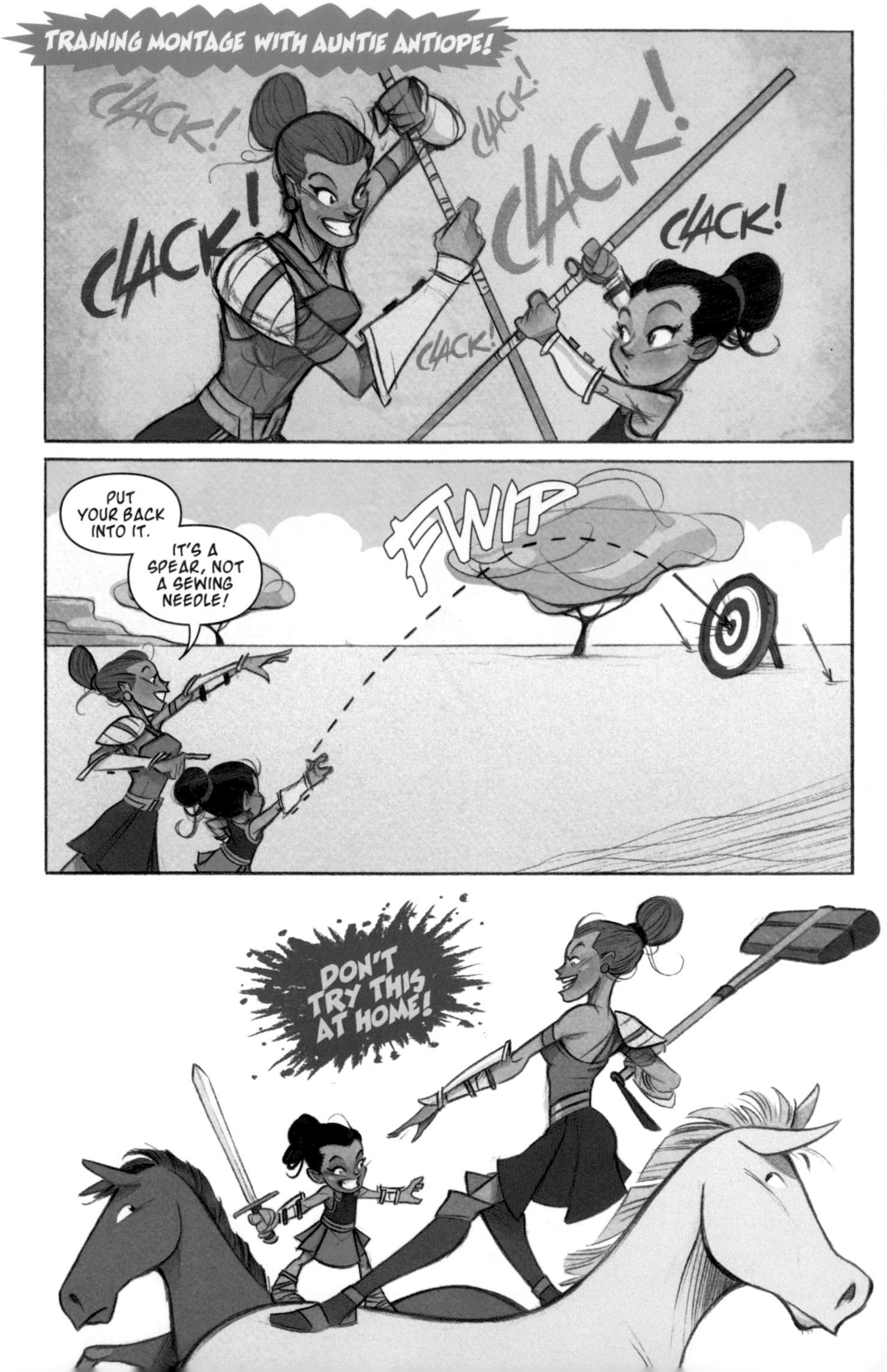
TRAINING MONTAGE WITH AUNTIE ANTIOPE!
CLACK!
CLACK!
CLACK!
CLACK!
CLACK!
CLACK!
PUT YOUR BACK INTO IT.
IT'S A SPEAR, NOT A SEWING NEEDLE!
FWIP
DON'T TRY THIS AT HOME!

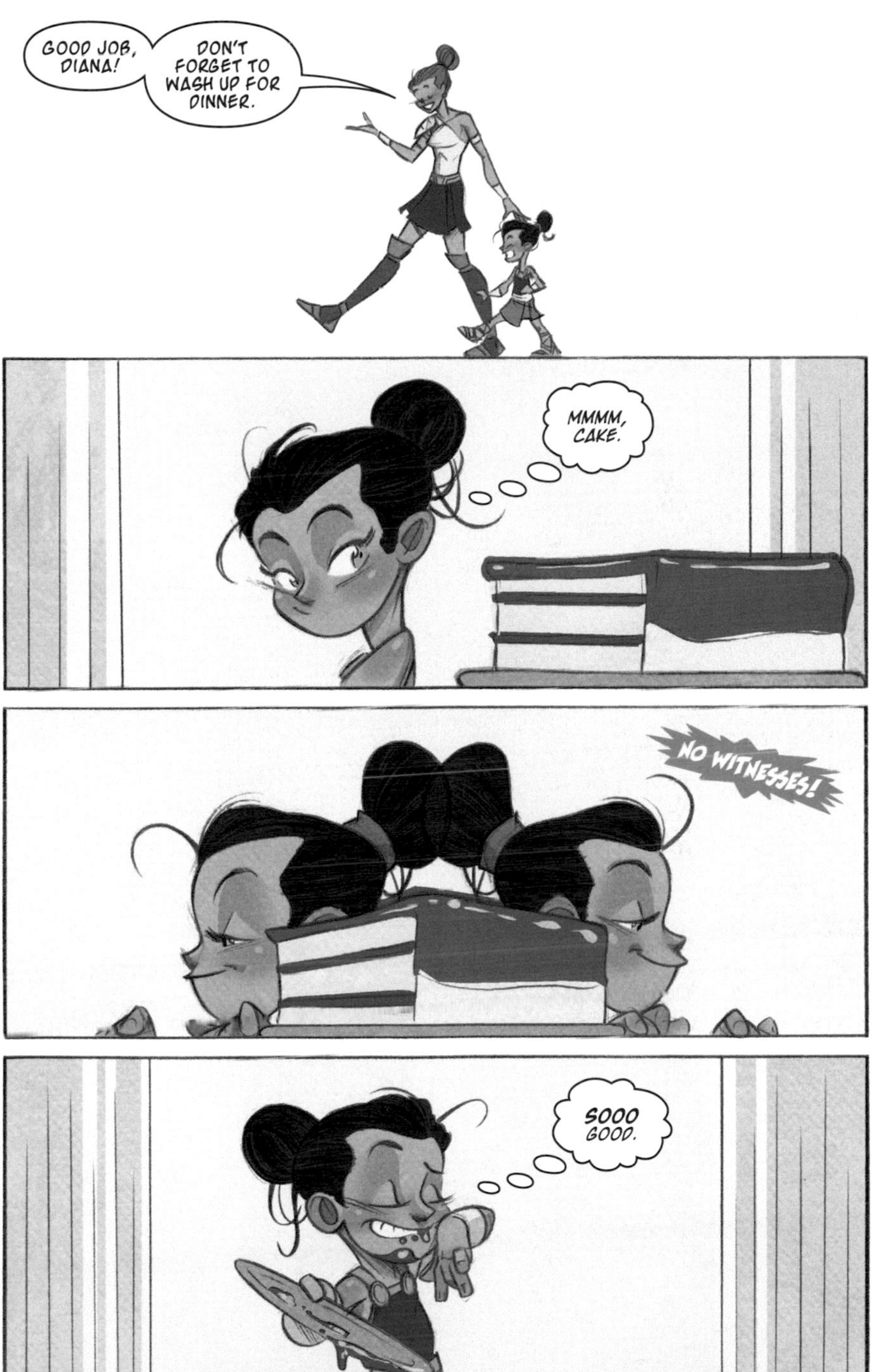
GOOD JOB, DIANA!
DON'T FORGET TO WASH UP FOR DINNER.
MMMM, CAKE.
NO WITNESSES!
SOOO GOOD.

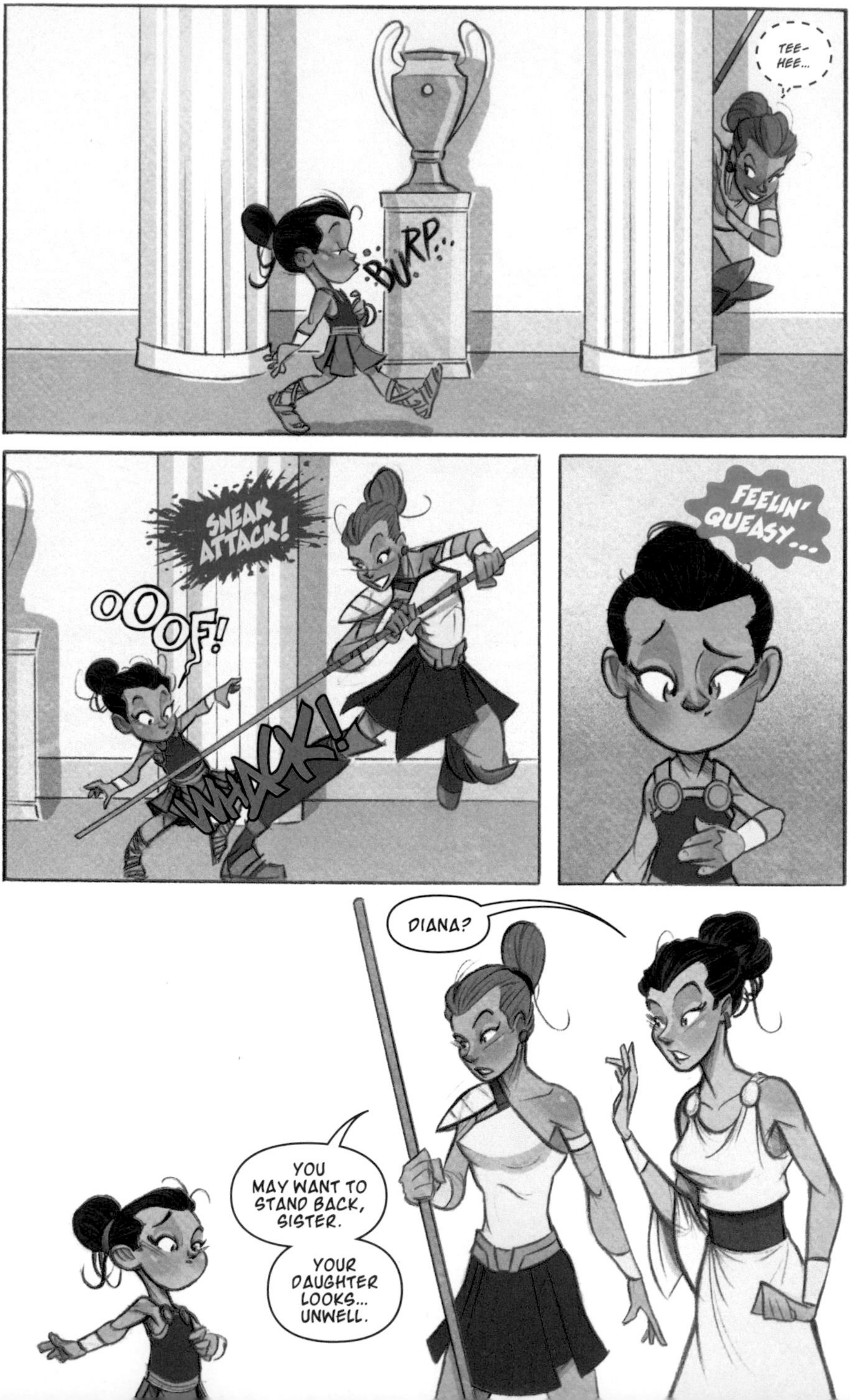
TEE-HEE...
BURP...
SNEAK ATTACK!
OOOF!
WHAK!
FEELIN' QUEASY...
DIANA?
YOU MAY WANT TO STAND BACK, SISTER.
YOUR DAUGHTER LOOKS... UNWELL.

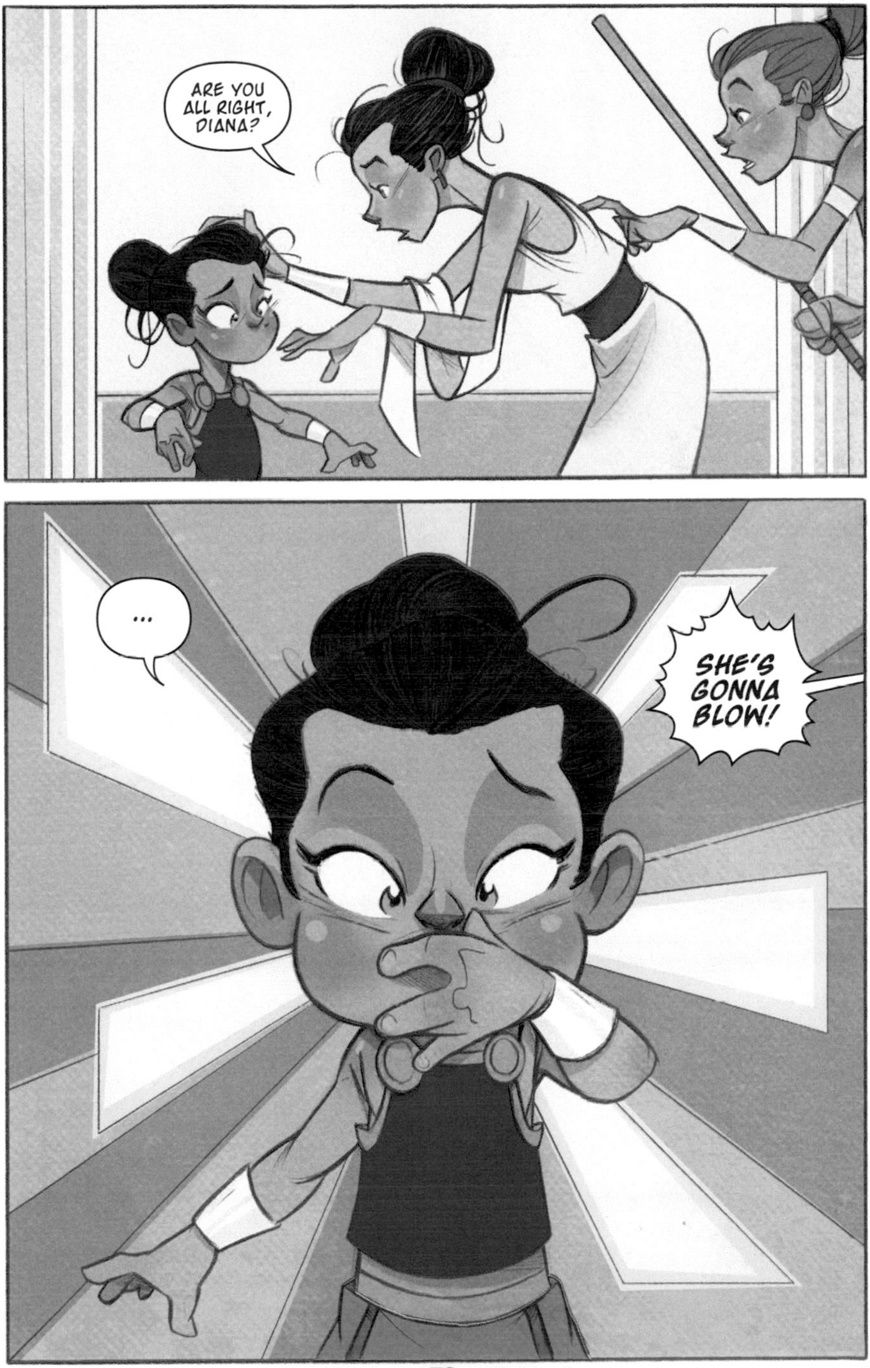
ARE YOU ALL RIGHT, DIANA?
...
SHE'S GONNA BLOW!

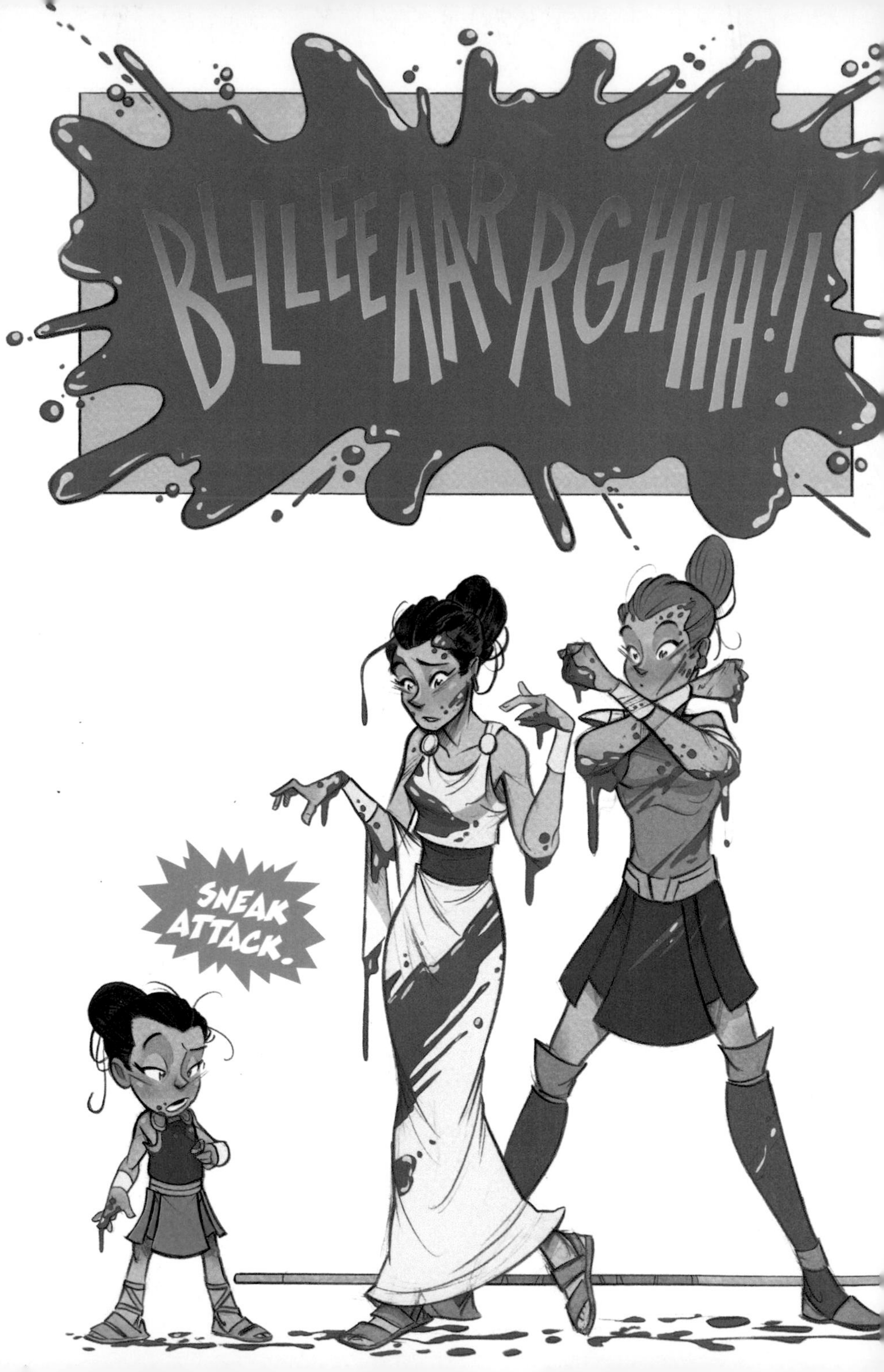
BLLLEEAARRGHHH!!
SNEAK ATTACK.

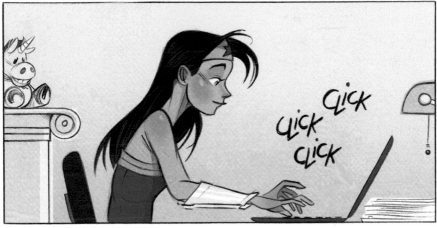

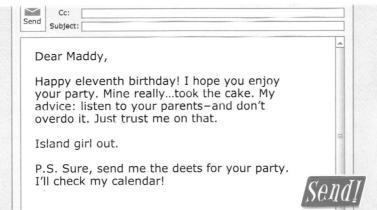

CLICK
CLICK
CLICK
Cc:
Subject:
Send
Dear Maddy,
Happy eleventh birthday! I hope you enjoy your party. Mine really...took the cake. My advice: listen to your parents–and don't overdo it. Just trust me on that.
Island girl out.
P.S. Sure, send me the deets for your party. I'll check my calendar!
Send!
You have 3,999 unread messages.
IT'S GOING TO BE A LONG DAY.

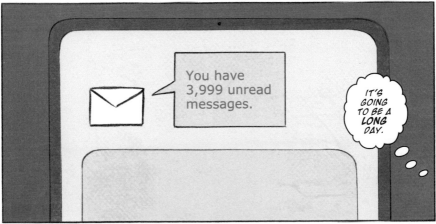

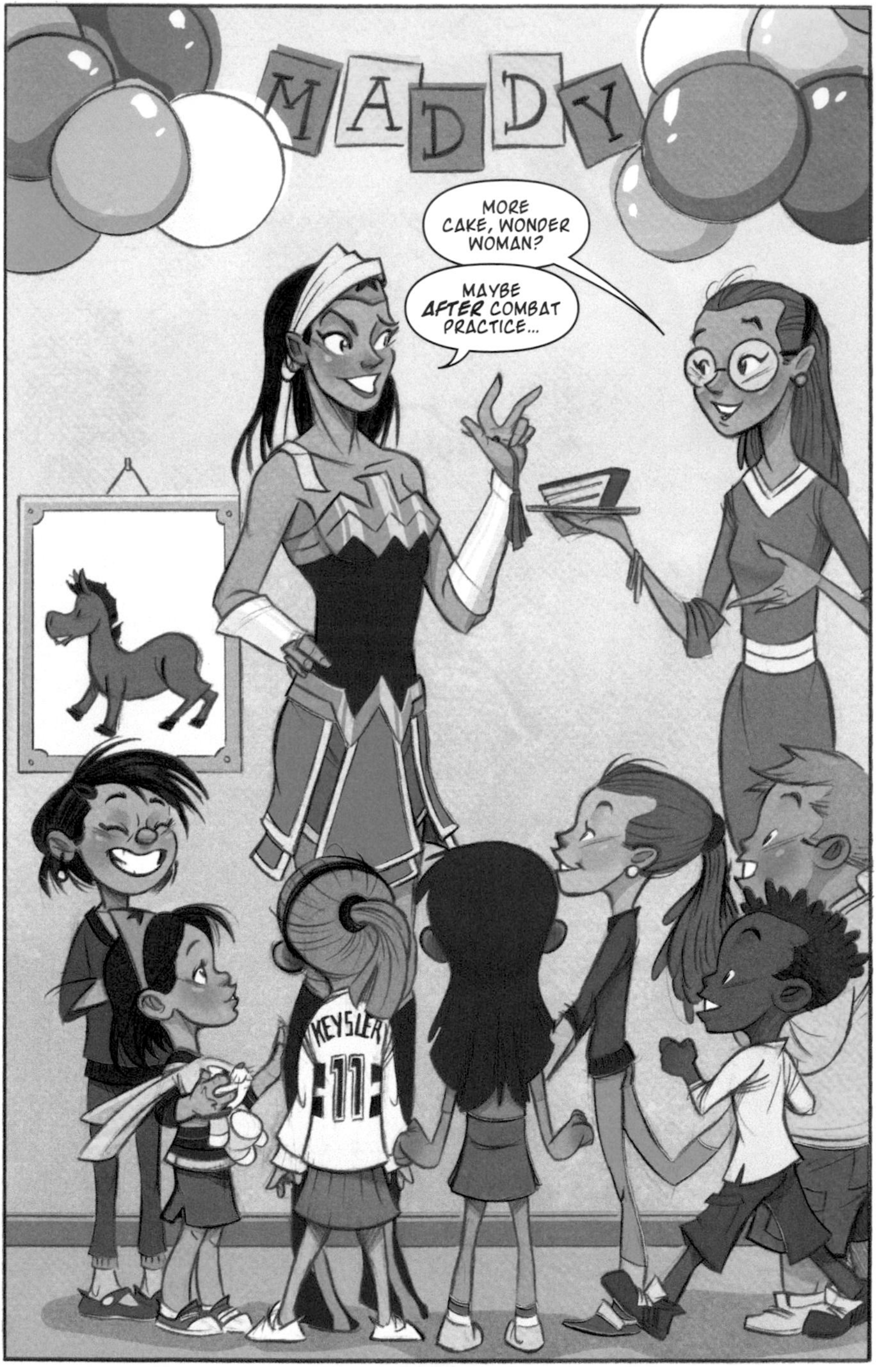
MADDY
MORE CAKE, WONDER WOMAN?
MAYBE **AFTER** COMBAT PRACTICE...
KEYSLER
11

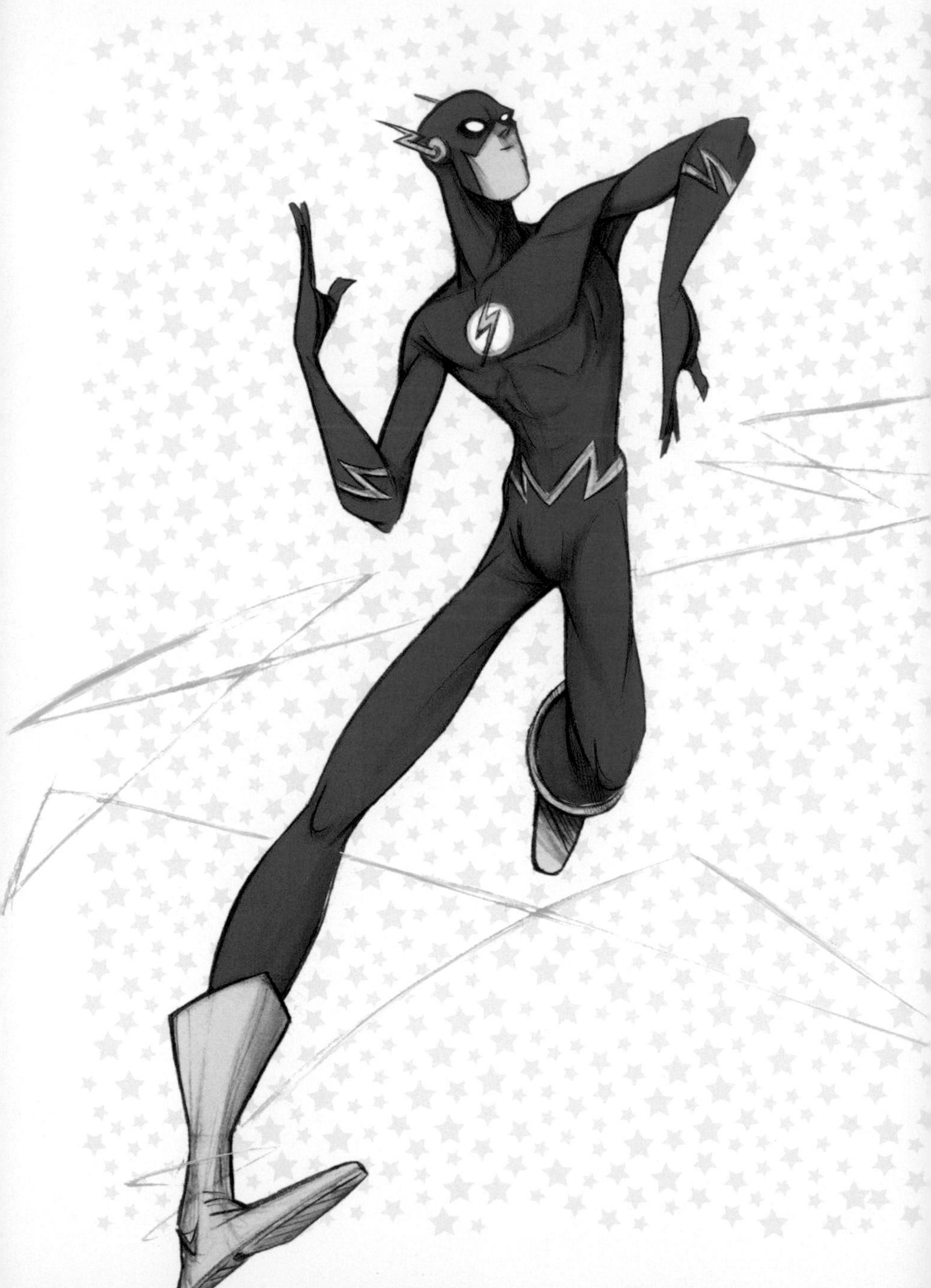

CHAPTER 5

Dear FLASH

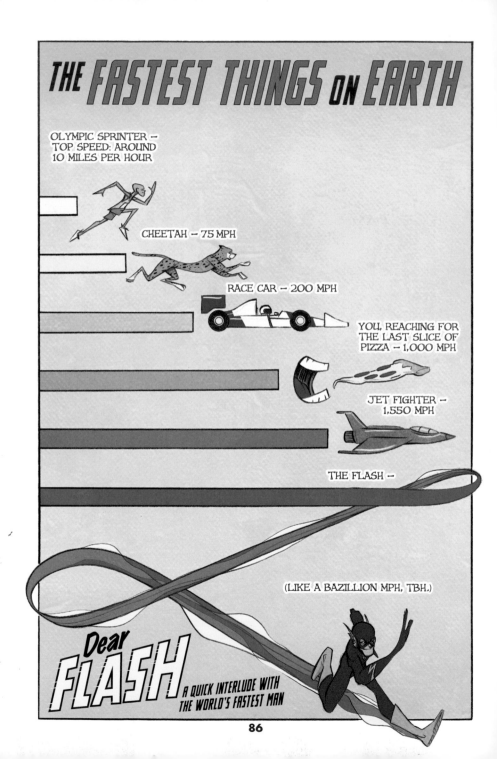

THE FASTEST THINGS ON EARTH

OLYMPIC SPRINTER —
TOP SPEED: AROUND
10 MILES PER HOUR

CHEETAH — 75 MPH

RACE CAR — 200 MPH

YOU, REACHING FOR
THE LAST SLICE OF
PIZZA — 1,000 MPH

JET FIGHTER —
1,550 MPH

THE FLASH —

(LIKE A BAZILLION MPH, TBH.)

Dear FLASH
A QUICK INTERLUDE WITH
THE WORLD'S FASTEST MAN

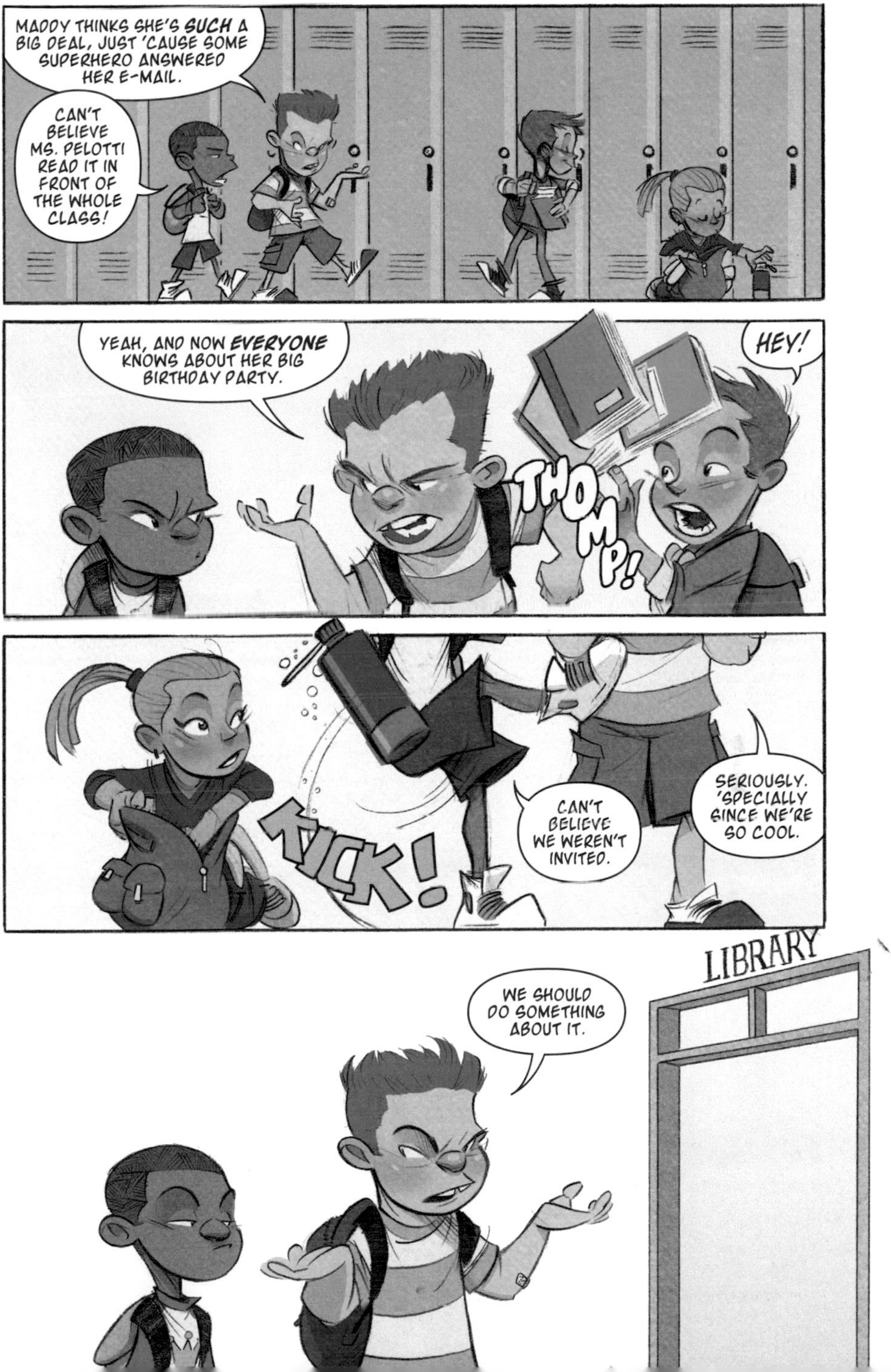
MADDY THINKS SHE'S SUCH A BIG DEAL, JUST 'CAUSE SOME SUPERHERO ANSWERED HER E-MAIL.
CAN'T BELIEVE MS. PELOTTI READ IT IN FRONT OF THE WHOLE CLASS!
YEAH, AND NOW EVERYONE KNOWS ABOUT HER BIG BIRTHDAY PARTY.
HEY!
THOMP!
KICK!
CAN'T BELIEVE WE WEREN'T INVITED.
SERIOUSLY. 'SPECIALLY SINCE WE'RE SO COOL.
LIBRARY
WE SHOULD DO SOMETHING ABOUT IT.

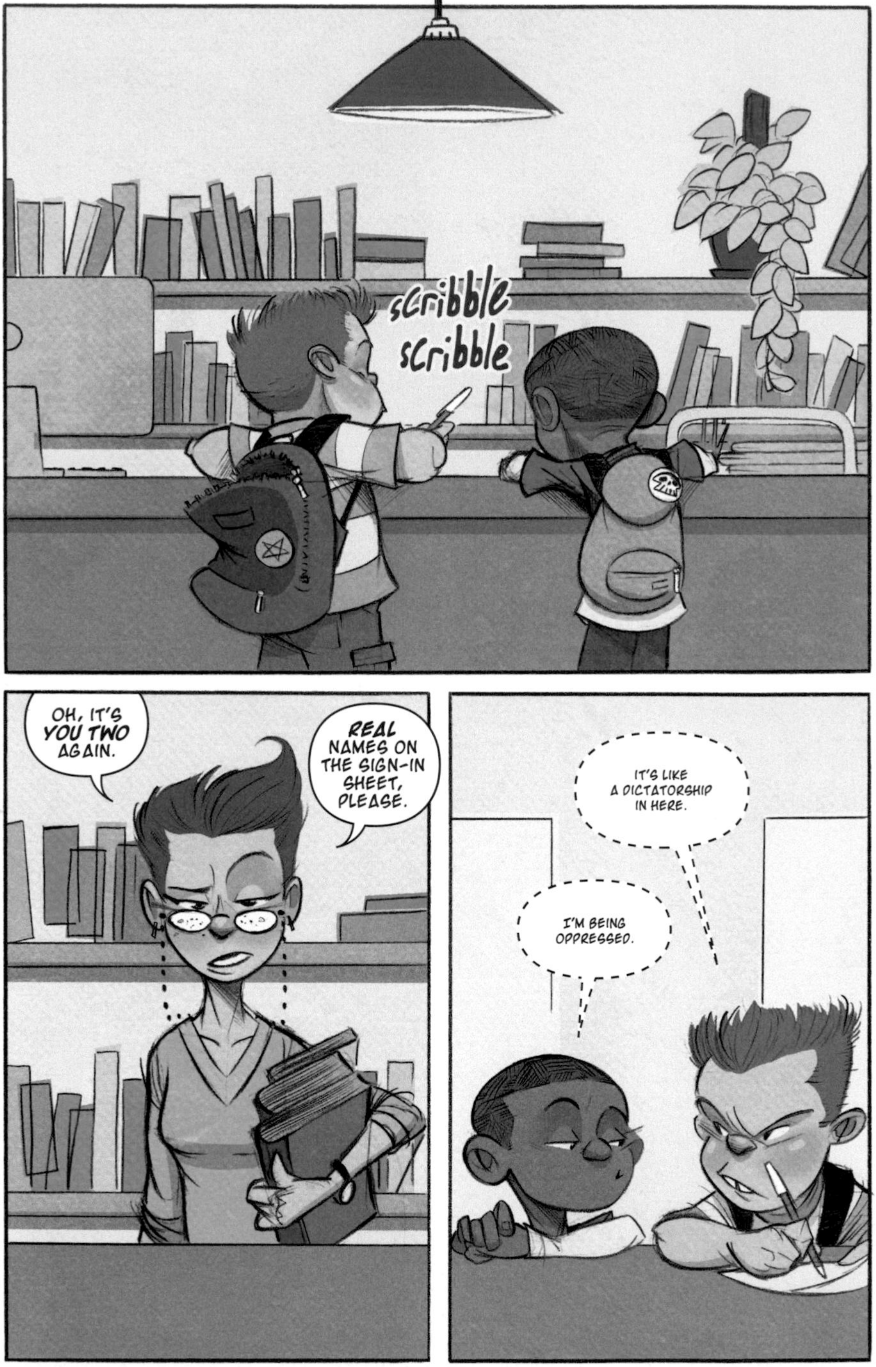
SCRIBBLE
SCRIBBLE
OH, IT'S YOU TWO AGAIN.
REAL NAMES ON THE SIGN-IN SHEET, PLEASE.
IT'S LIKE A DICTATORSHIP IN HERE.
I'M BEING OPPRESSED.

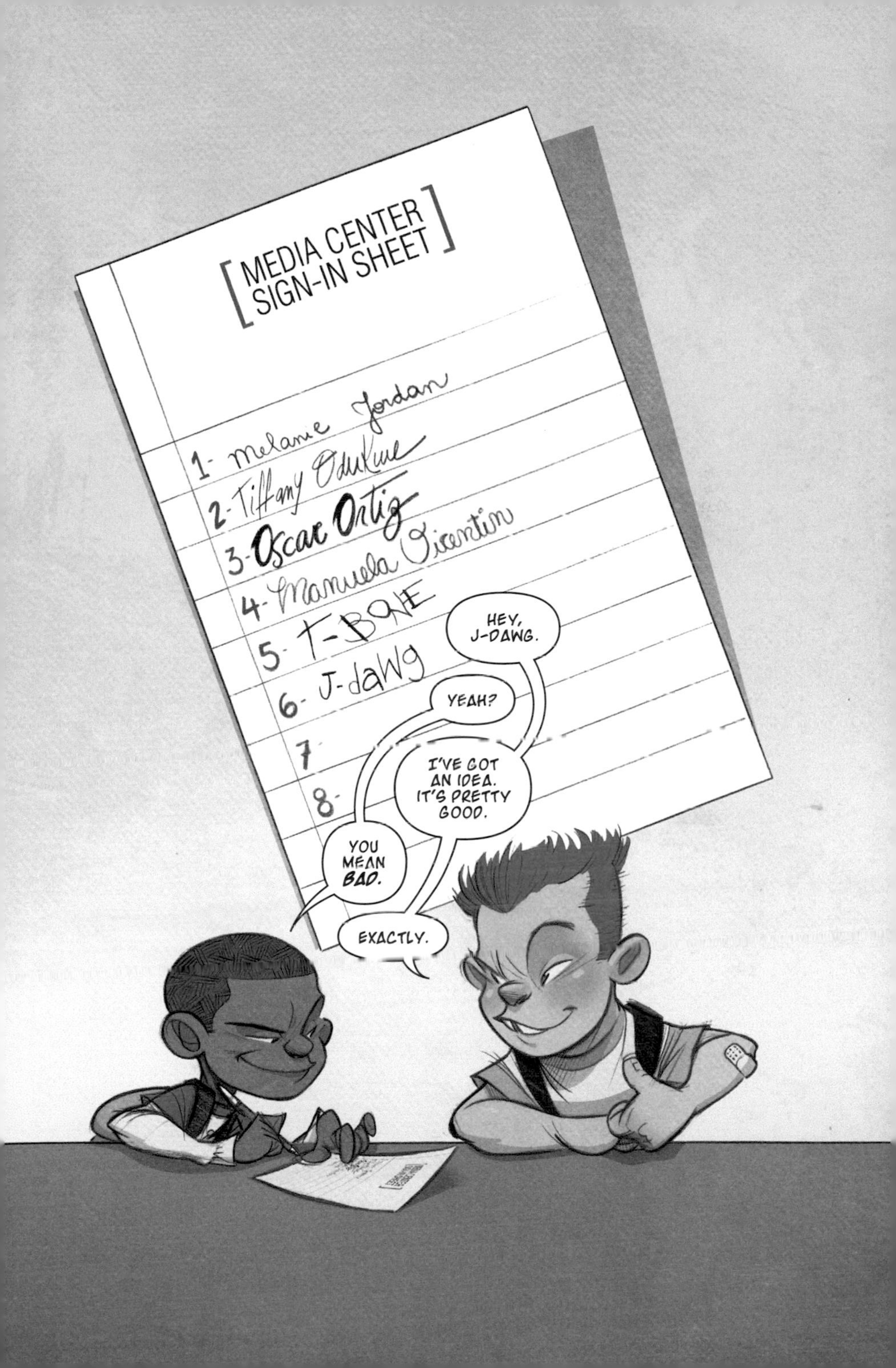
MEDIA CENTER SIGN-IN SHEET
1- Melanie Jordan
2- Tiffany Odukwe
3- Oscar Ortiz
4- Manuela Vicentin
5- T-BONE
6- J-dawg
7-
8-
HEY, J-DAWG.
YEAH?
I'VE GOT AN IDEA. IT'S PRETTY GOOD.
YOU MEAN BAD.
EXACTLY.

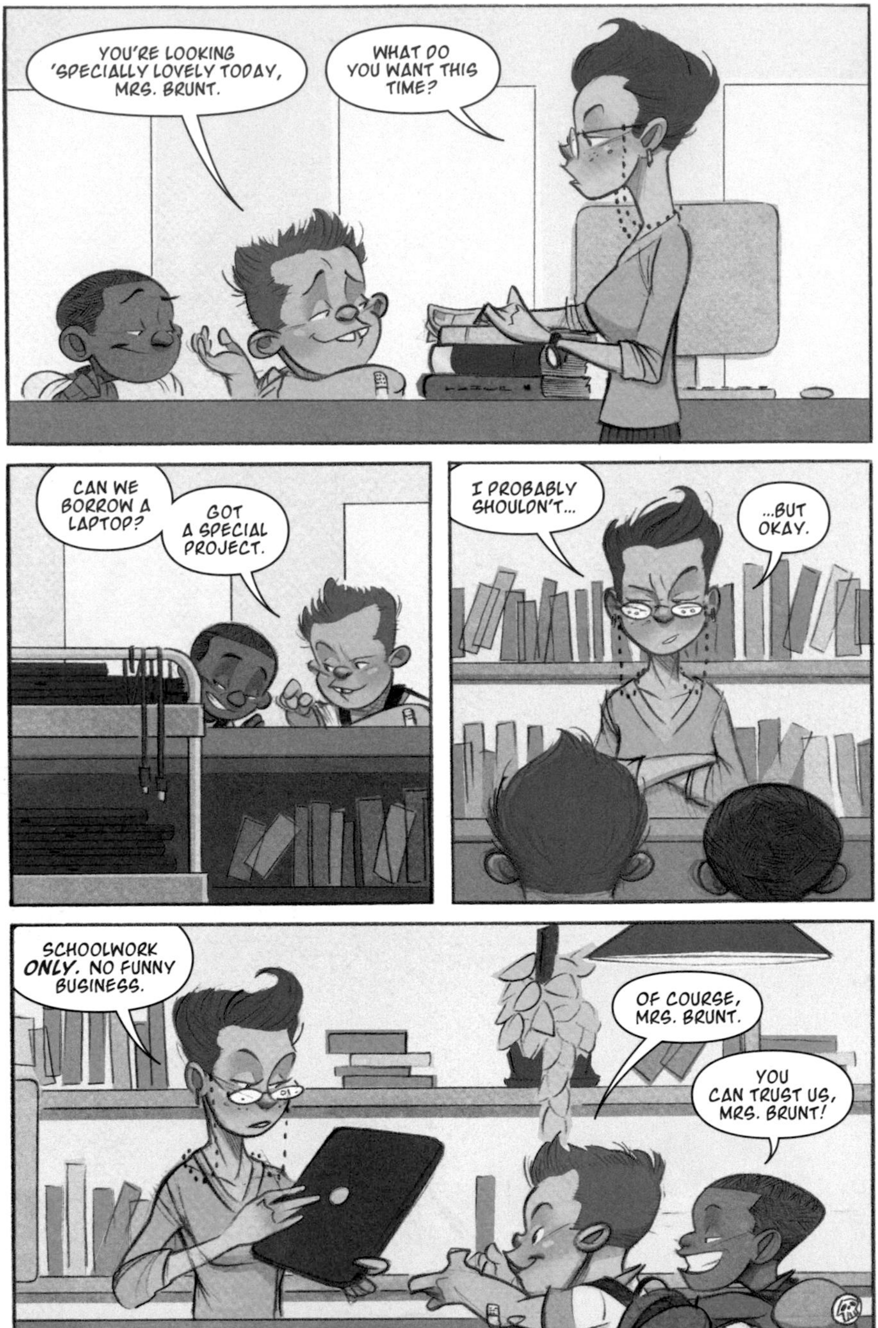
YOU'RE LOOKING 'SPECIALLY LOVELY TODAY, MRS. BRUNT.
WHAT DO YOU WANT THIS TIME?
CAN WE BORROW A LAPTOP?
GOT A SPECIAL PROJECT.
I PROBABLY SHOULDN'T...
...BUT OKAY.
SCHOOLWORK ONLY. NO FUNNY BUSINESS.
OF COURSE, MRS. BRUNT.
YOU CAN TRUST US, MRS. BRUNT!

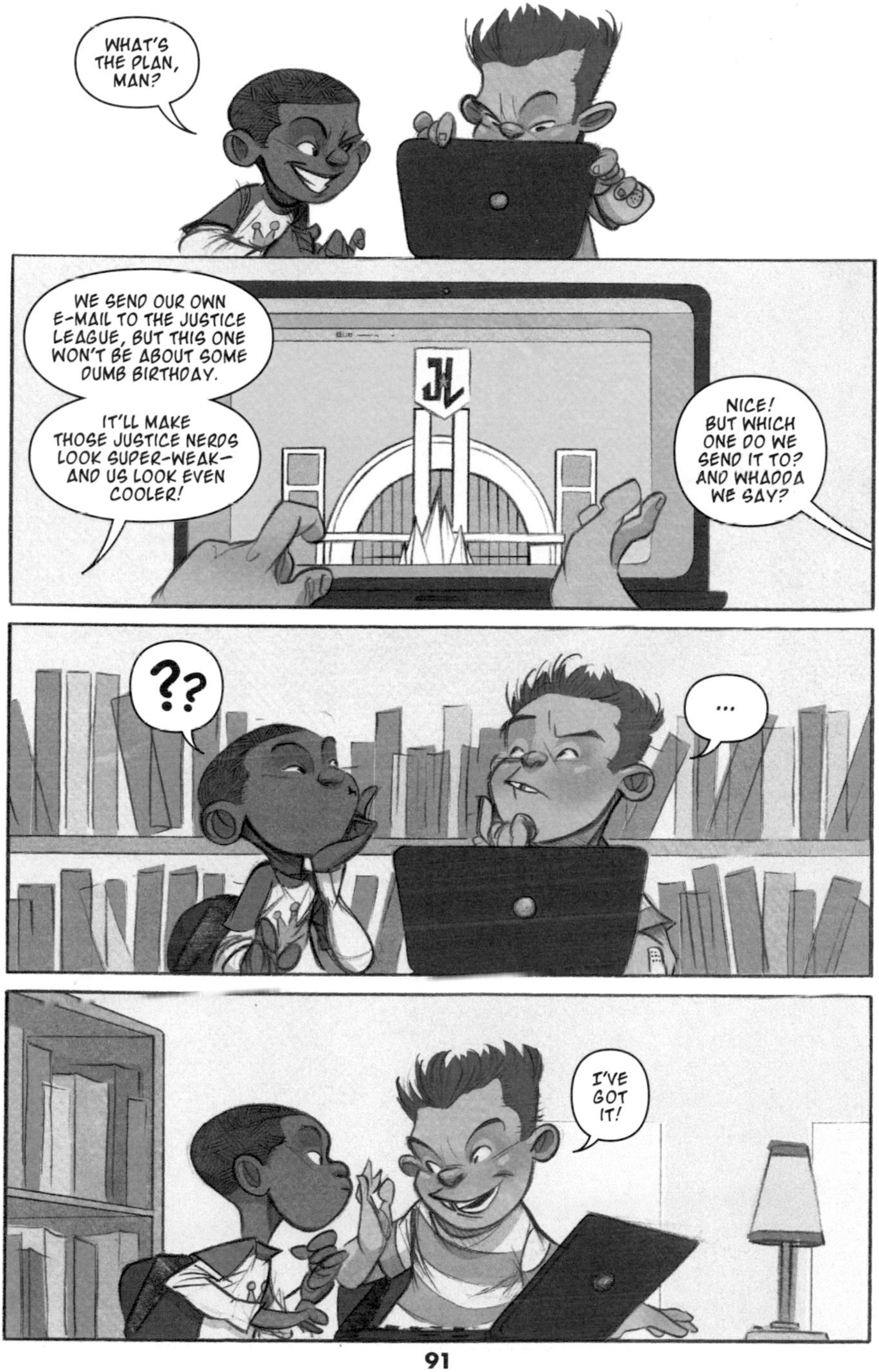
WHAT'S THE PLAN, MAN?
WE SEND OUR OWN E-MAIL TO THE JUSTICE LEAGUE, BUT THIS ONE WON'T BE ABOUT SOME DUMB BIRTHDAY.
IT'LL MAKE THOSE JUSTICE NERDS LOOK SUPER-WEAK—AND US LOOK EVEN COOLER!
NICE! BUT WHICH ONE DO WE SEND IT TO? AND WHADDA WE SAY?
??
...
I'VE GOT IT!

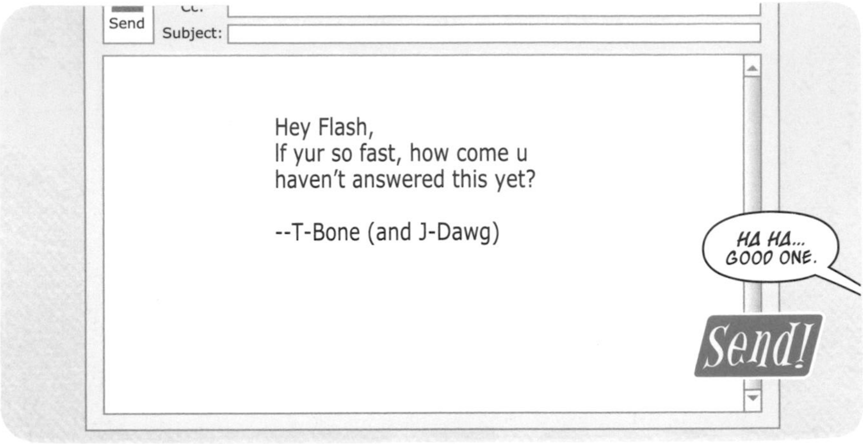
Send
Subject:
Hey Flash,
If yur so fast, how come u
haven't answered this yet?
--T-Bone (and J-Dawg)
HA HA... GOOD ONE.
Send!

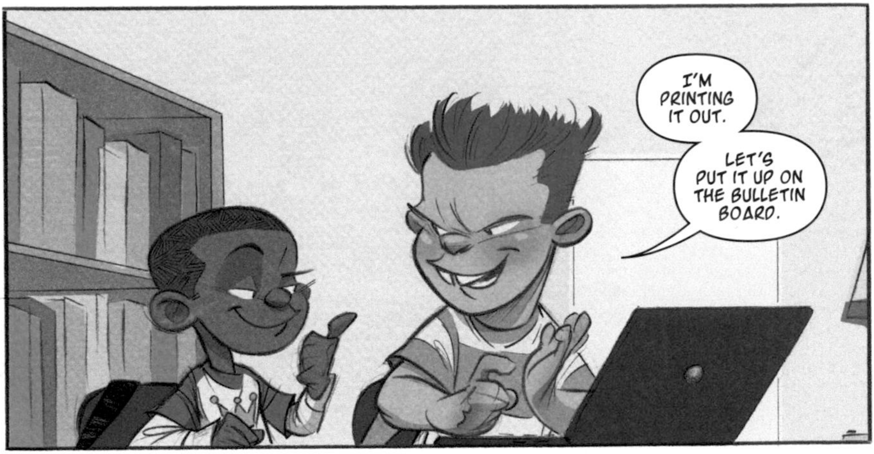
I'M PRINTING IT OUT.
LET'S PUT IT UP ON THE BULLETIN BOARD.

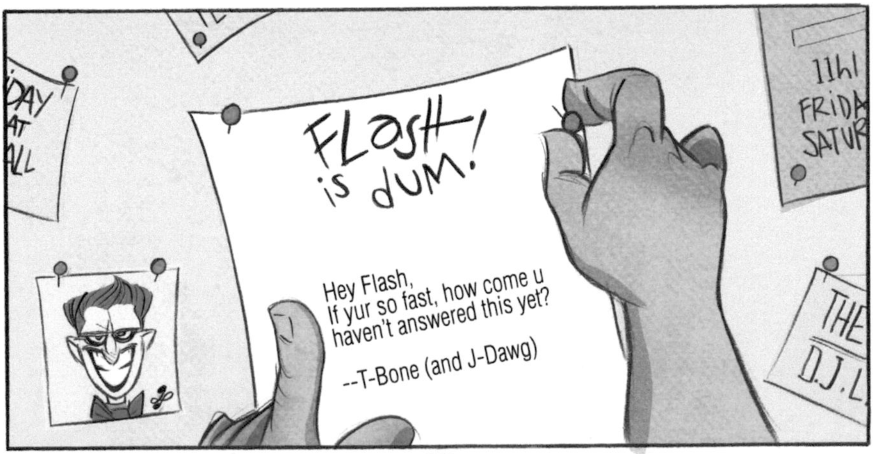
FLASH! is dum!
Hey Flash,
If yur so fast, how come u
haven't answered this yet?
--T-Bone (and J-Dawg)

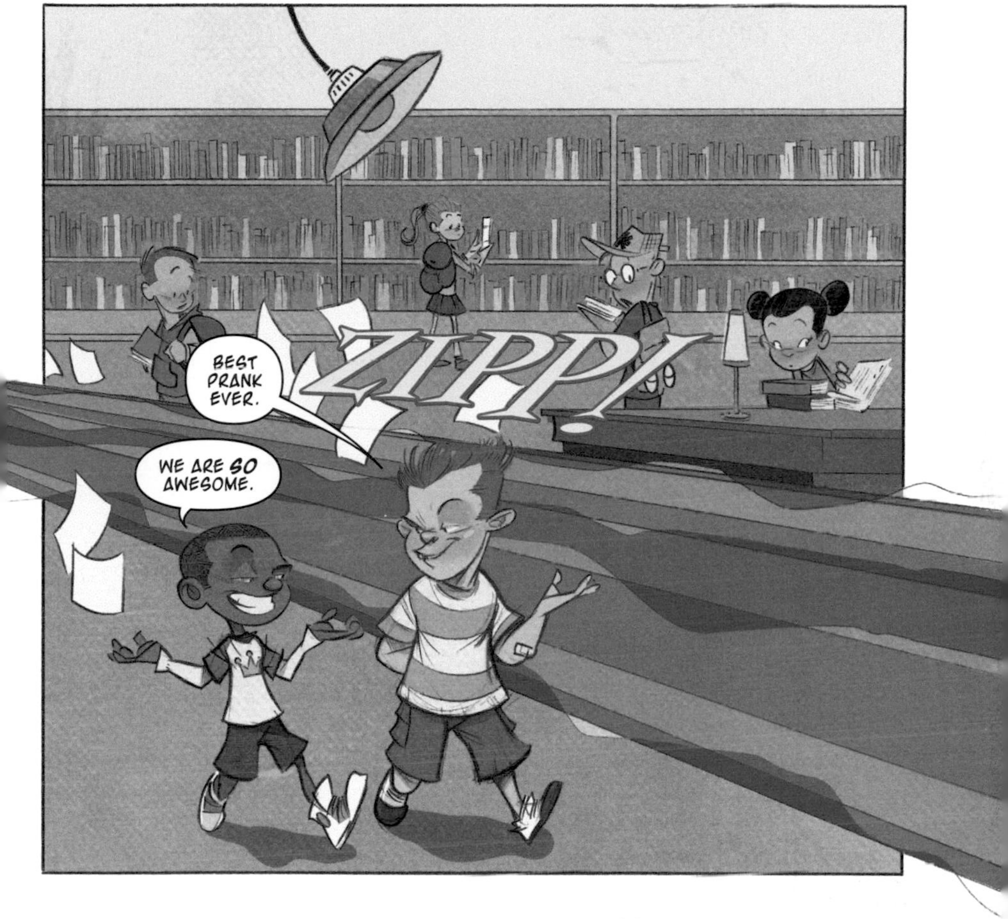
ZIPP!
BEST PRANK EVER.
WE ARE SO AWESOME.

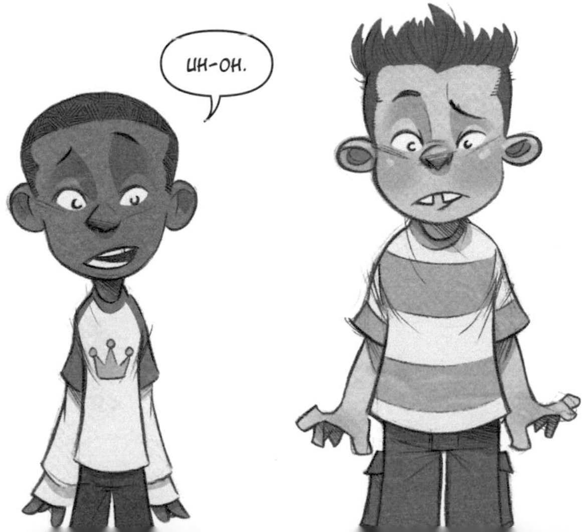
UH-OH.

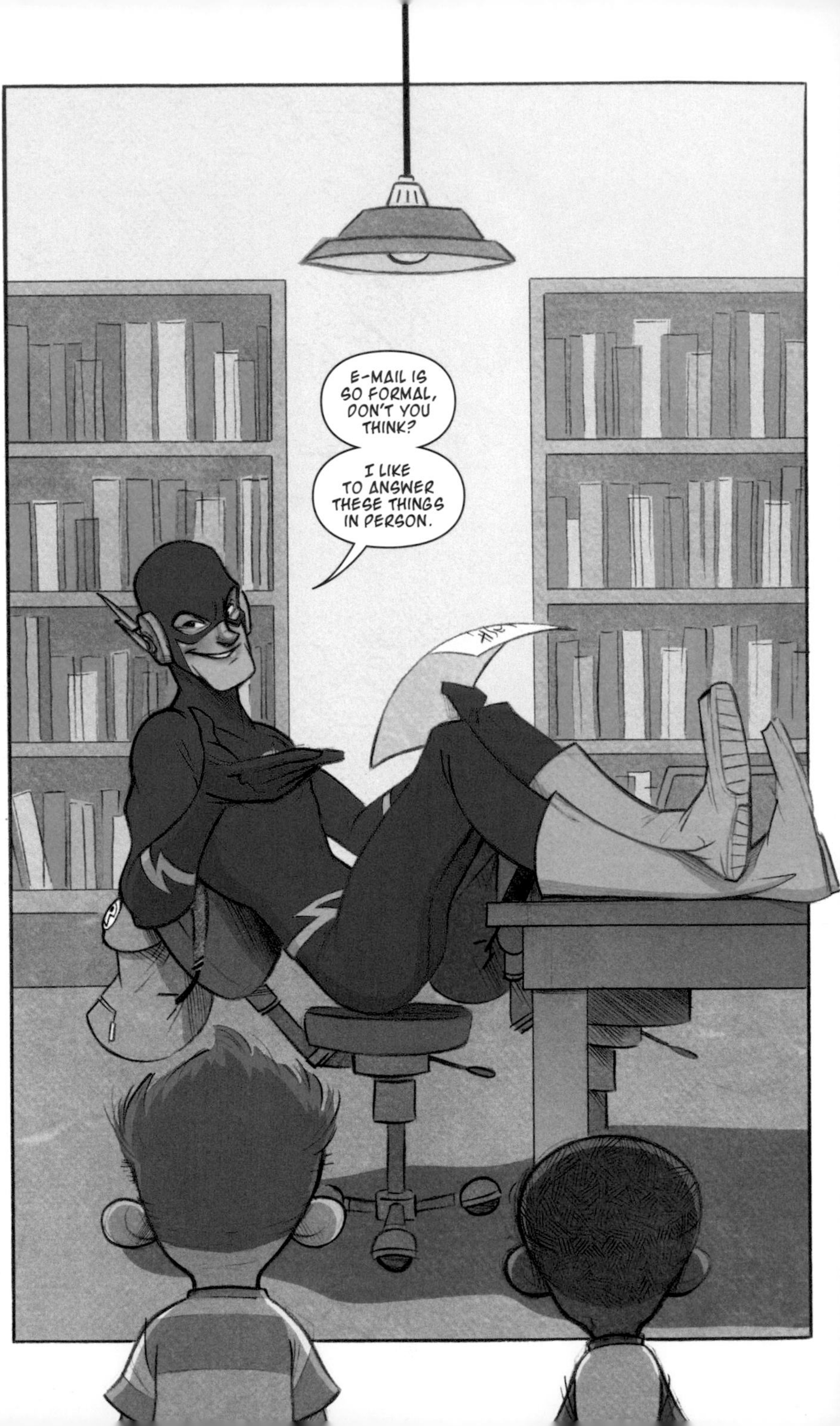
E-MAIL IS SO FORMAL, DON'T YOU THINK?
I LIKE TO ANSWER THESE THINGS IN PERSON.

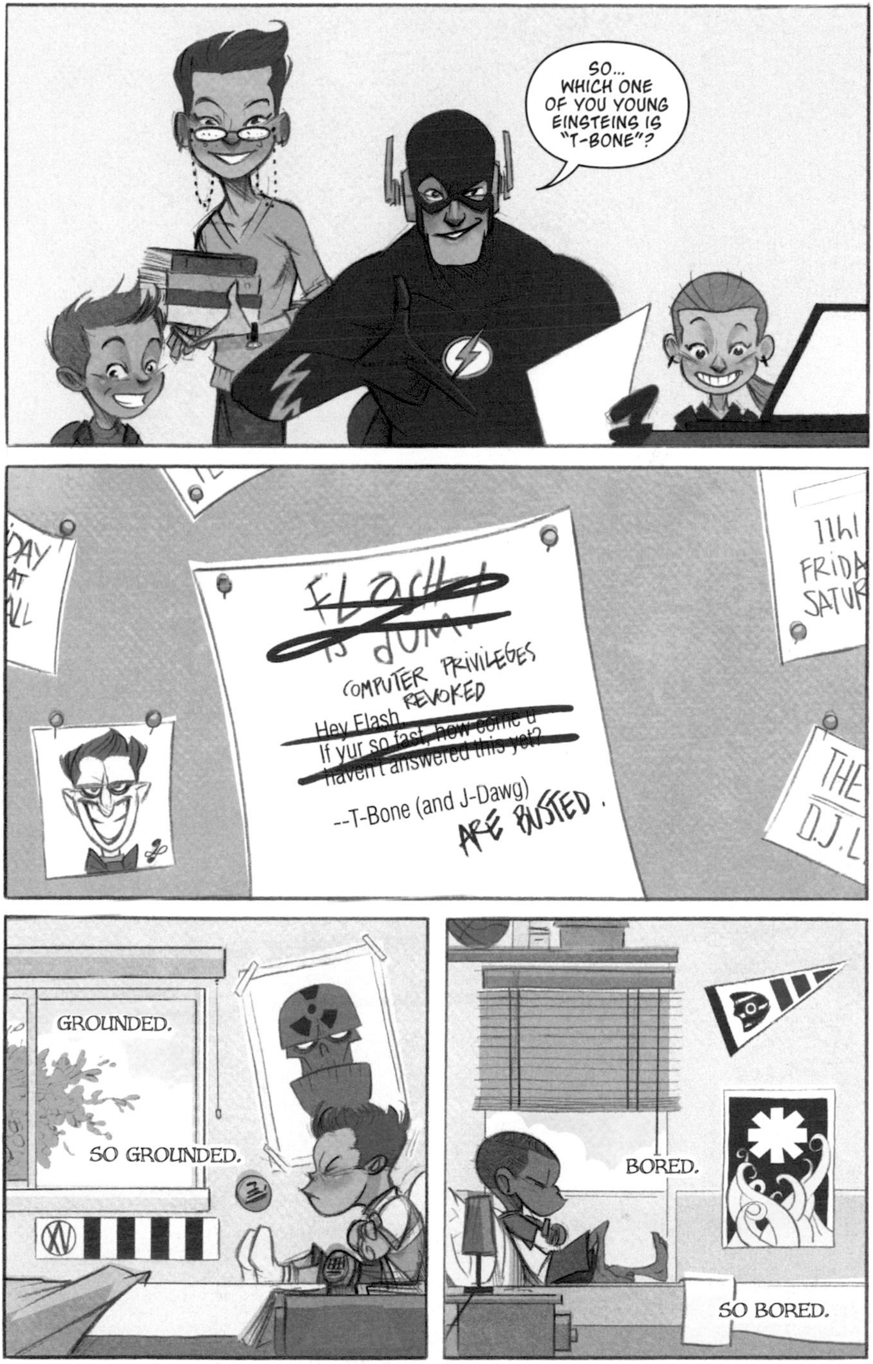

SO... WHICH ONE OF YOU YOUNG EINSTEINS IS "T-BONE"?
Flash is dum!
COMPUTER PRIVILEGES REVOKED
Hey Flash, If yur so fast, how come u haven't answered this yet?
--T-Bone (and J-Dawg)
ARE BUSTED.
GROUNDED.
SO GROUNDED.
BORED.
SO BORED.

CHAPTER 6

DEAR GREEN LANTERN

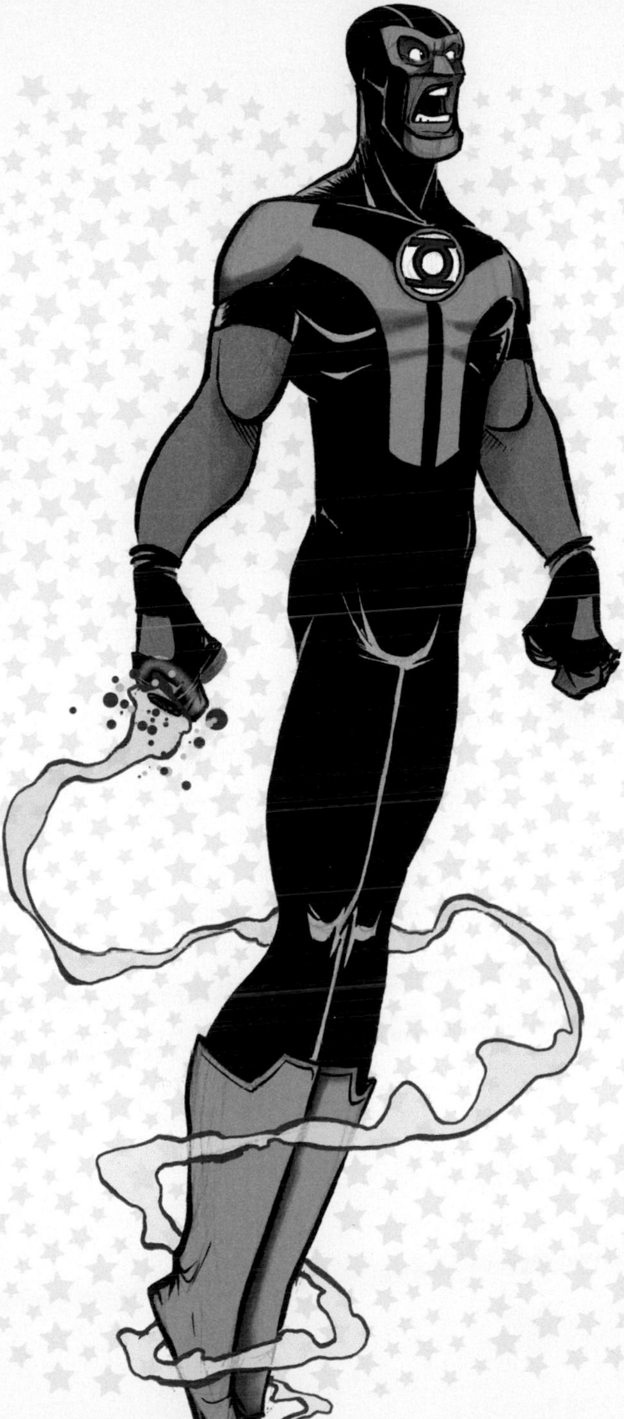

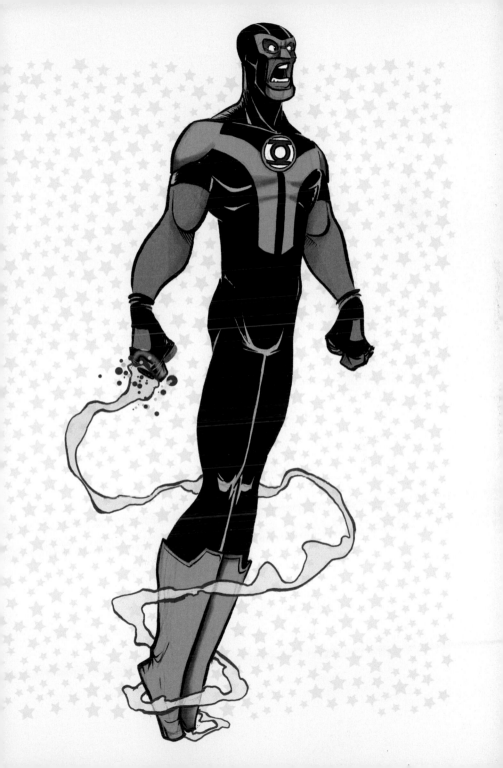

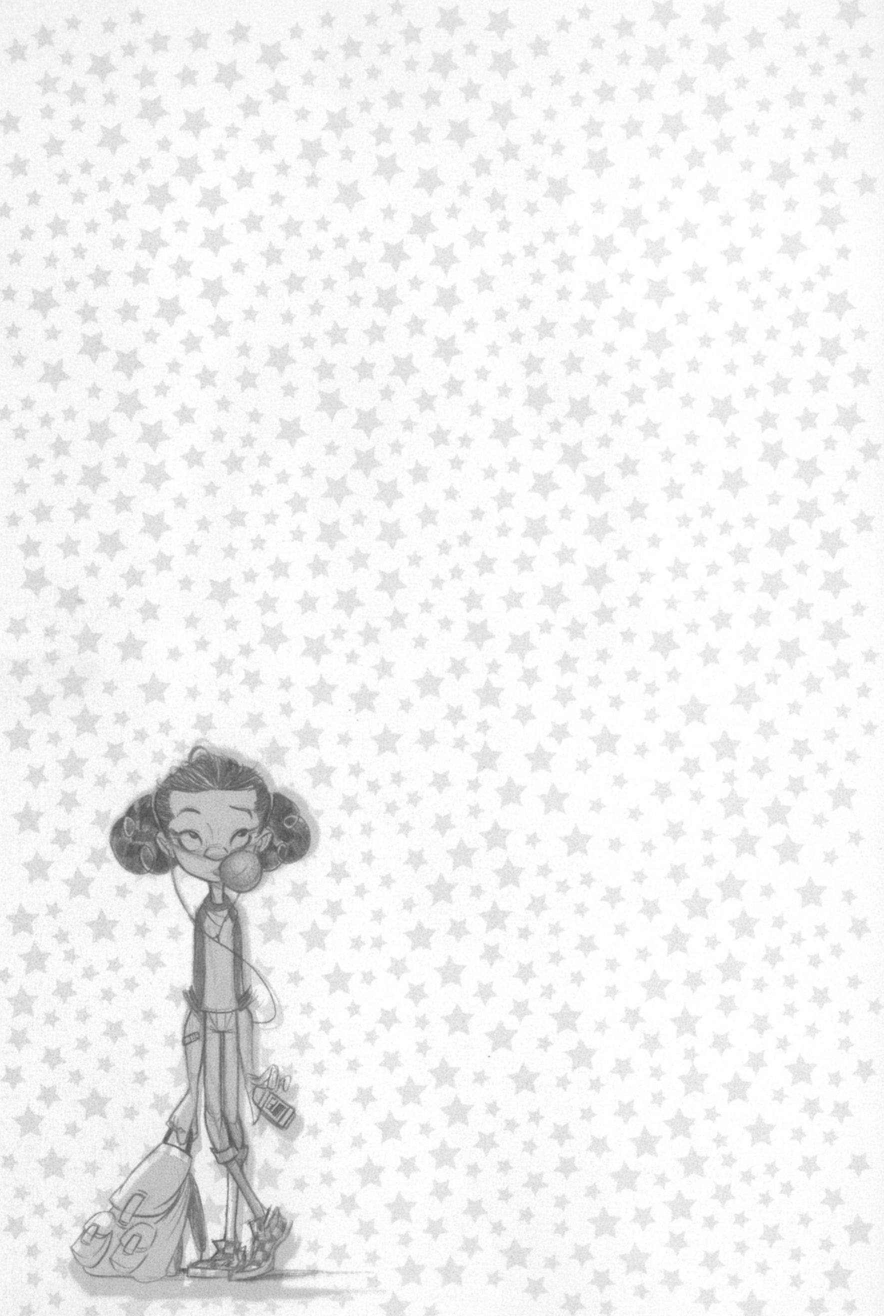

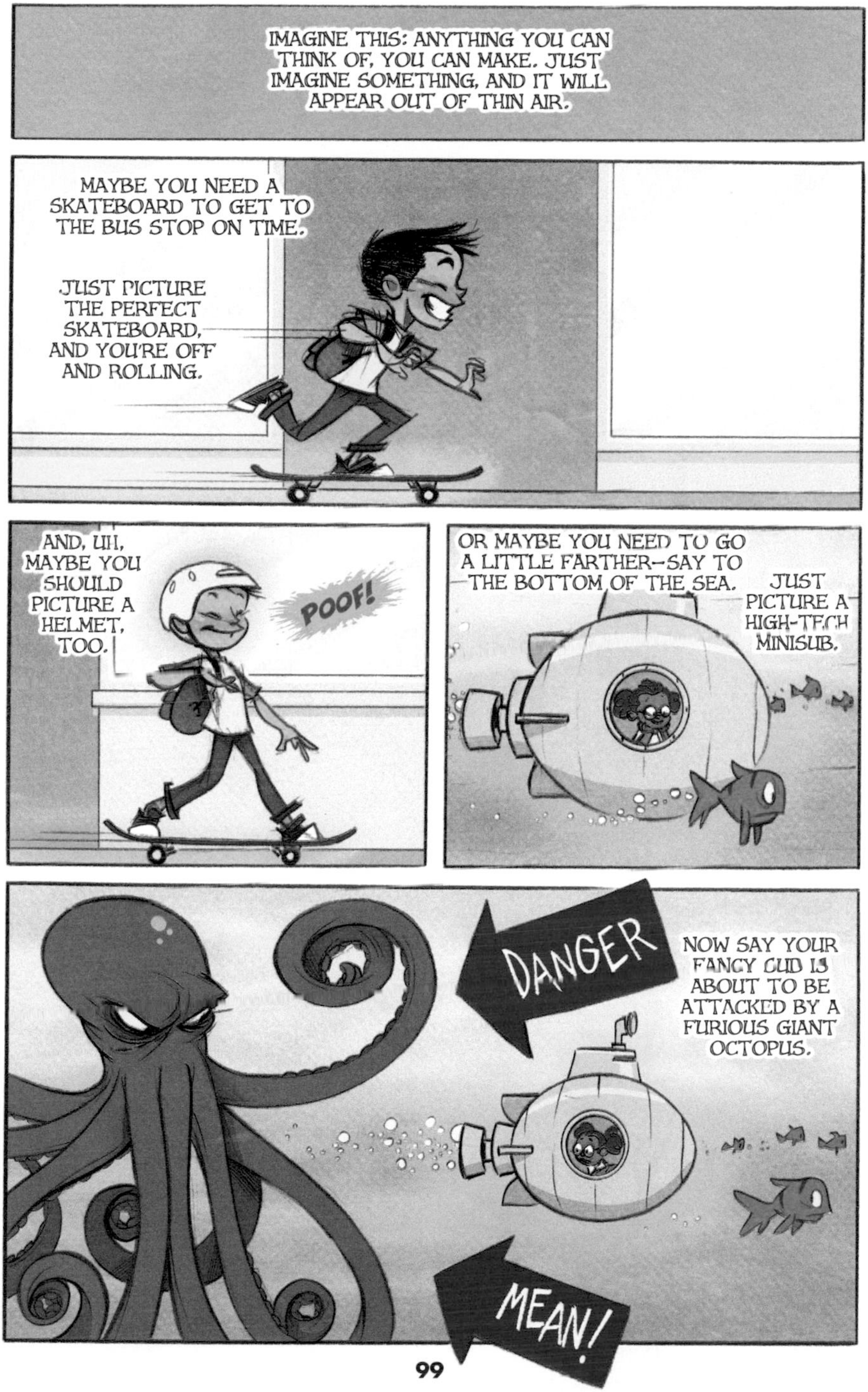
IMAGINE THIS: ANYTHING YOU CAN THINK OF, YOU CAN MAKE. JUST IMAGINE SOMETHING, AND IT WILL APPEAR OUT OF THIN AIR.
MAYBE YOU NEED A SKATEBOARD TO GET TO THE BUS STOP ON TIME.
JUST PICTURE THE PERFECT SKATEBOARD, AND YOU'RE OFF AND ROLLING.
AND, UH, MAYBE YOU SHOULD PICTURE A HELMET, TOO.
POOF!
OR MAYBE YOU NEED TO GO A LITTLE FARTHER--SAY TO THE BOTTOM OF THE SEA.
JUST PICTURE A HIGH-TECH MINISUB.
DANGER
NOW SAY YOUR FANCY SUB IS ABOUT TO BE ATTACKED BY A FURIOUS GIANT OCTOPUS.
MEAN!

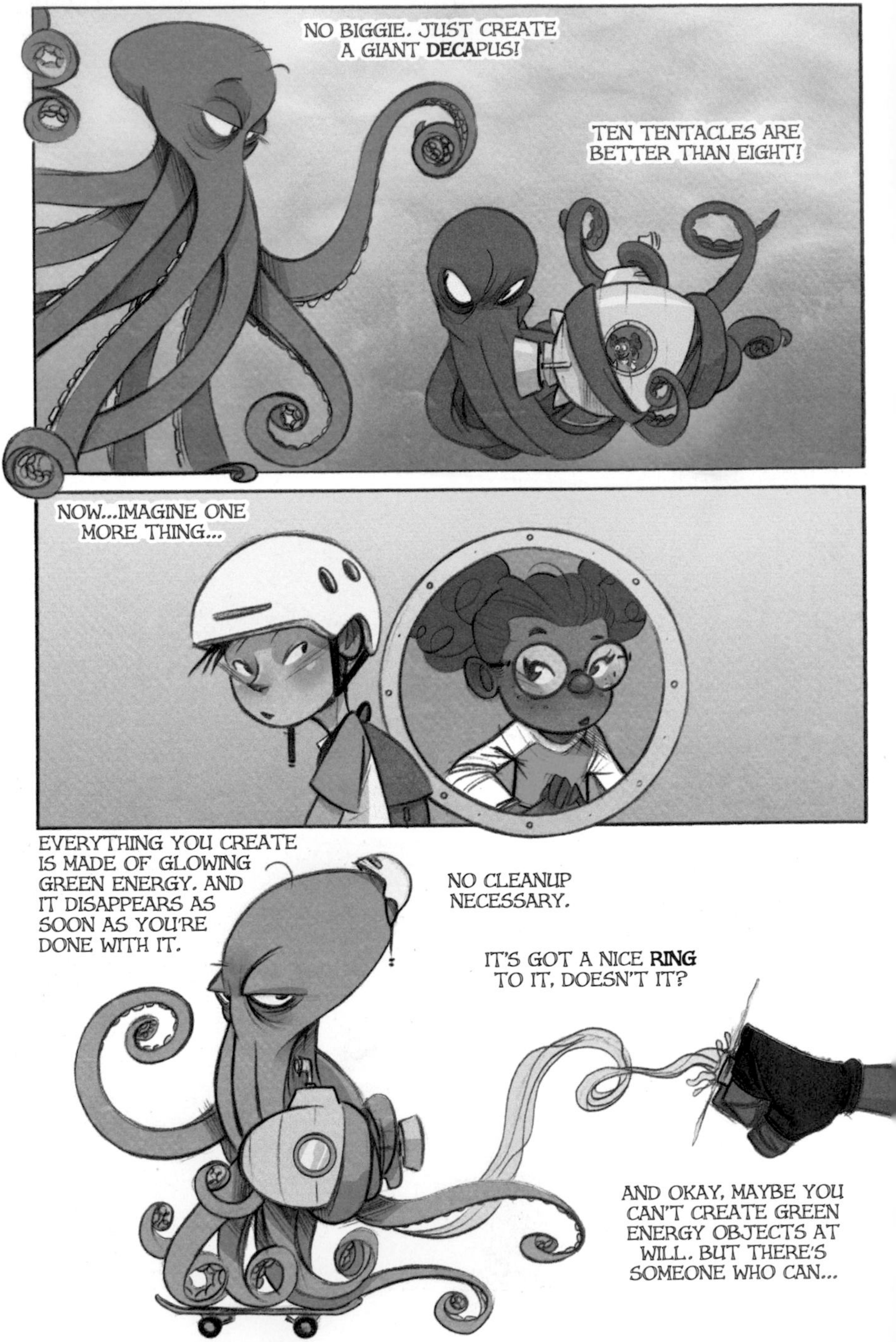
NO BIGGIE. JUST CREATE A GIANT DECAPUS!
TEN TENTACLES ARE BETTER THAN EIGHT!
NOW...IMAGINE ONE MORE THING...
EVERYTHING YOU CREATE IS MADE OF GLOWING GREEN ENERGY. AND IT DISAPPEARS AS SOON AS YOU'RE DONE WITH IT.
NO CLEANUP NECESSARY.
IT'S GOT A NICE RING TO IT, DOESN'T IT?
AND OKAY, MAYBE YOU CAN'T CREATE GREEN ENERGY OBJECTS AT WILL. BUT THERE'S SOMEONE WHO CAN...

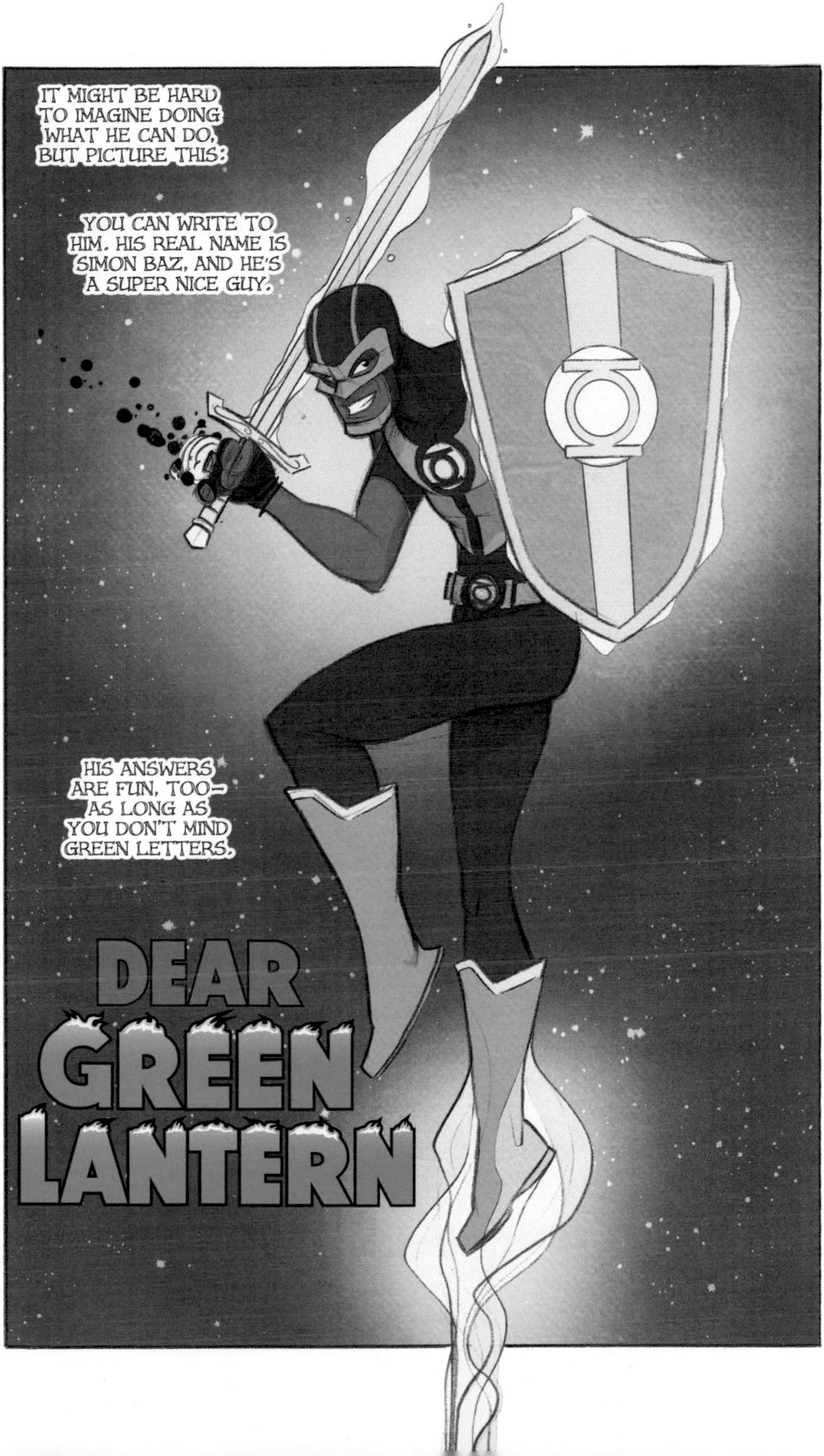
IT MIGHT BE HARD TO IMAGINE DOING WHAT HE CAN DO, BUT PICTURE THIS:
YOU CAN WRITE TO HIM. HIS REAL NAME IS SIMON BAZ, AND HE'S A SUPER NICE GUY.
HIS ANSWERS ARE FUN, TOO—AS LONG AS YOU DON'T MIND GREEN LETTERS.
DEAR GREEN LANTERN

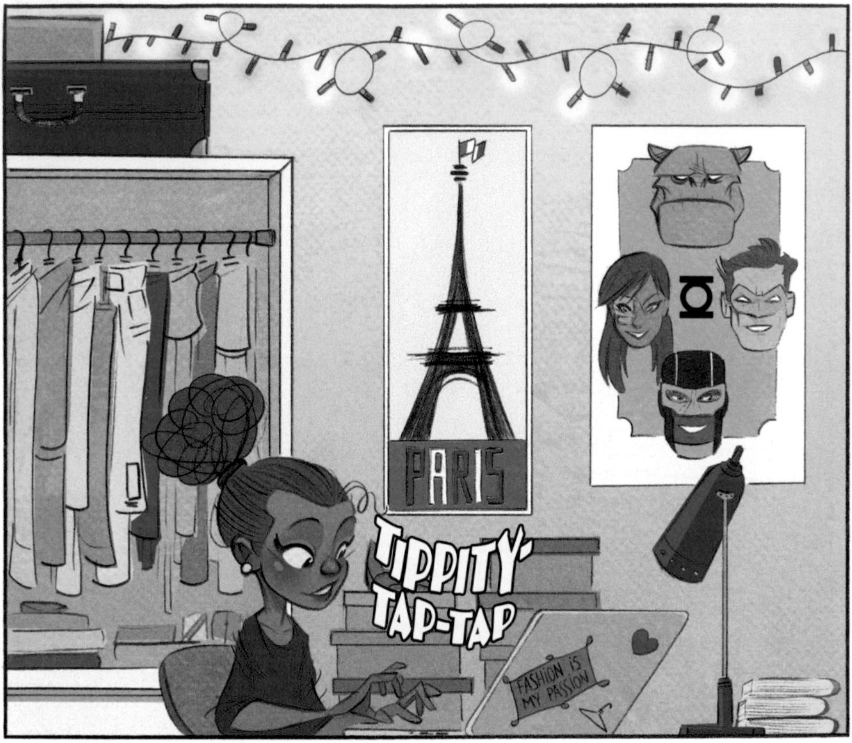
PARIS
TIPPITY-TAP-TAP
FASHION IS MY PASSION

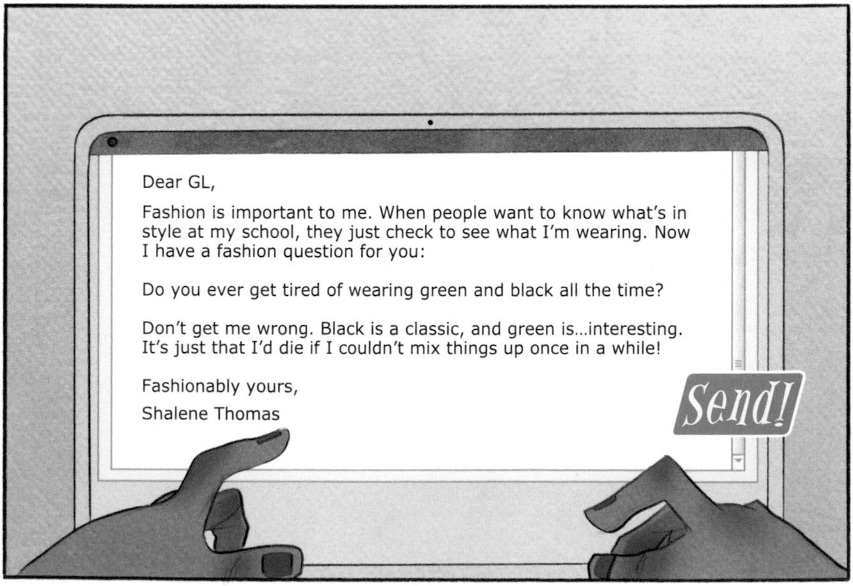
Dear GL,
Fashion is important to me. When people want to know what's in style at my school, they just check to see what I'm wearing. Now I have a fashion question for you:
Do you ever get tired of wearing green and black all the time?
Don't get me wrong. Black is a classic, and green is...interesting. It's just that I'd die if I couldn't mix things up once in a while!
Fashionably yours,
Shalene Thomas
Send!

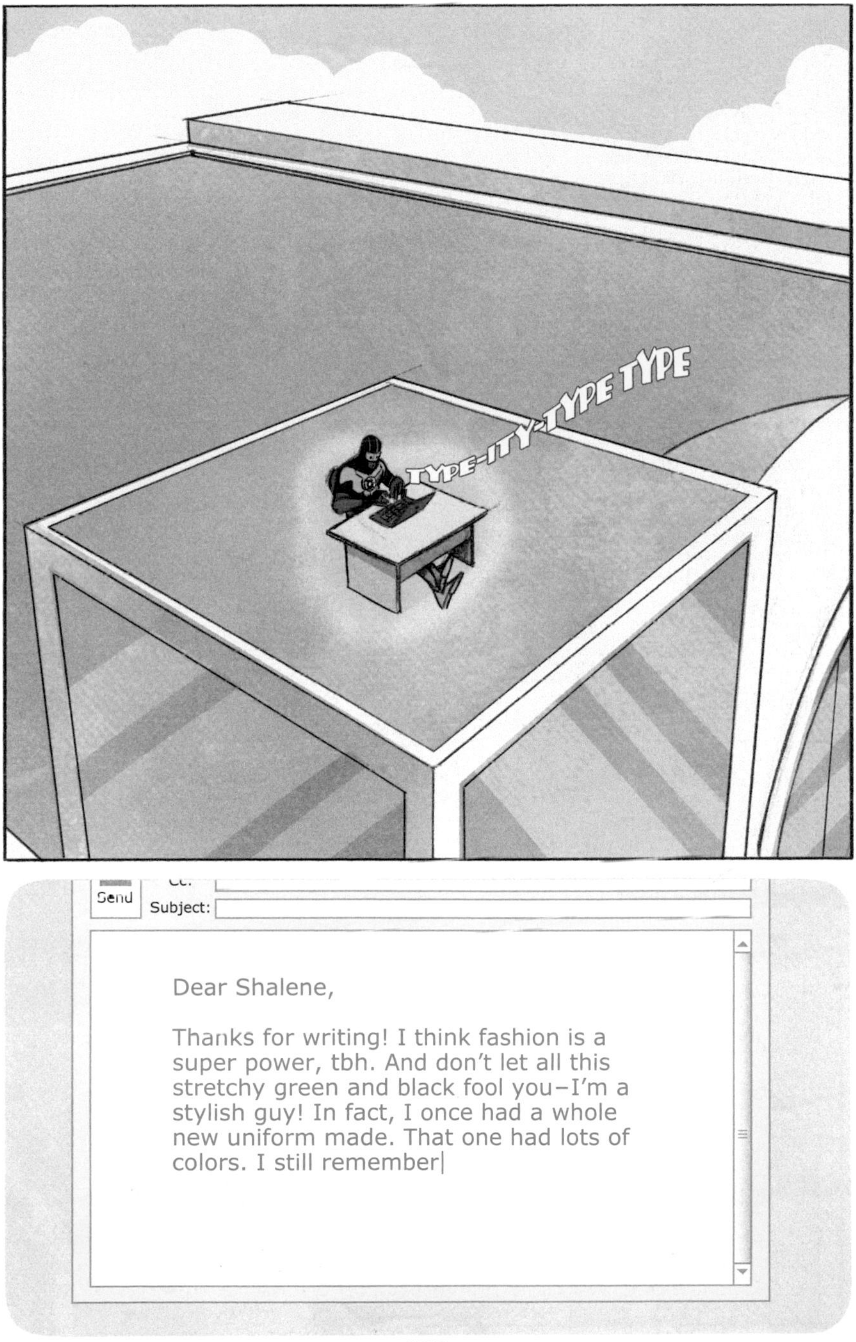
TYPE-ITY-TYPE TYPE
Send
Subject:
Dear Shalene,
Thanks for writing! I think fashion is a super power, tbh. And don't let all this stretchy green and black fool you–I'm a stylish guy! In fact, I once had a whole new uniform made. That one had lots of colors. I still remember

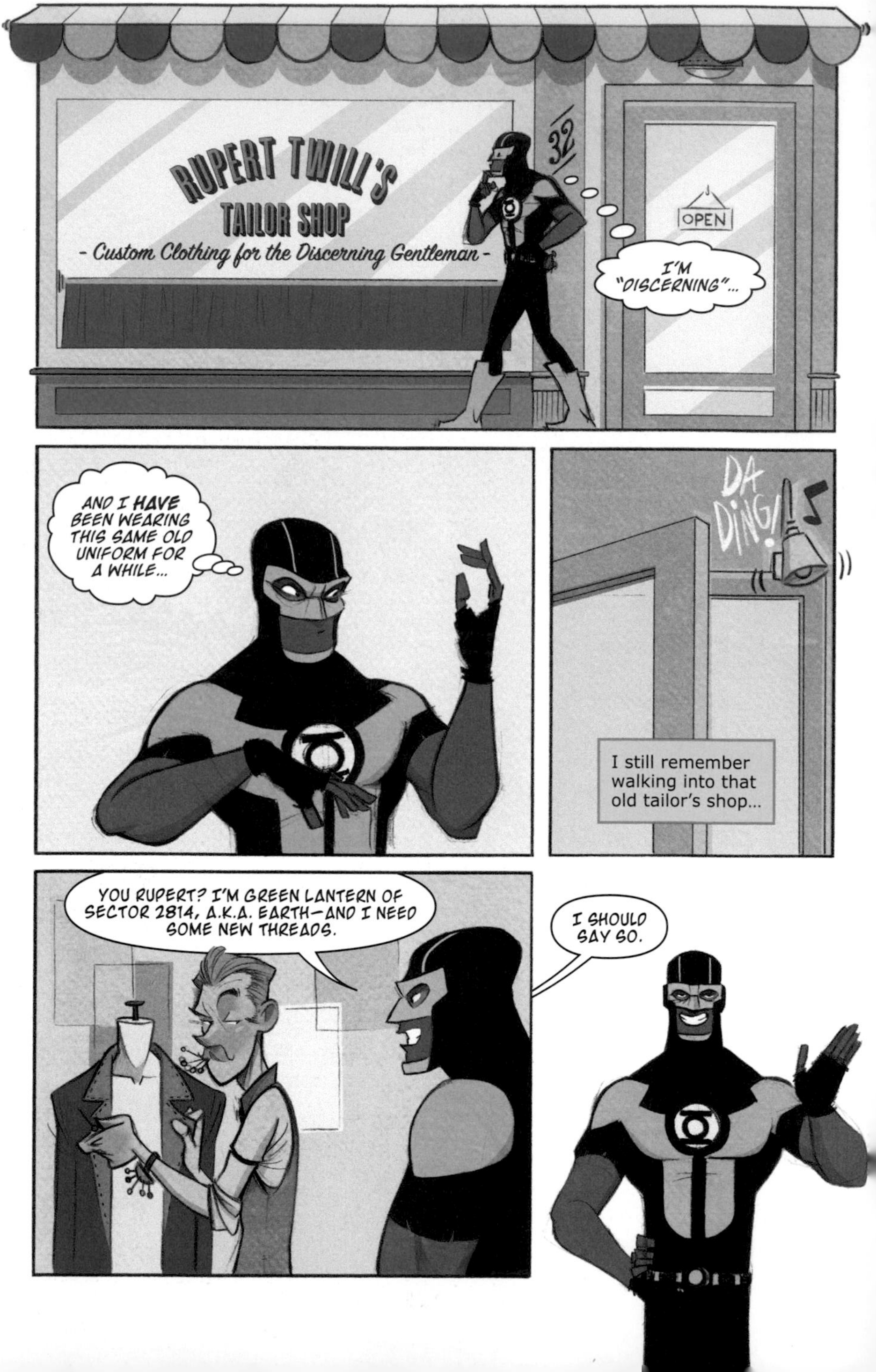

RUPERT TWILL'S
TAILOR SHOP
- Custom Clothing for the Discerning Gentleman -
32
OPEN
I'M "DISCERNING"...
AND I HAVE BEEN WEARING THIS SAME OLD UNIFORM FOR A WHILE...
DA DING!
I still remember walking into that old tailor's shop...
YOU RUPERT? I'M GREEN LANTERN OF SECTOR 2814, A.K.A. EARTH—AND I NEED SOME NEW THREADS.
I SHOULD SAY SO.

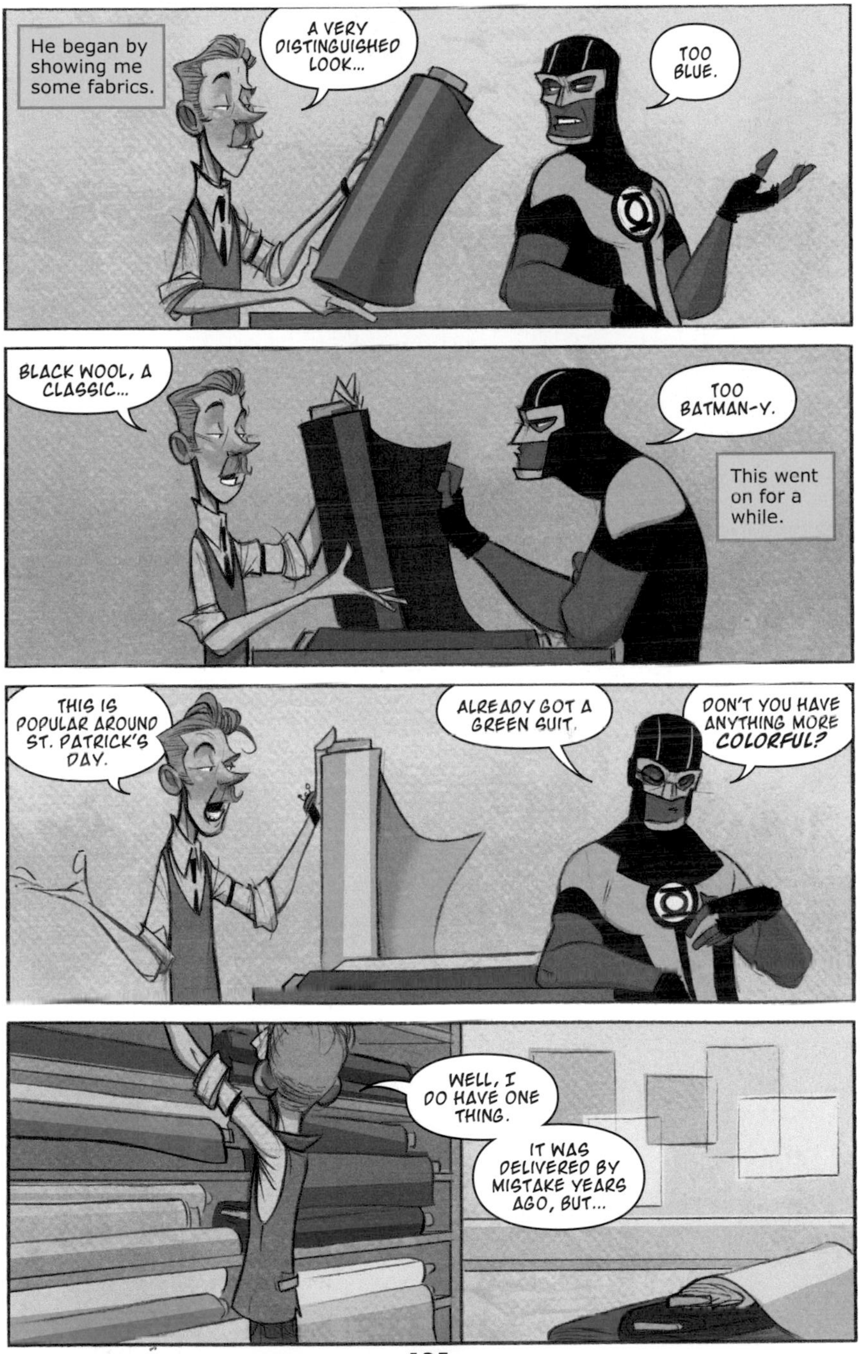
He began by showing me some fabrics.
A VERY DISTINGUISHED LOOK...
TOO BLUE.
BLACK WOOL, A CLASSIC...
TOO BATMAN-Y.
This went on for a while.
THIS IS POPULAR AROUND ST. PATRICK'S DAY.
ALREADY GOT A GREEN SUIT.
DON'T YOU HAVE ANYTHING MORE COLORFUL?
WELL, I DO HAVE ONE THING.
IT WAS DELIVERED BY MISTAKE YEARS AGO, BUT...

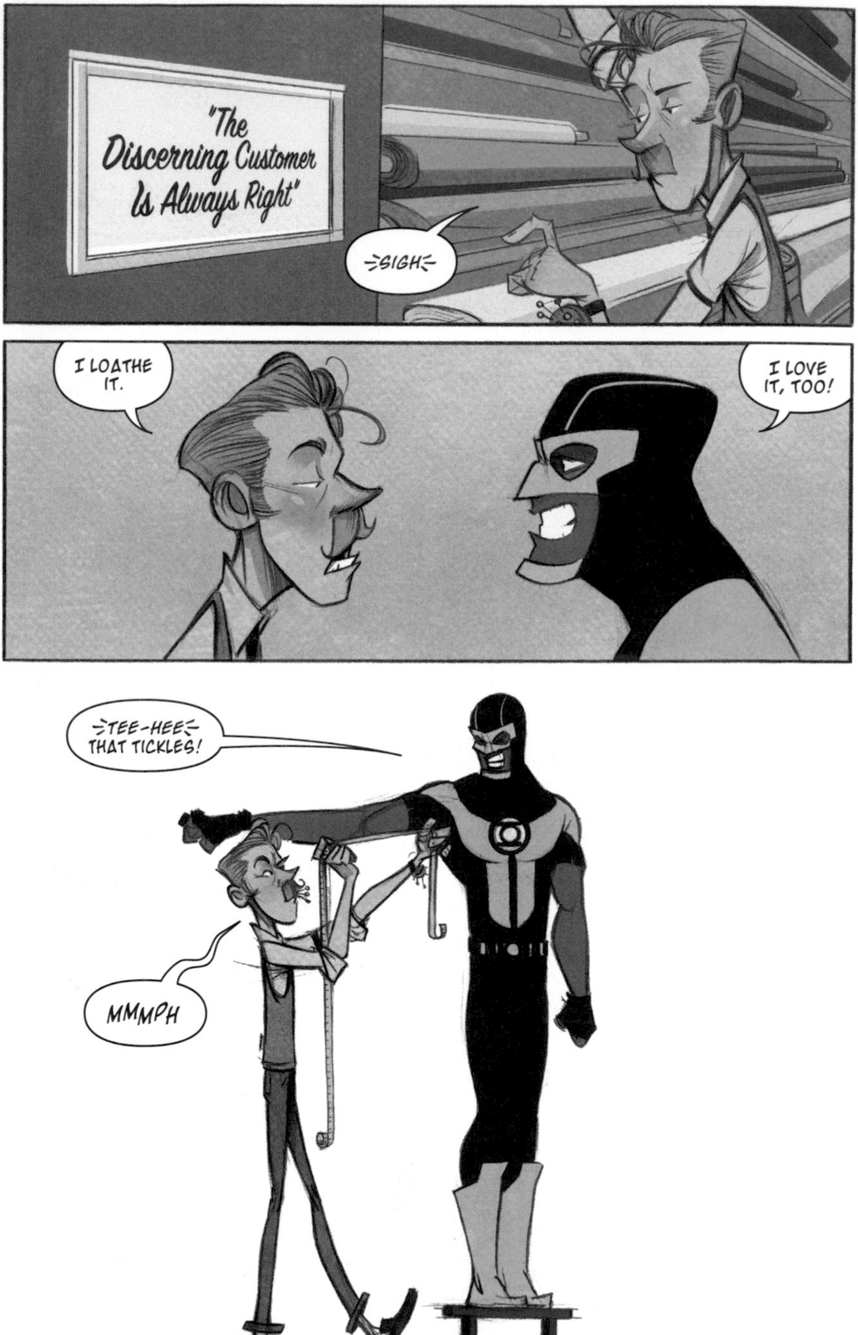
"The Discerning Customer Is Always Right"
SIGH
I LOATHE IT.
I LOVE IT, TOO!
TEE-HEE THAT TICKLES!
MMMPH

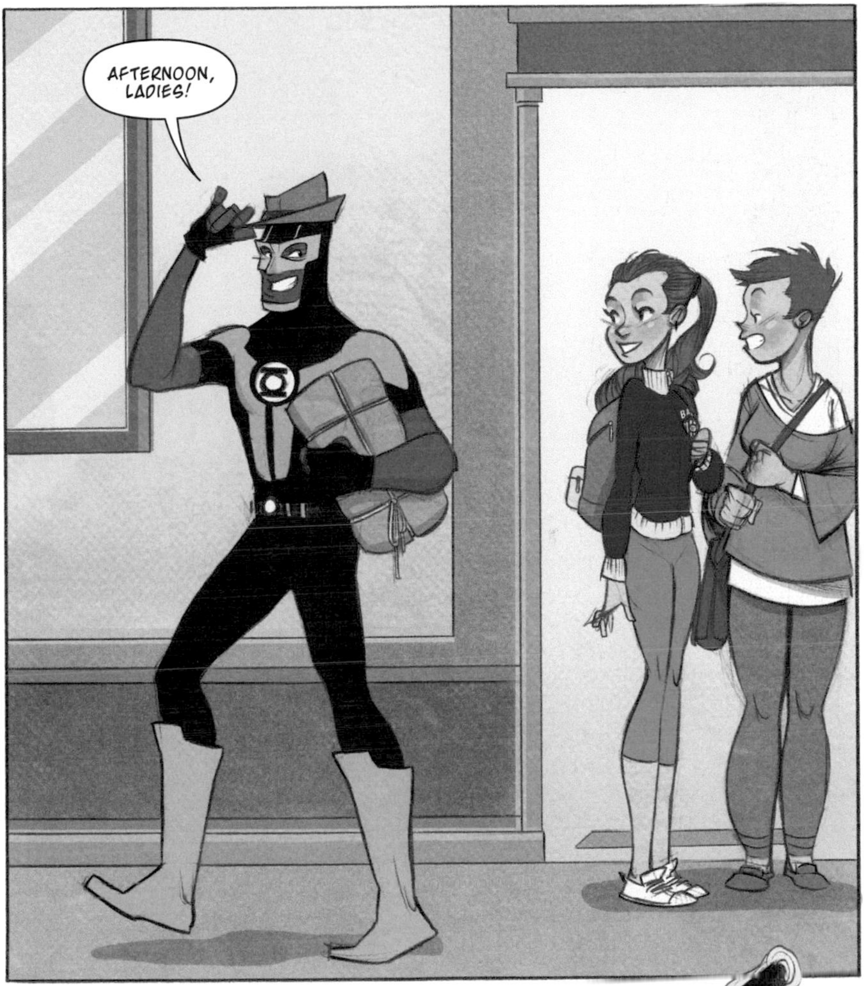
AFTERNOON, LADIES!

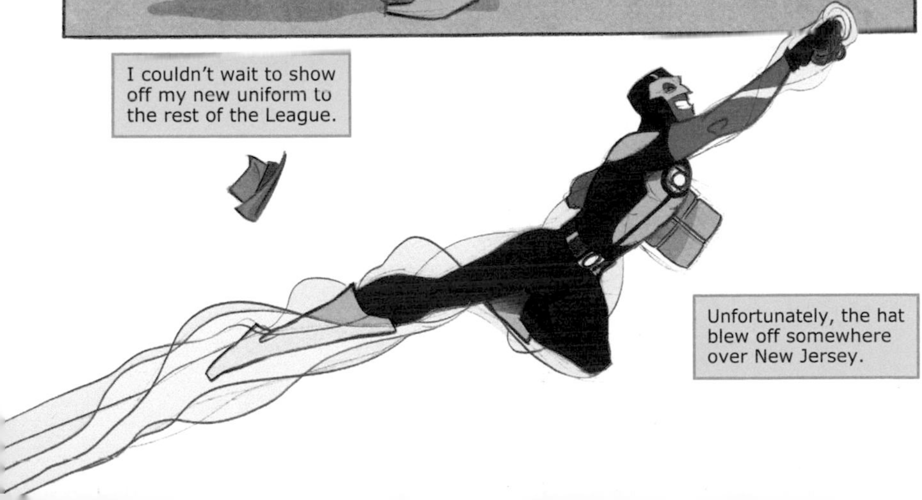
I couldn't wait to show off my new uniform to the rest of the League.
Unfortunately, the hat blew off somewhere over New Jersey.

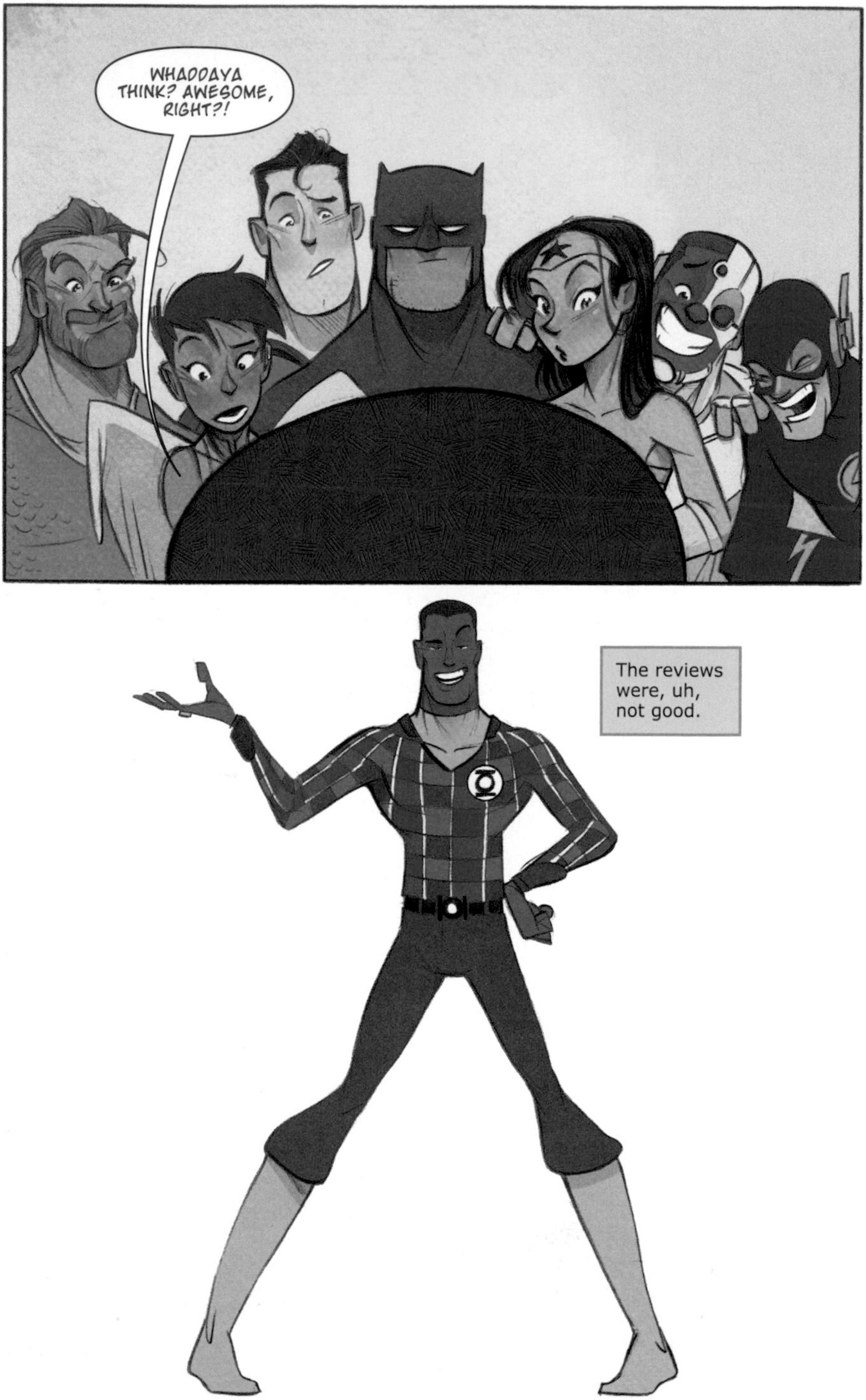
WHADDAYA THINK? AWESOME, RIGHT?!
The reviews were, uh, not good.

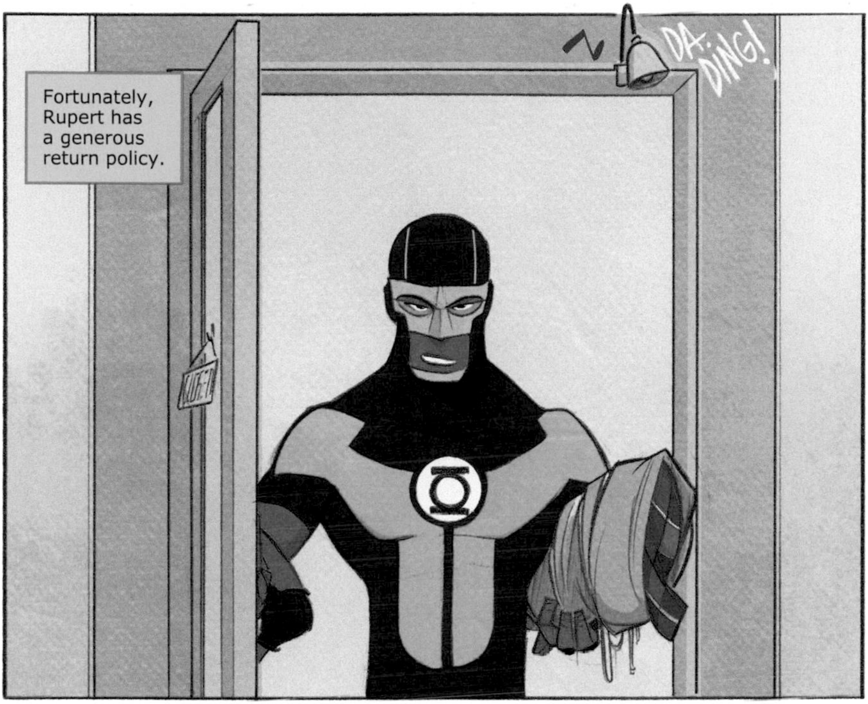
Fortunately, Rupert has a generous return policy.
DA-DING!

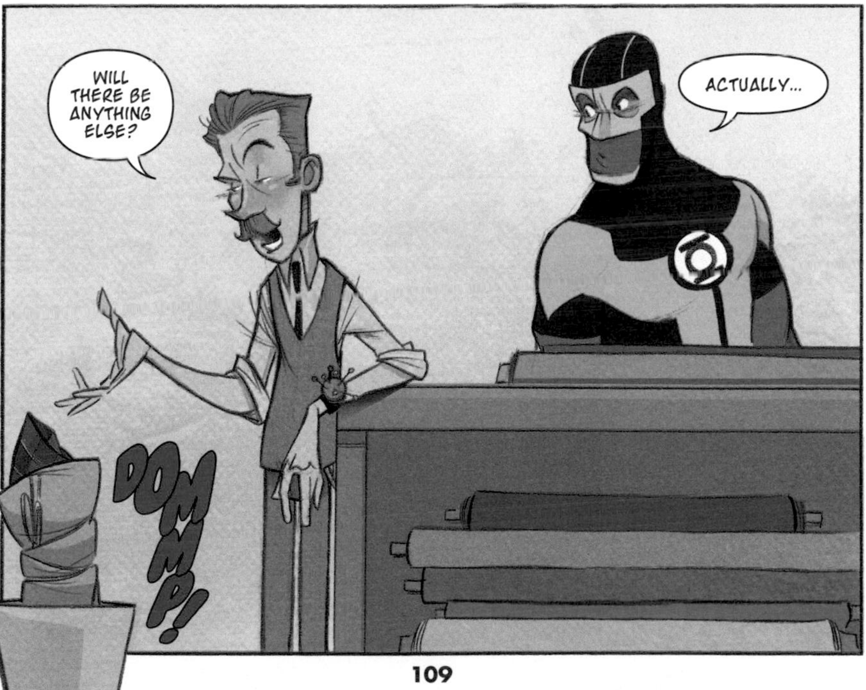
WILL THERE BE ANYTHING ELSE?
ACTUALLY...
DOMMMP!

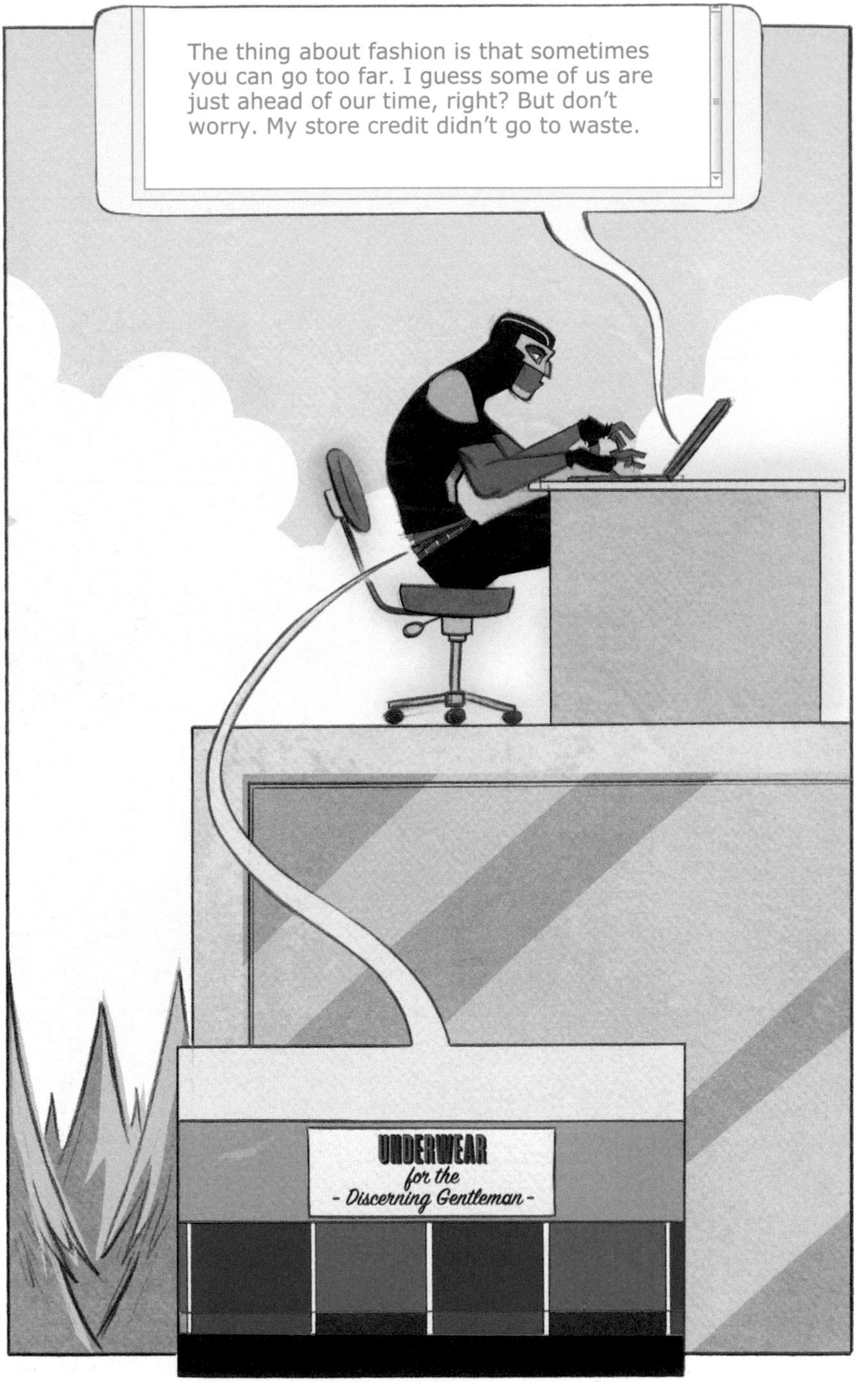
The thing about fashion is that sometimes you can go too far. I guess some of us are just ahead of our time, right? But don't worry. My store credit didn't go to waste.
UNDERWEAR
for the
- Discerning Gentleman -

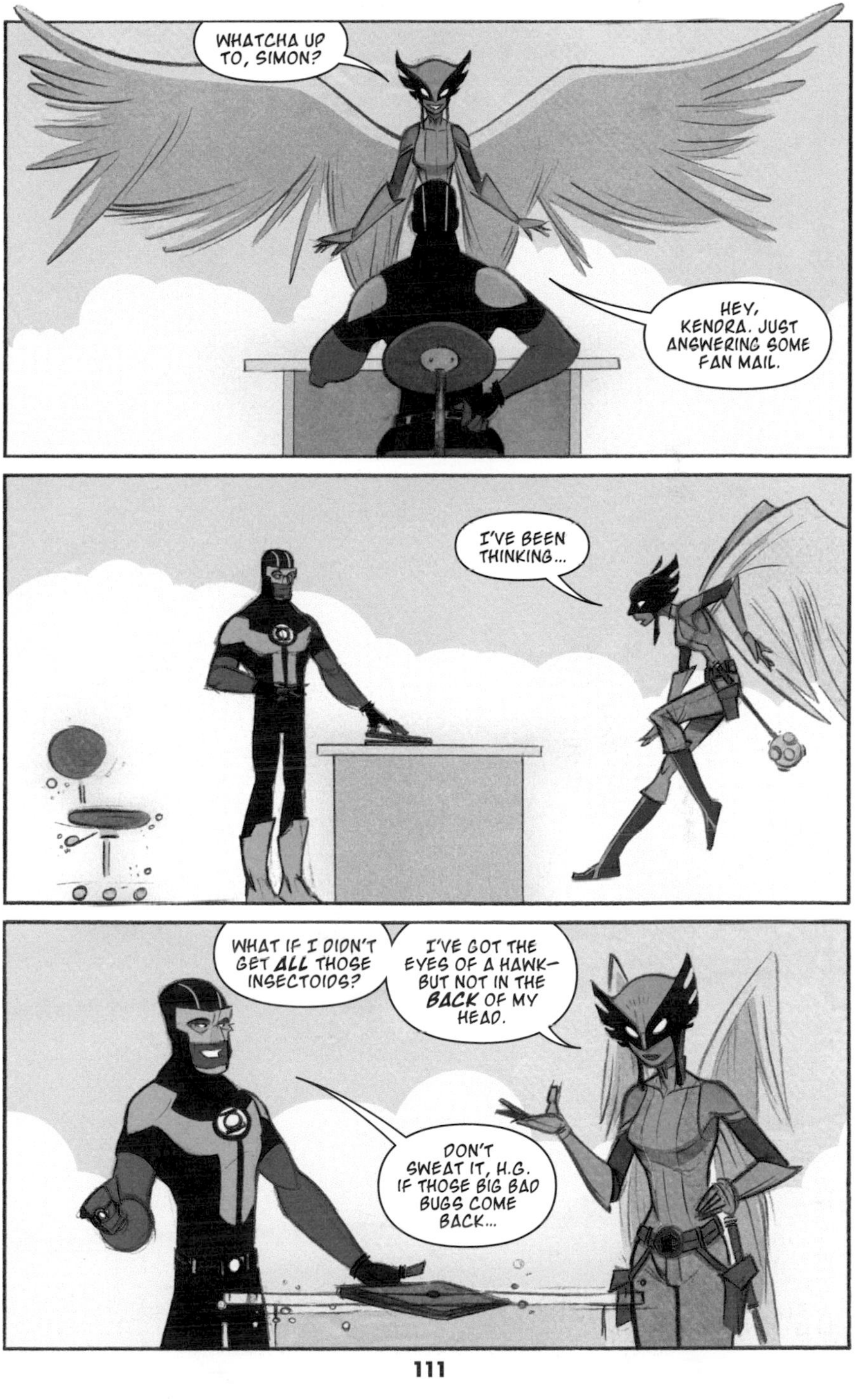
WHATCHA UP TO, SIMON?
HEY, KENDRA. JUST ANSWERING SOME FAN MAIL.
I'VE BEEN THINKING...
WHAT IF I DIDN'T GET **ALL** THOSE INSECTOIDS?
I'VE GOT THE EYES OF A HAWK—BUT NOT IN THE **BACK** OF MY HEAD.
DON'T SWEAT IT, H.G. IF THOSE BIG BAD BUGS COME BACK...

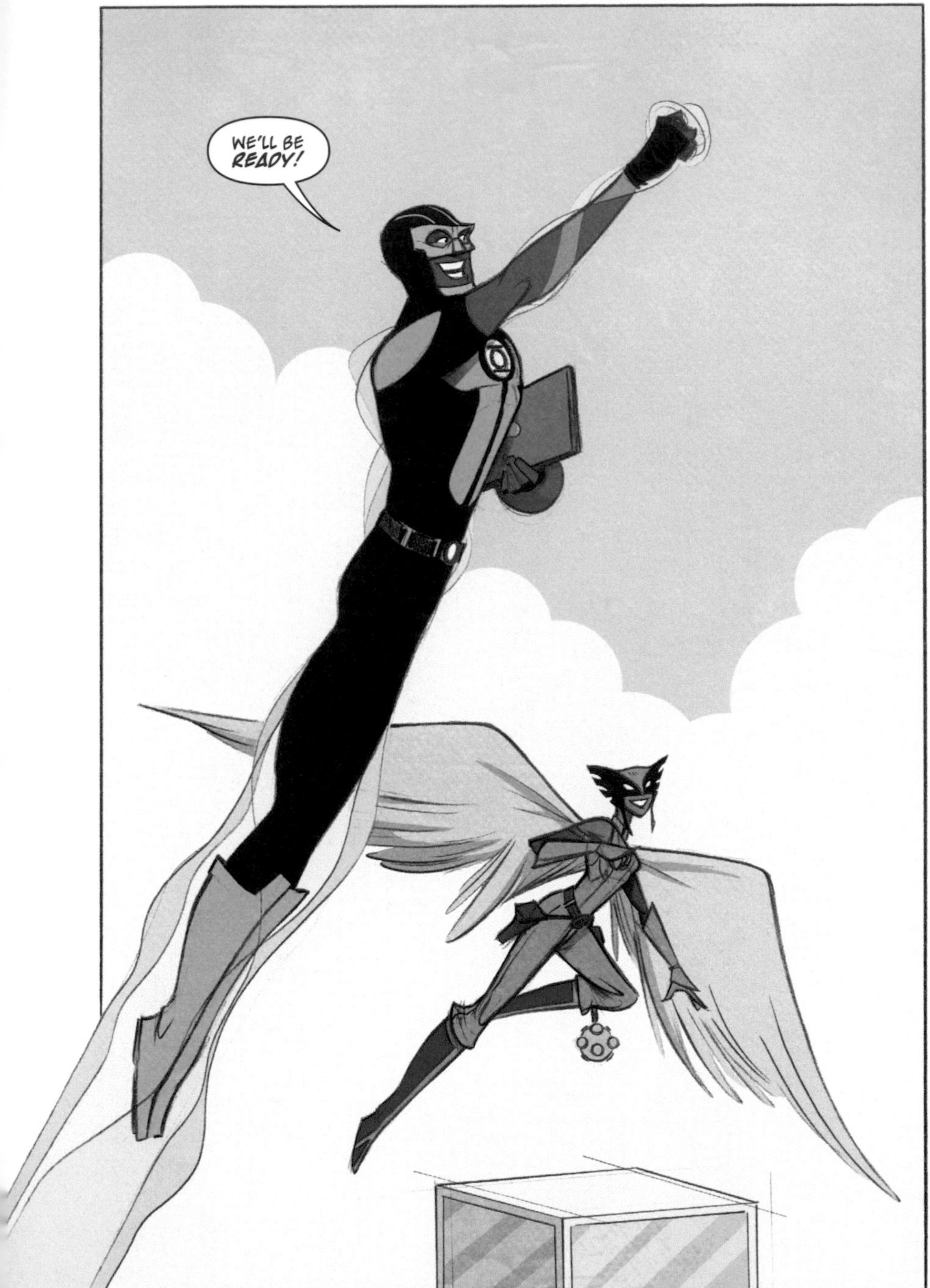
WE'LL BE READY!

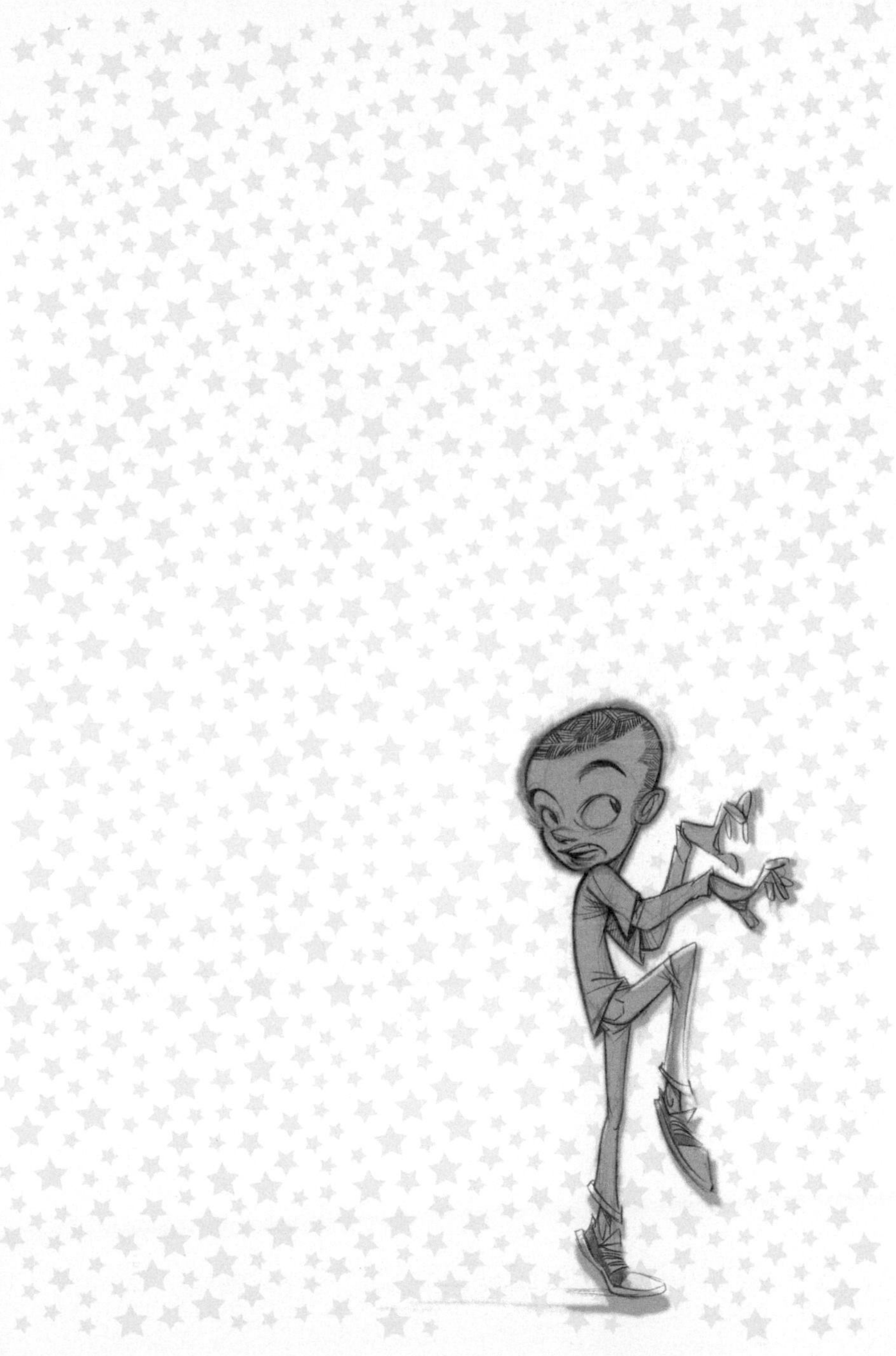

CHAPTER 7

DEAR CYBORG

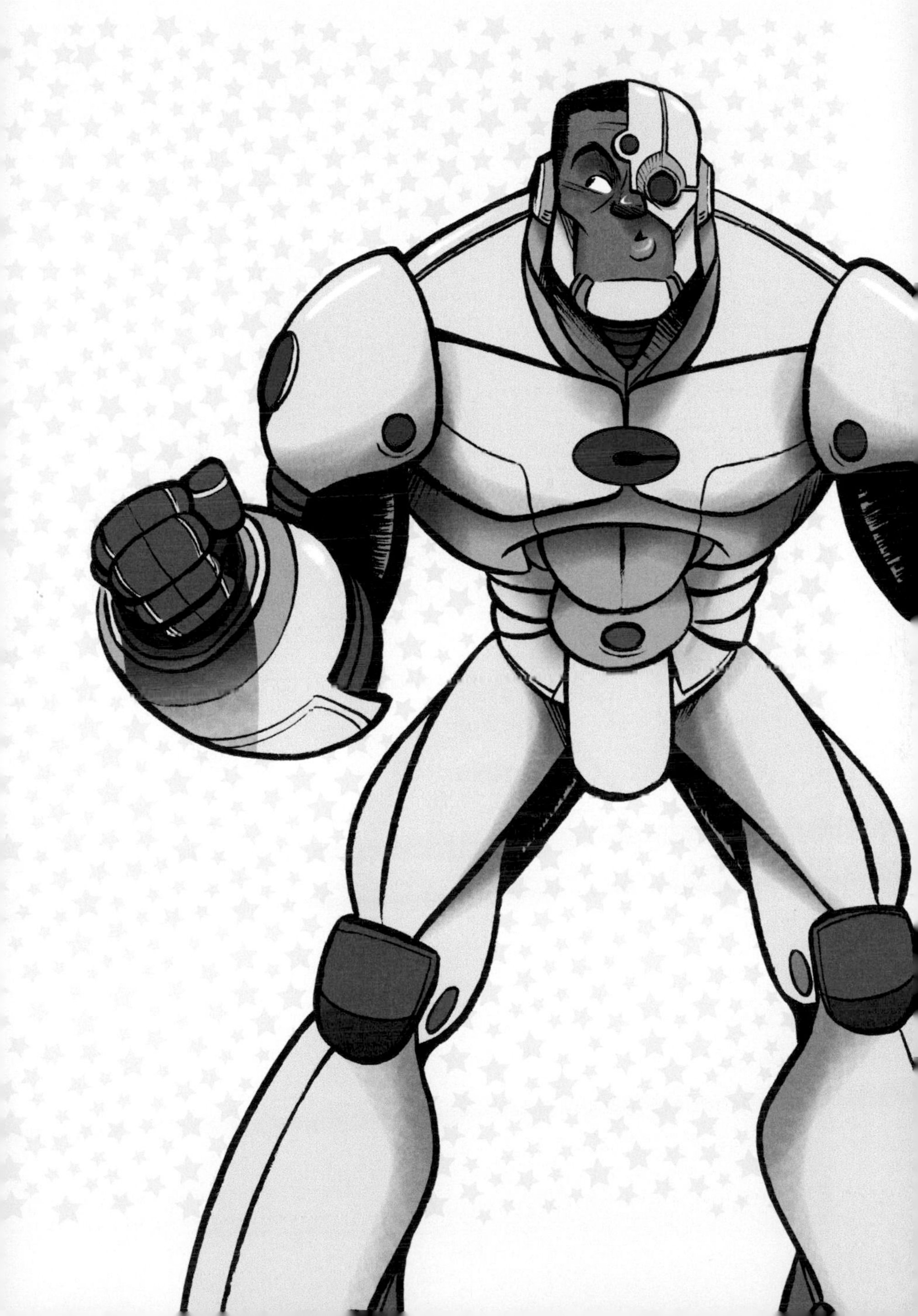

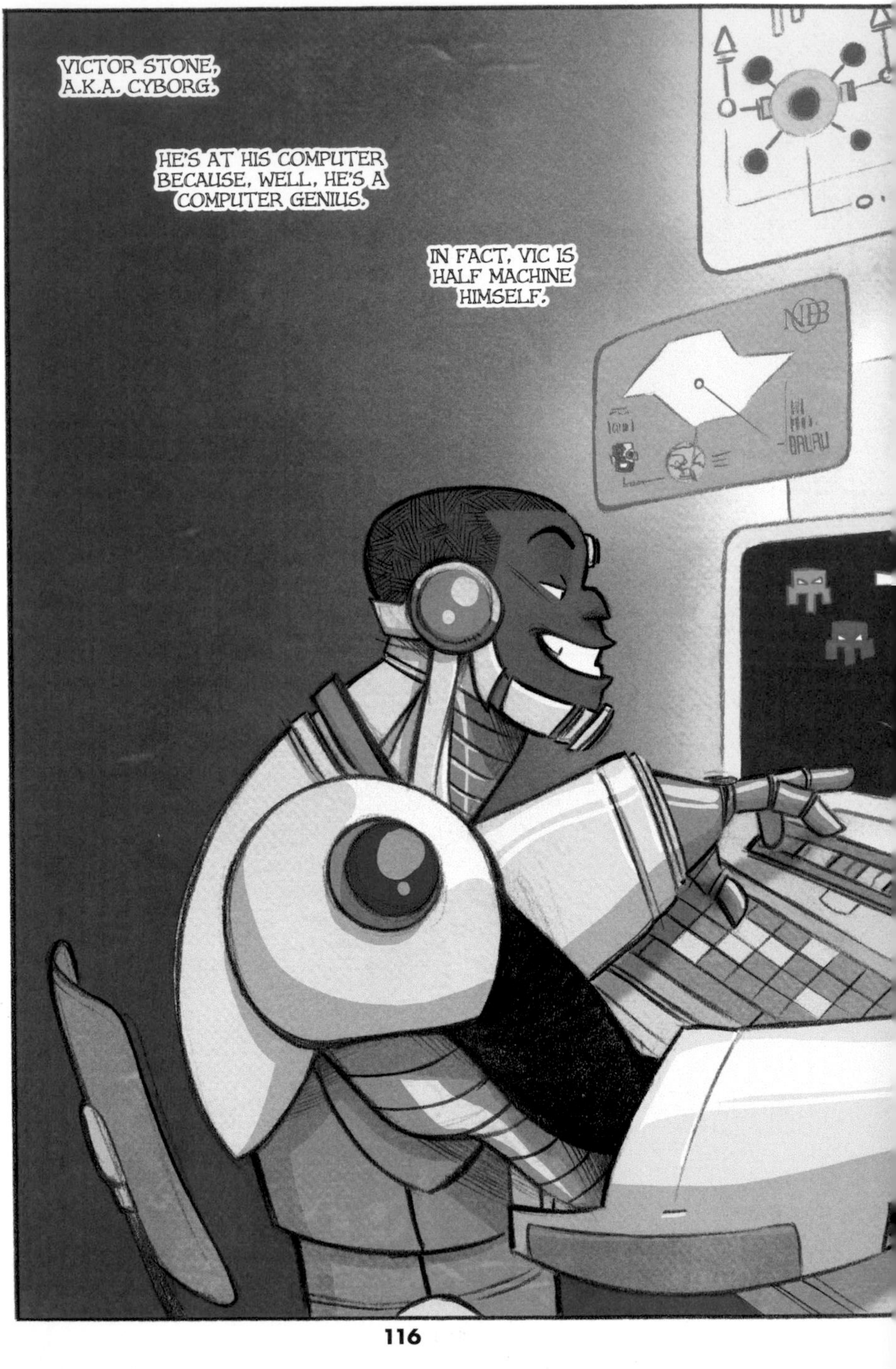
VICTOR STONE, A.K.A. CYBORG.
HE'S AT HIS COMPUTER BECAUSE, WELL, HE'S A COMPUTER GENIUS.
IN FACT, VIC IS HALF MACHINE HIMSELF.

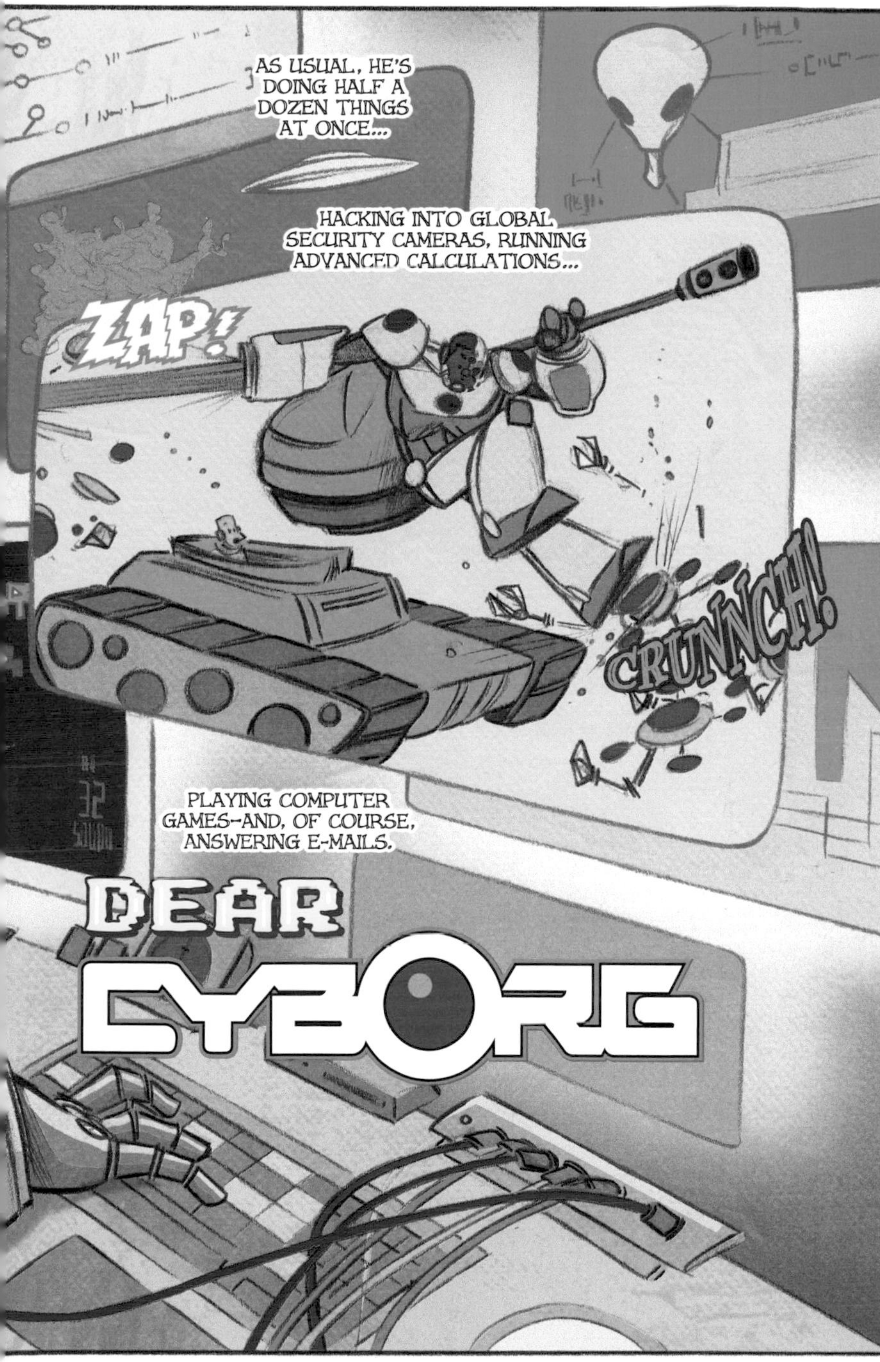
AS USUAL, HE'S DOING HALF A DOZEN THINGS AT ONCE...
HACKING INTO GLOBAL SECURITY CAMERAS, RUNNING ADVANCED CALCULATIONS...
ZAP!
CRUNNCH!
PLAYING COMPUTER GAMES--AND, OF COURSE, ANSWERING E-MAILS.
DEAR CYBORG

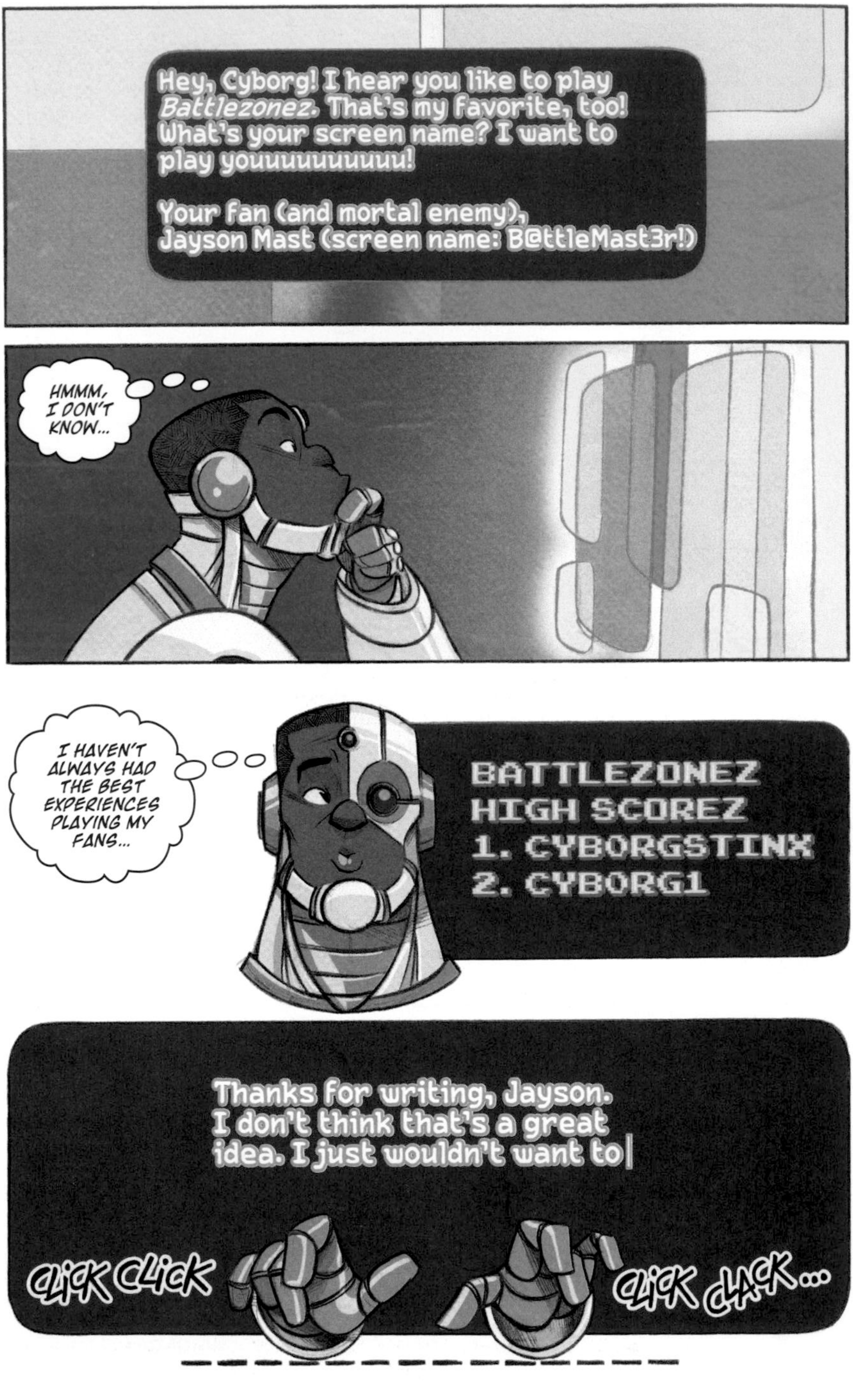
Hey, Cyborg! I hear you like to play *Battlezonez*. That's my favorite, too! What's your screen name? I want to play youuuuuuuuuu!
Your fan (and mortal enemy),
Jayson Mast (screen name: B@ttleMast3r!)
HMMM, I DON'T KNOW...
I HAVEN'T ALWAYS HAD THE BEST EXPERIENCES PLAYING MY FANS...
BATTLEZONEZ HIGH SCOREZ
1. CYBORGSTINX
2. CYBORG1
Thanks for writing, Jayson. I don't think that's a great idea. I just wouldn't want to
CLICK CLICK
CLICK CLACK...

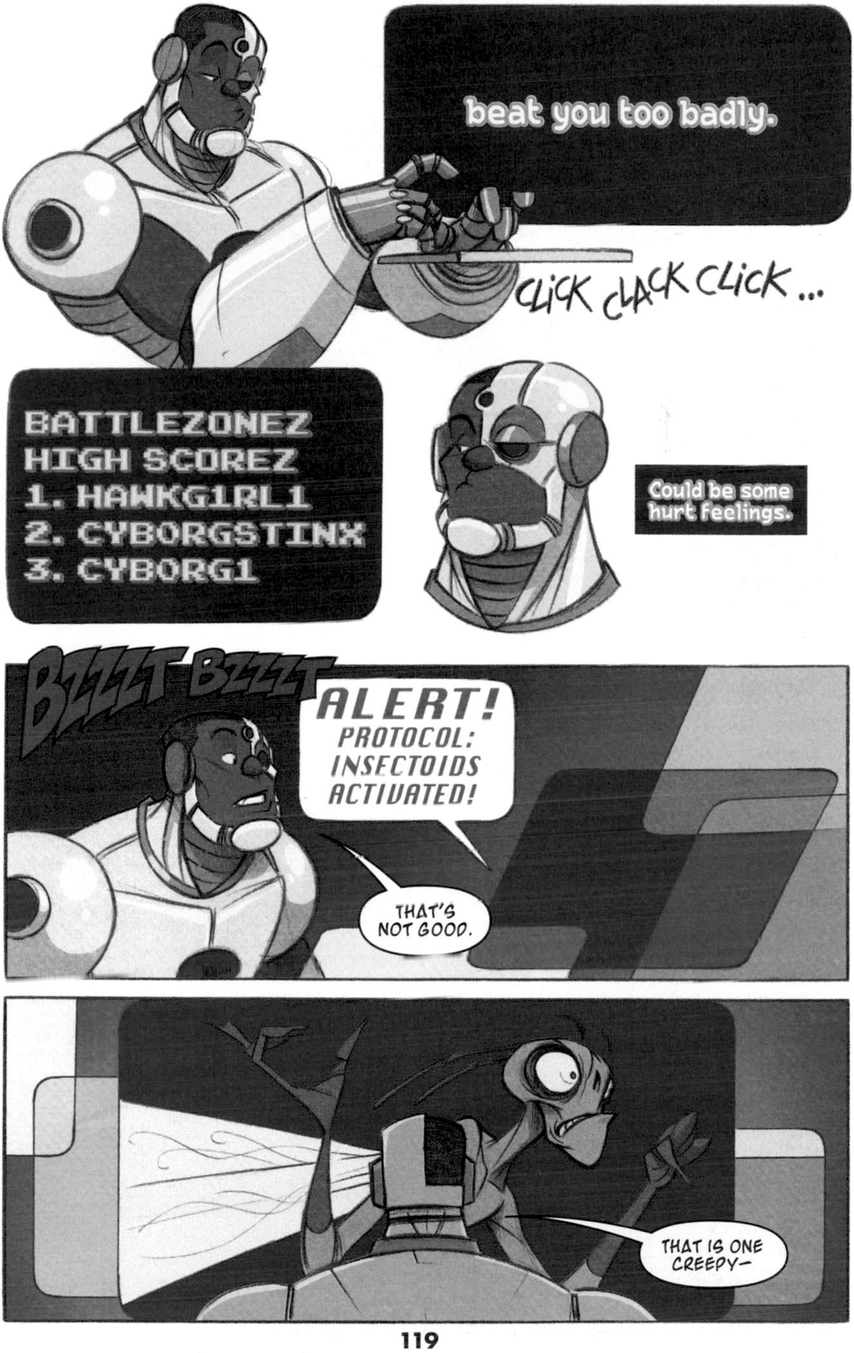
beat you too badly.
CLICK CLACK CLICK...
BATTLEZONEZ
HIGH SCOREZ
1. HAWKG1RL1
2. CYBORGSTINX
3. CYBORG1
Could be some hurt feelings.
BZZZT BZZZT
ALERT! PROTOCOL: INSECTOIDS ACTIVATED!
THAT'S NOT GOOD.
THAT IS ONE CREEPY—

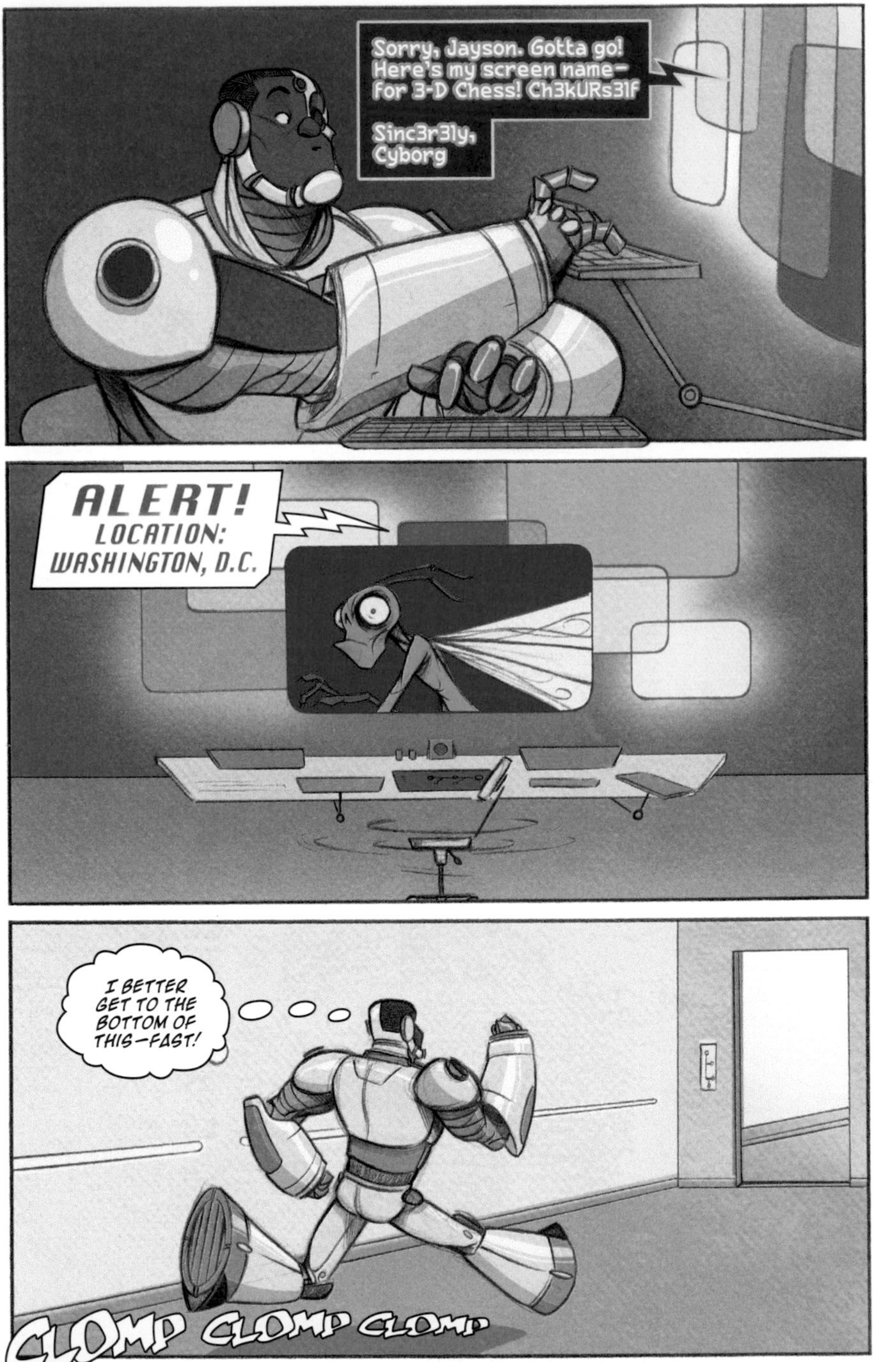
Sorry, Jayson. Gotta go! Here's my screen name—for 3-D Chess! Ch3kURs3lf
Sinc3r3ly, Cyborg
ALERT! LOCATION: WASHINGTON, D.C.
I BETTER GET TO THE BOTTOM OF THIS—FAST!
CLOMP CLOMP CLOMP

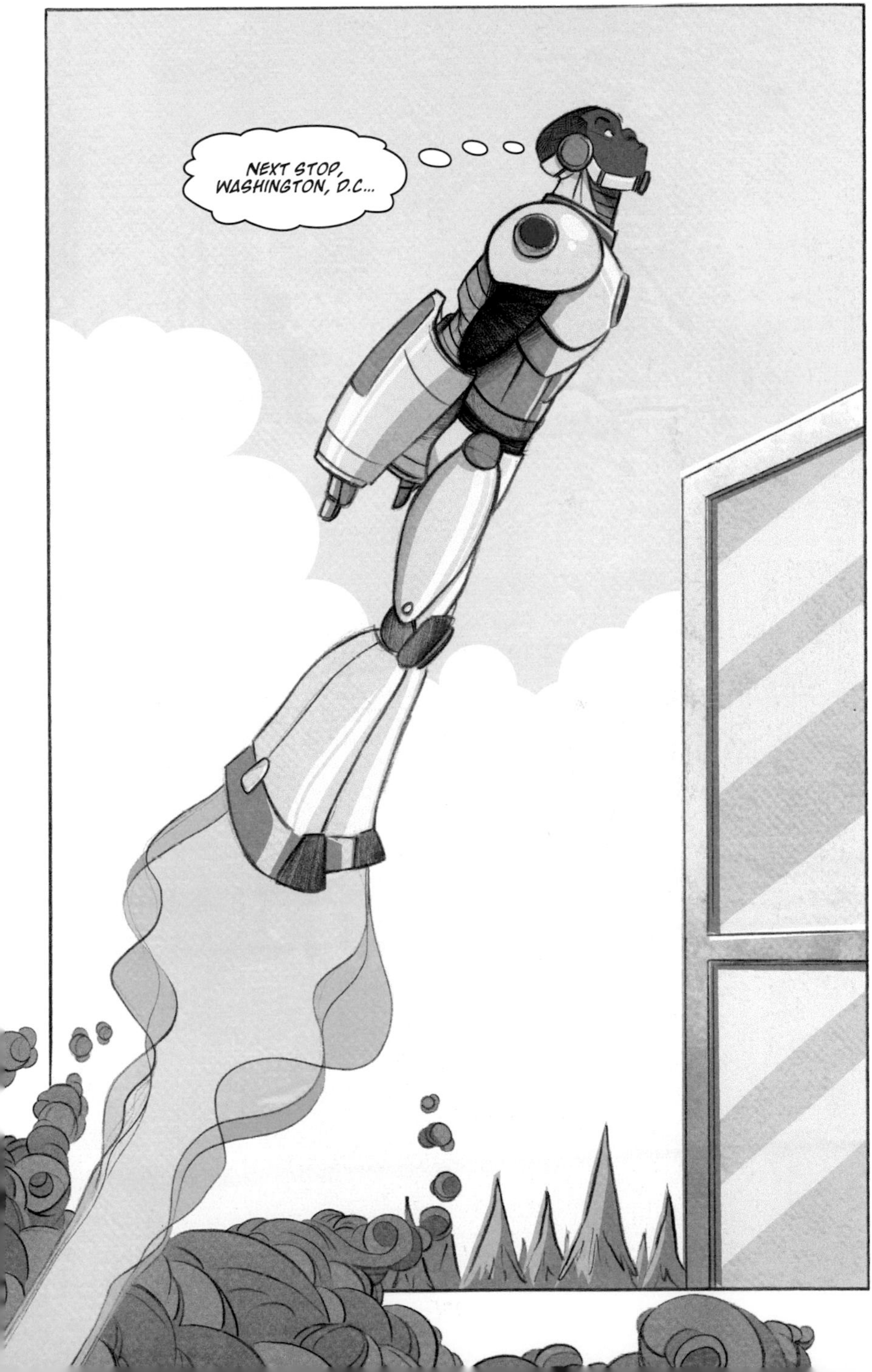
NEXT STOP, WASHINGTON, D.C...

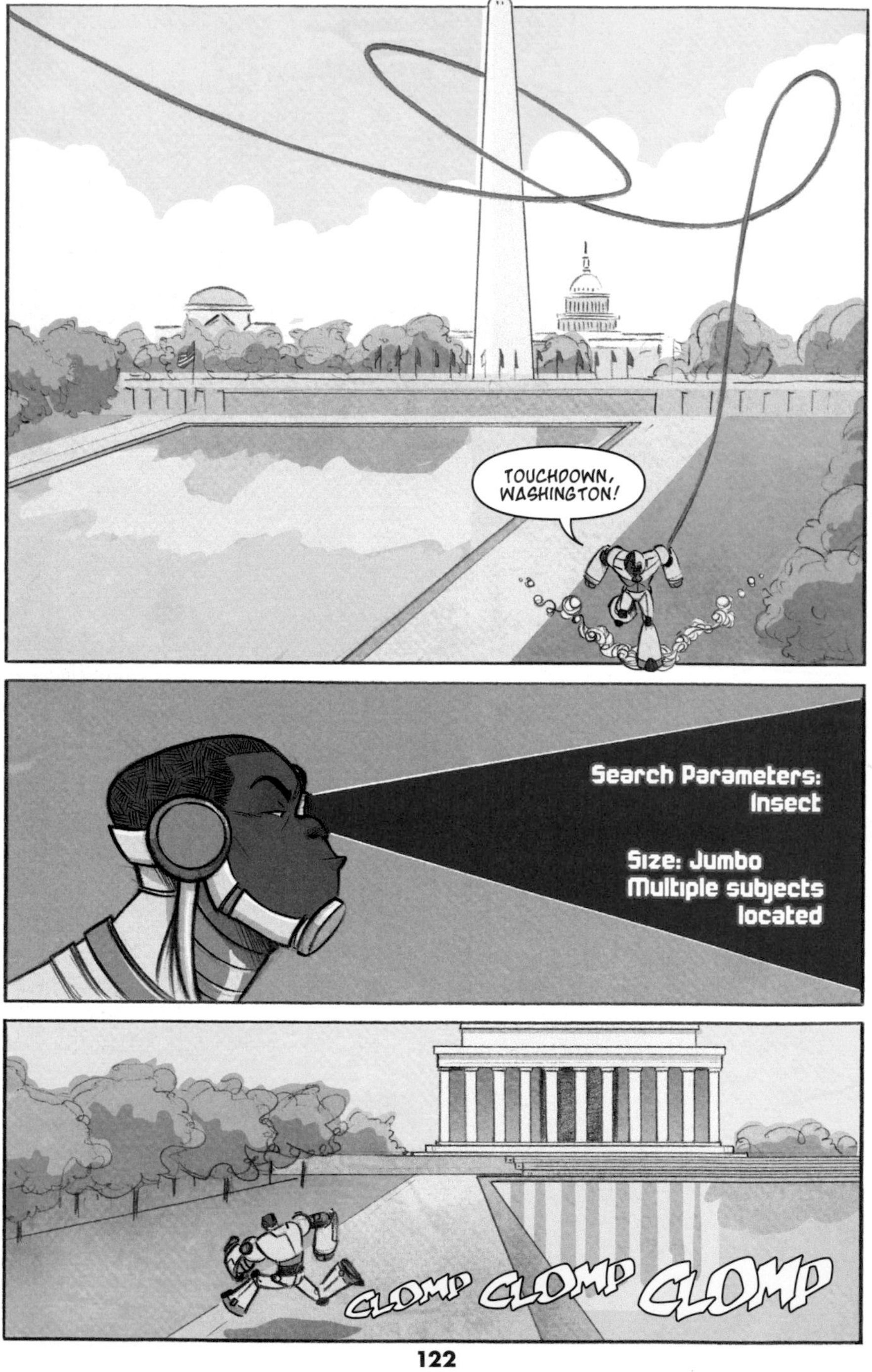
TOUCHDOWN, WASHINGTON!
Search Parameters: Insect
Size: Jumbo
Multiple subjects located
CLOMP CLOMP CLOMP

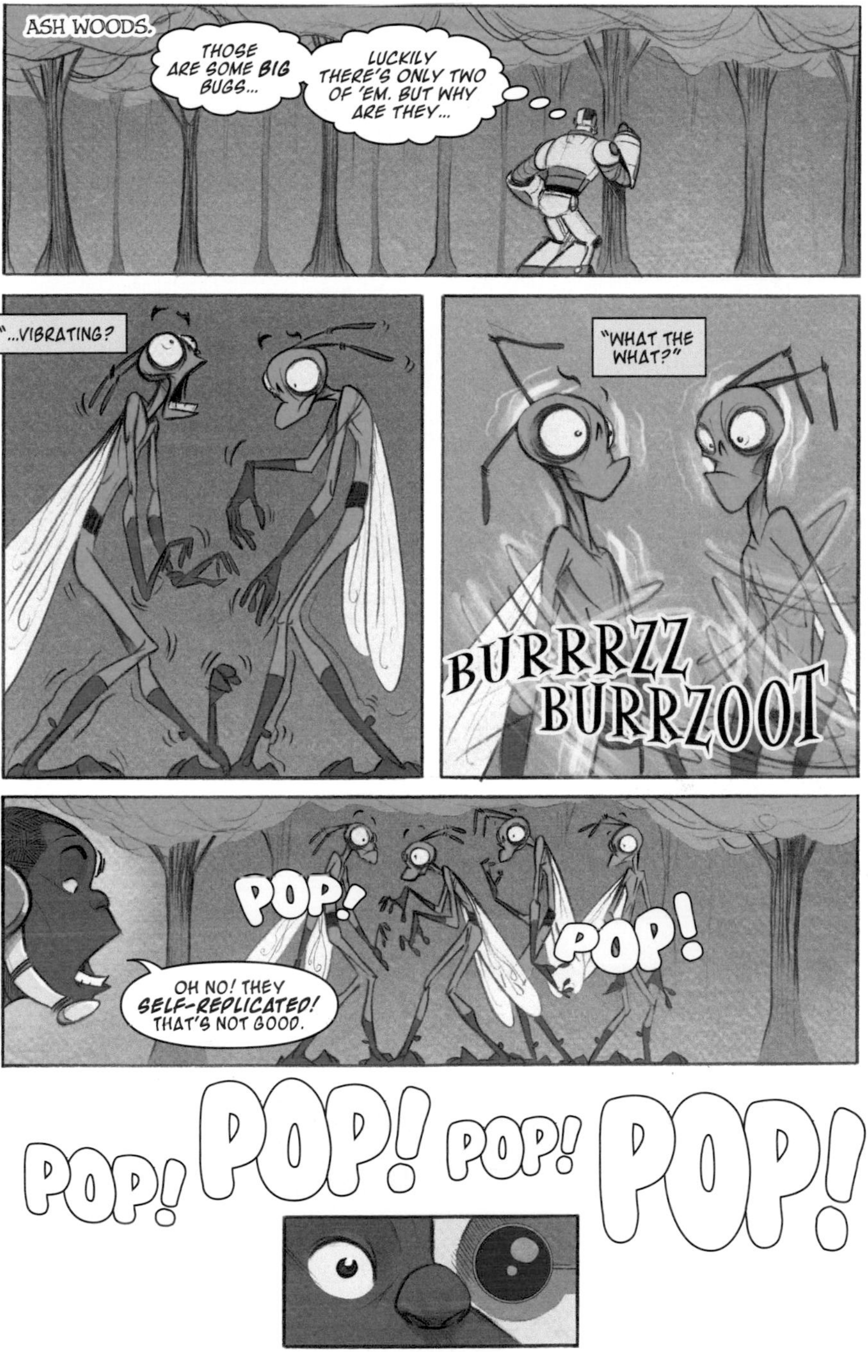
ASH WOODS.
THOSE ARE SOME BIG BUGS...
LUCKILY THERE'S ONLY TWO OF 'EM. BUT WHY ARE THEY...
"...VIBRATING?
"WHAT THE WHAT?"
BURRRZZ
BURRZOOT
POP!
POP!
OH NO! THEY SELF-REPLICATED! THAT'S NOT GOOD.
POP! POP! POP! POP!

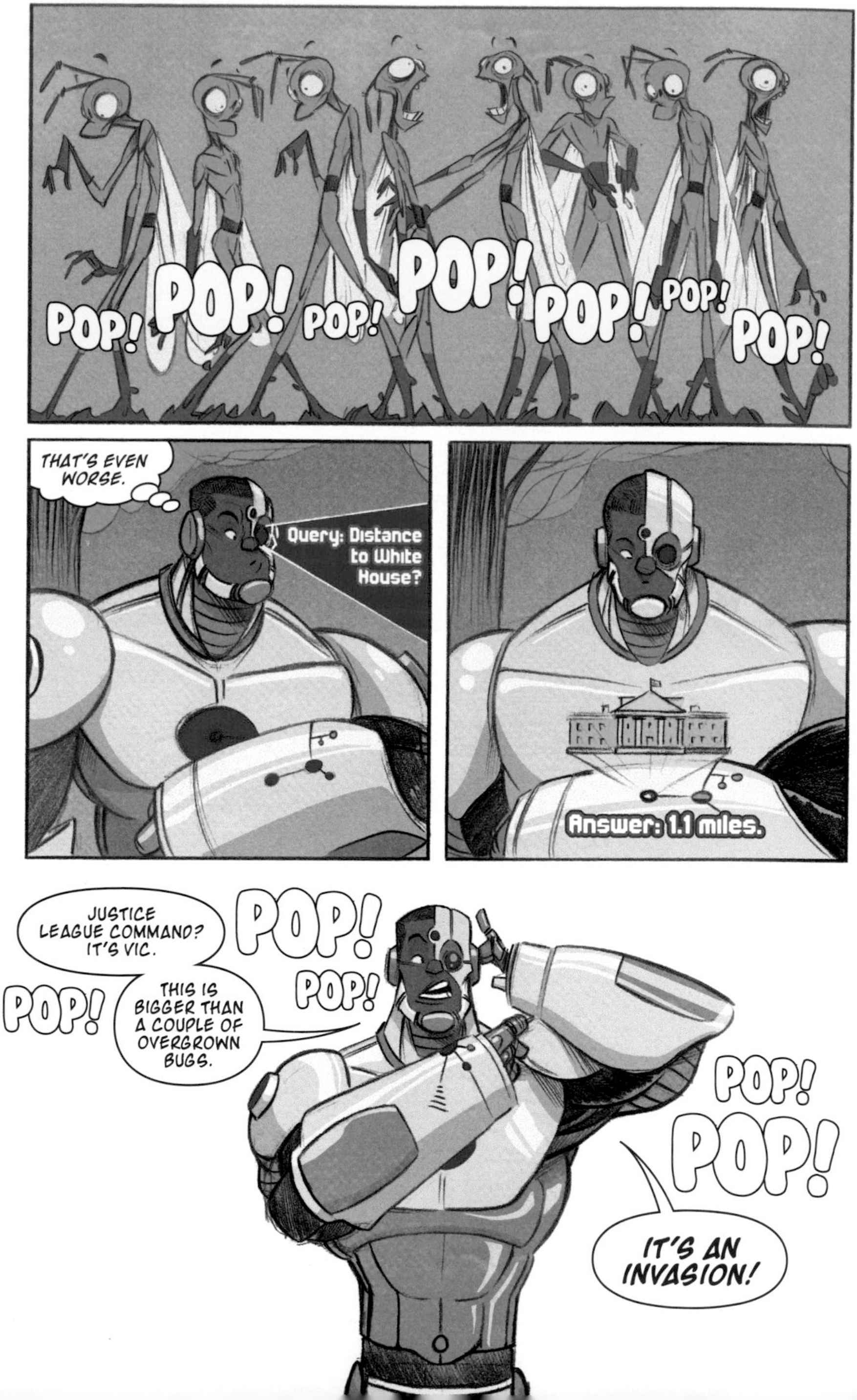
POP! POP! POP! POP! POP! POP! POP!
THAT'S EVEN WORSE.
Query: Distance to White House?
Answer: 1.1 miles.
JUSTICE LEAGUE COMMAND? IT'S VIC.
POP!
POP!
POP!
THIS IS BIGGER THAN A COUPLE OF OVERGROWN BUGS.
POP!
POP!
IT'S AN INVASION!

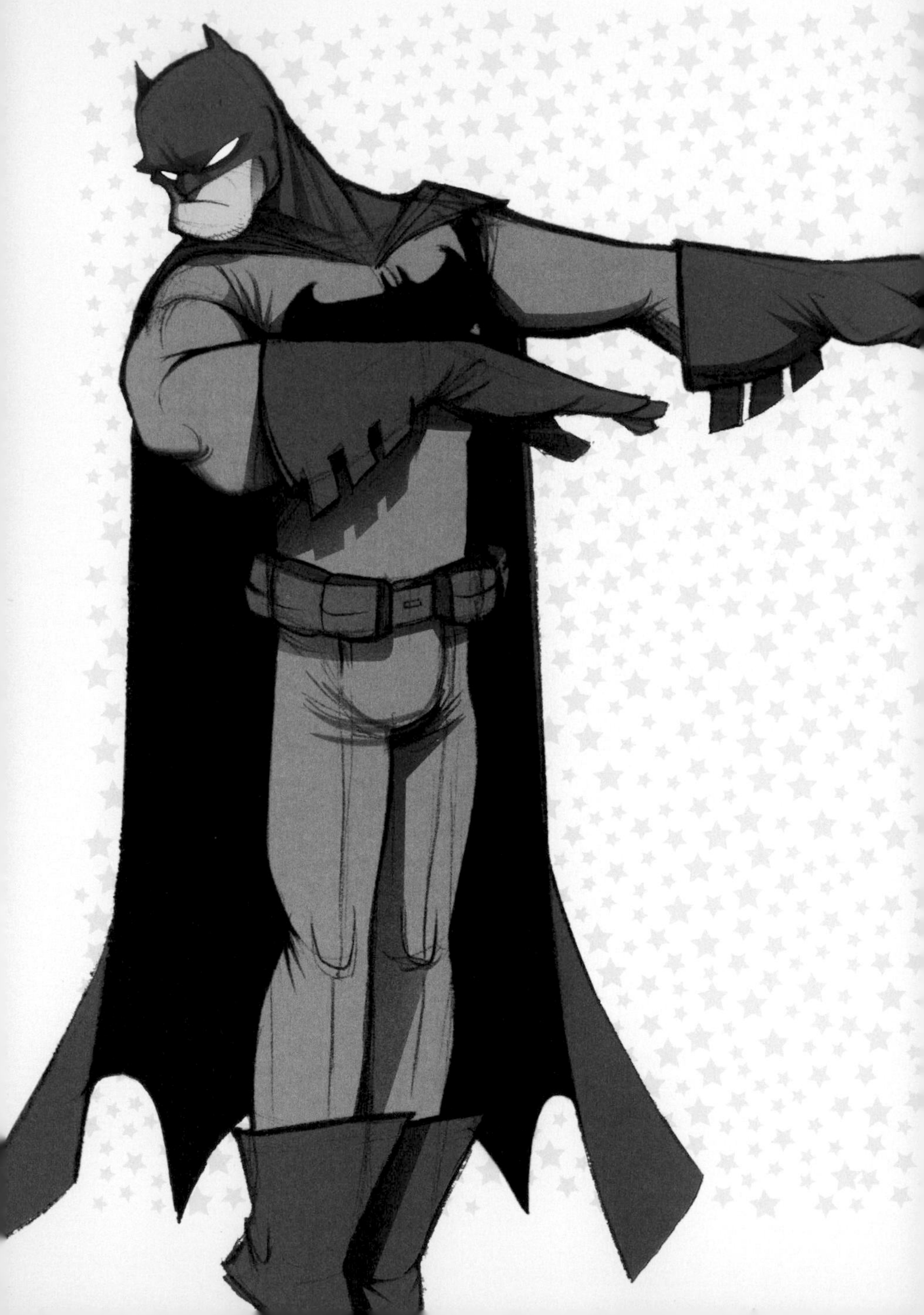

CHAPTER 8

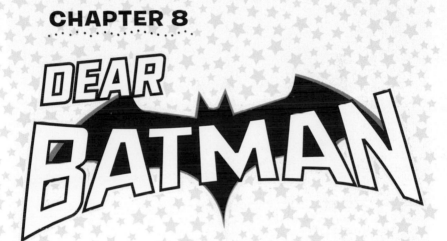

DEAR BATMAN

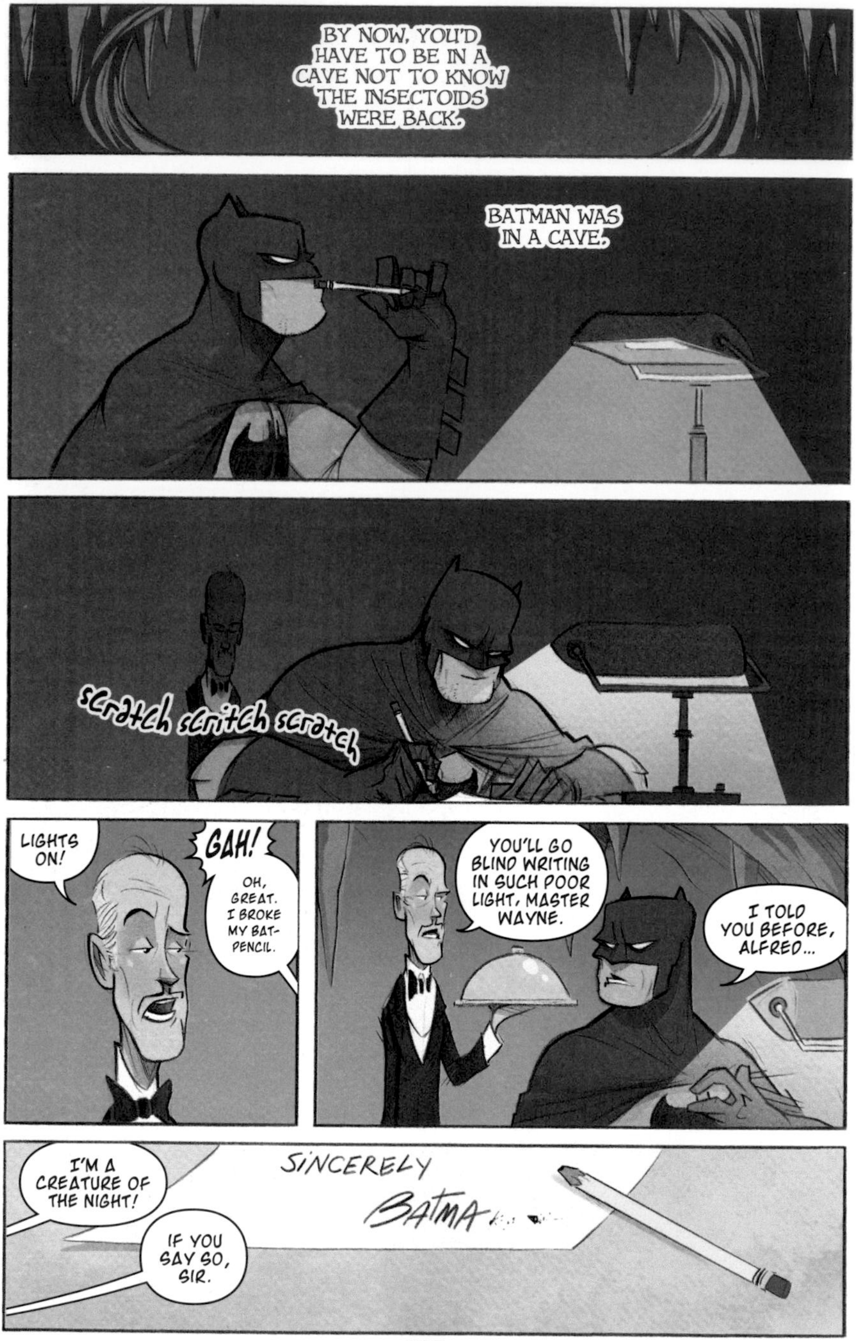
BY NOW, YOU'D HAVE TO BE IN A CAVE NOT TO KNOW THE INSECTOIDS WERE BACK.
BATMAN WAS IN A CAVE.
scratch scritch scratch
LIGHTS ON!
GAH!
OH, GREAT. I BROKE MY BAT-PENCIL.
YOU'LL GO BLIND WRITING IN SUCH POOR LIGHT, MASTER WAYNE.
I TOLD YOU BEFORE, ALFRED...
SINCERELY
BATMA
I'M A CREATURE OF THE NIGHT!
IF YOU SAY SO, SIR.

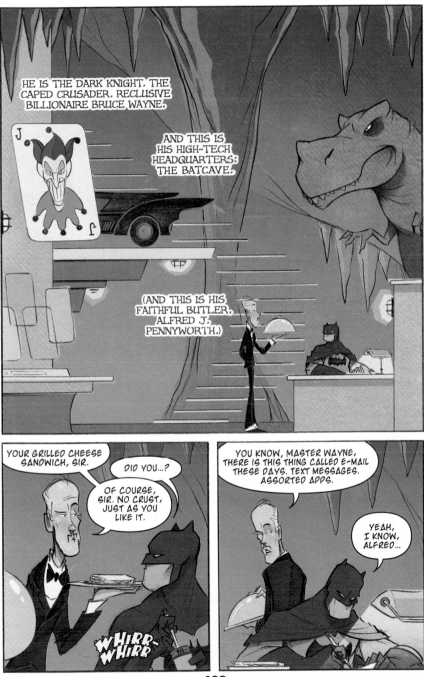

HE IS THE DARK KNIGHT. THE CAPED CRUSADER. RECLUSIVE BILLIONAIRE BRUCE WAYNE.

AND THIS IS HIS HIGH-TECH HEADQUARTERS: THE BATCAVE.

(AND THIS IS HIS FAITHFUL BUTLER, ALFRED J. PENNYWORTH.)

YOUR GRILLED CHEESE SANDWICH, SIR.

DID YOU...?

OF COURSE, SIR. NO CRUST, JUST AS YOU LIKE IT.

YOU KNOW, MASTER WAYNE, THERE IS THIS THING CALLED E-MAIL THESE DAYS. TEXT MESSAGES. ASSORTED APPS.

YEAH, I KNOW, ALFRED...

WHIRR-WHIRR

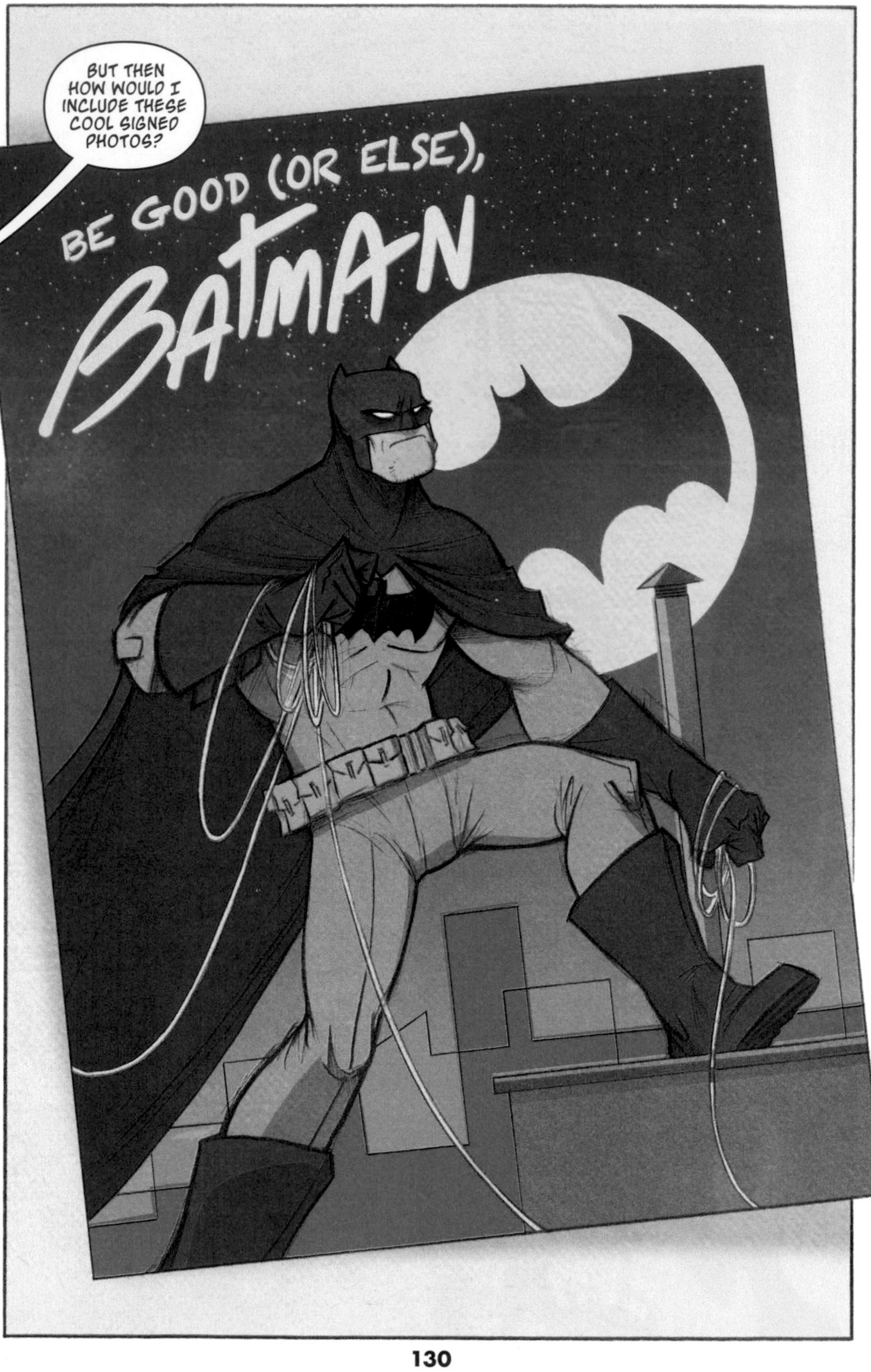
BUT THEN HOW WOULD I INCLUDE THESE COOL SIGNED PHOTOS?
BE GOOD (OR ELSE),
BATMAN

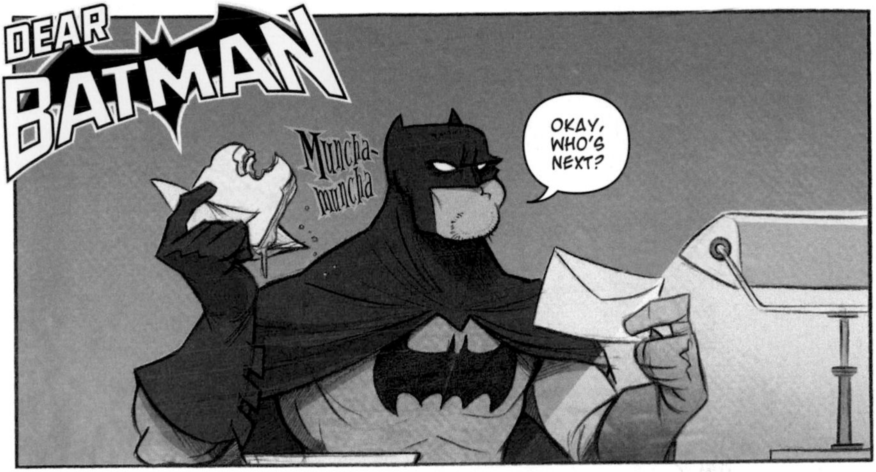

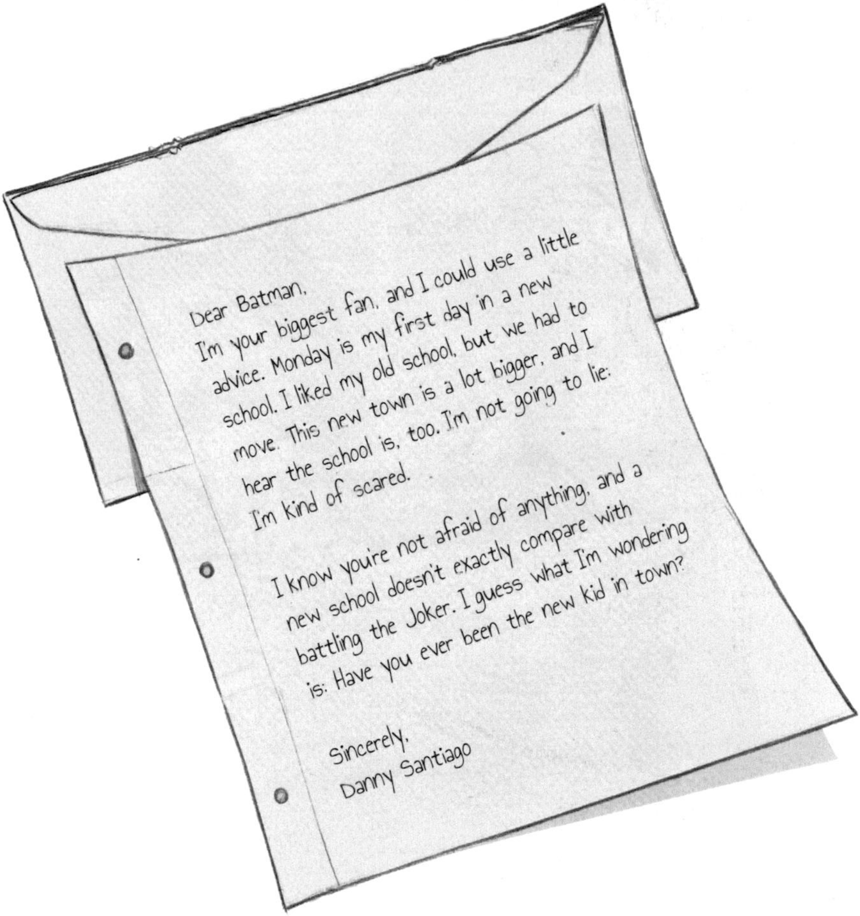
Dear Batman,
I'm your biggest fan, and I could use a little advice. Monday is my first day in a new school. I liked my old school, but we had to move. This new town is a lot bigger, and I hear the school is, too. I'm not going to lie: I'm kind of scared.

I know you're not afraid of anything, and a new school doesn't exactly compare with battling the Joker. I guess what I'm wondering is: Have you ever been the new kid in town?

Sincerely,
Danny Santiago

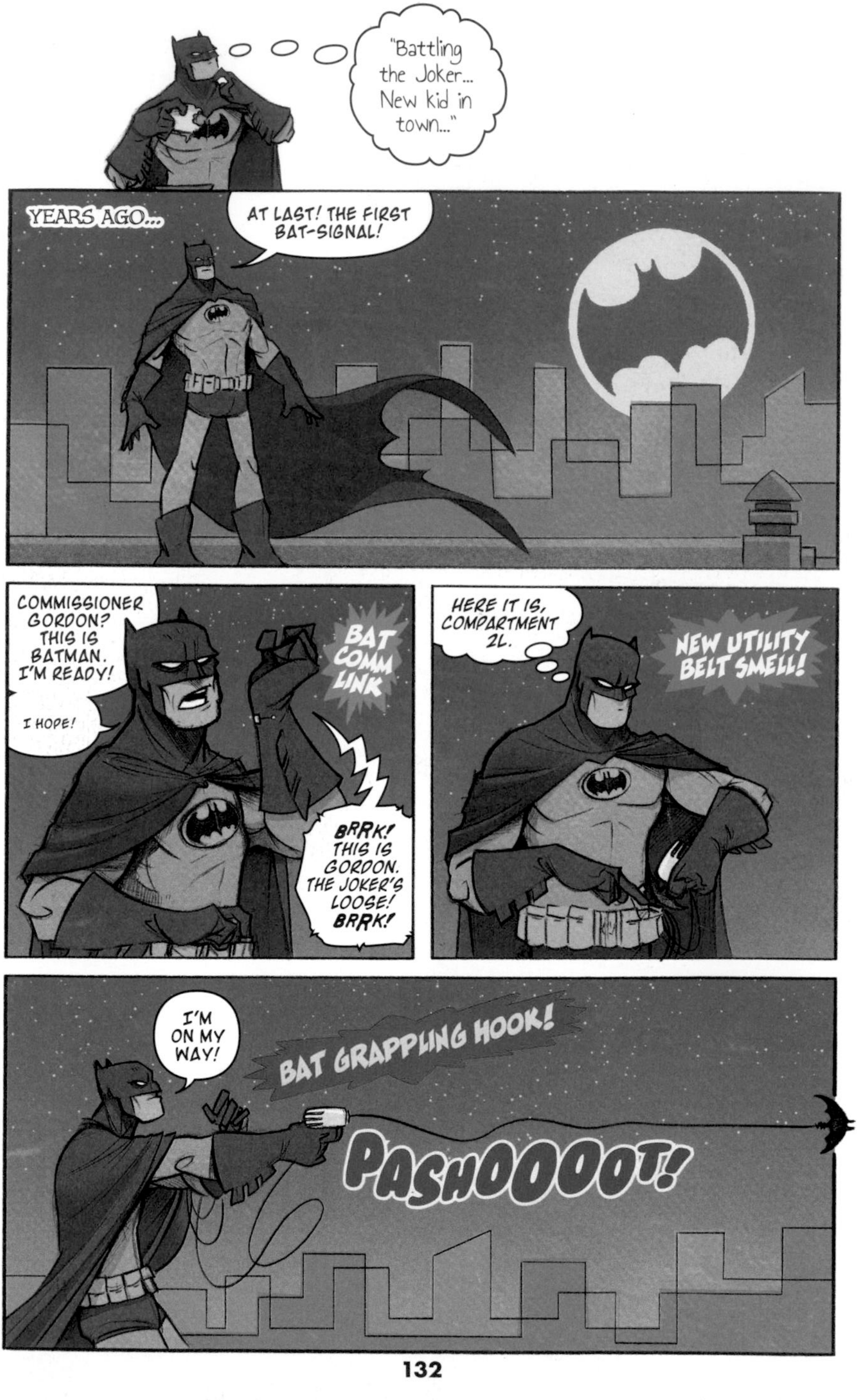
"Battling the Joker... New kid in town..."
YEARS AGO...
AT LAST! THE FIRST BAT-SIGNAL!
COMMISSIONER GORDON? THIS IS BATMAN. I'M READY!
I HOPE!
BAT COMM LINK
BRRK! THIS IS GORDON. THE JOKER'S LOOSE! BRRK!
HERE IT IS, COMPARTMENT 2L.
NEW UTILITY BELT SMELL!
I'M ON MY WAY!
BAT GRAPPLING HOOK!
PASHOOOOOT!

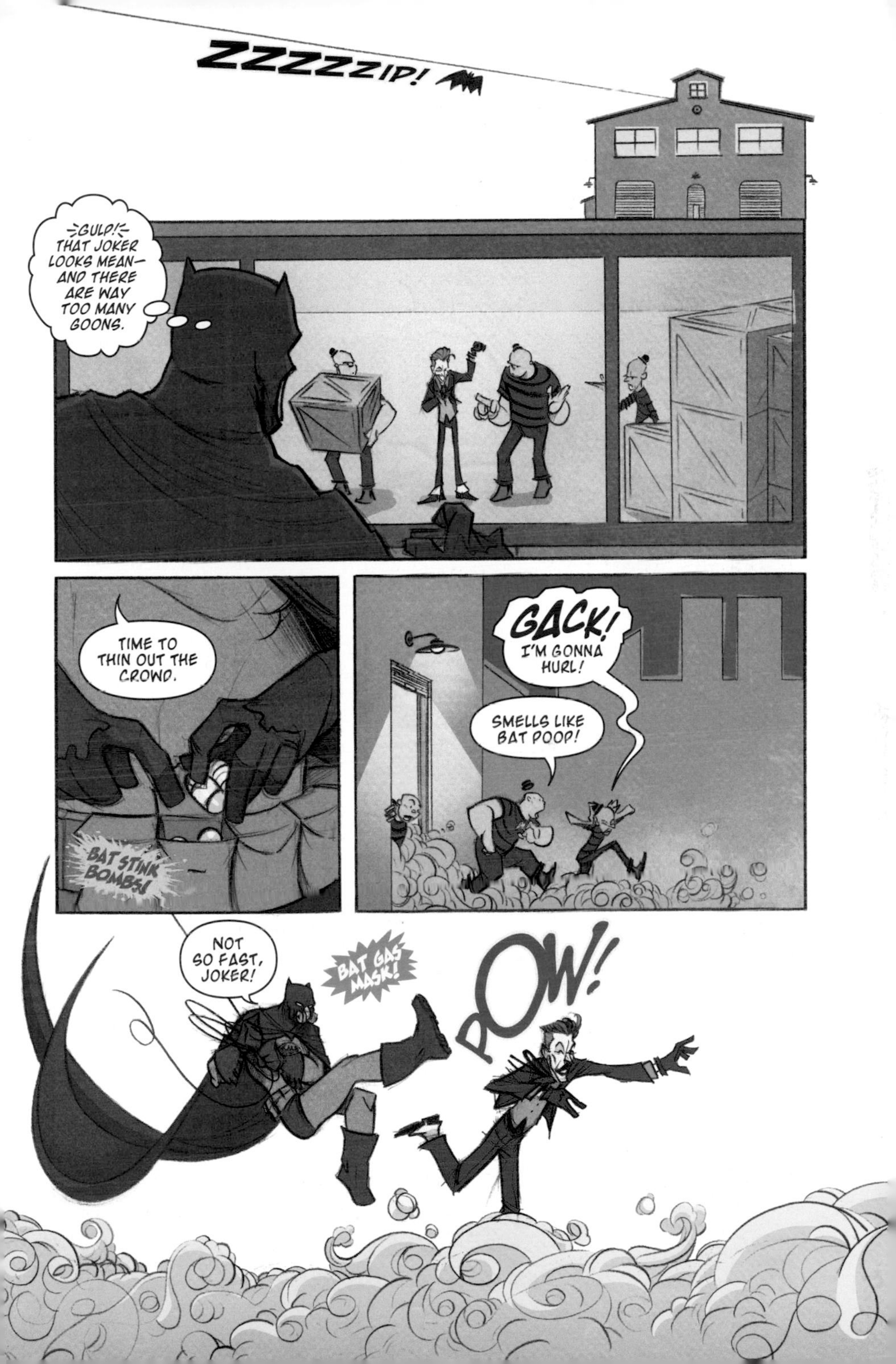
ZZZZZZIP!
-GULP!- THAT JOKER LOOKS MEAN— AND THERE ARE WAY TOO MANY GOONS.
TIME TO THIN OUT THE CROWD.
BAT STINK BOMBS!
GACK! I'M GONNA HURL!
SMELLS LIKE BAT POOP!
NOT SO FAST, JOKER!
BAT GAS MASK!
POW!

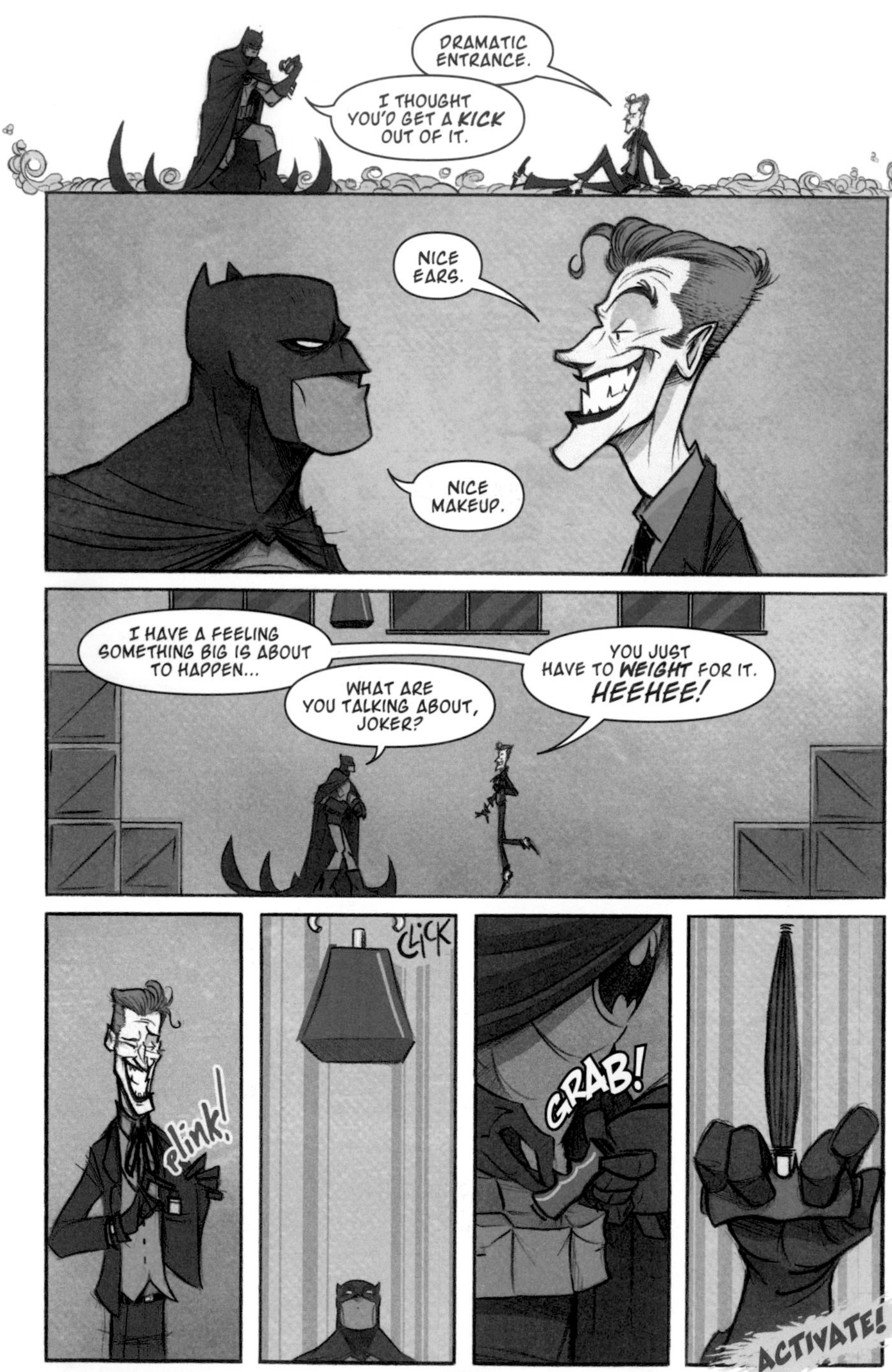
DRAMATIC ENTRANCE.
I THOUGHT YOU'D GET A KICK OUT OF IT.
NICE EARS.
NICE MAKEUP.
I HAVE A FEELING SOMETHING BIG IS ABOUT TO HAPPEN...
WHAT ARE YOU TALKING ABOUT, JOKER?
YOU JUST HAVE TO WEIGHT FOR IT. HEEHEE!
plink!
CLICK
GRAB!
ACTIVATE!

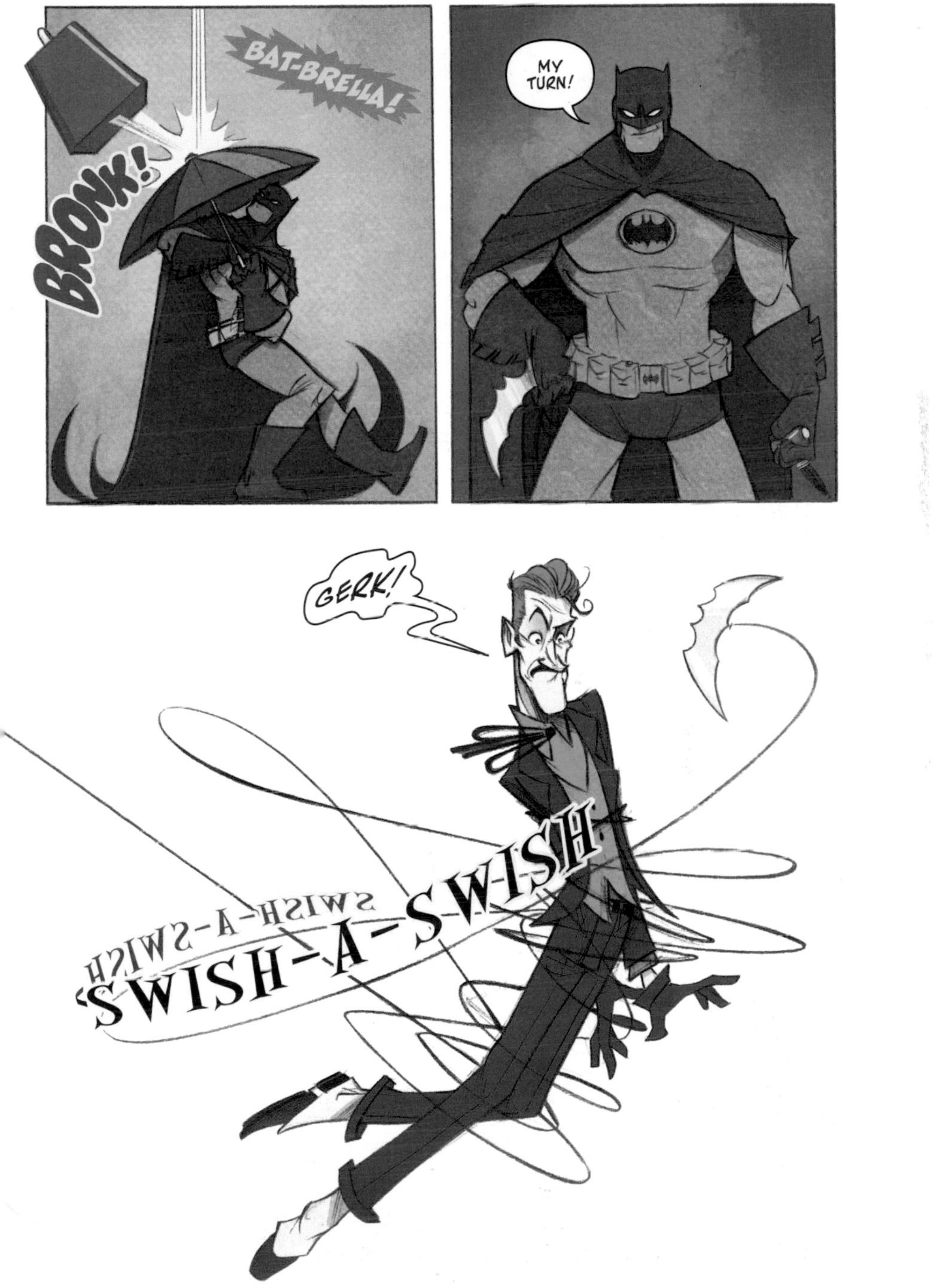
BAT-BRELLA!
BRONK!
MY TURN!
GERK!
SWISH-A-SWISH

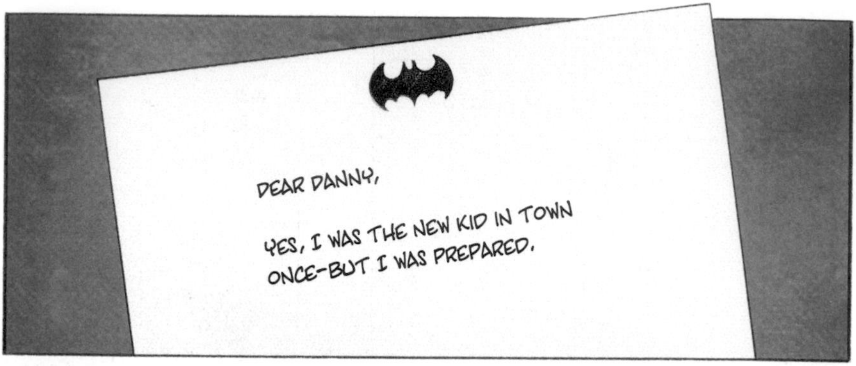
DEAR DANNY,
YES, I WAS THE NEW KID IN TOWN ONCE-BUT I WAS PREPARED.

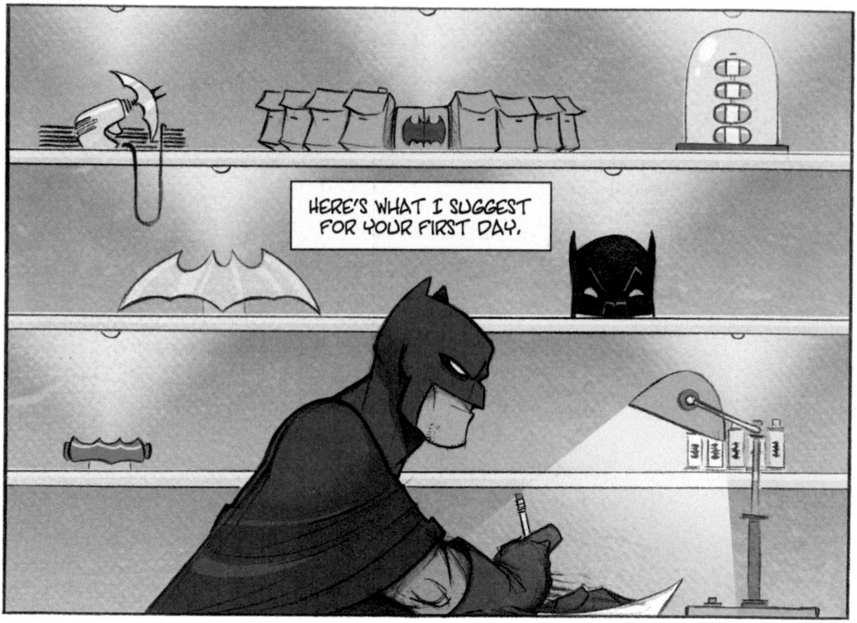
HERE'S WHAT I SUGGEST FOR YOUR FIRST DAY.

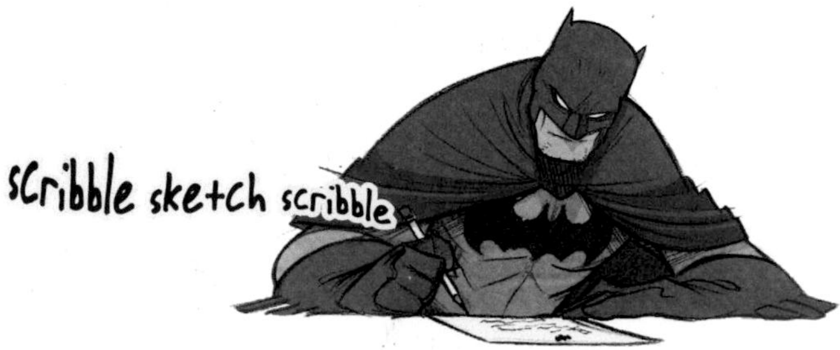
scribble sketch scribble

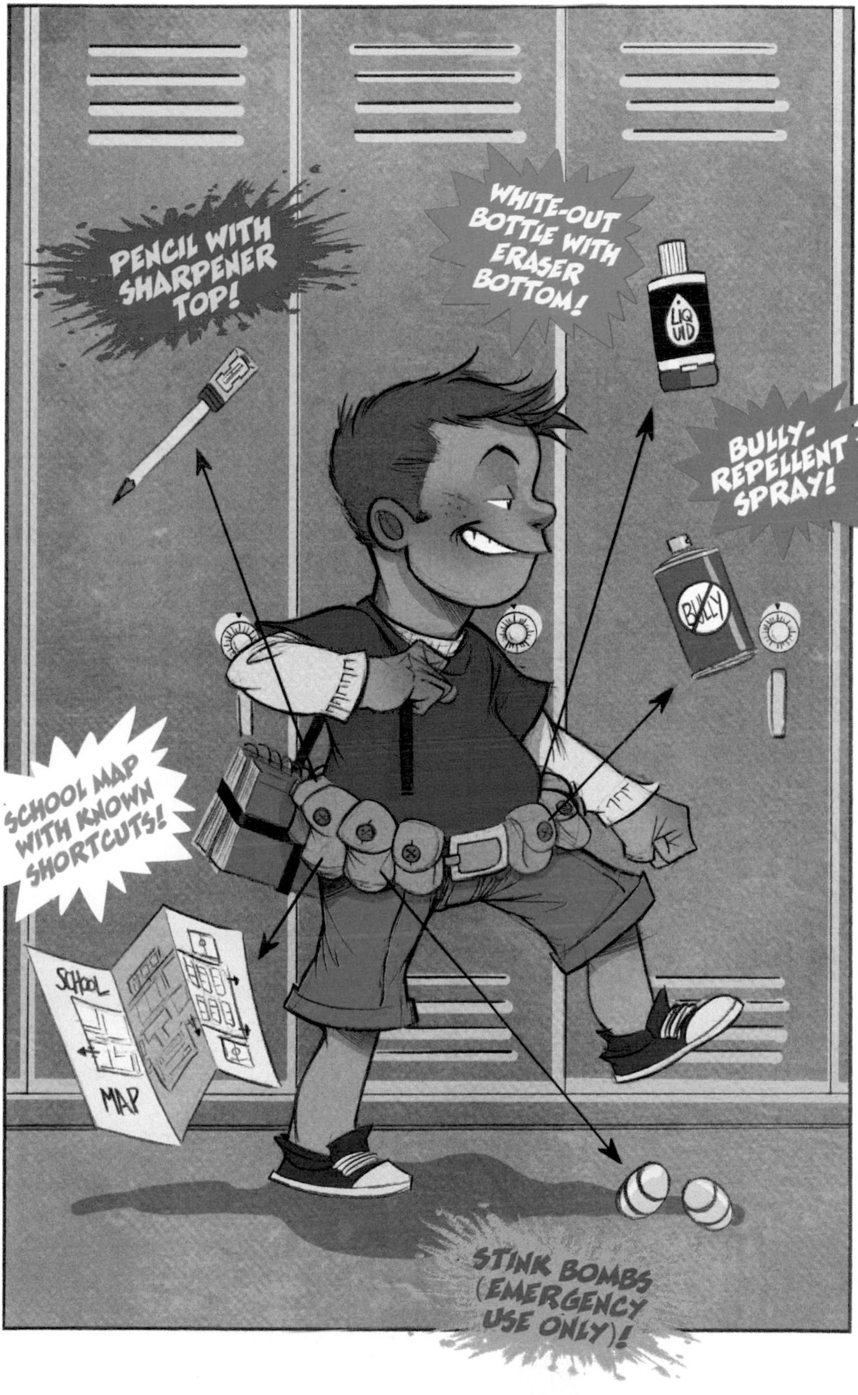
PENCIL WITH SHARPENER TOP!
WHITE-OUT BOTTLE WITH ERASER BOTTOM!
LIQUID
BULLY-REPELLENT SPRAY!
BULLY
SCHOOL MAP WITH KNOWN SHORTCUTS!
SCHOOL
MAP
STINK BOMBS (EMERGENCY USE ONLY)!

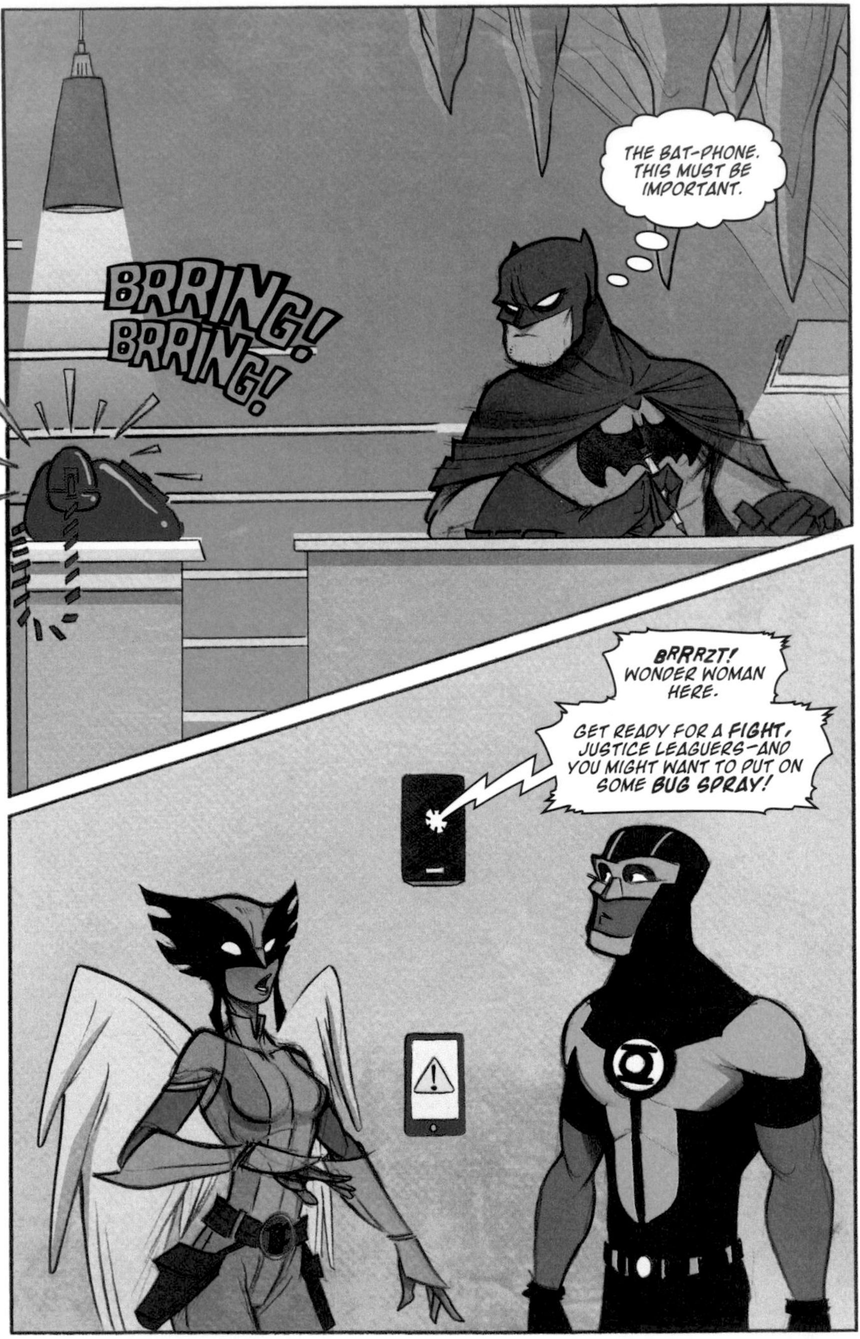
THE BAT-PHONE. THIS MUST BE IMPORTANT.
BRRING! BRRING!
BRRRZT! WONDER WOMAN HERE.
GET READY FOR A FIGHT, JUSTICE LEAGUERS—AND YOU MIGHT WANT TO PUT ON SOME BUG SPRAY!

CHAPTER 9

DEAR JUSTICE LEAGUE

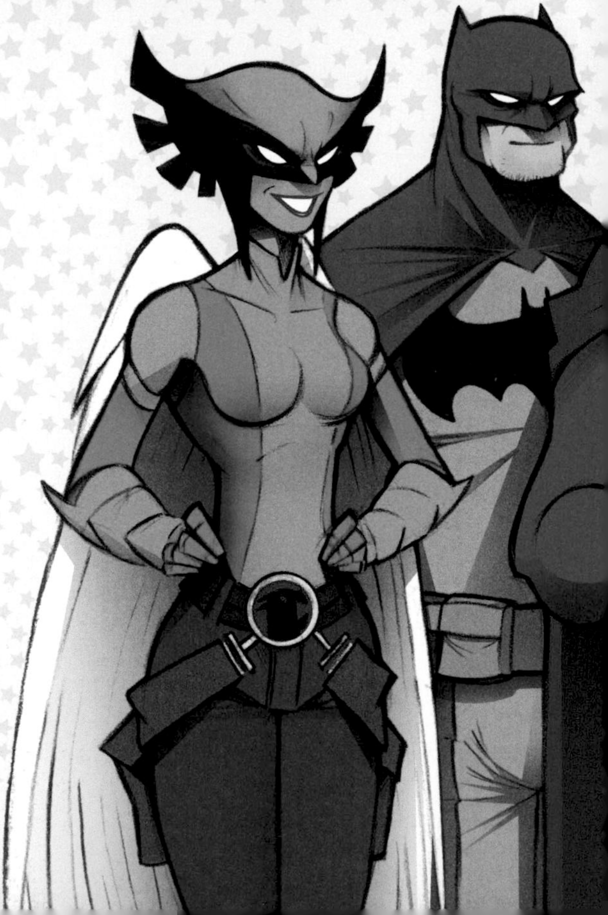

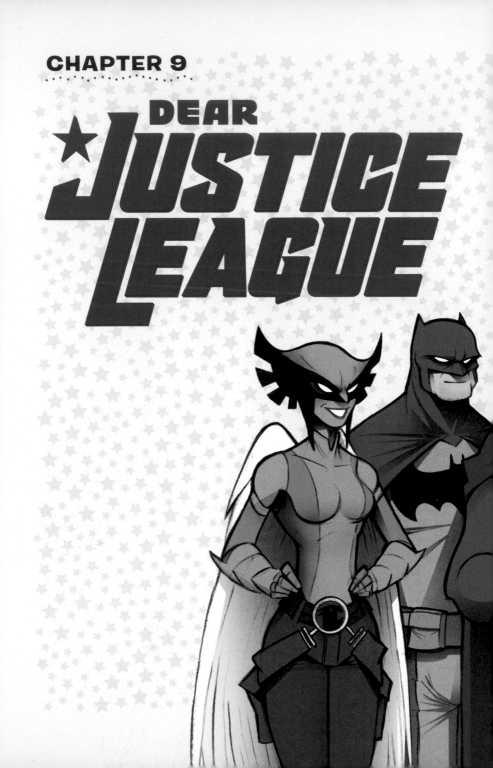

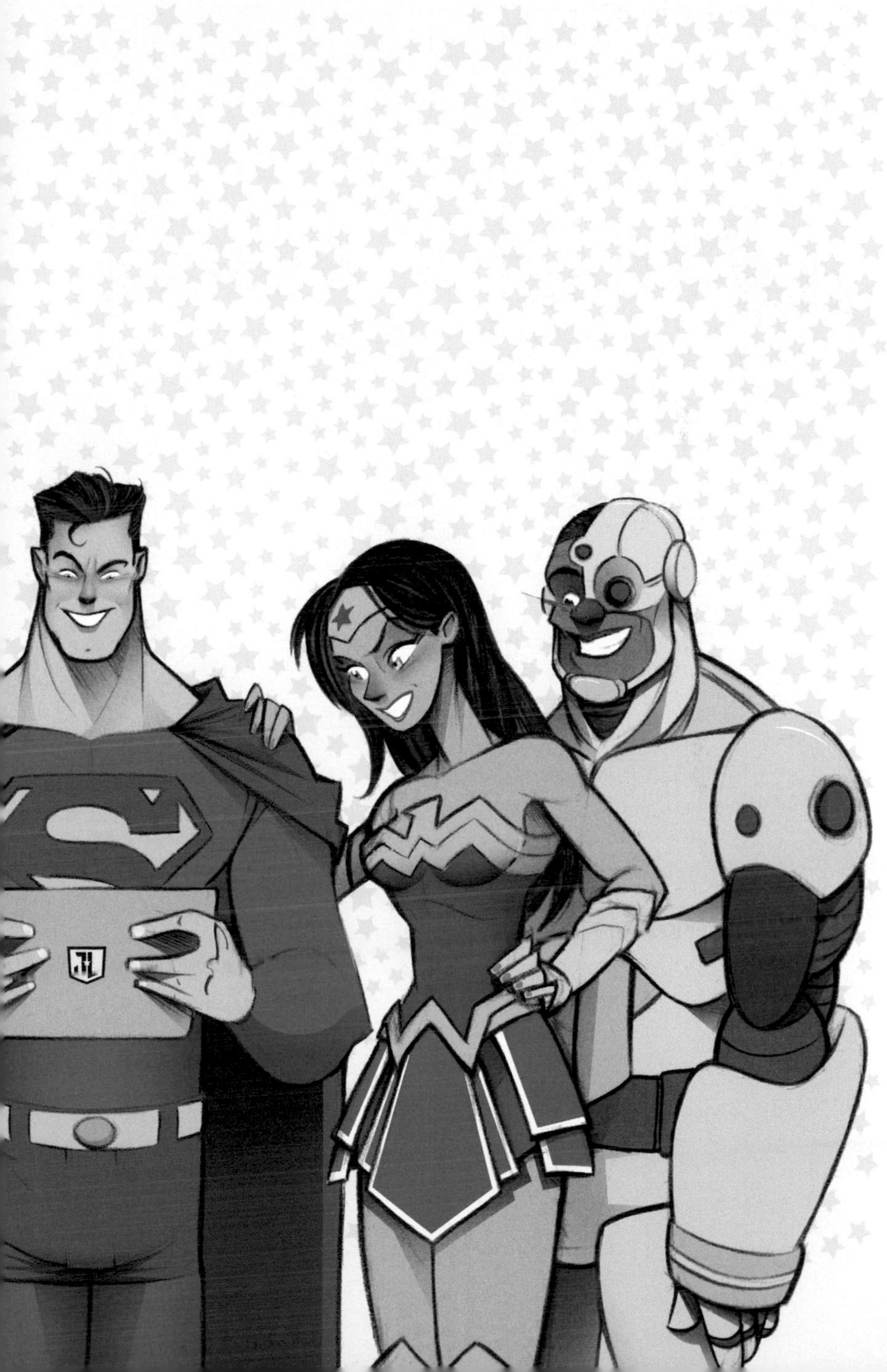

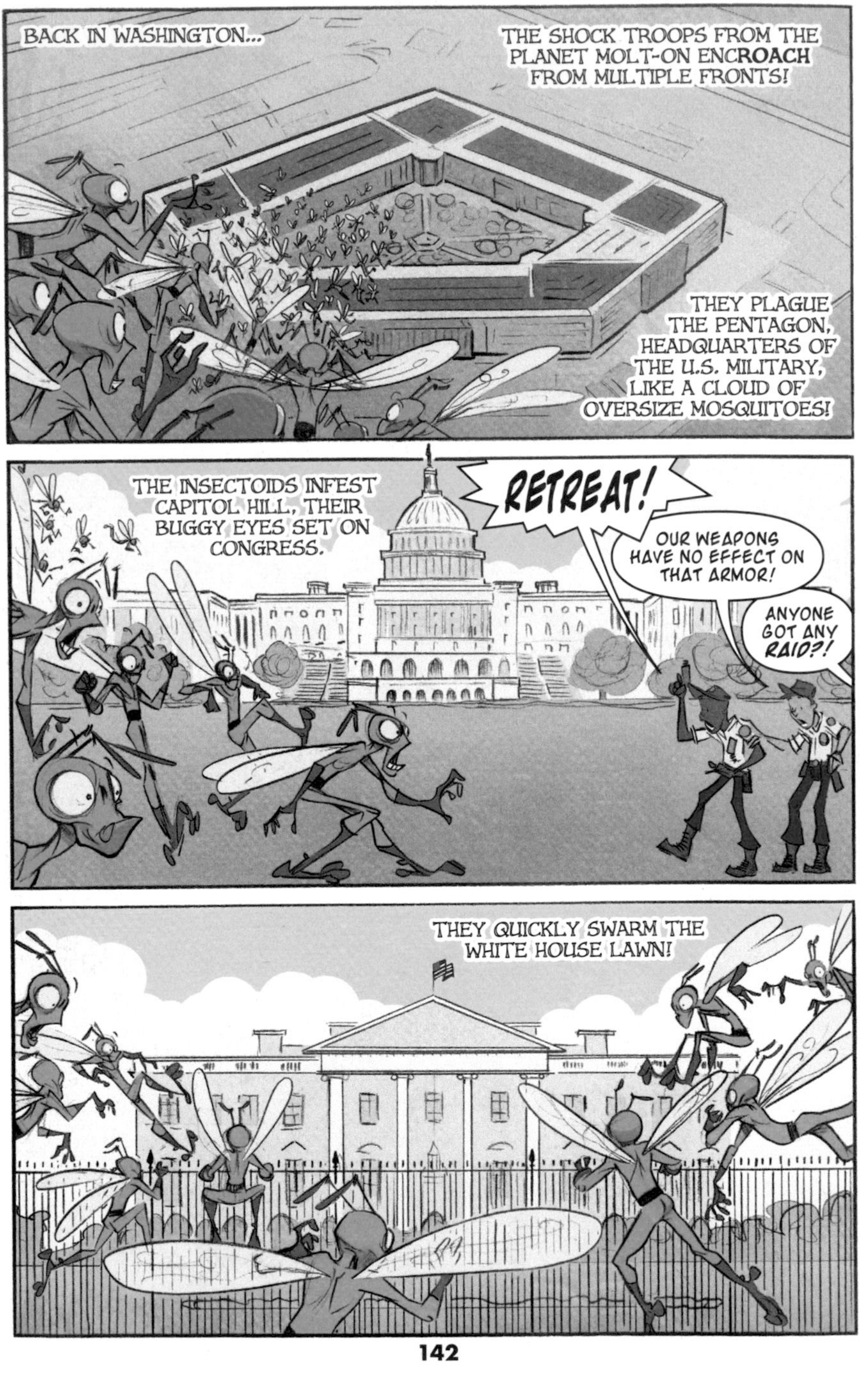
BACK IN WASHINGTON...
THE SHOCK TROOPS FROM THE PLANET MOLT-ON ENCROACH FROM MULTIPLE FRONTS!
THEY PLAGUE THE PENTAGON, HEADQUARTERS OF THE U.S. MILITARY, LIKE A CLOUD OF OVERSIZE MOSQUITOES!
THE INSECTOIDS INFEST CAPITOL HILL, THEIR BUGGY EYES SET ON CONGRESS.
RETREAT!
OUR WEAPONS HAVE NO EFFECT ON THAT ARMOR!
ANYONE GOT ANY RAID?!
THEY QUICKLY SWARM THE WHITE HOUSE LAWN!

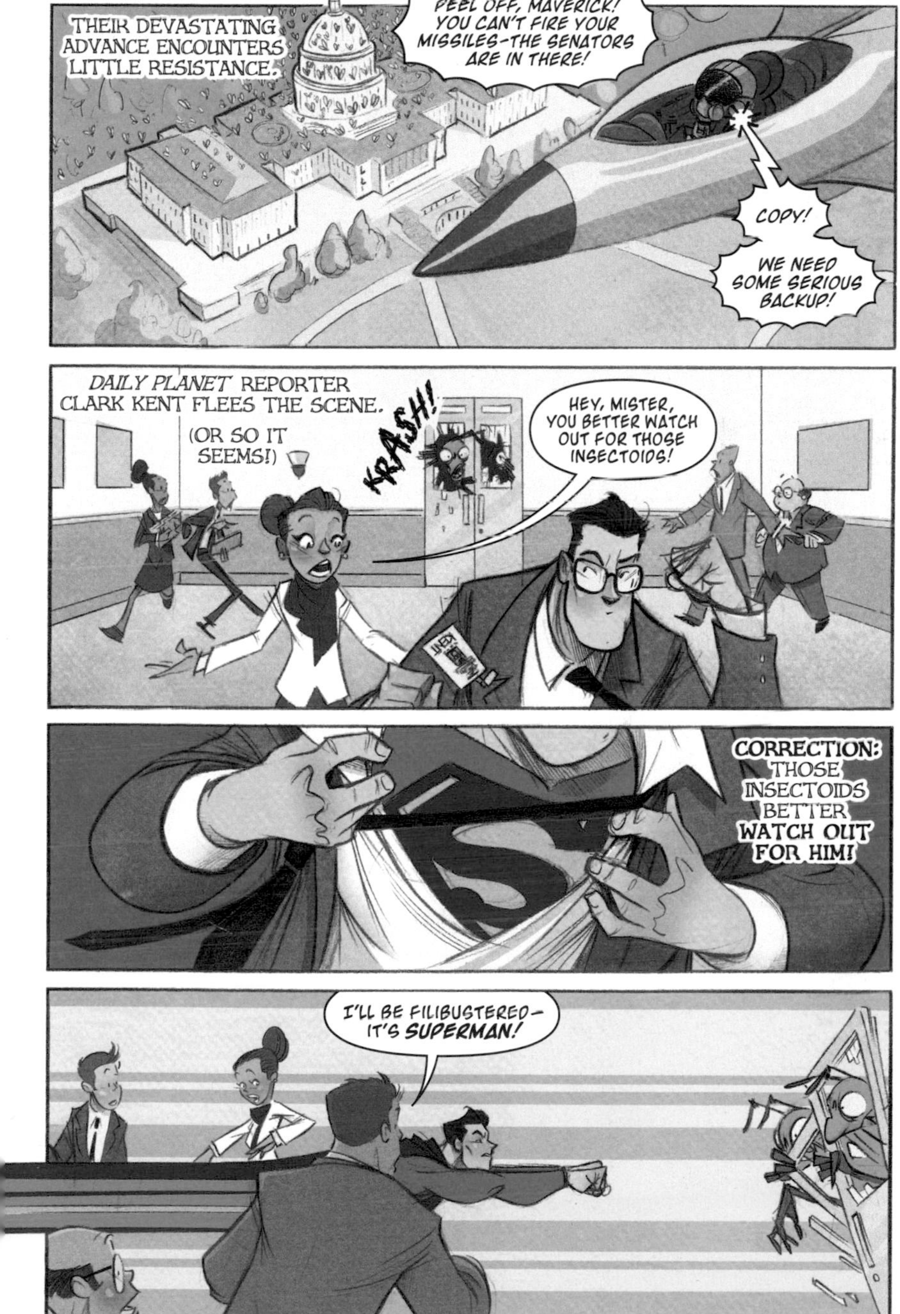

THEIR DEVASTATING ADVANCE ENCOUNTERS LITTLE RESISTANCE.
PEEL OFF, MAVERICK! YOU CAN'T FIRE YOUR MISSILES—THE SENATORS ARE IN THERE!
COPY!
WE NEED SOME SERIOUS BACKUP!
DAILY PLANET REPORTER CLARK KENT FLEES THE SCENE.
(OR SO IT SEEMS!)
KRASH!
HEY, MISTER, YOU BETTER WATCH OUT FOR THOSE INSECTOIDS!
CORRECTION: THOSE INSECTOIDS BETTER WATCH OUT FOR HIM!
I'LL BE FILIBUSTERED—IT'S SUPERMAN!

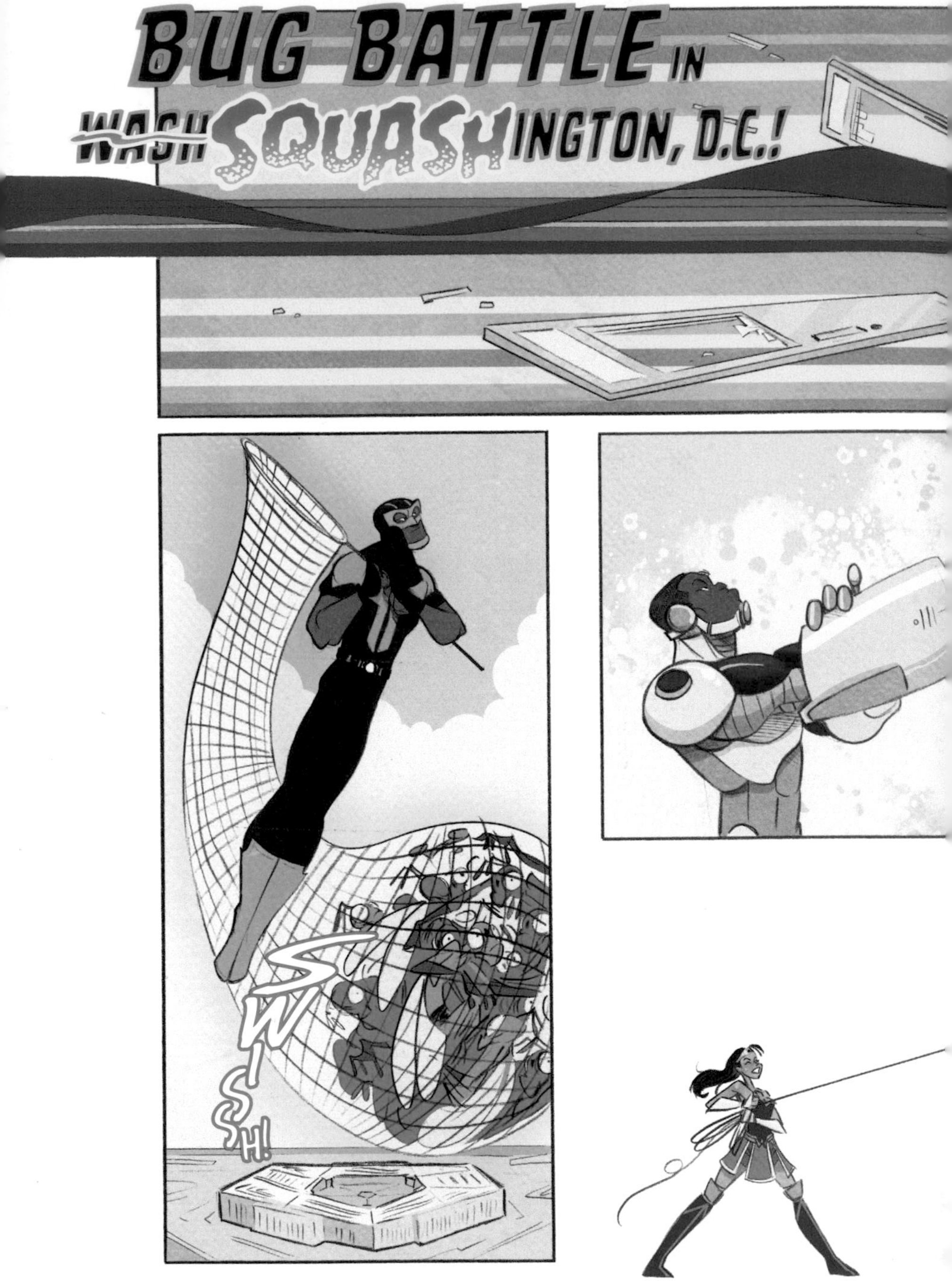
BUG BATTLE IN WASH SQUASHINGTON, D.C.!
SWISSH!

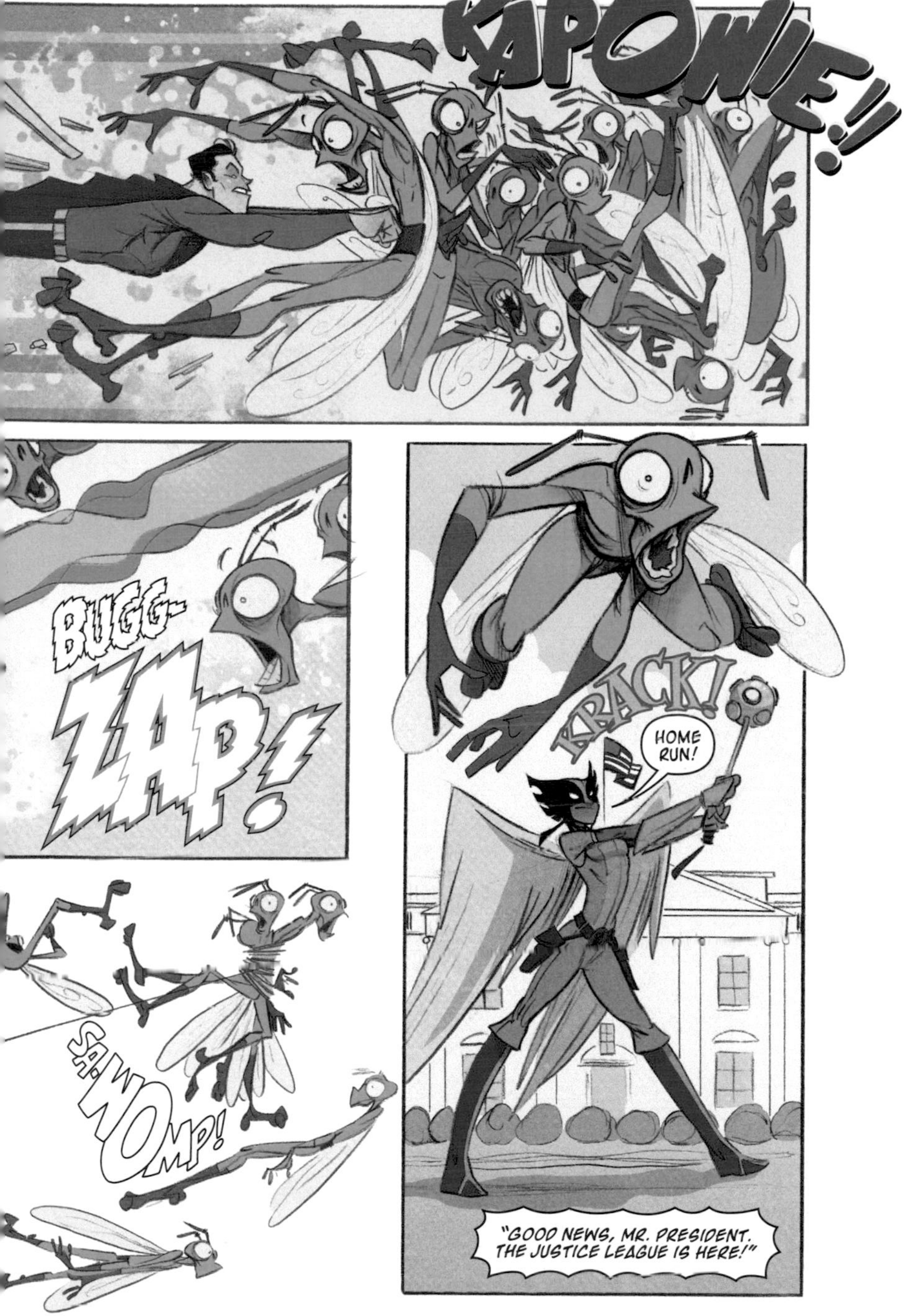
KAPOWIE!!!
BUGG-ZAP!
SA-WOMP!
KRACK!
HOME RUN!
"GOOD NEWS, MR. PRESIDENT. THE JUSTICE LEAGUE IS HERE!"

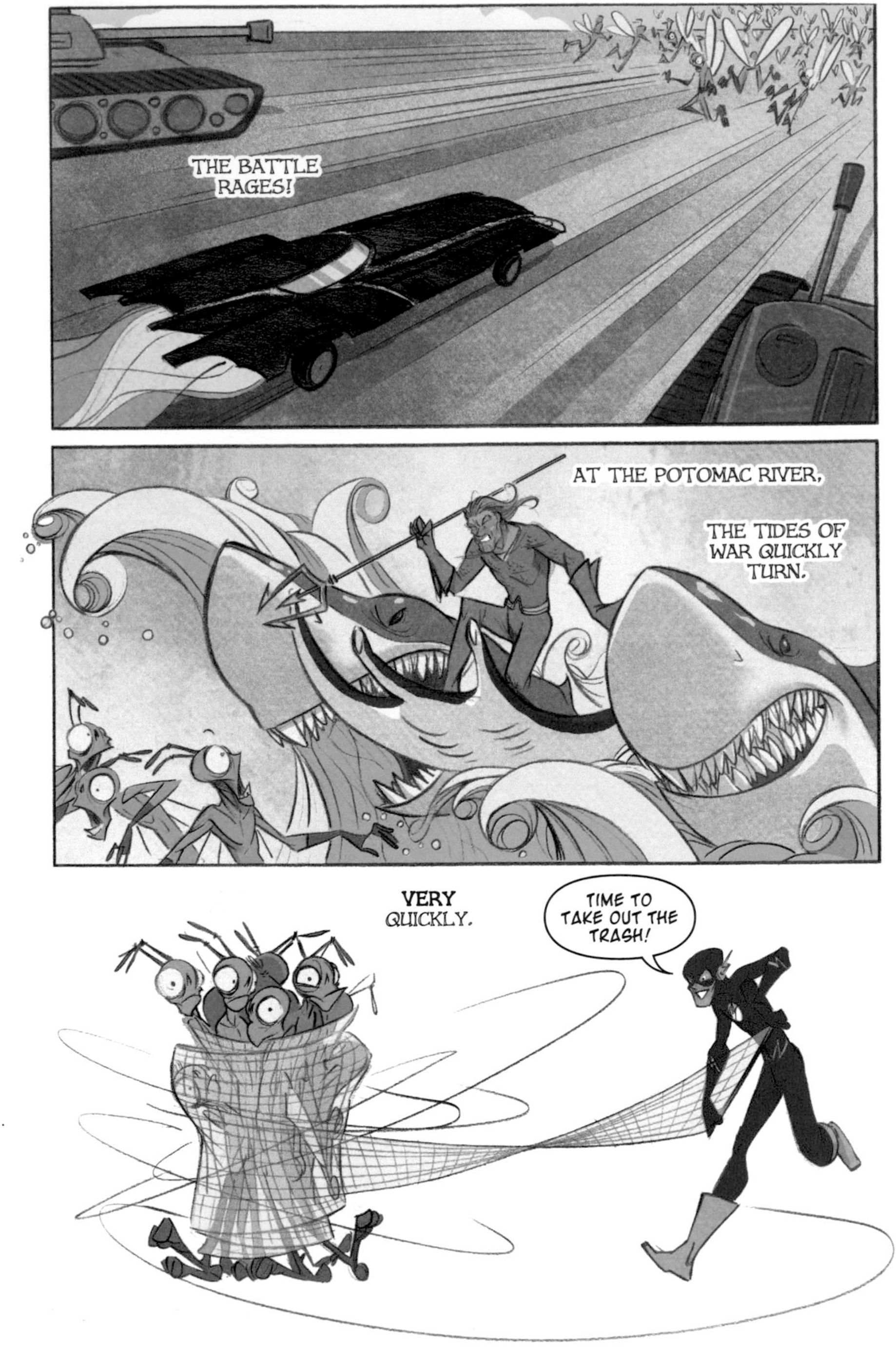
THE BATTLE RAGES!
AT THE POTOMAC RIVER,
THE TIDES OF WAR QUICKLY TURN.
VERY QUICKLY.
TIME TO TAKE OUT THE TRASH!

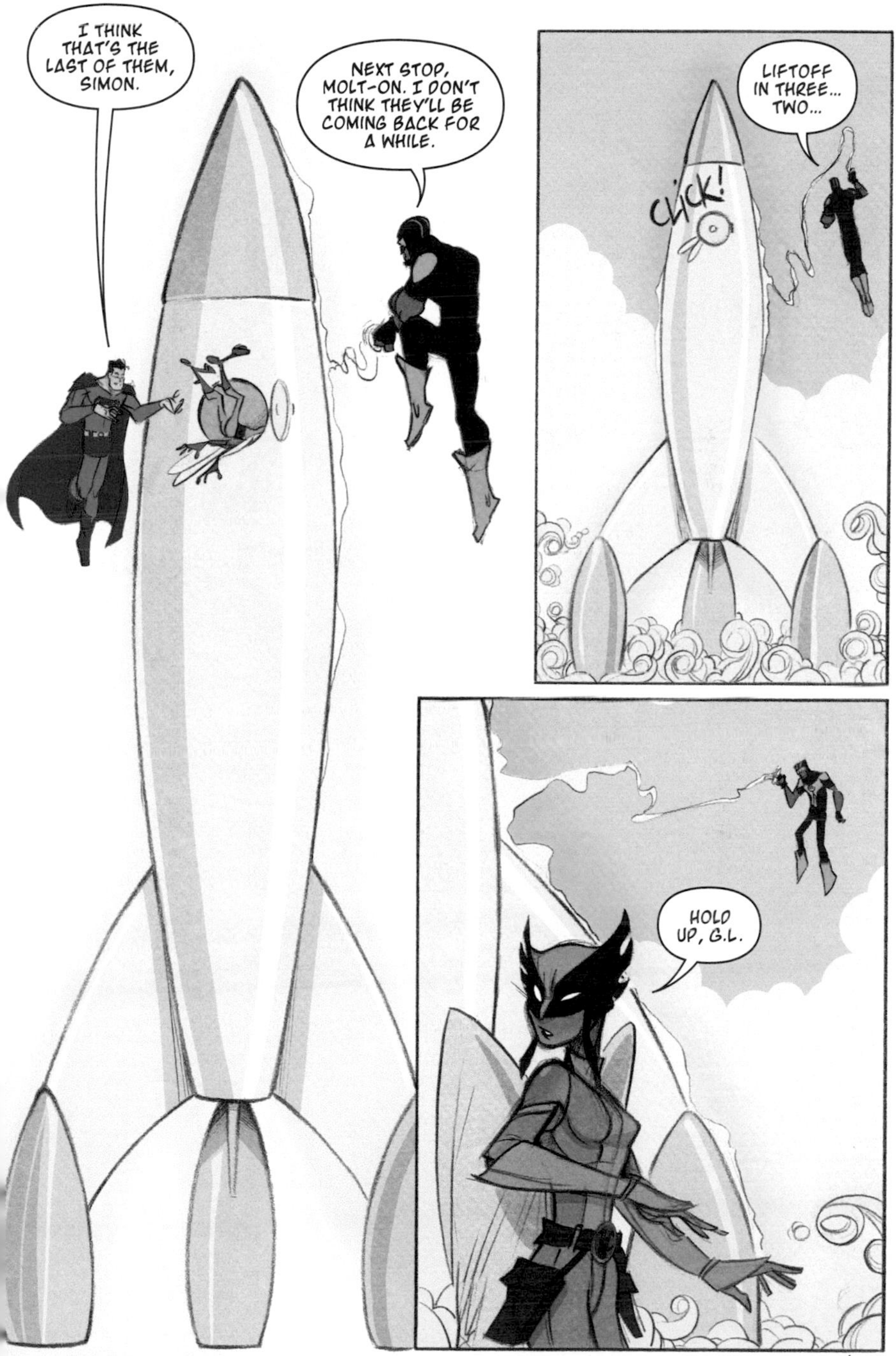
I THINK THAT'S THE LAST OF THEM, SIMON.
NEXT STOP, MOLT-ON. I DON'T THINK THEY'LL BE COMING BACK FOR A WHILE.
LIFTOFF IN THREE... TWO...
CLICK!
HOLD UP, G.L.

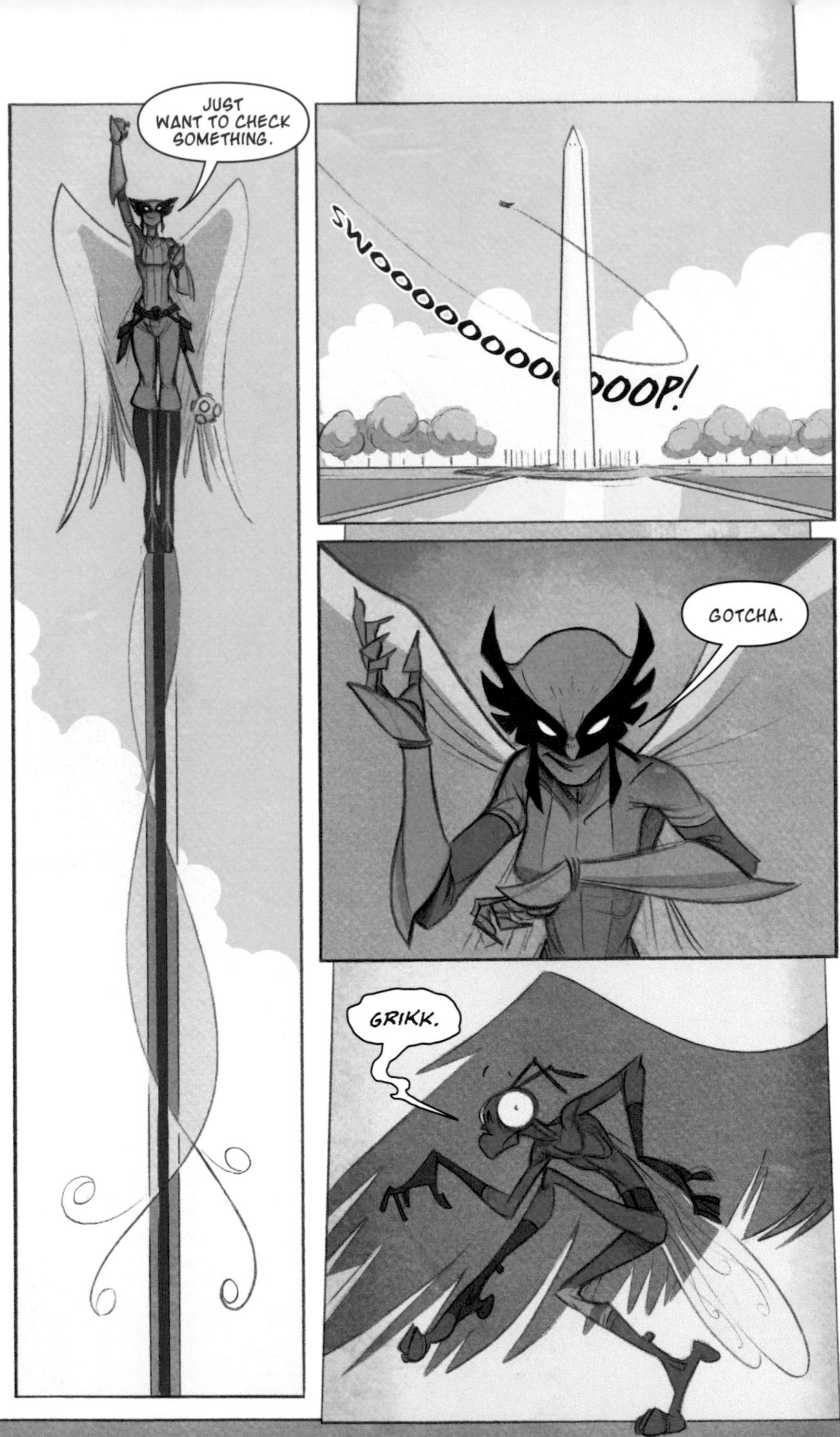

JUST WANT TO CHECK SOMETHING.
SWOOOOOOOOOOOOOOP!
GOTCHA.
GRIKK.

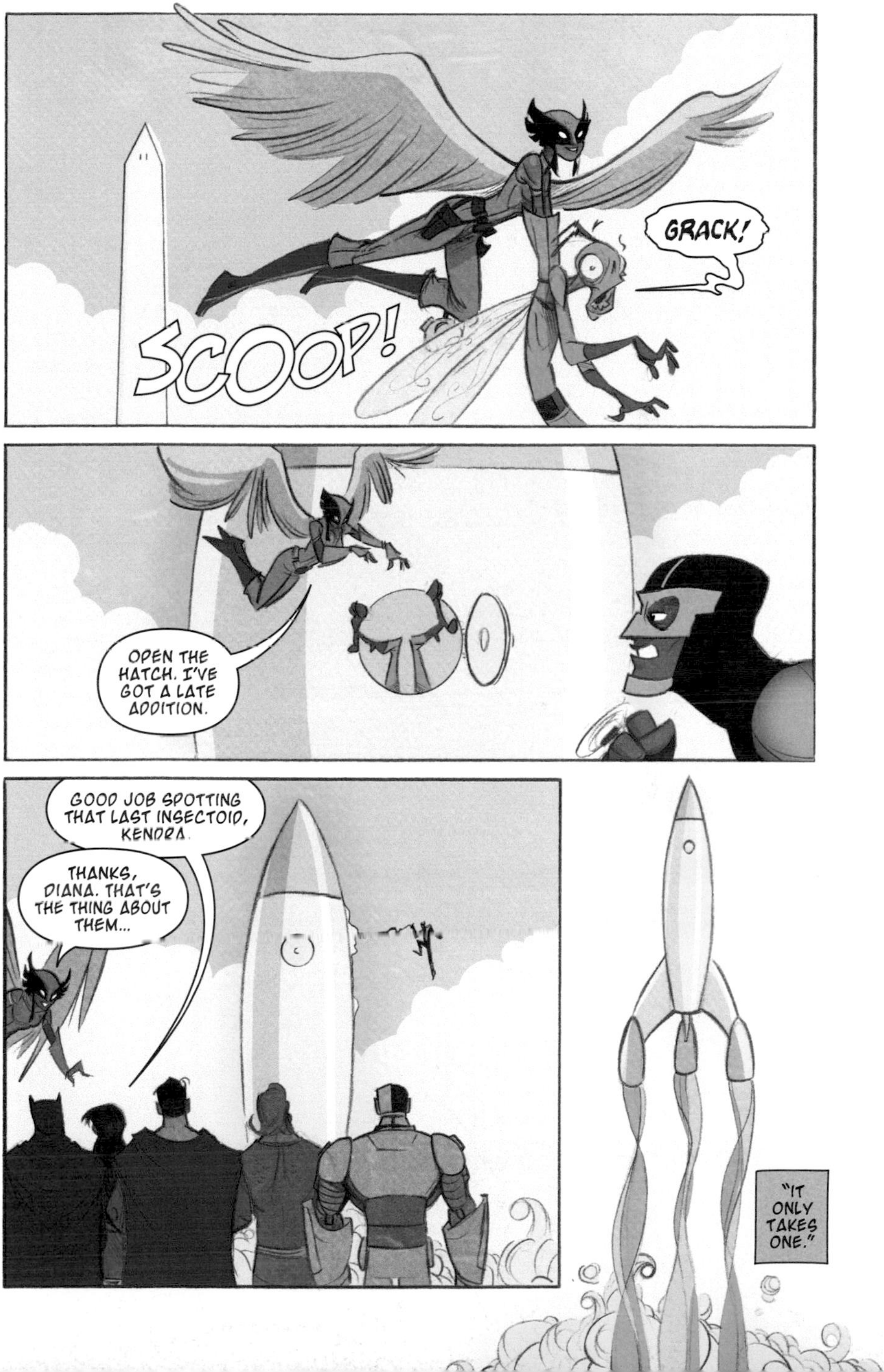
GRACK!
SCOOP!
OPEN THE HATCH. I'VE GOT A LATE ADDITION.
GOOD JOB SPOTTING THAT LAST INSECTOID, KENDRA.
THANKS, DIANA. THAT'S THE THING ABOUT THEM...
"IT ONLY TAKES ONE."

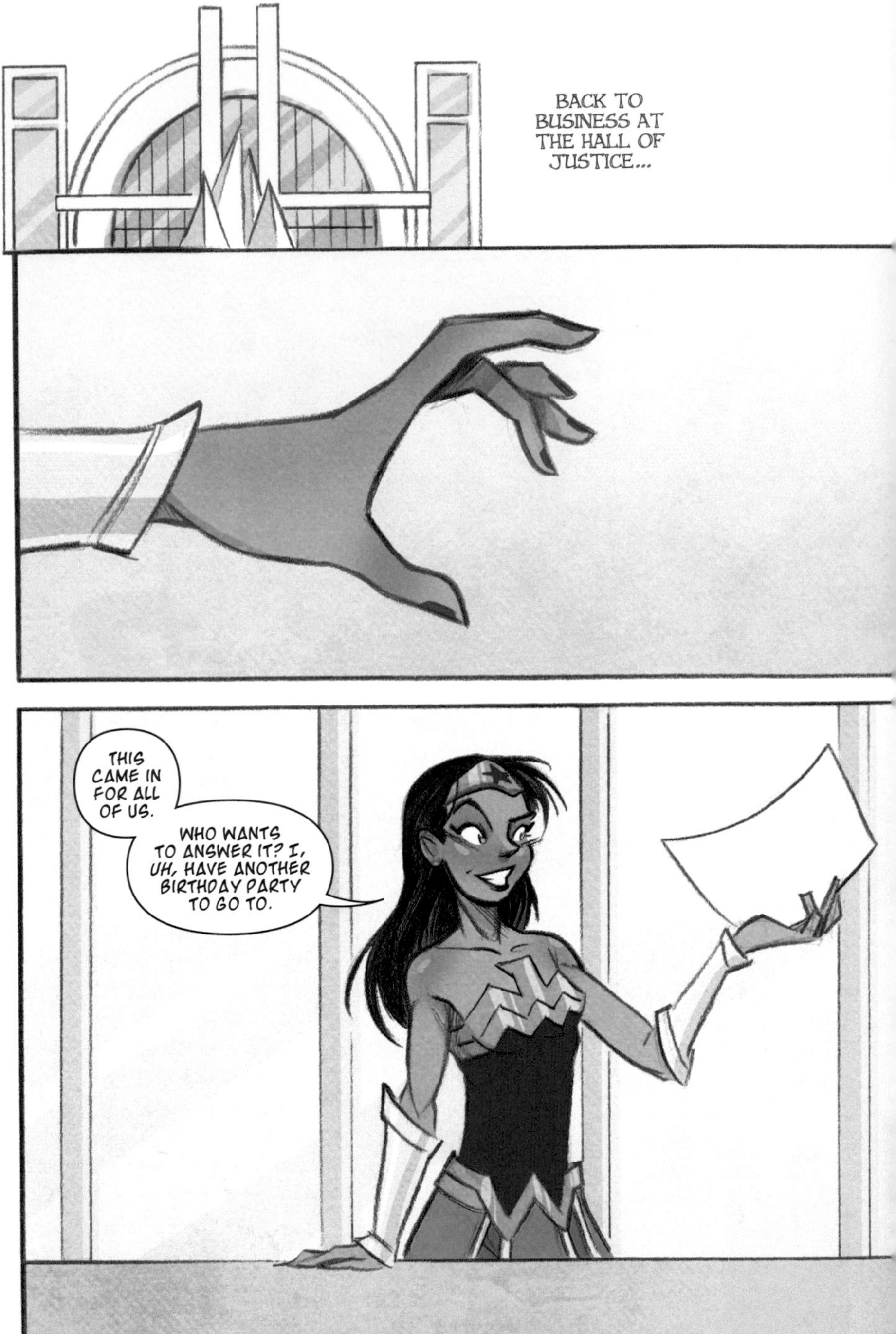
BACK TO BUSINESS AT THE HALL OF JUSTICE...
THIS CAME IN FOR ALL OF US.
WHO WANTS TO ANSWER IT? I, UH, HAVE ANOTHER BIRTHDAY PARTY TO GO TO.

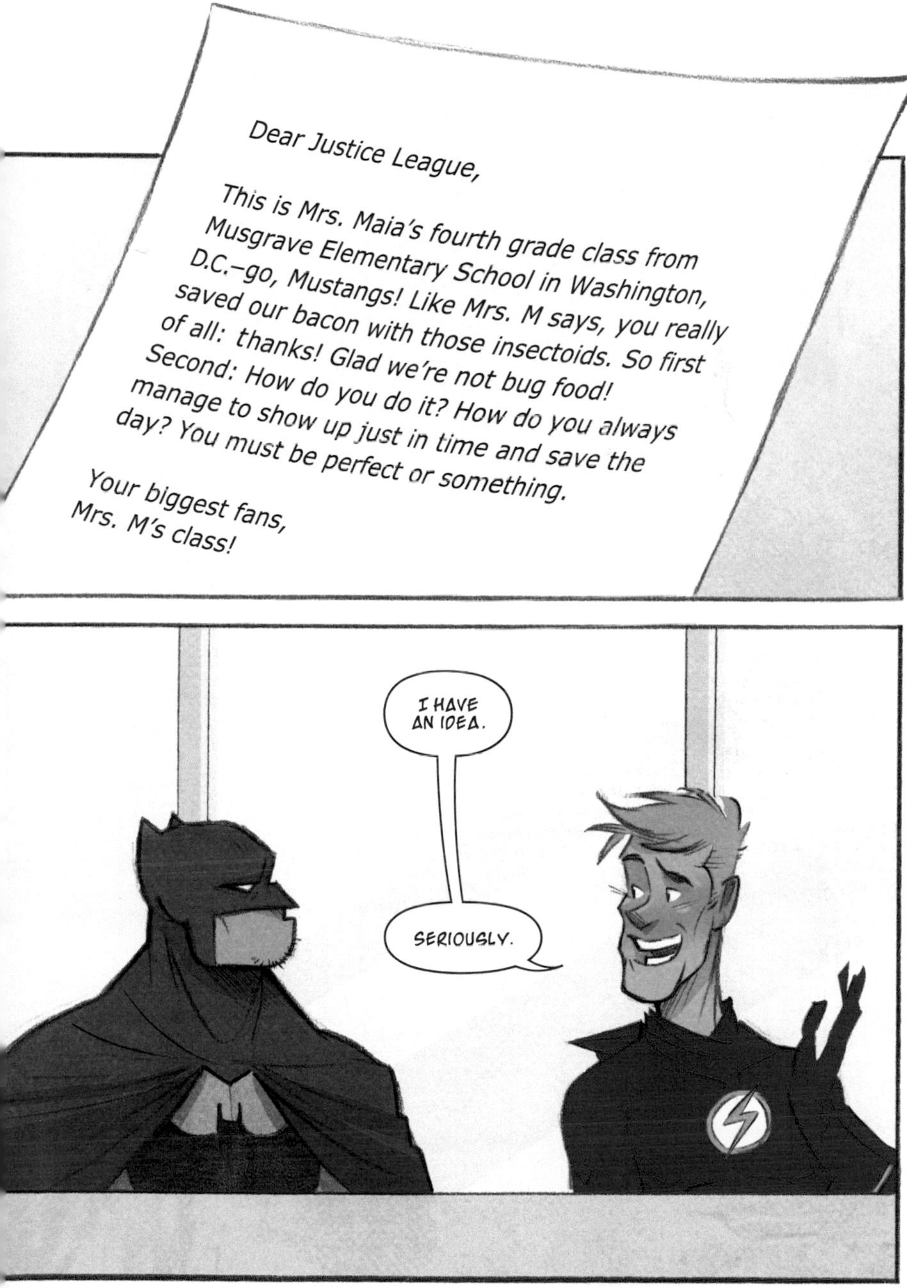
Dear Justice League,
This is Mrs. Maia's fourth grade class from Musgrave Elementary School in Washington, D.C.–go, Mustangs! Like Mrs. M says, you really saved our bacon with those insectoids. So first of all: thanks! Glad we're not bug food! Second: How do you do it? How do you always manage to show up just in time and save the day? You must be perfect or something.
Your biggest fans,
Mrs. M's class!
I HAVE AN IDEA.
SERIOUSLY.

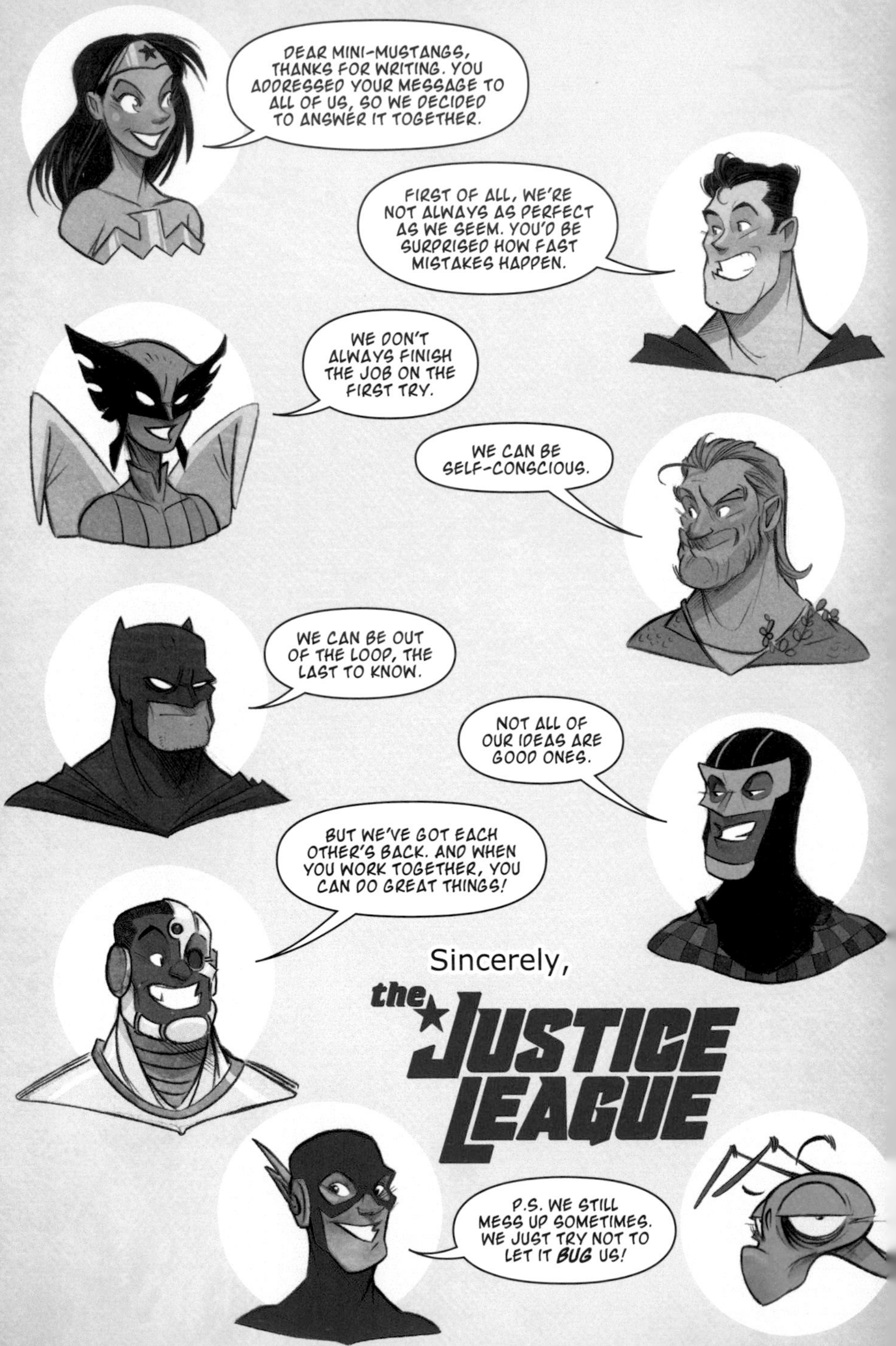
DEAR MINI-MUSTANGS, THANKS FOR WRITING. YOU ADDRESSED YOUR MESSAGE TO ALL OF US, SO WE DECIDED TO ANSWER IT TOGETHER.
FIRST OF ALL, WE'RE NOT ALWAYS AS PERFECT AS WE SEEM. YOU'D BE SURPRISED HOW FAST MISTAKES HAPPEN.
WE DON'T ALWAYS FINISH THE JOB ON THE FIRST TRY.
WE CAN BE SELF-CONSCIOUS.
WE CAN BE OUT OF THE LOOP, THE LAST TO KNOW.
NOT ALL OF OUR IDEAS ARE GOOD ONES.
BUT WE'VE GOT EACH OTHER'S BACK. AND WHEN YOU WORK TOGETHER, YOU CAN DO GREAT THINGS!
Sincerely,
the JUSTICE LEAGUE
P.S. WE STILL MESS UP SOMETIMES. WE JUST TRY NOT TO LET IT BUG US!

Hall of Justice Top Secret Files

NO PEEKING!

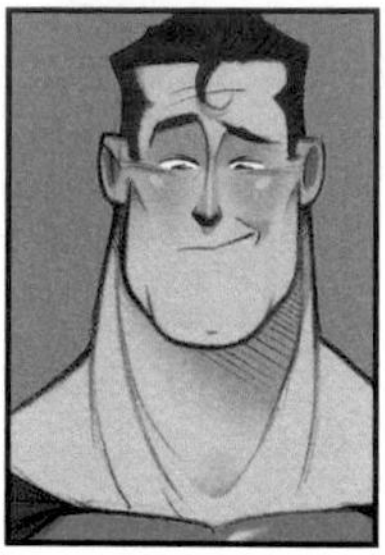

SUPERMAN

Secret identity: Clark Kent

Powers: Super-strength, super-speed—you name it, he's super at it. He also has the power of flight and invulnerability, plus X-ray vision, heat vision, and freeze breath.

Weakness: Kryptonite. Only stony remnants of his home planet, Krypton, can rock the Man of Steel.

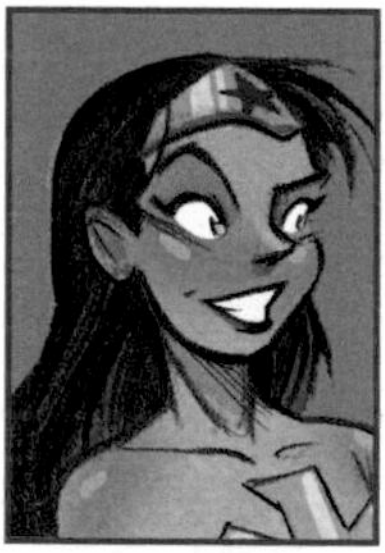

WONDER WOMAN

Secret identity: Princess Diana, Diana Prince

Powers: Super strength, speed, and agility. Epic combat training. Bulletproof bracelets. Magic lasso. Wisdom of the ages (seriously, she's like Yoda with better grammar).

Weakness: For such a wise woman, she sure works with a bunch of...*wise guys.*

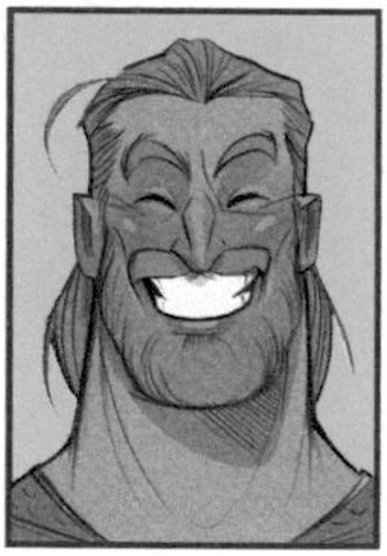

AQUAMAN

Secret identity: Arthur Curry

Powers: Super strength, agility, and durability. Hypersonic swimming. Aquatic telepathy (ability to command sea life). Fully amphibious.

Weakness: Requires periodic contact with water to maintain strength (and hygiene).

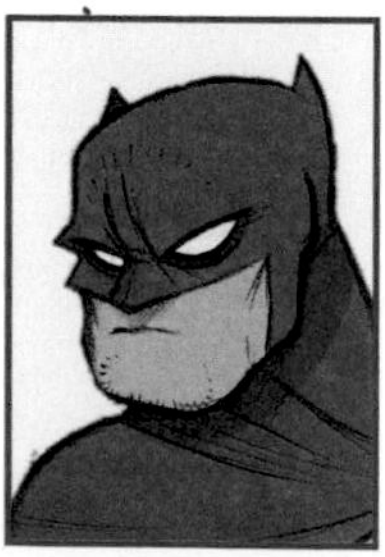

BATMAN

Secret identity: Bruce Wayne

Powers: This super-rich genius has a vast array of inventions and devices. He's also a martial arts expert and master detective.

Weakness: Often the only one in the room without innate superpowers.

CYBORG

Secret identity: Victor "Call Me Vic" Stone

Powers: Part human, part cybernetic machine. Super strength, speed, durability, and shininess. Flight. Energy beams. He's also a computer genius.

Weakness: A computer virus, maybe?

THE FLASH

Secret identity: Barry Allen

Powers: The Fastest Man Alive. Hyper-speed running. Super-reflexes to prevent light-speed splats. Can control his molecules and pass through solid objects.

Weakness: Extreme cold slows down his molecules. BRRRR!

GREEN LANTERN

Secret identity: Simon Baz

Powers: His power ring can create green energy objects, shoot energy beams, and generate force fields, and it allows him to fly.

Weakness: Powerless against the color yellow.

HAWKGIRL

Secret identity: Kendra Saunders

Powers: You may have noticed the wings? Flight. Enhanced strength, agility, sight, and durability. Nth metal (like, really strong metal) mace.

Weakness: Well, she's a teenager so...YouTube?

AUXILIARY MEMBERS!

HAMLET

Hawkgirl's hamster

Powers: Cute as a button, great stress reliever, and if you drop something down a pipe, Hamlet can get it.

Weakness: Can't resist the nom-noms.

PURDY

Aquaman's goldfish

Powers: Excellent swimmer, surprisingly good conversationalist.

Weakness: Bowl-bound.

JUSTIE

The Justice League cat; Head Mouser, Hall of Justice

Powers: Agile, stealthy, adorable.

Weakness: Cat naps.

JUMPA

Wonder Woman's Kanga, an Amazonian kangaroo

Powers: Jumbo size, with spring-loaded hops.

Weakness: Low ceilings.

PHOTO BY FRANCINE DAVETA

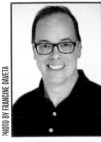

MICHAEL NORTHROP

Author of DEAR JUSTICE LEAGUE

Powers: Word wrangling. Story conjuring. Punishing puns. Perfect speling.

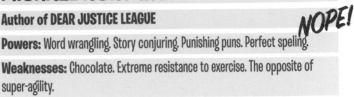

NOPE!

Weaknesses: Chocolate. Extreme resistance to exercise. The opposite of super-agility.

Michael Northrop is the *New York Times* bestselling author of Scholastic's new multi-platform series *TombQuest*. His first young adult novel, *Gentlemen*, earned him a Publishers Weekly Flying Start citation, and his second, *Trapped*, was an Indie Next List selection. His first middle grade novel, *Plunked*, was named one of the best children's books of the year by the New York Public Library and was selected for NPR's Backseat Book Club. He is originally from Salisbury, Connecticut, a small town in the foothills of the Berkshire mountains, where he mastered the arts of BB gun shooting, tree climbing, and field goal kicking with only moderate injuries. After graduating from NYU, he worked at *Sports Illustrated Kids* magazine for 12 years, the last five of those as baseball editor.

Who approved these members? -WW

PHOTO BY JOSI VICENTIN

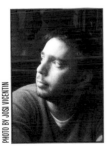

GUSTAVO DUARTE

Artist of DEAR JUSTICE LEAGUE

Powers: Turning ink into superheroes. Filling pages with adventure. Super-humor.

Weaknesses: Inability to wake up early. Total immunity to alarm clocks. Warning: May turn into zombie.

Gustavo Duarte is a Brazilian cartoonist, graphic designer, and comics creator and currently resides in São Paulo. For the last 20 years, Duarte's cartoons and illustrations have been published in some of the most popular publications in Brazil. In 2009, Duarte began publishing his own comics like *Monsters!*, *Có!*, *Birds*, and others. In addition to his own works, Duarte has also written and illustrated comics for major publishers including DC (BIZARRO) and Marvel (*Guardians of the Galaxy* and *Lockjaw*), among others.

DEAR MICHAEL NORTHROP!

The author of DEAR JUSTICE LEAGUE received a letter from his younger self, age 10.

Dear Older Me,

Nice to meet you—I mean, me. I hear you're writing about superheros. That sounds pretty cool. But I thought our plan was to BE a superhero. What happened?!

Sincerely,

Younger (and cooler) you

P.S. Here's a better headshot for your book.

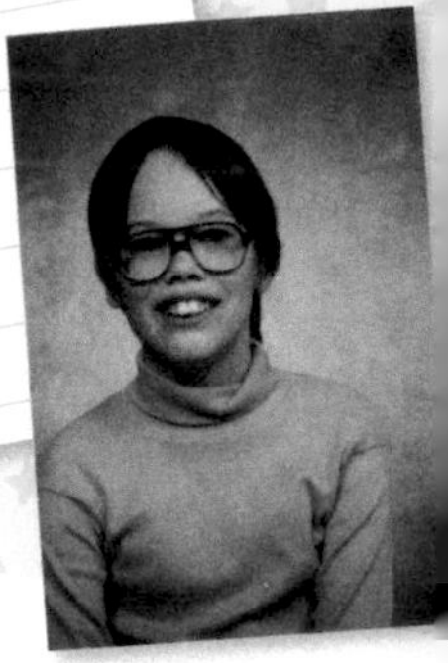

Dear Younger Me,

Listen, little buddy, I tried. You probably remember the part about tying a towel around our neck, jumping off a chair, and attempting to fly. We even threw in a few SHAZAMS! Still no dice. When we got too tall for the chair thing, we graduated to telekinesis: moving objects with our mind. Long after most kids had given up on finding their superpower, we were still staring at salt shakers in McDonald's and trying to make them move. Weirdly, it didn't work. So yeah, we had to move on to plan B—as in Books.

It's not so bad, though. If you think about it, reading is a superpower, too.

Fondly,

Older (and taller) you

Dear ______________________________,

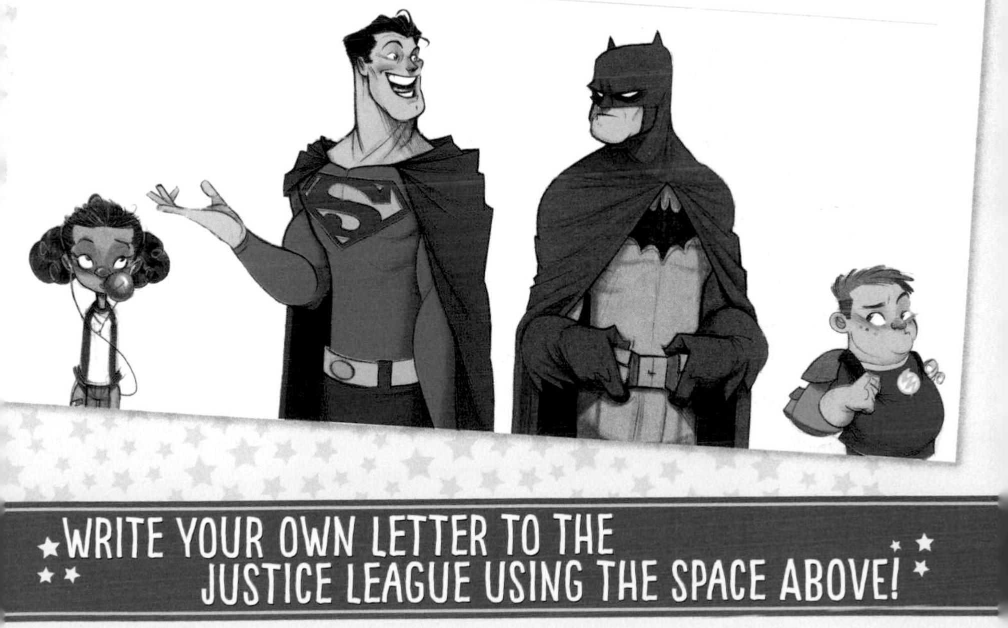

★WRITE YOUR OWN LETTER TO THE JUSTICE LEAGUE USING THE SPACE ABOVE! ★

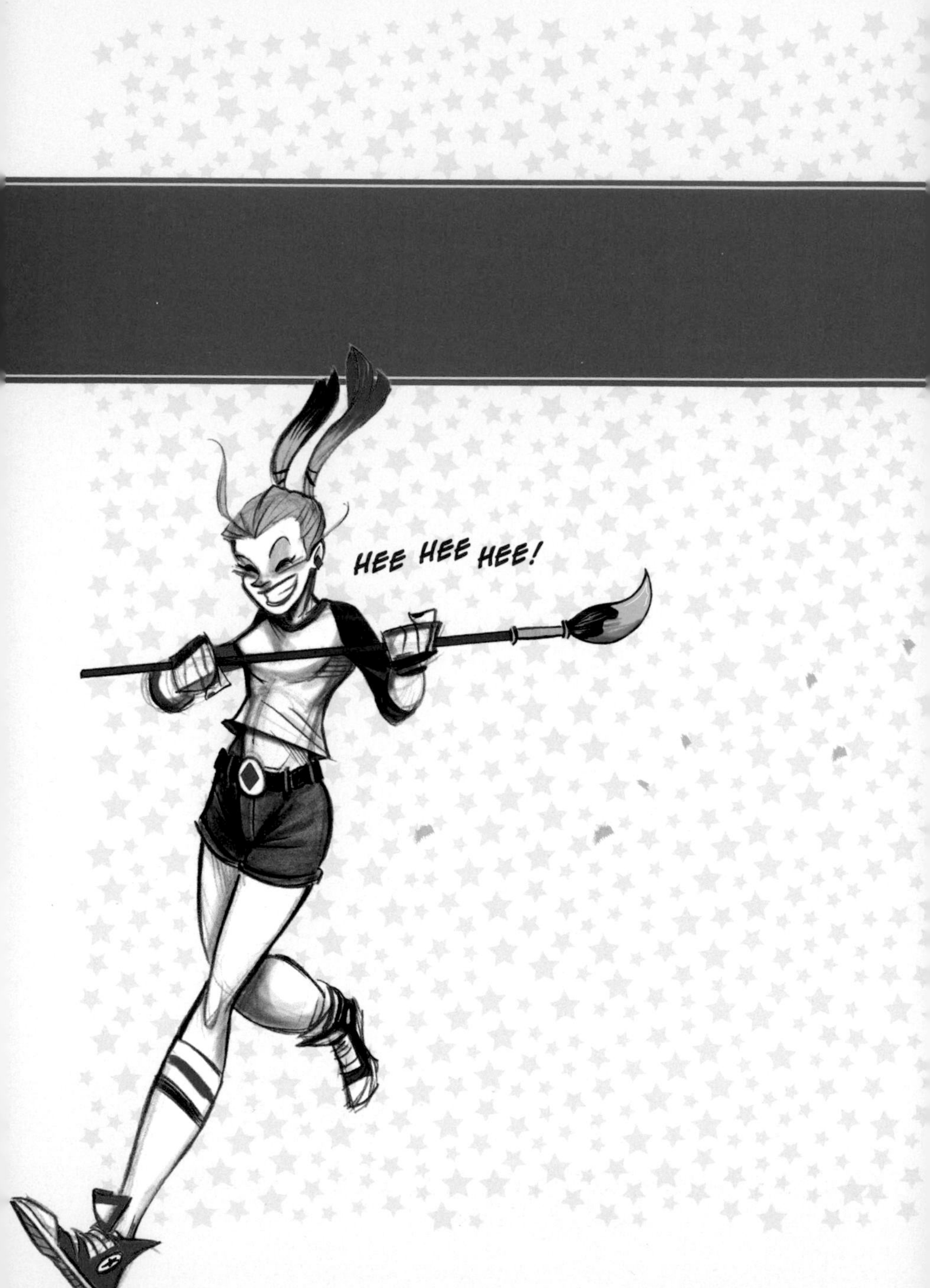
HEE HEE HEE!

DEAR ~~JUSTICE LEAGUE~~ SUPER-VILLAINS

You thought only
heroes got fan mail?
Think again!

Keep reading for an evil sneak peek at

DEAR SUPER-VILLAINS

the next book from Michael Northrop and Gustavo Duarte!
Coming Fall 2020.

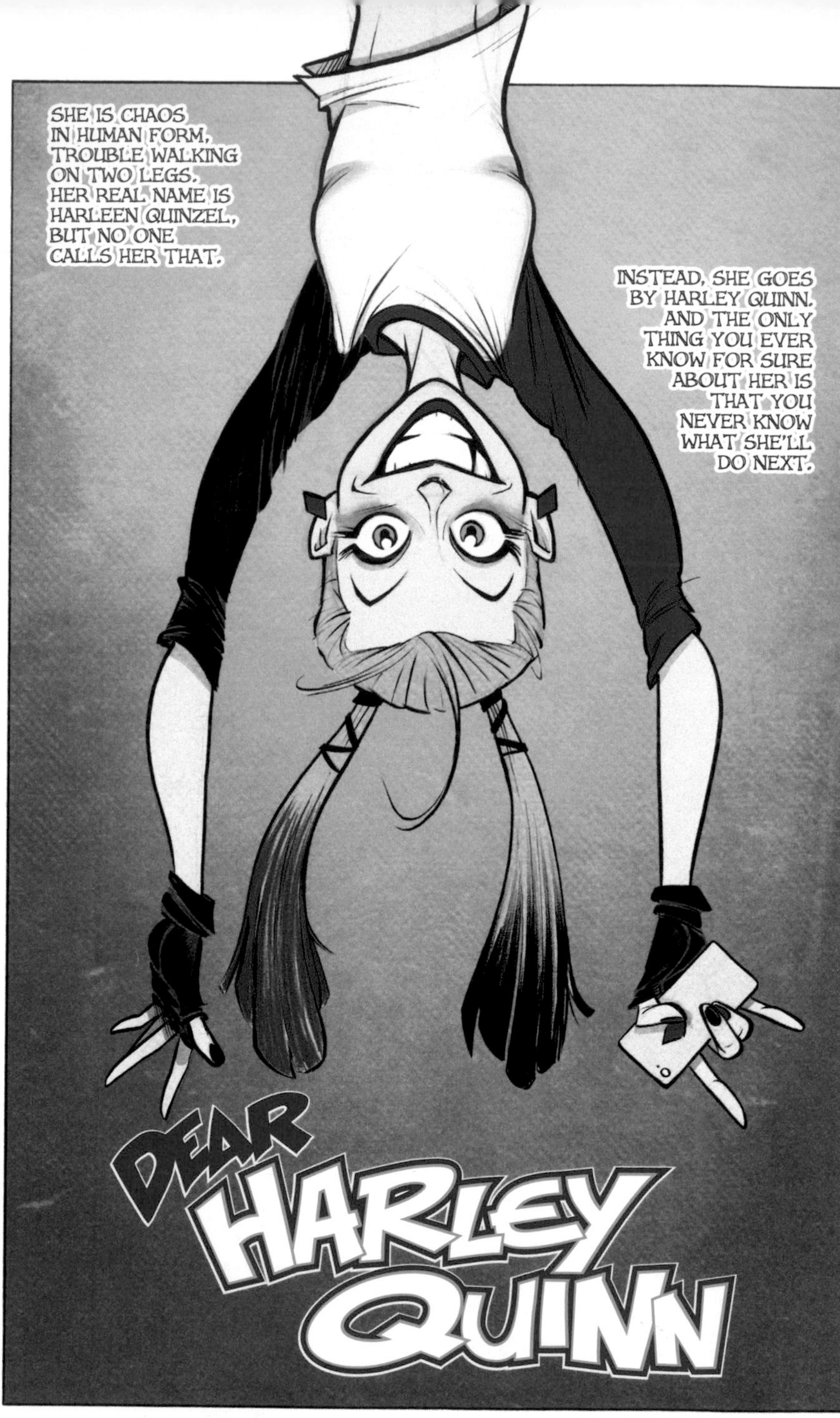
SHE IS CHAOS IN HUMAN FORM, TROUBLE WALKING ON TWO LEGS. HER REAL NAME IS HARLEEN QUINZEL, BUT NO ONE CALLS HER THAT.
INSTEAD, SHE GOES BY HARLEY QUINN. AND THE ONLY THING YOU EVER KNOW FOR SURE ABOUT HER IS THAT YOU NEVER KNOW WHAT SHE'LL DO NEXT.
DEAR HARLEY QUINN

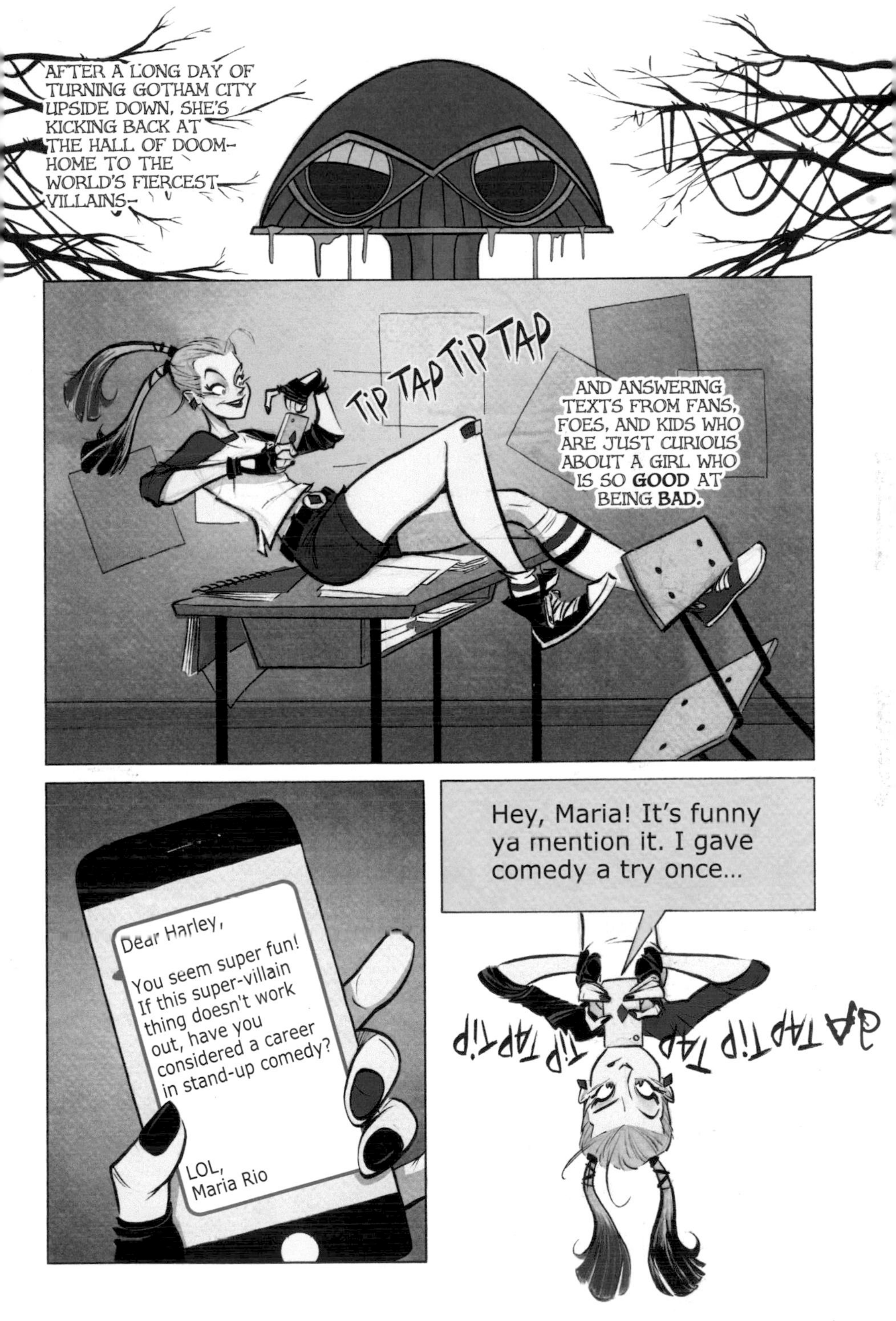
AFTER A LONG DAY OF TURNING GOTHAM CITY UPSIDE DOWN, SHE'S KICKING BACK AT THE HALL OF DOOM–HOME TO THE WORLD'S FIERCEST VILLAINS–
TIP TAP TIP TAP
AND ANSWERING TEXTS FROM FANS, FOES, AND KIDS WHO ARE JUST CURIOUS ABOUT A GIRL WHO IS SO GOOD AT BEING BAD.
Dear Harley,
You seem super fun! If this super-villain thing doesn't work out, have you considered a career in stand-up comedy?
LOL,
Maria Rio
Hey, Maria! It's funny ya mention it. I gave comedy a try once...
TIP TAP TIP TAP

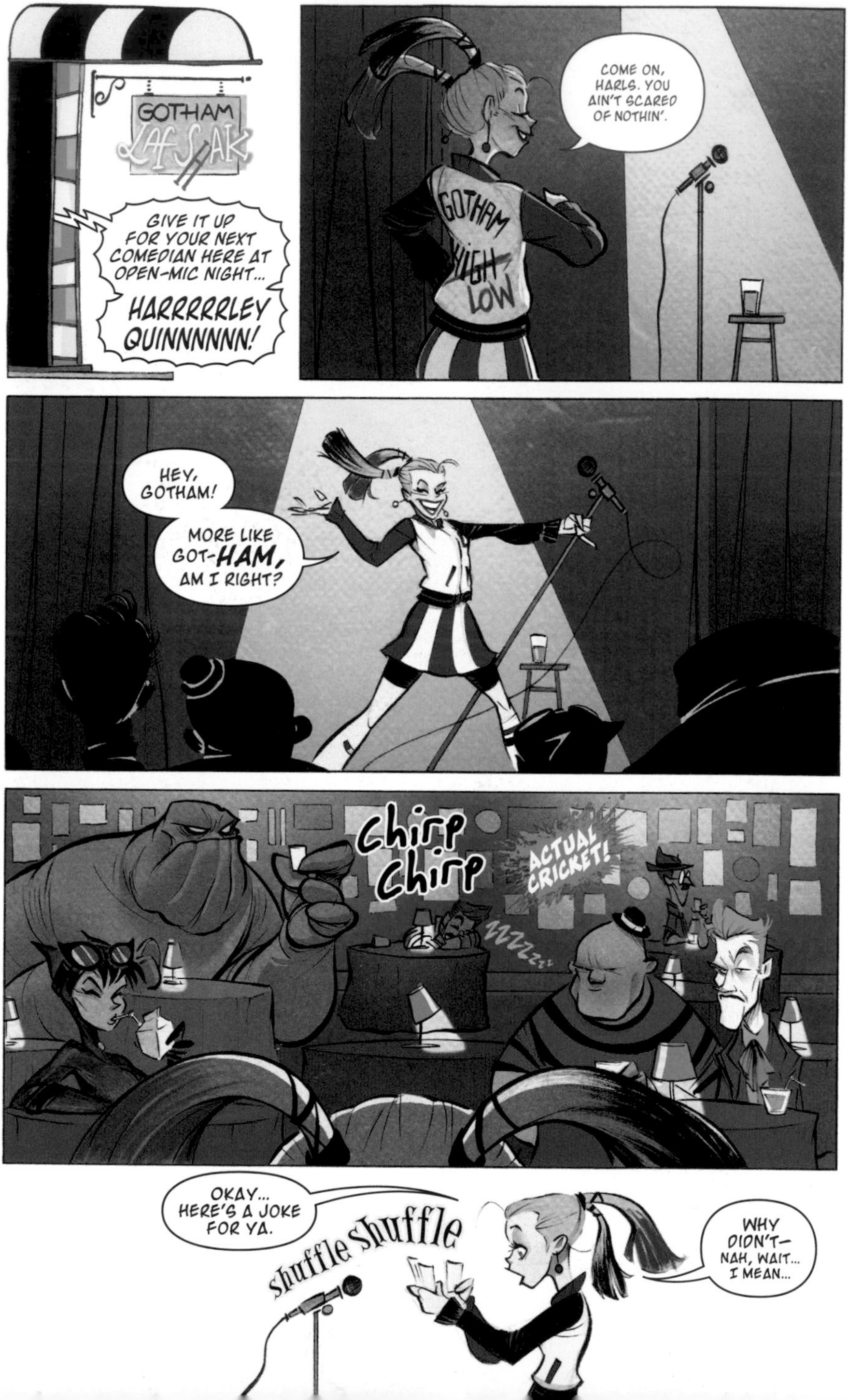
GOTHAM LAF SAK
GIVE IT UP FOR YOUR NEXT COMEDIAN HERE AT OPEN-MIC NIGHT...
HARRRRRLEY QUINNNNNN!
COME ON, HARLS. YOU AIN'T SCARED OF NOTHIN'.
GOTHAM HIGH LOW
HEY, GOTHAM!
MORE LIKE GOT-HAM, AM I RIGHT?
Chirp Chirp
ACTUAL CRICKET!
ZZZZzzz
OKAY... HERE'S A JOKE FOR YA.
shuffle shuffle
WHY DIDN'T— NAH, WAIT... I MEAN...

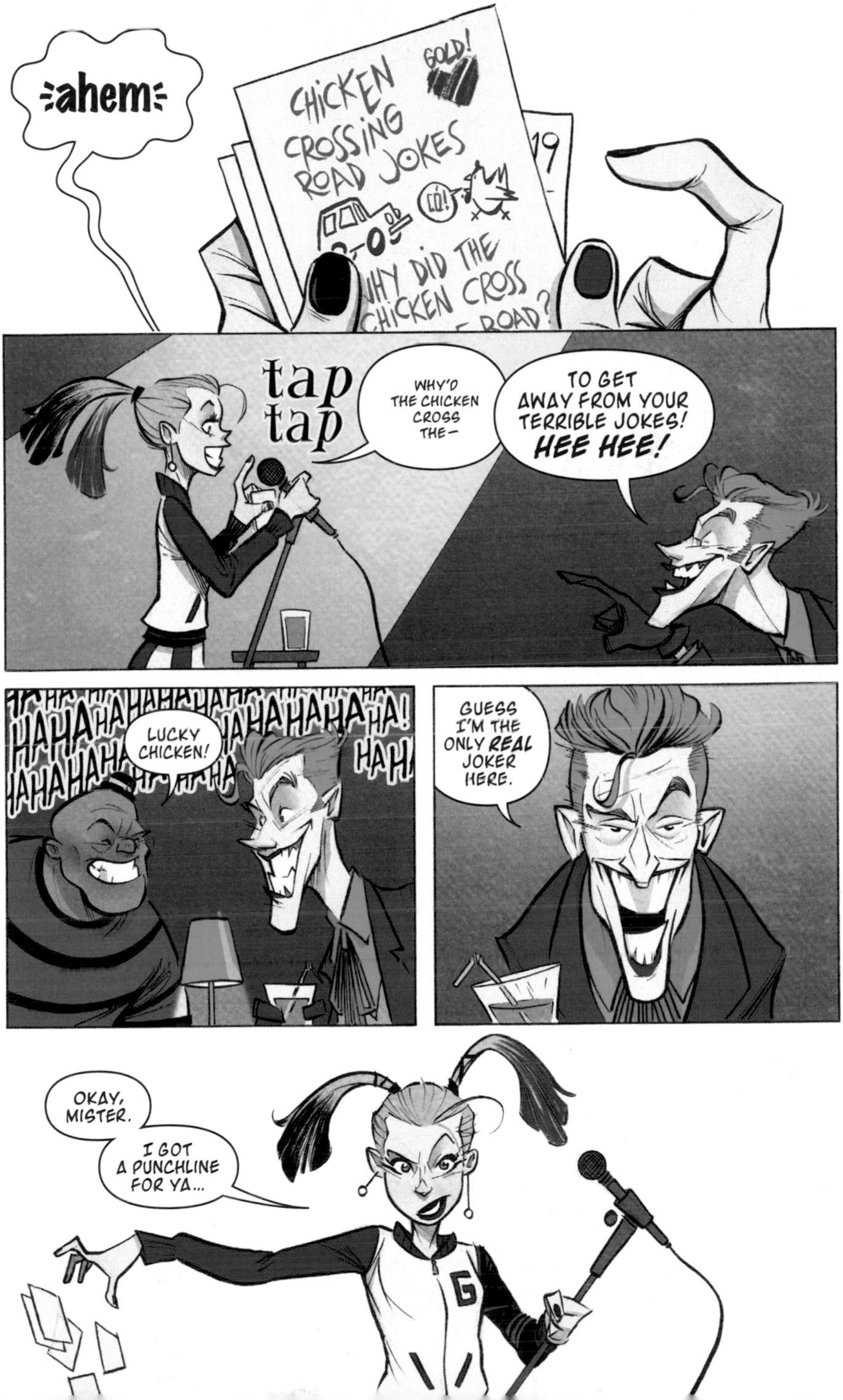
ahem
CHICKEN CROSSING ROAD JOKES
GOLD!
CO!
19
WHY DID THE CHICKEN CROSS
tap tap
WHY'D THE CHICKEN CROSS THE—
TO GET AWAY FROM YOUR TERRIBLE JOKES! HEE HEE!
HAHAHAHAHA
LUCKY CHICKEN!
GUESS I'M THE ONLY REAL JOKER HERE.
OKAY, MISTER.
I GOT A PUNCHLINE FOR YA...
G

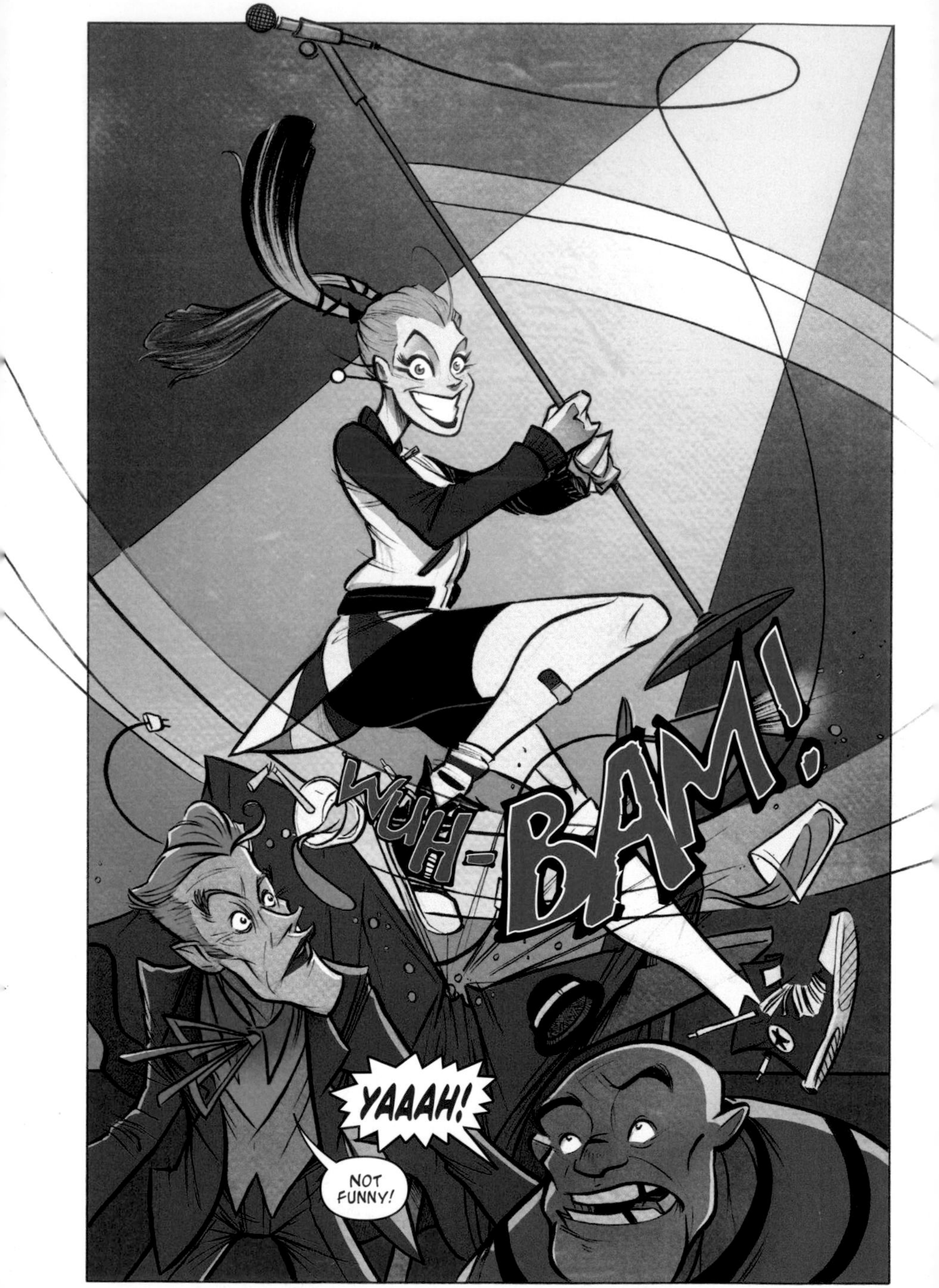
WUH-BAM!
YAAAH!
NOT FUNNY!

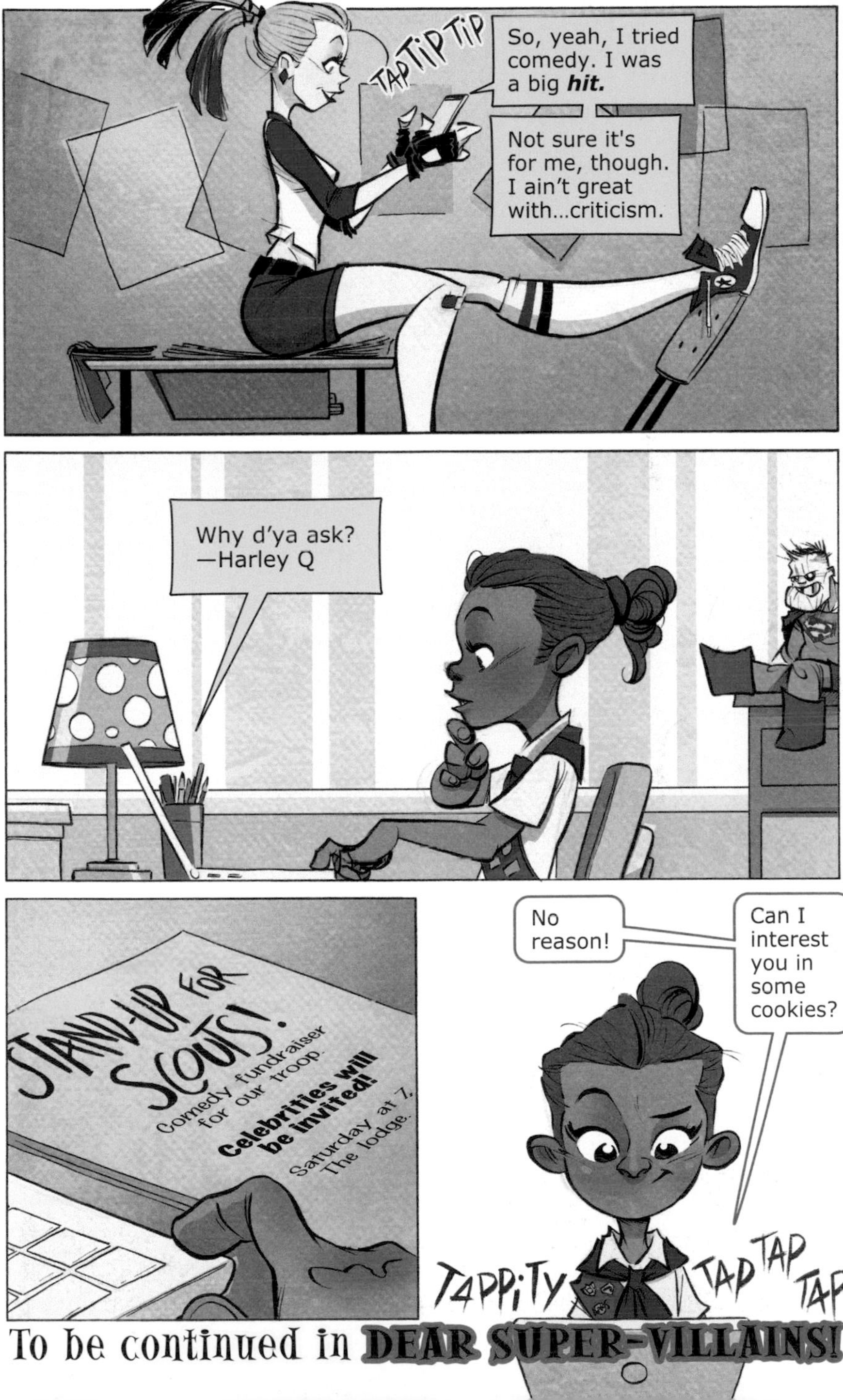
TAP TIP TIP
So, yeah, I tried comedy. I was a big ***hit.***
Not sure it's for me, though. I ain't great with...criticism.
Why d'ya ask? —Harley Q
STAND-UP FOR SCOUTS!
Comedy fundraiser for our troop.
Celebrities will be invited!
Saturday at 7. The lodge.
No reason!
Can I interest you in some cookies?
TAPPITY TAP TAP TAP TAP

To be continued in **DEAR SUPER-VILLAINS!**

Don't miss the next adventure from DC Zoom!
Turn the page for a super sneak preview.

Can Superman keep Smallville from going to the dogs?

From the *New York Times* bestselling creators of TINY TITANS comes the hilarious story of Clark Kent as he navigates aliens, disappearing hot dog carts, and middle school.

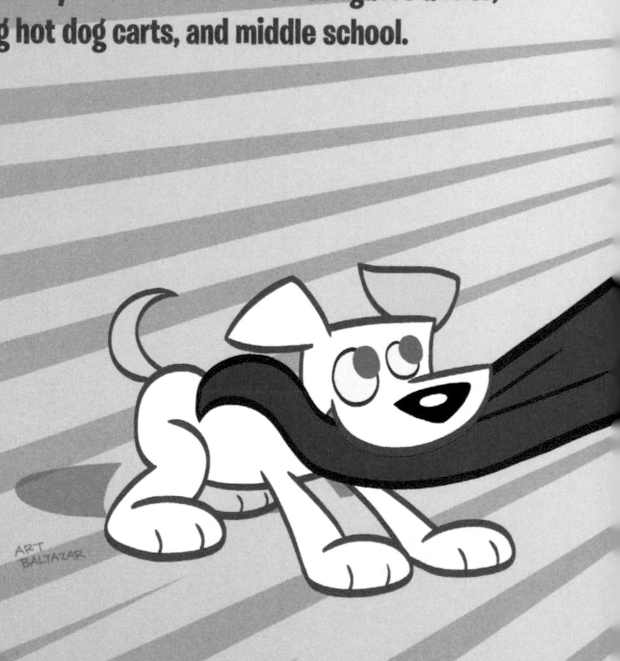
ART BALTAZAR

On sale 9/3/2019

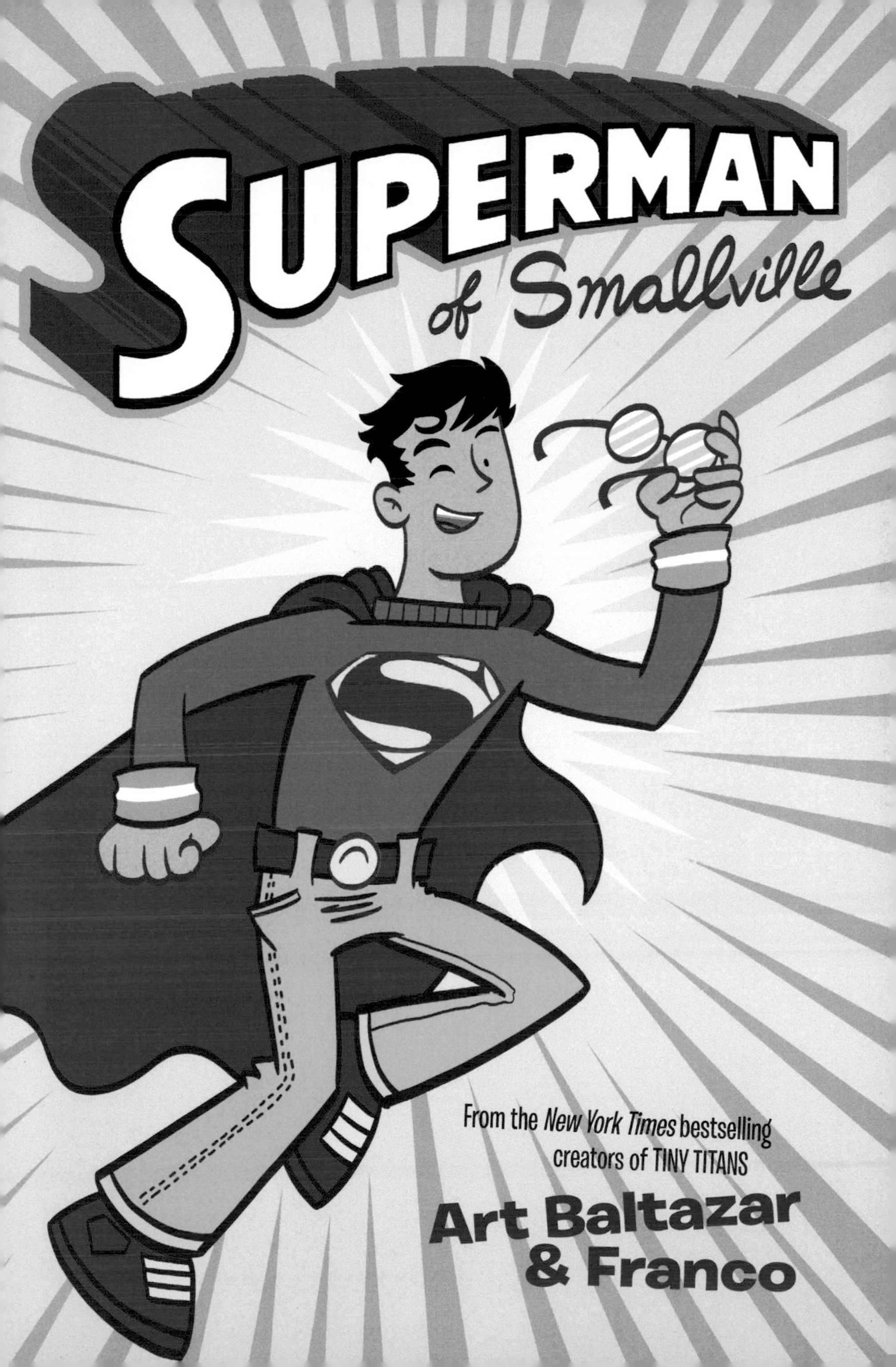
SUPERMAN
of Smallville
From the New York Times bestselling
creators of TINY TITANS
Art Baltazar
& Franco

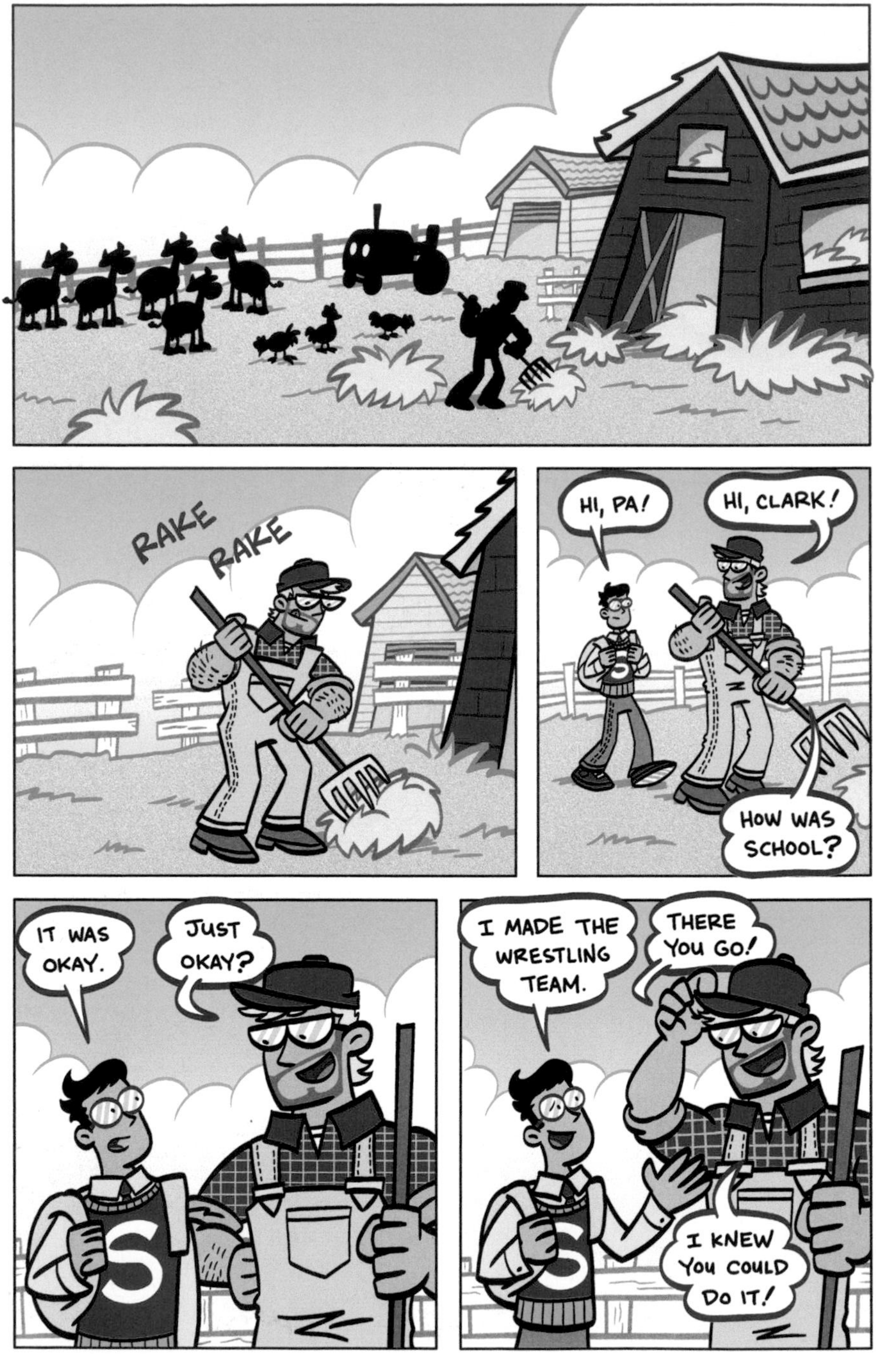
RAKE
RAKE
HI, PA!
HI, CLARK!
HOW WAS SCHOOL?
IT WAS OKAY.
JUST OKAY?
I MADE THE WRESTLING TEAM.
THERE YOU GO!
I KNEW YOU COULD DO IT!

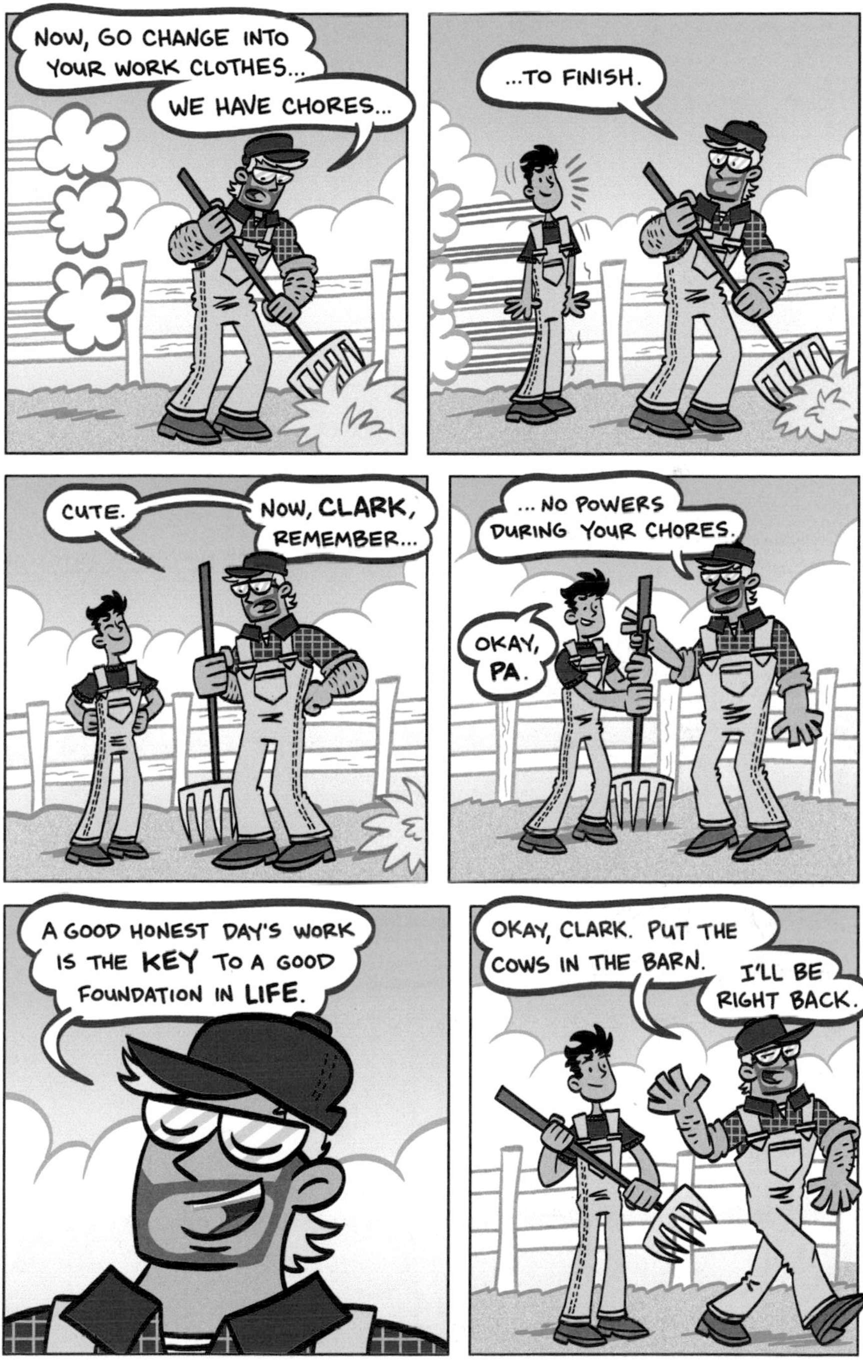
NOW, GO CHANGE INTO YOUR WORK CLOTHES...
WE HAVE CHORES...
...TO FINISH.
CUTE.
NOW, CLARK, REMEMBER...
... NO POWERS DURING YOUR CHORES.
OKAY, PA.
A GOOD HONEST DAY'S WORK IS THE KEY TO A GOOD FOUNDATION IN LIFE.
OKAY, CLARK. PUT THE COWS IN THE BARN.
I'LL BE RIGHT BACK.

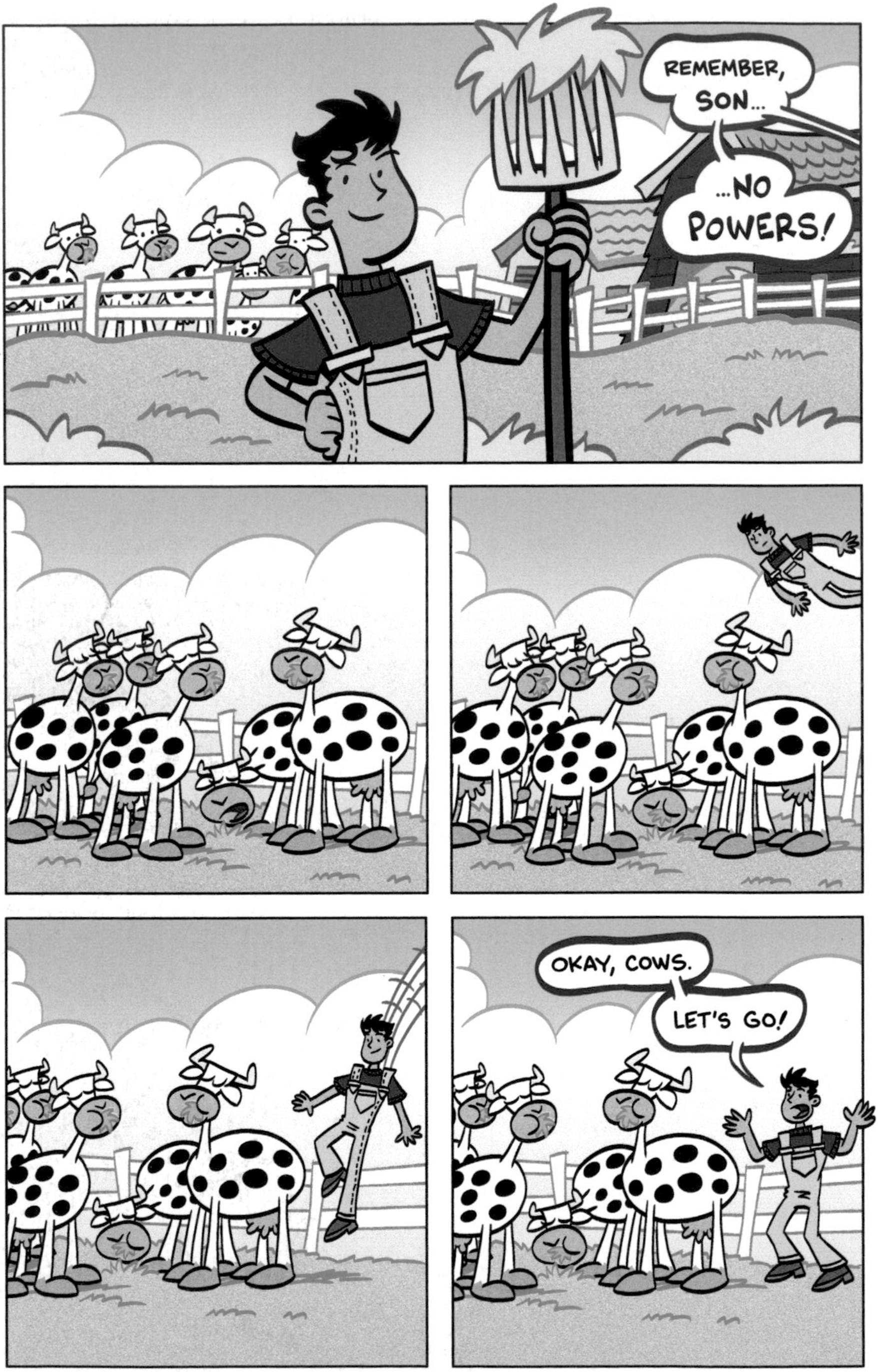
REMEMBER, SON...
...NO POWERS!
OKAY, COWS.
LET'S GO!

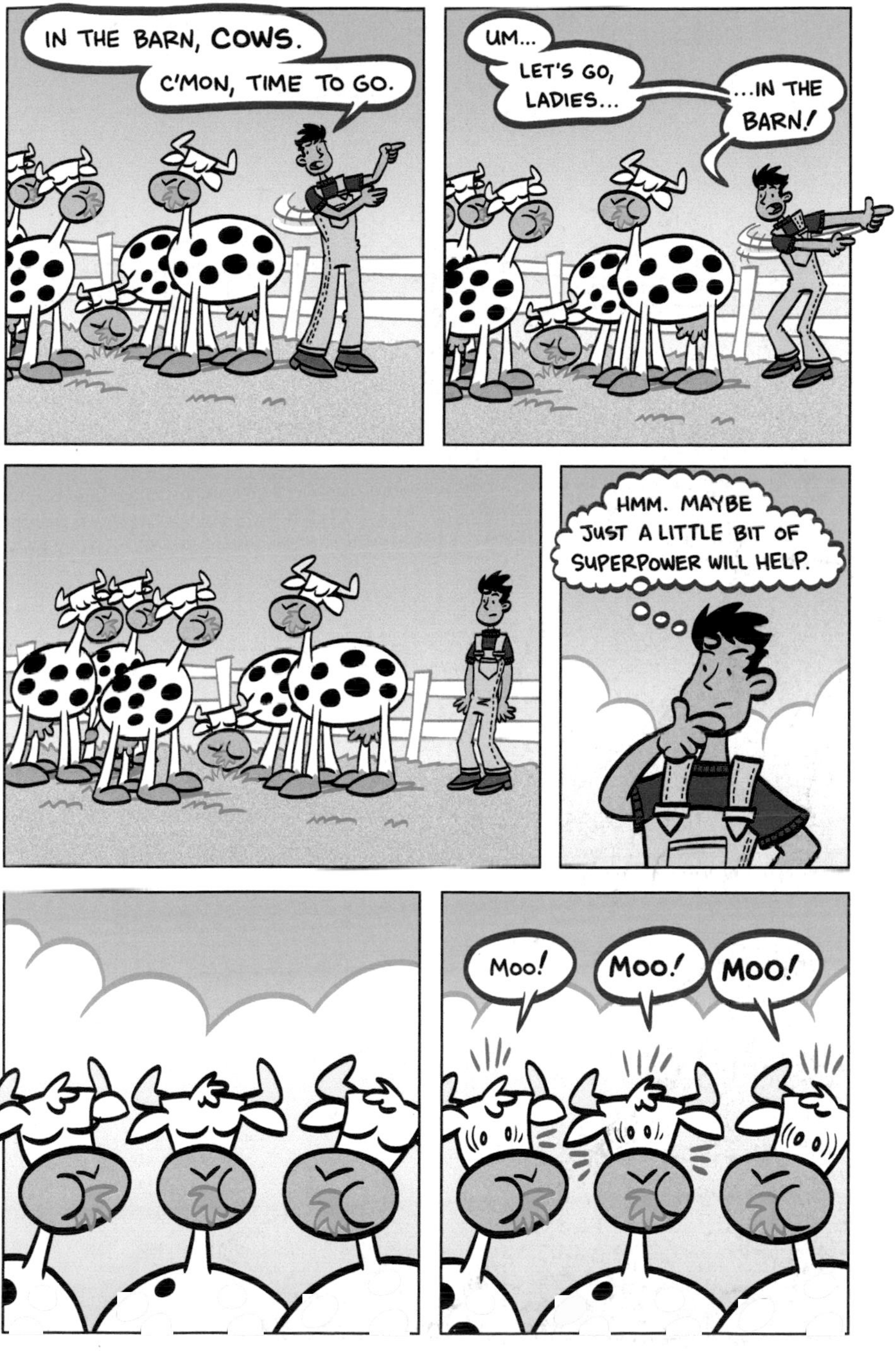
IN THE BARN, COWS.
C'MON, TIME TO GO.
UM...
LET'S GO, LADIES...
...IN THE BARN!
HMM. MAYBE JUST A LITTLE BIT OF SUPERPOWER WILL HELP.
Moo!
MOO!
MOO!

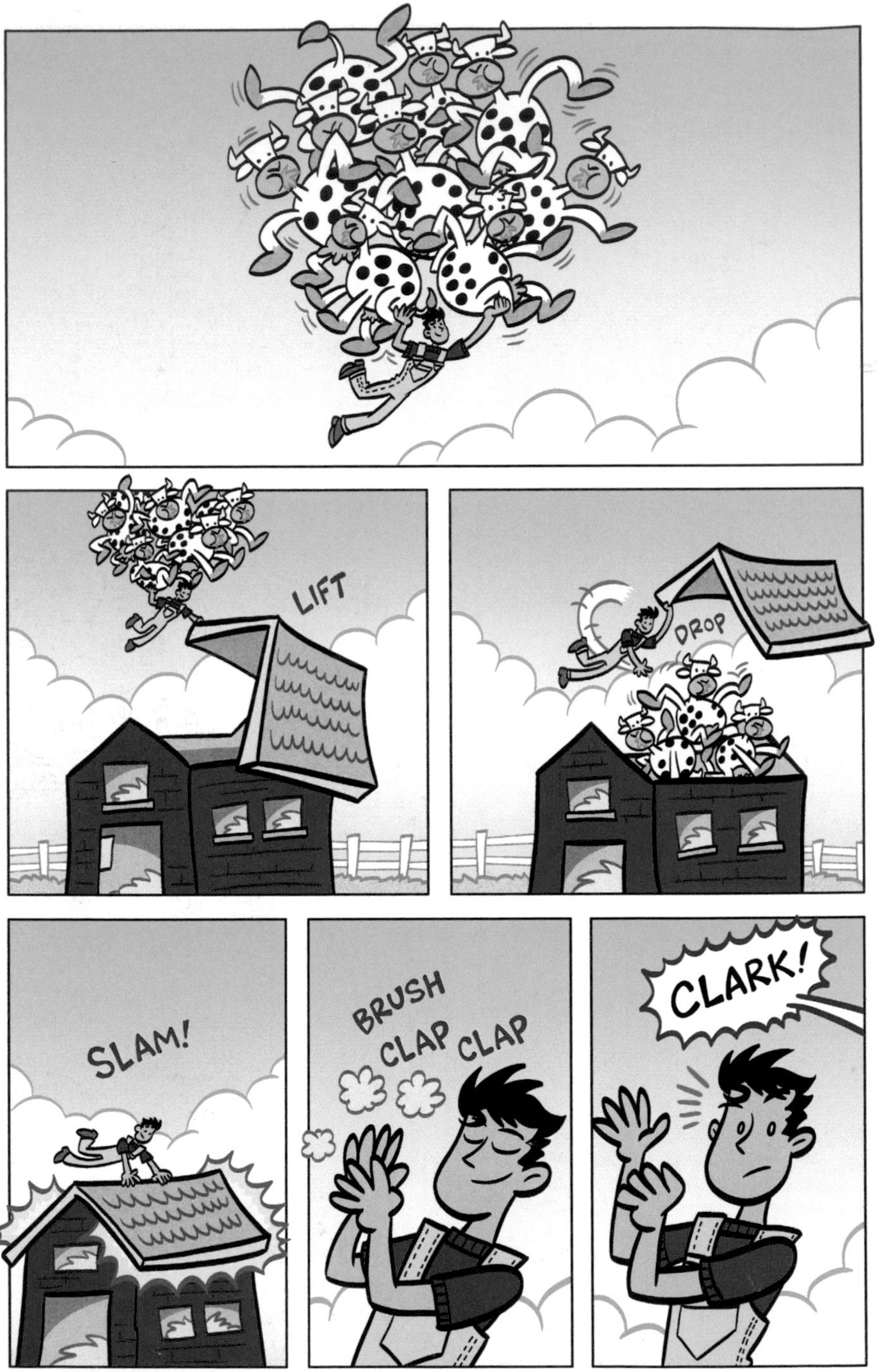
LIFT
DROP
SLAM!
BRUSH
CLAP
CLAP
CLARK!

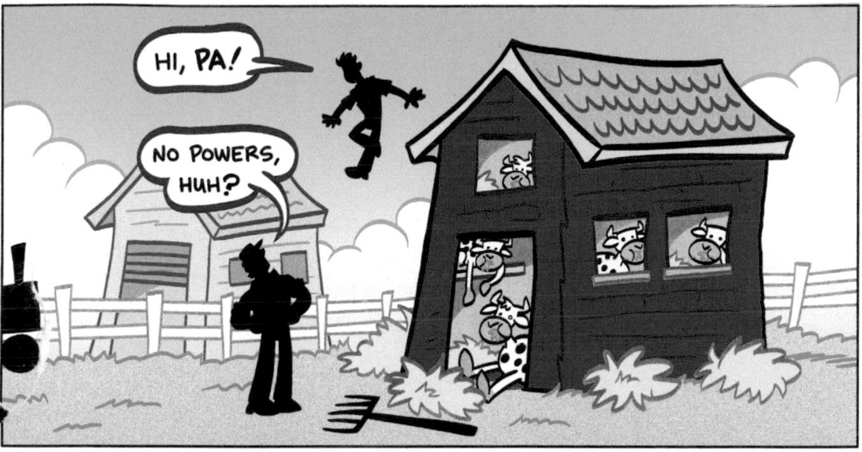
HI, PA!
NO POWERS, HUH?

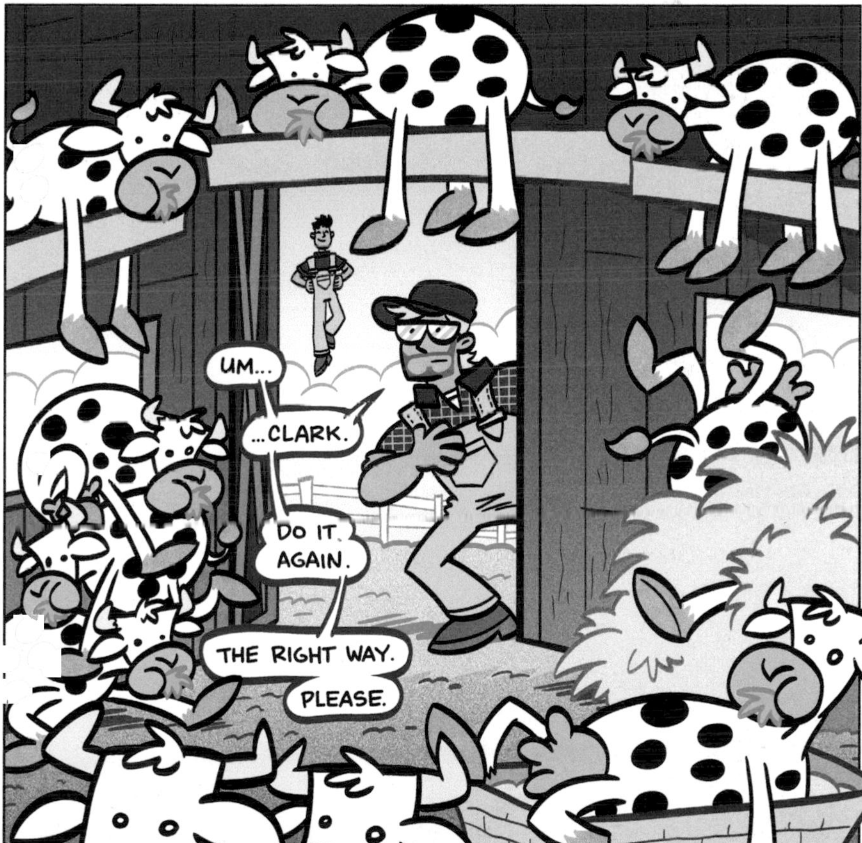
UM...
...CLARK.
DO IT AGAIN.
THE RIGHT WAY.
PLEASE.

THE FUN CONTINUES IN SUPERMAN OF SMALLVILLE!

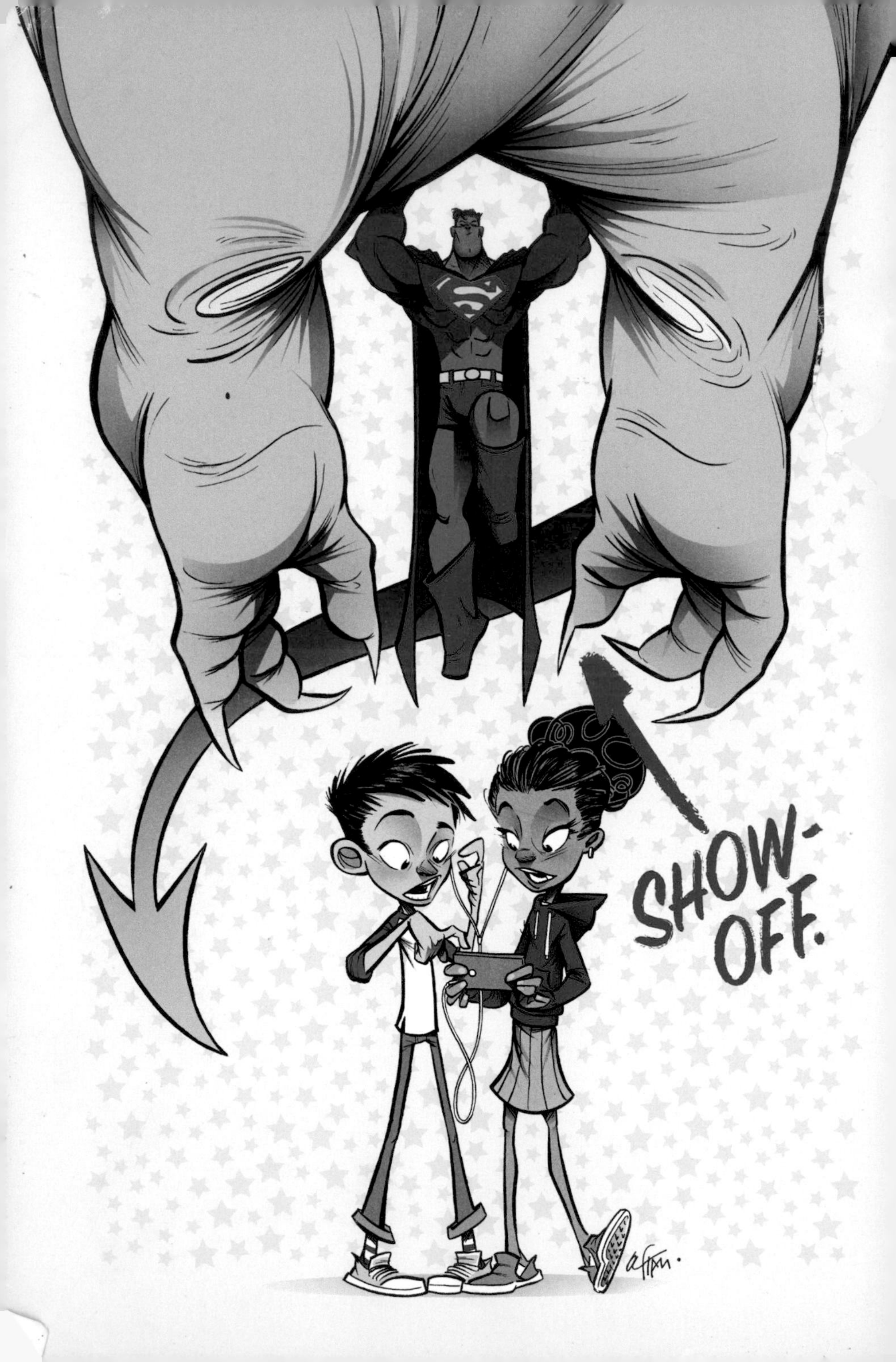
SHOW-OFF.